Hi Linda -
much success with your
writing project -- it
sounds like a winner.
Enjoy your journey with
"Shelbi and me." Best wishes
Paul

Copy number: 709

5-3-96

Meet the people of *Shelee and Me:*

SHELEE OSBORNSON: Definitively self-assured. An independent woman of extraordinary talent and beauty. Passionately in love with Phil Sloan, devoted to her family and profession, but denied the one womanly role she most desires.

PHIL SLOAN: A skilled physician, possessing great strengths and compassion, who enriches all who know him. Though friendships define his being, he is often overwhelmed by the women in his life.

MANNY WESTON: Premier American mystery writer. An author who weaves tales of incredible power and intrigue. What stories lie beyond his most personal and terrifying mystery?

GLORIA BURNS: Glamorous, retired movie star, now the guru of Wall Street. Gloria, America's wealthiest businesswoman, collects corporations as some collect stamps.

DUNCAN COLE: Gloria's husband. Duncan's multibillion-dollar corporate empire of broadcasting, sports teams, and publishing, dominates his sector of the business world.

JONAH THORNTON: Murderer and child molester, a community's worst nightmare. His maniacal focus: to destroy those who have exposed his crimes.

LUCKY OSBORNSON: Much more than Shelee's uncle. Warrior, gambler, boxing champion, and mentor to young Phil Sloan.

SERENA MARTIN and SARAH ANDREWS: Phil Sloan's distant love interests, affecting the life he now knows.

* * * * *

*If you hunger for good food and fine wines, if you crave honest conversation and insightful dialog, if you enjoy personal intimacy and great sex, if you welcome a spiritual vacation to both city and countryside, and—more important—if you take uncommon pleasure in an exciting story, then this book is written for you. Enjoy!*

# Shelee and Me

## *Journeys of Intimate Discovery*

Paul D. Cohn

BURNS-COLE PUBLISHERS
Bozeman New York

A Sloan/Osbornson Book
A Division of Burns-Cole Publishers

*Shelee and Me – Journeys of Intimate Discovery*

Grateful acknowledgment is made for permission to reprint excepts from the following previously published material:

Excerpts from *Paddle-to-the-Sea,* copyright © 1941, renewed 1969, by Holling Clancy Holling. Reprinted by permission of Houghton Mifflin Co. All rights reserved.

Excerpts from the following works, reprinted by permission of the author:
*Wrong Man Twice?* copyright © 1995 by Paul D. Cohn.
*YellowStone,* copyright © 1995 by Paul D. Cohn.
*SABOR - Sisters and Brothers of Revenge,* copyright © 1995 by Paul D. Cohn.
*Mikie and Mike,* copyright © 1995 by Paul D. Cohn.


Cover art and design: Armin Mühsam
Text design: Alexsandra Hamilton
Cover models: Seabring Paty, Neal Chandler



Library of Congress Catalog Card Number: 95-75735

ISBN 0-9645876-3-7

First edition - Publication date: February 14, 1996

A *Copy number:* citation and numeral inscribed inside the front cover designates the unique copy number for this book.



PUBLISHED AND PRINTED IN THE UNITED STATES OF AMERICA

## ACKNOWLEDGMENTS

There are many people who, in a great variety of ways, made unique contributions to this book. I wish to thank Ken Williams who generously shared his psychological insights, concepts, and encouragement; artist Janie Camp who provided many painting and artistic perspectives; Darragh Huggins and brother Jeff for healthy family patterns and attitudes; Dr. Doug Alvord, trauma consultation; artist H. Steve Oiestead whose family—at great personal peril—is honored in this book for protecting political refugees in Norway during WWII; Chrysti Mueller, The Word Smith, and husband Steve Mueller, for sharing the delightful wedding sequence; Lynn Anderson who made music come alive in Minneapolis; Professor Michael Ivie for enlightening me about the uncommon and beautiful net-winged midge; Julie Phinney for typesetting; my daughters Jill Cohn, Melinda Lucas, and Dr. Lisa Shaffer for their suggestions, input, and reviews; The Floating Restaurant on Lake Pend Oreille in Hope, Idaho; Anna Golinski who generously helped me with the Russian language; and the following individuals who provided consultation and ideas: Patty Anderson who introduced me to the Sons of Norway; Joe Albro, Antoine J. Bastien, Erin Barrett, M. Paul Burns, Professor Ada Giusti, Teddy Gerlinger, brothers Bill and John Guza, Justin Hettinger, Beth Harlow, Dr. Barbara Honeyman, Arne Hovin, Buddy Howard, Professor Greg Keeler, Gretchen Rupp, sons-in-law David Lucas and Jeff Shaffer, Julie Tabler, computer wizards Larry Washburn and John Benediktson, J.H. who "banned" the book in Salt Lake City even before it was published, many other folks whom I may have overlooked, and last and least the women of the local authors' group who booted me out for reasons they will never understand.

*Special thanks* go to Dave and Lee Ann Hale for their sparkling plot ideas; to author and editors Toni Volk and Durrae Johanek for their invaluably creative editorial review, opinions, and detailed editing; and to Armin Muhsam for his inspired cover design and artwork. And also special thanks to Kathy Anderson for her outstanding editorial advice.

. . . For C. and L.S.

"The time has come for you to sit on this snowbank and wait for the Sun Spirit to set you free. Then you will be a real Paddle Person, a real Paddle-to-the-Sea."

"Ho!" he called. "You have started on your journey! Good-by, Paddle-to-the-Sea!"

—Holling Clancy Holling

Theirs was a duet
like no other.

—Tien Bhota, *Nocturnes*

# Shelee and Me

*Journeys of Intimate Discovery*

*"There ain't many folks in this world I love, 'cept my family and Phil Sloan, maybe a few women, too. That Shelee girl, she's like my own daughter. 'Course, she don't know the truth and I ain't quite sure neither.*

*"Knowin' now what Thornton's scheme was, I should have planned on killin' him first time I heard his name on our way to Montana. I sort of killed people before. After what Thornton done, dying's not good enough for him. Somethin' like Thornton should never happen—it never should, by god . . . never should!"*

*—Lucky Osbornson*

## One / Phil

I remember looking at Shelee with considerable lust when we were kids together up at her Uncle Lucky's, soon after I discovered my dick had multiple functions. I'd seen her a few times before, but she was almost two years older than I was—when you're a kid, that's an important difference. I guess she was pretty then, but I perceived her as foul-mouthed, snooty, and a real smart-ass. Also, she was taller than I was. For sure, I couldn't match her verbal acrobatics . . . still can't keep up with her when she's on a roll.

Coincident with my genital revelation and my fresh view of Shel, was another distraction, a girl named Linda, the daughter of Lucky's girlfriend—Lucky had lots of girlfriends then. Linda, with her unforgettable blue eyes and long, jet black hair, always smelled of hay dust and lilacs.

The beautiful old lilac trees at Lucky's—they're still there—had a hammock hanging between two of the larger ones. They'd been planted by homesteaders who owned Lucky's spread seventy years earlier. We were in the middle of our first hay cutting, when one evening I found myself in the hammock with

Linda. We necked for a while until I finally got enough courage to put an inquisitive hand between her legs and was startled to find a damp spot where it came to rest. Immediately, she pulled my hand away and went into the house. I didn't care, for at that moment my interest in women was forever burned into my being.

Linda kept her distance while flirting with me all summer, though she refused to join me again in the hammock.

But the hammock in the lilac trees became a sanctuary for me, a place where I often chose to sleep through those humid July and August nights. And a few times I dreamed of a girl who sang twilight songs with the crickets of our long summer evenings. Twenty-five years would pass, then I would see her face in a photograph.

What I recall most about the first few times with Shelee—almost ten years ago when I returned to Minneapolis to set up my medical practice—was going back to Lucky's after all those years. I picked her up one Saturday morning for the hour-and-a-half drive to her uncle's farm. We stopped for lunch at a floating restaurant on Lake Minne Belle and left with a dessert to eat later at Lucky's.

When we arrived at the farm, Shel set out the dessert and a special wine she'd brought, and started the coffee. I put our stuff away, which took about a minute. Then, as I looked around for Shelee, I realized I hadn't been here since my first year at college, and a number of treasured memories came to mind. Soon, Shel, who had wandered into the woods behind the cabin, returned with a bouquet of cottonwood boughs.

I can see her now, walking from the edge of the trees, the marvelous peasant blouse and full skirt she wore, her red hair and freckles, and those loving brown eyes. We sat next to each other at the picnic table in front of the cabin, enjoying lemon cake, the thirteen-year-old Muscat Canelli, and our coffee.

"Was it fate that brought us up here?" Shel said solemnly.

"No," I answered with a smile, "it was your uncle walking in on us the other evening."

She smiled back. "That, too, of course."

We moved close together, so the sides of our legs touched, and we looked out at the lake. The cottonwood boughs lay on the table, and Shel played with them while we talked. The cottonwoods were just leafing out, and their nascent buds were covered with a sticky yellow balm that gives off an intoxicating smell. The air at Lucky's, I recall from my boyhood, was always full of this natural perfume early each spring.

We sipped quietly from a shared glass of wine. Then Shelee picked up a bough, brushing the buds across her breast.

"I understand Indian maidens did this to attract their men," she said. The buds left pollen-yellow traces on her blouse and skin.

"See what you think," Shel continued, taking my hand and touching the perfume on her skin. She placed my fingers underneath my nose and against my mouth, and I tasted the sweet balm of the cottonwoods. The hollow of her throat blushed as she moved even closer to me.

"An Indian woman told me this yellow is the color of desire," she said. Still holding my hand, Shelee moved it to her face, kissing my fingertips. Then she kissed me full on the mouth.

That single kiss will forever be my most vivid memory.

University classes had just resumed after spring break when Dena was referred to me by the student health service. I've had some success with similar cases, so the Women's Center or health service sends me two or three referrals each year. Dena Lewis, the nervous young woman sitting in my office on Thursday morning, told me she was an animal science major and hoped someday to have a ranch of her own. Dena had a squeaky-clean look, impeccably groomed and boyish, and was currently being treated for stomach ulcers. She unhappily related her story of growing up, slaving on a farm with a demanding, angry father and a compliant mother.

Dena went on to describe her love for animals, beginning with those on the farm—the livestock responded with non-demanding affection. Soon words hurried along, overrun by emotion, and she burst into tears.

"I need your help, Dr. Sloan," she sobbed. "My friend and her sister—she's only eleven!"

"Who's only eleven?" I asked gently.

"Trudy Thornton!" Dena said, jumping to her feet, her face twisting in anger. "You don't know the *half* of it, Dr. Sloan!" she cried. "They only live a few miles from us. I've known them most of my life. Carol's down here at college doing pre-vet, and her little sister's at home . . . at home getting . . . getting screwed by her father!"

"I know what needs to be done," I said. "Tell me what *you* want to do." Still sitting, I extended my hands. She reached for me briefly, then pulled away.

Dena continued to cry as she shifted from one foot to the other. "I'm so scared," she said. "Carol's situation is terrible. Her bastard father told her if she tells, he'll kill her and Trudy, then himself. I don't know what to do!"

"Would your friend be willing to come in and talk with me?" I asked.

"I don't know. I'm supposed to meet her at eleven."

"The situation sounds dangerous. Let's see what we can work out. Has anyone discussed this with the authorities?" I asked.

"No!" Dena answered, shaking her head as she sat down. "We're all too scared."

I walked to my desk and nudged the phone in Dena's direction, offering her my chair. "I'm obligated to report suspected child abuse to Youth Protection," I said, glancing at my appointment calendar. "Maybe Carol can come here at noon. Could you call her?"

"She's in class now," Dena said, "but I could have her phone as soon as I see her."

"I'm available from noon on," I said, "plus this evening's free. It's important that I talk with Carol—I'll fit her in. And Trudy needs immediate protection, so please don't say anything to anyone about our conversation. Caution Carol also," I added. "Part of the interviews will be used for complaint motions. Do you think Carol will sign a statement about her father?"

Dena shuddered. "She probably will, Dr. Sloan, but Mr. Thornton could come down here to kill us all, including you. The whole family's terrified of him!"

"My experience is that offenders usually back down as soon as the authorities are involved," I assured her. "I can make arrangements for Carol to move into a women's shelter just in case. If you feel threatened, then you can stay there, too. The location is kept confidential, so you can't be found."

Dena nodded.

"I'm sorry, I have another client waiting," I said, "but I want to see you tomorrow." Dena picked up her backpack, and we walked out together. She made an appointment for 9:00 A.M.

Before my next appointment, I called the local youth authority and Minneapolis Family Services, alerting both of them to a possible problem, asking also about the youth shelter facility in Jefferson County. Then I dialed Shel's number.

"Hi, Trish, is Shelee available?" I asked, knowing she was most likely in class. "Please tell her this afternoons plans are unavoidably on hold—problem here at the office. I'll call back as soon as I know my schedule. Thanks."

I greeted my new client, a very overweight African-American man with Native American features who looked like a bum. We shook hands and went into my office. I closed the door and then asked, "What can I do for you, Mr. . . . uh, Manny?"

"Manny is my first name, Doctor," he said and smiled, settling into the chair next to my desk. "I would like to talk with you for an hour."

I must have looked surprised, because he said, "I can pay you in advance." He pulled four $100 bills out of his shirt pocket and pushed them across the desk at me.

"That's twice my hourly fee," I said as I pushed the money back. "You can pay me when we're finished—if I've been helpful."

He put the bills into his pocket with his cigarettes. "I'm doing some research for a book," he said, "and I heard you testify at a hearing a few weeks ago—you were billed as an expert." He paused and began to fidget.

I tried to recall which hearing he was talking about. His manner of speech was formal and scholarly, quite unlike his appearance. "How can I help you?" I asked.

"I want to discuss child abuse."

"All right. What would you like to know?"

"Well, I'm interested in the psychology of it," he said, "and how it affects personality development. But let's start with a basic question: Do abused children grow up to be abusive adults?"

"Not always."

Manny extracted a crushed notepad out of his back pocket, borrowed a pen from me, and made a few entries as we talked. His questions were thoughtful and focused, and I tried to answer them, sometimes exploring subjects at length. About halfway through the hour he looked fidgety again.

"Could we go outside and sit at the picnic table so I could smoke?" he asked.

"Why not?" I said, getting up and following him out of the office. "We'll be outside if you need us," I said to my astonished secretary. Manny lumbered down the hall ahead of me, lighting a cigarette the moment he hit the outside door.

We sat at the table on the grass strip by the parking lot. "Thanks," he said, sighing a cloud of smoke, flicking an ash onto the newly green grass.

"What are we going to do when it's fifteen below?'

Manny flashed a smile. "We'll figure that out when it happens," he said. "This is quite helpful; may I come to see you weekly? Sort of a consulting arrangement?" I nodded. He pulled a decrepit, overflowing leather wallet from the inside of his jacket, and absentmindedly searched through it, finding and unfolding a smudged check. Manny made out the check as we continued to talk.

At the end of the hour, we agreed on an appointment for the following Thursday. "My accountant hates it when I pay cash for business activities," he said, and handed me his check.

"But Manny," I said, looking at the amount—one thousand dollars. "This is—"

"In advance," he interrupted.

Then I noticed his name on the check. "My god! Of course, Manny Weston, the writer. I guess I knew you lived in Minneapolis. You write . . ."

His eyes twinkled. "Mysteries."

"I'll be pleased to be your consultant," I said. We shook hands, and I walked back to my office as he headed for his car. And I wondered if there were other reasons why Manny Weston had come to see me.

When I returned to my office, Molly was waiting for me and had things closed up. "I assume your afternoon is back on track," she said. "Carol Thornton called and said you wanted to see her. She's coming in tomorrow morning with Dena Lewis. I took the liberty of calling Ms. Osbornson."

"Thank you."

"Do you realize who that last client was?" she asked.

"I do now."

## Two / Shelee

In celebration of our balmy spring day, I left work early and drove to Phil's office. His afternoon schedule was now free, so we could go ahead with our hurried trip to Lucky's for morel hunting and perhaps fishing and get back to Minneapolis in the late evening.

He was already in the parking lot when I arrived, and grinned at me when I drove up. He dropped his jacket and change of clothes in the backseat, then got in.

"Nice to see you," I said, kissing him on the cheek. "What's up?" I knew that grin.

"You'll never guess who came to pick my brains today."

"Don't make me guess."

"Manny Weston."

"You're kidding! The most famous mystery writer in America?"

"That's the one."

"Amazing! For therapy?"

"No, or I wouldn't tell you about it. He's researching a book."

"What's he like?"

"I didn't even know it was him." Phil laughed. "I thought he was some bum wanting to discuss his drug problem."

"That doesn't surprise me," I said. "I went to a talk he gave at school—he *does* look like a derelict. Was he shy?"

"No, why?"

"Well, he sure was when I saw him. He gave three short readings, answered a couple of questions, and left the room. No goodbyes or anything."

"I'm starving," Phil said. "Let's stop up ahead." He took off his necktie and tossed it into the back.

I pulled into a McDonald's and we loaded up. Our Manny Weston discussion continued as I drove back onto 394 West.

"I had no idea he was black," Phil said between bites of food. "There certainly aren't any people of color in his books."

"He's Indian, too." I said. "I read in one of his rare interviews that his mother was a Kahama Indian, from somewhere near Port Angeles. I think he grew up around there, too, and went to the University of Washington. Anyway, invite him for dinner."

When we arrived at Lucky's, Sloan did a little striptease, changing his clothes while I got our 'shrooming stuff out. We headed for the woods.

For the uninitiated, mushrooming sounds totally stupid. It's not, it's more like an adult Easter egg hunt, which can be very productive, a complete bust, or something in between. One always gets a nice walk in the woods, and if you find mushrooms, particularly morels, you've got something good to eat. There's no better place to find them than at my uncle's.

Though the property has always been called that—Uncle Lucky's—it belongs to my parents as well. But Lucky was the one who found it. When the Germans first invaded Norway, he managed to get out of the country, escaping to Great Britain. He planned to stay in England and fight the Nazis from there, then changed his mind when he got the chance to come to America earlier than expected as a merchant seaman on a U.S. cargo ship.

Lucky and my father worked out a deal before the invasion. Stewart, my dad, had just married my mom, and they agreed to stay in Norway and take care of the family farm and our relatives. Lucky's part of the deal—his given name is Lars—was to go to America and pave the way for the rest of the family.

It was good that Lucky left Norway. He was so pugnacious I'm sure the Germans would have shot him sooner or later. As a noncitizen, he lied his way into the U.S. Navy and ended up on a carrier in the Pacific. He never had a chance to fight the Nazis.

He moved to the farm after the war, buying it with savings he'd stashed while in the service, and with money Dad sent over. Probably more of Lucky's money came from poker playing than his navy pay. My dad's a skilled machinist and ended up working in town, leaving Lucky to run the farm. A few years ago, Lucky leased the cattle and hay operation to a local farmer and moved to Minneapolis, saying he needed to be closer to the action. I assume that meant women and poker. Lucky stays active up here with his home, garden, and fishing lake; he also hunts here in the fall. In any case, the farm is an absolute paradise, and by four o'clock, Phil and I had several pounds of morels.

Phil decided to fish, and I continued to mushroom hunt, although now I had another activity in my mind. After a few minutes of tromping through the cottonwoods, finding more mushrooms and enjoying the breezy April afternoon, I walked back quietly, stopping a short distance inside the woods, close to where Phil was fishing. I wore a flour sack dress. That's what my sister, Abby, and I call them because we use a soft cotton fabric with a faded flower print. I took my panties off, poked them between my breasts, lifted the front of the dress just so, and dumped the morels into the skirt. Then I walked to the open lakeshore where Phil was fishing.

"Look at the mushrooms I found."

Phil leaned his fish pole against a tree, and walked over. "My, you've a nice bunch there," he said, smiling broadly. "Looks as if you've lost your panties again."

"Not only that, but I don't know what to do with these mushrooms," I said dreamily. "Could you help me?"

Phil knelt on the ground, and put a handful of morels into our bucket. Moments later, he began kissing me in a very private way, scattering most of the mushrooms in the grass. I held his head and pressed myself against his face and chest, playing with his hair and getting quite aroused. Forcefully pushing him to me, I opened my legs farther. The sensation became so exquisite that I was having trouble standing. But Phil stood and took my hand, leading me back into the woods where he took off his shirt and pants.

"I've got to tell you that mushroom hunting really turns me on," I whispered, brushing my mouth across his chest. He didn't bother to take my dress off, just pushed it up around my chin. We lay on his clothes and made insane love.

Afterward, Phil caressed my face and hair, talking softly. Then he lifted me gently and pulled my dress back down. He held me and we dozed for a few minutes.

Next morning, when I drove to my office on the Minneapolis campus, I arrived at the Creative Arts Building feeling intoxicated by our second fine spring day in a row. A brief rush of wind stripped a flurry of crab apple blossoms from the trees that line our sidewalk. I pulled the building's door open while the petals swirled around the entrance. I smiled—art everywhere, I thought. I hiked up my skirt and ran the three flights of stairs up to our suite—as I like to refer to it—a group of three small offices for three professors, and a larger office for the assistant department head—or just Asshead, as I often refer to him.

Trish Lathrop, our secretary and my best friend, was sitting at her desk in our outer office as I breezed through the open door; she looked totally beautiful as usual.

"Hey, how are you?" I asked.

"Oh, I'm fine, Dr. O.," she said. "Are we breathless again?"

"Yeah."

"Well, you're in luck. No messages, no kids waiting."

"Just the break I needed," I said as I walked into my office and closed the door. I was laying out my morning's work when the phone rang.

"Guess who?" Trish announced.

"Put him on," I told her, looking at my watch. It was a few minutes past 8:30. "Phil, I was just thinking about you."

"Good! Then think about lunch today," he said. "My eleven o'clock canceled."

"I can't, Phil. It's Friday. You know the morning class goes until one."

"Okay, Shel. You've missed another golden opportunity."

"As golden as yesterday?" I teased.

"I admit, you've taught me a new way to make love."

"My contribution to the artistry of our passion," I replied. "And that's *all* I'm going to say, Philip." My shrink boyfriend loves to talk about our relationship. I don't want to discuss it—simply too precious to mess with. The man works incredible wizardry with me, and I'd love to know the magic that happens in his office.

"Wait a second," I said, "the damned phone just rang again."

Trish poked her head in. "Two students wanting to see you, Dr. Osbornson."

"Thank you, Ms. Lathrop," I said. Then to Phil, "We'll make it up this evening. I love you. Gotta go."

My favorite student, Naomi Anderson, and her boyfriend, Mitch, walked in. They were both smiling. "What's up, you guys?" I asked.

"We're having our spring celebration next weekend and we'd like you to come."

This young woman, a Rouland Indian from a reservation northwest of here, is the best artist we've had at our school in years. She has a fine, natural talent, and an innate understanding of painting techniques. Naomi started as a freshman with excellent, illustration-style oils—painting from her head, photos, or in the field, moving composition and light around at will. I do mostly abstracts, and was delighted when she asked me to be her advisor—we have some outstanding representational painters on our faculty whose artwork is much closer to Naomi's genre.

"I'd love to," I said. "Mind if I bring Phil?"

"Of course not ," she said. "You can stay at the Guest Lodge Motel. My folks would love to meet him."

"Mine, too," added Mitch. "They think you're a celebrity, Ms. Osbornson."

"I *am* a celebrity," I assured them, dialing Phil's number while they waited.

"Yes," Phil said eagerly, "but don't include me in any plans for this weekend. I may have to work."

"Okay, kids," I said, "the trip's on. We'll be there next Friday. Take my reservation, please," I added, walking them to the door. They both groaned as they left.

Naomi sells enough artwork to support herself; and a self-supporting artist at twenty-two is practically unheard of. Her work, which includes a great variety of subjects, has evolved into a loose, realist mode. Her art career has really blossomed, quite unlike my sputtering start. It was almost by accident that I got even with the art establishment and started making real money from my paintings.

I grew up in Minneapolis and went straight through college at the U of M. It was in the middle '70s, when there was enough turmoil on campus to make life interesting, and free love did abound. I became rather cynical during those years, often finding myself, like most students, at odds with the faculty. Still, when my graduate work was finished, I applied for an instructor's position in the School of Fine Arts. So it was an unexpected pleasure when the school offered me the job. Oh yeah, I was married briefly in the late '70s. Big mistake.

My art sold but never at a rate or prices I felt it deserved. And I knew my work was better than most of the stuff available in the contemporary market. I had paintings in a couple of galleries around town, and priced my stuff mid-range. National exposure, I decided, was what I needed and hoped to get a shot at it in the annual show at the Twin Cities Art Institute.

The art institute's a big deal—it's the main art museum in town, and has major national status. Every spring they have a show and sale of paintings and sculpture from all over the country. It's an honor to be juried in, but they give a little leeway to works from the locals and the colleges, probably because so many of the institute's staff—mostly artists themselves—are associated with local schools. The show receives a lot of publicity and many works sell. It's a good fund-raiser for the museum, and the 25 percent commission is reasonable. I always tried to submit my best work, and sometimes I got two pieces in the show, the most allowed each artist.

While my show pieces usually sold, they never won so much as an honorable mention, and I was irritated that my gallery sales didn't improve in spite of the institute publicity. So my cynicism caught up with me one spring when I got crazy with my submittal to the Fat Fart Institute's show: I decided to paint with a shotgun.

At the bookstore on campus where I buy my art supplies, I found a few cans of acrylic spray paints, mostly with glitter and primary colors. I bought a can of bright yellow and a can of blue glitter but wanted the rest of the colors to be pastels. So I mixed up my own and took them to an auto body shop in my neighborhood. The owner happily installed my mixtures into pressurized cans.

I took a 30-by-36-inch stretched canvas, hung several warmed cans of spray paint in front of it, and gave them a blast of number 4's with Uncle Lucky's 12-gauge. Paint went everywhere, dripping from the canvas. Remnants of the cans flapped in the breeze. They swung against the canvas and made some strange arcs in the paint. I took the painting down and let it dry face-up on the picnic table so the colors would run together.

The result was surprisingly good, and I christened my masterpiece VØLM I. My regular paintings have great color and composition, and I labor to create as much mood and depth as is possible with abstracts. The shotgun painting had none of those qualities. It was simply a bright, disorganized splash of colors.

The more I looked at the VØLM, the more I liked it. So I filled in the pellet holes, framed it, and gleefully submitted it to the show with a $10,000 price tag on it. It not only sold, it won the Best of Show. They know I'm Scandinavian and the exotic name on the piece may have impressed them. For all I know it means BARF I in Swedish. My high-end art career was launched, allowing me to sell VØLMs at will. My other paintings began to sell faster, too, and at higher prices. No one knew how I produced the VØLMs with the exception of Lucky. The art press went crazy speculating about my technique, but I simply kept quiet and smiled a lot. I've refined and improved the process since then, but it's remained basically the same.

I had worked for almost an hour, then walked out to see Trish. "Phil and I got invited to the Rouland reservation," I said. "Their spring powwow is a week from tomorrow."

"See if you can figure out how that girl turned such a talent," Trish said. "Maybe the secret's up there in the woods."

The loudspeaker chimed. Class time was in a few minutes, and I had to pee.

## Three / Phil

A weekend visit to the Rouland tribe suggests all kinds of possibilities. I've always wanted to fish up there, and the reservation has several hot bass lakes reserved for tourists. Maybe Mitch will show me around, and I bet Shel will go fishing, too.

My first client, Ms. Thornton, just checked in with Molly, so I walked out and introduced myself.

A half hour later, Carol Thornton, twenty years old and at a major crossroads in her life, sat in my office, her hands covering her face, the statement charging her father with criminal assault in her lap. "This is all so depressing," she said. "I hurt so bad.

My father's going to go berserk. And what's Trudy going to do about school? She's only in sixth grade."

"We'll work that out with the child protection folks," I said, "but wherever she moves, there are schools nearby. It might be disruptive to her classwork but she needs to be away from home for a while. Anything's better than her present environment."

"Can she move in with me?" Carol asked.

"Ask that when you meet with Trudy's social worker," I said.

Carol appeared emotionally exhausted. "This is going to destroy my family . . . I've put off doing this for so long." Carol sat for a minute, then sighed and signed the statement.

We sat in silence a few more minutes. "Much of what we do in life involves feelings that are conflicting," I said. "Though you may feel you're tearing your family apart, it has to be done for you and Trudy. And believe it or not, for your mom and dad, too. Some things need to be unraveled before they can be mended."

Carol shifted her position on the couch, tears again welling in her eyes. She cried softly.

"It's painful and depressing now but these feelings are temporary. Would you consider a viewpoint that can help you get beyond them?"

She nodded, and I continued.

"You have the option of getting through this with only minor depression, if you understand that gloom won't benefit anyone or improve the outcome. Being depressed won't help the passage to happier times. So you have a choice here. Will you consider it in those terms?"

Carol shrugged. "Yes, okay," she said with a fragile smile.

We both stood and I offered her my hand.

"Thanks for having the courage to help yourself and your sister. Please bring Trudy in as soon as possible, and phone me any time." I opened the office door. "Remember, Trudy doesn't need to know about any of this until she gets away from your father and arrives here safely."

"I know," she said. "Thanks."

Dena Lewis, who had been waiting in the outer office, stood and hugged her friend.

"I'm calling home," Carol said with firm resolve. "I think it's spring break at Trudy's school next week. My mom can put her on the bus tomorrow morning. 'Bout time for another visit with her big sister in Minneapolis," she concluded.

Carol left quickly and Dena walked into my office, settling again onto the couch.

"Is it okay that I switched times with Carol?" Dena asked.

"Of course," I said. "Your willingness to help your friends is admirable. Now let's talk about why you're here."

"Don't you know why?"

"Psychiatry is not mind reading," I said gently. "How long have you had ulcers?"

"You're really going to help the Thornton girls, aren't you?"

I nodded. "I will do my *absolute best*."

"Then help me, too, Dr. Sloan!" Dena sobbed into her hands. "Help me, too! . . . since I was a little girl . . . and my mother and grandparents would *not* believe me."

Dena's stomach problems started about a year earlier, when she first talked to her mother about her father's abuse, and now the entire family refused to believe Dena. They began to protect themselves, ridiculing Dena about her complaints, and denying everything.

"I finally confronted both my parents at dinner one evening," Dena said as she paced around the office. "It was the night before I came back to school after Christmas break, a year ago. All my stuff was in the car and I was ready to hit the road if I had to." She recited her story with little emotion.

"What happened?"

"My father denied it. He's become more of a tyrant at home and he won't talk to me. I didn't even go home over spring break last week, just worked here in town. Mom blames me for his shitty behavior. Actually, he hasn't bothered me for several years, since before I was a freshman. I told him I'd kill him if he touched me again."

"You called him a tyrant. Has he always been a tyrant?" I asked.

"They're both tyrants in a way," she said, returning to the sofa. "My folks are paying for school, so I'm sort of tied to them." Now she was beginning to show emotion again, her voice breaking, alternating between sadness and anger.

"When I finally got up the courage to tell my mother, I thought she'd understand and protect me. If I had a little sister or a brother to talk to . . . it's always been just me and my folks . . . I feel so alone and betrayed!" Dena began to sob, drawing into herself.

I wanted to reach out to Dena, but I stayed in my seat.

"Unfortunately," I said, "it's often the pain and sense of aloneness that brings the courage to face the greater inner pain."

"I mean, maybe I shouldn't have told you about Carol's family, or any of this," she said. "The Women's Center up at school has been so helpful. I'm in a support group there, but my damn stomach keeps getting worse." Dena again rose from the couch and paced nervously around the office. "I need to do something—anything—will this help me feel better?"

"Quite possibly," I answered, remembering that letting the patient struggle sometimes gives clues, provides direction for the client's healing.

"Dena, do you want to sign a complaint against your father?"

"Yes."

After Dena's visit, I walked across the street and bought Manny Weston's latest mystery, picked up some fast food at the local burger joint, and settled in my office for lunch and paperwork—almost two hours until Sid gets here, and Sid's never late. I would have much preferred lunch with Shel, but I could use some downtime to recover from my sessions with Dena and Carol.

I finished my fish sticks and hamburger, put my work away, and opened the Weston mystery. Alternating between a strawberry yogurt shake and dregs from my coffeepot, I lay on the couch reading. But after a short time I became sleepy, so I closed the book, reached over my shoulder to the side table, and extracted a picture of Shel from the drawer. Resting the framed photo on my chest, I looked at Shel smiling at me in the morning sun, framed in the doorway of Lucky's cabin, the snapshot taken that summer ten years ago, when we reconnected.

Shelee and I lost track of each other after I finished high school. Years later, when I returned to Minneapolis to set up my practice, we met after Lucky sort of fixed us up. Shel had been married briefly and was between boyfriends. At a pub that caters to the late crowd, we spent our first date eating dinner and catching up. We hung out there, talking and drinking wine until the place closed. Shel was surprisingly candid in discussing her personal life, seemingly burned out on relationships. And I was sitting there falling in love with her face—flowers romanced by sunshine, wild in the mountain breeze.

"You said you were married almost four years. Were you two just so different that things couldn't work?" I asked. "Uh, sorry," I said, feeling the wine, wanting to keep the conversation going. "I withdraw that."

"No, I don't mind." She smiled sadly. "It wasn't that we were so different. I simply lost interest in him, in us really, in everything but school. It's still a mystery to me, and poor Mark was so bewildered by the breakup—I treated him terribly. It's just lucky we didn't have any kids."

Shelee paused and sipped her wine. "We tried to get pregnant the first year or so; it never happened. Turns out I had a pelvic infection that left me . . . well, anyway I can't have kids

"I'm sorry," I said. She appeared on the verge of tears.

"You probably don't remember," she continued, "I was in the hospital for a week with the damn thing, when I was seventeen. You were . . . what, fifteen then? What'd you eat? How did you get so large?" she asked, her mood brightening. "No, I mean tall. Shit, I've had too much to drink." She grabbed the edge of the table. "Long as I'm at it, what size shoes do you wear?"

I remember every word of this conversation. At that happy moment, Shelee blushed in the hollow of her throat, a tantalizing rose patch mingling with her freckles. This memory ranks somewhere above Linda Sorenson and the lilacs. Shelee Osbornson didn't seem to be anything like the girl I knew so many years before, although the more I reflected about the woman who sat across the table from me, the more I saw she had those special qualities way back then. She was now brilliant both in looks and wit, an absolute visual treat, medium tall with dark red hair—luxurious and long, and blessed with amazing brown eyes. Her breasts and figure are as generous as her attitude. And I think she doesn't believe me when I tell her I like a woman with meat on her bones.

I went over to her house for dinner on our second date. Turned out Shel could cook and owned quite a wine collection. Also, I met her cats, Fellini and Jesusa, who introduced themselves by jumping into my lap. "How'd you come up with this cat's name?" I asked as I lifted Jesusa, the black cat, off my lap. Shelee used the Spanish pronunciation for Jesusa.

"You mean, Jesusa Epstine? She's a black, Hispanic female, who happens to be Jewish—also an animal."

I laughed. "A woman for equal opportunity," I said.

"Yeah, except when it makes no sense."

"When's that?"

"I'll tell you," she said, pausing to eat paté, "when you're forced to promote and hire based on ethnicity and gender rather than artistic competency.

"For example," she continued, pointing with a cracker, "we had this big equal opportunity directive at school. It completely pissed me off—the art department already has the most diverse faculty and staff at the university. We sort of thrive with all the cultural differences. Anyway, the directive required that since we're an urban campus, our ethnic makeup had to reflect a cross section of Minneapolis and St. Paul. Give me a break! It was particularly insulting to our foreign faculty members. And all new hires had to be female, of course, to provide gender balance."

Shel picked up the hors d'oeuvres and glasses. Dinner was almost ready.

"So what happened?" I asked, following her into the kitchen.

"Oh, we appealed the stupid thing and got it modified so artistic and teaching skills had equal weight."

"Is the cat's middle name Ming Toy?" I asked.

"No, why?"

"It's an inside joke, Shel."

"Well, if it is, damned if I haven't improved on it."

Among the things Shelee dished up that night was her version of Lucky's venison meat loaf with a marinara sauce. It was delicious, and I told her so.

"I got the recipe from *The Rocky Horror Picture Show*."

"Are you familiar with the concept of derivative personality?" I asked.

"Hey, none of that shrink talk here." She smiled flirtatiously.

"In my line of work," I said, "we also call it goofball syndrome."

## Four / Phil

After some convincing, Trudy Thornton came in Tuesday morning, accompanied by her sister, Carol, and a local youth protection officer from the Hennepin County Children's Shelter.

Susan Tucker, a social worker who's worked with me before, spent Sunday afternoon talking with the two Thornton girls.

The police had done their part, placing Trudy in the shelter and preparing documentation for possibly charging the father. This was not the vacation poor Trudy had in mind. The youth officer gave the partly completed report to me, then left after a brief conference.

These sessions with abused kids are always disquieting. Carol sat with Trudy and the three of us worked through it. I arranged for Susan Tucker to meet us after the interview so we could complete the next, and perhaps most painful, part of the process. Trudy needed to be examined by a doctor for evidence of sexual abuse.

I admire how strong these young women are in the face of what must be impossible heartbreak. Carol and Susan went with Trudy to see a gynecologist in my building. They stopped by my office after the exam, and the doctor's report confirmed the abuse. Carol waited with Trudy in the outer office while I talked privately with Susan.

"You've manipulated the system again, haven't you?" I said, smiling.

"Damn right," Susan said. "Kids come first!"

Susan had delayed checking in with Youth Protection until midafternoon on Monday, extending Trudy's stay in Minneapolis by more than a day. When the mandatory, three-day hold at the emergency shelter is over, Trudy will be sent back to a Jefferson County facility.

"The only youth home in Jefferson County is in Stone Lake," Susan said, "and it sucks! This kid should stay in Minneapolis. Her father sounds like a crazy son of a bitch."

I shrugged. "Good luck. Hennepin's going to require that Jefferson County pay for it."

"Not if she moves in with Carol," Susan said. "Trudy wants to stay here, and I can arrange to get most of her expenses covered. The setup at Carol's looks pretty good to me."

I shook my head. "Susan, if you can pull this one off, I'll buy you lunch at any restaurant in town."

"You're out at least seventy-five bucks, Doc."

"Go for it!" I said, standing and giving her a high-five. "I'll recommend it in my report."

Molly just left and I'm sitting at her desk, finishing the documents. Carol remains quite apprehensive about her father's potential violence, and I plan to alert the Jefferson County sheriff to that. By three o'clock I'd talked with the sheriff's office in Stone Lake, faxed the signed statements, and sent the originals by overnight mail.

Jonah Thornton sat in his white 1978 Buick slant-parked in front of the Jefferson County Courthouse in Stone Lake, Minnesota. He rested his head on the car's cracked-blue steering wheel as murderous thoughts festered in his mind. Jonah placed Dena Lewis on the top of his list, followed by his two ungrateful daughters, and that big-city Jew-faggot Dr. Sloan. His mood smoldered as he picked at the sun blisters on the dashboard. How could his children turn on him like this? Should have never let that Carol bitch go off to college. He needed a plan—Judge Boyer had ordered him not to leave the county. I'll show the fucking judge, too, Jonah reflected. That bastard's first mistake was letting me out on bail.

Molly was talking with my answering service when I got to my office Thursday morning. She pushed a note into my hand and pointed to my door, continuing with her phone conversation.

The note said that Harris Martinsdale, the symphony director, was in a panic and to call him immediately. I dialed Harris on our other line.

"You know we're having a special concert series that starts Friday evening?" he said anxiously.

"Yes, I think so," I answered.

"Can you help us with a major crisis?" Harris asked. "Our guest conductor, Byron Ehlrich, was a close friend of Alexander

Godunov. He went into a real tailspin when Godunov died last week. Said he couldn't conduct this weekend. The four concerts are sold out, and he says he can't go on!"

"That *is* a crisis," I said. "How can I help?"

"Will you see him?"

"Yes, and tell me what else you feel is relevant."

"What's to tell?" Harris said. "Ehlrich rehearsed with the orchestra all last week, missed one day traveling to and from the funeral, and then made this announcement yesterday afternoon. I spent three hours last night convincing him to see you."

"I'm pleased you thought of me, Harris—I'll do what I can. Please hold a minute." I walked out to check my appointments and found Thursday full, including three new patients.

"I can see him at four o'clock this afternoon," I said.

"No earlier?"

"The day's totally booked, Harris."

"Thanks," Martinsdale said, "I'll ask him to call and confirm."

The moment I hung up, Molly came into the office. "There was an ugly phone call last night," she said, "and you'd better—

"I'll be with you in a moment," Molly called to my first client who'd just entered the outer office. Then she continued quietly, looking mildly concerned. "The answering service recorded it, and they're sending it over by messenger."

"Thanks," I said. "Can you stay through lunch? We'll deal with it then."

"Listen to it!" Molly frowned, waving the cassette. "I think it's from Dena or Carol's father. You want to send it to Jefferson County?"

"Maybe."

The message was typical of the threatening calls I've received in the past, but assuming it might be Lewis or Thornton, I called the sheriff's office and talked with Deputy Matthew Hartung, the detective who arrested both Morton Lewis and

Jonah Thornton the previous day. I played the recording for him.

"It sounds more like Thornton than Lewis," he said. "It's pretty muffled, but send it up. Any other folks who might be threatening you, Dr. Sloan?"

I said no, and he explained that the men had been released on bail, since they didn't currently pose threats to their children and because they have farms to look after.

"What about the wife battering charges against Thornton?" I asked.

"Yeah, I saw that in Carol's affidavit," he said, "and the county attorney has reviewed it. We interviewed Jonah's wife, and she's denying everything, including the incest. But she looks pretty scared, and we think she's lying. Right now there's no basis for charging him with battering. There's only been one previous complaint, and it was minor."

"Trudy's in an emergency shelter, and the two college girls are back in school," I told him, feeling frustrated. "But they can move to a women's shelter if they're in danger. What do you think?"

He was silent but I could hear him moving in his office. "Um, just a second," he said. I heard a door close. "Can we have a conversation that's completely off the record?" he asked.

"Of course."

"I saw in Trudy's paperwork that you and the social worker are recommending that she stay in Minneapolis. Possibly with her sister?"

"That's right," I said. "And last night's phone call reinforces that."

"Not returning an abused juvenile to the home county is highly unusual."

"I'll tell you what should be highly unusual, Deputy Hartung," I said, "is children being raped in their own home!"

"Please hear me out, Doctor. I've met the older two girls, and they're fine kids. I think this situation is terrible. My wife knows all three. She's been a 4-H adviser for twelve years, and Trudy's in my wife's group. I've got a ten-year-old who's a 4-H'er, too."

"What's your point?" I asked.

"Well, my wife, Elaine, has suspected something was bothering Trudy for some time. And, personally, I think it would be better for Trudy to stay down there. But the pressure's building here to return her after the three-day period."

"How's that?"

"Our child welfare bureaucracy doesn't want to foot the bill—it's cheaper to house her here. Then Jonah Thornton's attorney wants her up here for judicial convenience. You know, and return her to the environment she's used to. Maybe eventually move her back home."

"Screw that," I said. "We'll file a petition to keep her here."

"That's what I was going to suggest," Hartung said. "Your current recommendation is being ignored."

"Thanks for the feedback," I said, "but I don't like those guys out of jail. One of them is threatening me! It's great you made the arrests so quickly; *but* they got out too damn soon."

"You mentioned moving the older girls, Dr. Sloan," he said. "Do so if you want to, and I'll look into the phone call when I get your tape. Also, please send permission to access your phone records." I could hear him walking in his office. It sounded like he reopened his door. "We'll keep watch on both Lewis and Thornton. They're not supposed to leave the county without court permission, and they're restrained from any contact with their children."

"Thanks again," I said, and hung up, still angry that these two abusers were out of jail. I called Susan Tucker's office.

Nowadays I'm quite selective about my clients. But when I first started practicing, I'd see almost anyone who came through the door. It soon became evident that I could benefit only a few of those who sought me out, and fortunately I could afford to be choosy. During the last two years of my medical training in Washington, D.C., I banked a ton of money playing poker. The game's congressional contingent, gangsters, and other criminal types supplied me with a small fortune—I arrived in Minneapolis with about $1.5 million, so I didn't need a gigantic income from my practice.

I kept my rates low, made lots of referrals, and began enjoying more of my life. The medical community soon learned about my strengths and referred a good number of clients my way.

And then there's Sid. He's one of my racquetball partners. We played r-ball for some time before he hired me as a consultant—his way of denying he needs help. We both go along with the charade: I enjoy his company, and he's making a little progress. I prefer patients I can learn from as well as help, and Sid is always intriguing, but *I'm* the better racquetball player. That's how it is.

I try to understand people, figure them out before I get to know them. They told us in school never to prejudge it's a bad habit I have, a holdover from poker days. I was a little off the mark when it came to Sidney Simons—god, he hates his parents for that name. I figured him for a typical New Yorker. He's all the stuff compulsive people are about. Turns out he's from Chicago, even grew up and went to school there Sid has a master's in electronic engineering, worked as a circuit designer for a few years, then moved here. He started a company that makes custom, computer-driven stereo and home video equipment—high-end, expensive stuff. I guess the company's a success, because people from all over the world fly to Minneapolis just to buy systems and components from his factory salesroom.

Sid's divorced and has experienced several failed relationships since his divorce. He has two grown sons who live a long way from Minnesota, perhaps to distance themselves from their dad. I met Sid at our sports club, bashing away with the rest of the challenge court crazies. He's a tough racquetball player and has been known to lose his temper, but became easy to beat when I told him I was a shrink. Sid proposed the consultant arrangement with me, claiming it was for tax purposes. I was supposed to give him advice on "ideas he just wanted to kick around," as he put it. We met on alternating weeks for a while, now he comes in weekly. It's screwy for a psychiatrist and a client to socialize, even if it's now limited to racquetball. It's the only way it will work with Sid. If I told him to get another analyst, he'd quit therapy.

From my window, I could see Sid pull in next to the building. A patient's demeanor often is more revealing than most of what he says. Sid parked his sports car at an angle to take up two slots, then walked into the office and installed himself on the couch. He radiated intensity. "Doctor, Doctor, what's your advice for the day?" he said.

"Never park next to a Cadillac," I answered.

"I already know that, Phil. Tell me something I don't know."

"You may have a discount today for anything you already know," I said. "Maybe old Phil's out of advice." I moved out of my chair and sat on the couch next to him. He wouldn't look at me.

"No therapy," he said.

"It's your time, Sid. We can just sit here if you wish." I was totally bored with his bullshit. "You're a tough nut, Sidney."

Sid, who's around forty-five, has been in and out of counseling for ten years. He's too bright for effective therapy if he doesn't want it to happen. He instinctively figures ways to cover up whatever is bothering him. The session today was going nowhere, and we chatted along about nothing. Then I had an idea.

"Okay Sid, I think I have some advice for you. It has to do with an addictive behavior, one you may not be aware of. You know the psychobabble about addictions being ways to avoid reality?" I leaned forward slightly, remembering how much he values intellect. "Well, thinking . . . intellectualizing is an addictive behavior."

His Chicago accent surfaced. "Waddya mean?"

"I think all this intellectual stuff you do is a way to avoid your feelings," I said. "What do you think?"

Sid stood. "Enough for today! How much?"

"Half hour, a hundred bucks," I said, walking over to my desk. He handed me a check from his shirt pocket, then grabbed it back and filled in the amount.

"Goddamn Sid, I'm shocked you didn't have the dollar amount filled in, too. You're losing it."

"Fucking too smart for goyim," he sneered. "See you tomorrow for r-ball?"

"You bet," I said. "You get the court." Sid gave a quick nod, gave me the finger, and went straight out the door.

Not long after Sid left, a haggard and cheerless Byron Ehlrich sat on my sofa, talking with me about his friendship with Godunov, and the loss he felt at his friend's passing. Soon the conversation turned to the death of his own father many years before.

"I was about fifteen when my father died," Ehlrich said. "A few weeks before he passed away, he gave me a music box. It was in the shape of a pirate's treasure chest, made out of leather, from Italy, quite old, and it didn't work.

"I put it in a drawer and forgot about it," he said, staring out the window. "For some reason, I remembered the music box on the morning of his funeral. I removed the cover and discovered it had a simple mechanical problem. I fixed it easily." We both sat quietly until he could speak again.

"It worked then, but I have no idea what tune it played—a few of the sounding tines were broken off. Some of the pegs on the sound wheel moved full circle without making a note. Often I'll listen to the strangely fractured melody."

"Can you tell me why?"

"Old music boxes play ordinary tunes," he said. "This one does not."

"It still plays its tune," I said. "How does filling in the blanks make it ordinary?"

He stood and began to pace around the room, his words sad and intense. "I hear of fathers giving their sons good advice; mine did not. He was in his own little world. Perhaps my father had something to share with me, though he mostly talked about what he believed were his great accomplishments. But his accomplishments were just nonsense, and he blathered on so much, I quit listening to him."

"Maybe you quit listening to yourself," I suggested. "The death of your friend may be stimulating you to move on to new things, and to let go of your father's nonsense."

We sat quietly again. "Hum that music box melody for me," I said, breaking the silence.

Instead of the fragmented tune, he whistled the complete one.

"I never tried that before," he said "Must have known it all along."

We continued to talk about his family and music career. Byron decided he could add some ballet music and dedicate the weekend concerts to Godunov. I guessed the conducting problem was under control for the time being, and suggested he see a counselor at home in New York. When we were finished he asked about my fee; I told him it was my gift to the symphony.

It had been a long day and was after five-thirty when I finished putting my stuff away. I was about to leave the office when my spirits were raised by a call from Harris Martinsdale. "You have indeed given *us* a gift," he said. "I want to send you two free tickets to the '50s Ball when they're available, plus tickets to any concert of your choice."

"I'm glad I could help," I said. "The '50s tickets are thanks enough."

## Five / Shelee

Phil and I have this living arrangement that sort of evolved on its own. Though we each have our own home, about a ten-minute drive apart, we spend most evenings together. Tonight we're meeting at my house for dinner, and I hope we'll talk about Manny Weston. Phil says his appointments are on Thursdays.

Phil had a consulting arrangement with Sid Simons, too. But now Phil says Sidney's in therapy, so we don't see him socially. That's fine with me; Sid's a pig-and-a-half. About a year ago we went to dinner with Simons and his girlfriend, and he got into a noisy, pointless argument with the waitress about pasta, insisting she understand *his* definition of vermicelli. Ever since that evening, I've avoided doing things with Sid.

I'm jealous that Phil even gets to talk with Manny Weston. Weston's pretty shy and hardly ever gives an interview. I think I've seen but one interview in the *Minneapolis Post Express* during the ten years he's lived here, and never seen him on television. His books are fascinating.

"Did you see Manny Weston today?" I asked Phil as he walked through the doorway.

"I did," Phil replied, kissing me hello. "Dinner smells great."

"Talk about anything interesting?" I asked.

"Oh, not really. Just reviewing the psychology of growing up crazy. And we discussed some plot sequences."

"You invite him for dinner?" I asked.

"I was going to, Shel, but I want to wait. Manny's visit today felt like a prelude to therapy."

"I am disappointed," I said, tossing the salad. "I love his writing and it would be fun to get to know him. Is he married?"

"I think so," Phil said, helping me set the table.

"Oh, by the way, my sister asked if Fritz could go with us this weekend. All right with you?"

"Sure."

"I checked with Naomi and she said it'd be fine. There's lots of kids' stuff going on as part of the spring festival. Maybe we could eat dinner at the Sauk Fish Pier," I suggested. "You know, on the way to the reservation."

"Right," he said, as if he'd forgotten our plans. "I love the Fritzoid," he continued absently. "Although I think it's illegal to transport two related nuts in the same car."

"This nut loves you," I said. "Now open the wine and finish setting the table." I handed him the bottle from the fridge.

"Nice choice, Shel. What's the occasion?"

"We're having a pheasant I found in the freezer, one Lucky shot last fall. Let's toast the old fart." Phil opened the wine and offered me some. "That's aged nicely," I said.

Phil carried the salads and wine into the dining room, and I dished up the pheasant, rice, and vegetables.

Phil was staring out the window when I came in. He pulled out my chair and briefly rested his face in my hair as I sat down.

"You're so serious," I said. "Something on your mind?"

"Maybe so," he sighed. "Sorry."

"If you want more sex, it's fine with me."

He smiled. "You do have a way of lifting my spirits, Shelee."

"So what's bothering you?"

"Nothing really. Thinking about something a client said."

"Can you tell me?"

"He told me about his father's death, years ago. Then he was just a kid. Something related to that is still tormenting the guy —after all these years."

"Was he as young as you were when your dad died?" I asked quietly.

"Yes, even younger," Phil said. "Hey, I didn't mean to go morose on you. Did I tell you how good the morel sauce is?"

"Nope. And the fresh ones are all gone." Phil immediately seemed distracted again as he poured more wine.

"Oh, did you dry the rest?" Phil asked. "Maybe we can pick some more at the reservation this weekend." He drifted into his own thoughts.

"Good idea," I said, heading into the kitchen for seconds. "What time can you leave tomorrow?" I looked back at him for an answer as I left the room, but he wasn't listening.

I had seen Phil like this before, whenever the subject of fathers came up. Something was touching him very deeply, something more than the loss of his father—a loss that he's often talked about. But whether he'll ever tell me more than he already has, I don't know.

Later, after we'd gone to bed, Phil just lay there, perhaps thinking again about whatever was troubling him. I snuggled against him and tried to recall what I knew about Phil at the time of his father's death. Phil was probably a junior in high school, and though he was up at Lucky's a lot, it seems I hardly knew him. Lucky always hired a bunch of high school boys each summer to work on the farm. I briefly saw Phil coming out of the woods behind the cabin, not long after his father died.

It was near dusk one evening in late summer, and I was up at Lucky's collecting insect specimens for a summer biology class at the university. I wanted to speak to Phil, say something that might comfort him, but I could only stare and wonder. He didn't appear to see me. I had caught him unaware, in a private stupor of bewilderment and grief.

A dozen years later, soon after my divorce from Mark, I'd come to Lucky's for some self-understanding and peace. Poor Mark was truly devastated—I'd never meant to hurt him.

I walked beside the lakeshore one evening—again it was late summer—and headed up the limestone spring creek, the main one that feeds the lake. I sat down on a cottonwood log, in a grassy opening next to the creek, and watched the net-winged midges swarming over the rapidly moving water. Their strange behavior was familiar to me, an appreciating witness to their final and most important act.

Looking like oversized mosquitoes, almost an inch in length, with long, lacy wings, the midges appeared, emerging from the water to mate and die. First the males swarm over the stream, calling the females. Joined insects become double-ended, with wings at both ends, connected by their narrow bodies. In the orange light of the setting sun, to the sound of the swift-running brook, they performed a dance of creation and death.

The pairs first move their wings slowly, fluttering above the water and descending toward the stream. When close to the water, the male beats his wings rapidly, heading upward, overcoming the more tranquil wing strokes of his mate. Each duet, in the form of a winged *J*, ascends to ten feet or so above the stream. Then the descent begins again as the male drops below the female. Countless midge couples now danced over the water in their quiet rise and rapid fall.

Once the female is fertilized, the fatigued male makes one last attempt to rise as a couple. But now the female beats her wings faster, the couple separates, and the spent male drops into the water. The solo female continues the dance alone, laying her eggs perilously close to the moving creek, each time leaving the water's surface with a little less strength. Soon the exhausted female rests gently on the water, again joining her dying mate.

I continued to watch until the sun set into the forest, the western skyline streaked in tarnished silver. Even in the failing light, I could see small fish at the lake's inlet feeding on the dying insects, and I wondered about a life where one could fly and mating brings death.

Walking back to the cabin in the deepening twilight, I started to cry, something I don't do very often—then suddenly I recalled a young Phil Sloan coming out of these woods. At once I was crying harder than I can ever remember, sobbing out of control and unable to catch my breath. I stumbled along, frantically wiping the tears on both sleeves, crying into the crook of my arm. There was some comfort in the cool, wet pressure of my arm across my face, and I began to recover.

Uncomfortably damp and cold, I put on a sweatshirt and sat on the cabin's porch. Finally, I heated up some soup for dinner, changed into a flannel nightie, and went to bed early. Hugging my pillow, I imagined the stream's tumbling current and the midges' last, quiet song.

## Six / Phil

Friday afternoon I closed up the office early. When I got to Shelee's neighborhood of old Victorian homes, I could see her nine-year-old nephew, Fritz, buzzing around on his bike at the end of the street, speeding over driveways and jumping the curb. He bounced down hard when he saw me pull in, pedaled back quickly, and parked his bike behind the open tailgate of Shel's car.

"Hi," he said, out of breath. "Okay if we take my bike?"

"Sure. Are we taking Shel's car?"

"Yup." He grinned and ran into the house.

I put a load of things in the station wagon and followed Fritz inside.

Shelee kissed me as I walked in, and said loudly, "Fritz wants to show us something."

"Is this going to be one of Fritz's jokes?" I asked.

Shel nodded. "I come from a family of comedians."

A loony-looking Fritz came around the corner, wearing an old painting shirt of Shel's, tucked in at the waist. One of her cats was stuffed inside the shirt, humping around, making strange gurgling sounds.

"I'm not feeling well," Fritz said. "I haven't eaten for days."

Shelee smiled. "Poor thing, I can see you're all swollen up."

"I know," he said. "I don't know what's gotten into me." He flopped on his back in the middle of the room. He popped a button open and Fellini, Shel's tomcat, stuck his head out.

"They must have watched *Alien* together," I said to Shel.

The cat looked around, glared at Fritz, and bared his teeth, hissing. "Oh god!" Fritz screamed, "I'm giving birth to an alien baby." The cat struggled, trying to get out of the shirt. Fritz switched to a flat, mechanical voice, "Do not kill it. It is my baby and I love it."

"Some baby," I said, "it doesn't love *you*."

"It will in time," Fritz said, as the cat went berserk.

"Glad I trimmed his nails," Shel said, laughing. "Fritz, you'd better let him go."

"Your baby's a gut-munching, larval parasite," I pointed out.

"You may not speak that way about my baby," Fritz said, mimicking Shel. "It can never be a parasite." Fritz struggled with the cat, trying to keep it in the shirt. The cat thrashed free, trailing red ribbons that Fritz had tied to its hind legs.

"Cut the cords!" he yelled. The cat ran a few feet, became tangled in the ribbons, then turned and attacked Fritz the tormentor. "Oh, no, my baby hates me. It's trying to kill me!" Fritz fought to keep the cat from his head, then rolled over, face down. "It's turning on me! And after all I've done for it."

Shelee crawled over and grabbed the cat, holding her growling pet while Fritz pulled off the loosely knotted ribbons. "You're truly a funny kid," she sighed, wiping a tear on her sleeve. She set Fellini on the rug and he stalked off without a backward glance.

Fritz sat up, smiling broadly. She gave him a hug and said, "Let's load up and hit the road. I'm almost ready for dinner." We carried the rest of the things out to the car.

I drove, feeling the warmth of Shel's hand on my leg. Fritz sat in the middle of the backseat looking cheery and smug. We headed west on I-94, anticipating dinner at the restaurant in

Sauk Centre, over an hour away. I switched on the radio as the regional report came on NPR. Fritz perked up.

"You guys, here's a joke," he said. I turned the radio down. "Okay . . . these two North Dakotans are telling a joke and one asks, 'How many North Dakotans does it take to screw in a light bulb?' "

"Yes?"

"And the other replies, 'What's a light bulb?' "

Shel chuckled and said, "Very funny, Fritz. What would happen if you lived in North Dakota and told the joke about people who live in Minnesota?"

Fritz smiled. "What's a Minnesota?" he asked. This time I laughed.

Shelee turned and said to me, winking, "What do you suppose is the matter with Fritz? Professionally speaking?"

"Fritz is developmentally skewed," I answered. "In other words, Abby should have never named him Fritz. When you name a child Fritz, this is what you get. Fortunately there's not an analogous name for girls, except possibly Fritzina."

"Okay you guys, what's the name of the oldest living teriyaki pilot?"

"I think I've heard this one before," I said.

"Kamikaze Chicken!"

"You're going to like the Rouland folks, Zoid," I said to Fritz. "They give discount lobotomies. Auntie Shel is going to help me out with the costs."

"Will they put a tag around my neck so I'll get sent home?" Fritz asked.

"I'll be happy to pay the extra two dollars for the tag," Shel said.

Fritz picked up the Friday newspaper from the seat beside him and appeared to be reading. I waited for the kid's next joke. Shel dozed off, and Fritz, with an audience of just one, also snoozed.

When I turned north on 71, Shel woke up. She looked back at Fritz. "Wake up, bud, we're almost to the Fish Pier."

The kid was instantly awake. "Did I miss anything?" he asked.

"The only thing you missed," I told him, "was a motorcycle gang with naked mannequins strapped to the back of their bikes."

"Aw, you're kidding," he said. "Shel, did you see them?"

She yawned and stretched, "No but I wish I had; I was asleep, too." We pulled off the road into the parking lot of the restaurant. The place looked packed.

"Oh, no," Shel said, "I'm hungry. Hope we don't have to wait."

There was a table next to the water, just being set as we walked in, and to our surprise, no one was waiting for it.

"Not bad for no reservations," I said as we followed the hostess to the table. We looked over the menu, and I ordered one of their specialties, walleye with a lemon and mustard hazelnut sauce. Shelee decided on the fried black crappie, my second choice. Fritz ordered a hamburger and fries.

"You can order anything on the menu," I told him.

"No, he can't," Shel kidded. "I'm paying for this."

"Fine with me," I said. "Will you give me the money to pay for it? I love it when women give me money in public." Shelee just smiled. "You still could order anything," I said to Fritz.

"I'll just take a burger," he said.

"Are you pandering to us?"

"I'm not sure what that means, so you'll never know," he said. "Do you know Sean Gustafson's dad?" Fritz asked as the waiter left. "I think he's a shrink like you."

"If his dad's Homer Gustafson, then I do. He gave a talk at a psych seminar last month. Why?"

"Well Sean's always in trouble. Mr. Rickman kicked him out of English class the other day and said a funny thing after he left."

"What did he say?" Shel asked.

"He said psychiatrists' kids are always screwed up. Is that true, Phil?" Fritz asked, wrinkling his nose.

"The not-so-funny thing about it, Fritz my boy, it's often more true than not," I said. "Some mental health types depersonalize their children's problems. They've entered their profession hoping to get help with their own neuroses. As a result, they spatter their issues onto their children. Then when one of their kids has difficulties, they shrug it off as a typical kid problem."

Fritz looked at me and frowned. Just then the waitress arrived with our salads, a six-year-old Gavi for Shel and me, and a Coke for Fritz. Shelee tasted the wine. "This is extraordinary," she told the waitress.

I had a sip of wine, then turned to Fritz, "So anyway, these children get the message it's all right to be messed up, since the kid's part of his parents' therapy group, and he never has to take personal responsibility for change. At another level, he's fulfilling his family's wish, allowing his folks to work the problem at home with him. There's probably several unacknowledged agenda—"

Shel started waving her hand in front of her face, so I quit talking. Fritz crossed his eyes briefly, giving Shelee a sweet smile.

"I think I'll stick with shtick," Fritz said, shaking his head. "Sorry I asked."

I turned to Shel. "Thanks, this wine's a knockout. Let's take it with us if we don't finish it."

"I might finish it," she said, twirling her glass. Then to Fritz, "You want to taste it?"

"Naw," said Fritz, "I hate the stuff you drink." We finished our salads as the waitress brought the dinners. Shel and I split our fish and shared them. We offered some to Fritz, but he declined. "Remember, I'm a burger and fries kind of child?" he said, mimicking Shel. And a happy child, I mused, a happy child like Trudy Thornton should be—and I tried to visualize eleven-year-old Trudy keeping herself safe until she could leave home.

## Seven / Phil

We arrived at the Rouland reservation just before ten. The clerk, a pretty teen in a colorful Native American dress, greeted us. She handed Shelee a schedule of events and asked a few questions about the U of M. "Did you see the big mural behind the desk?" Shel asked. "That's one by my student," she explained.

When we got to our room, Shel called Naomi. A reproduction of the mural from the office hung above the couch. Fritz glanced at the print, sat down, and leafed through a comic book.

"Mitch and his dad want to take you boys fishing," Shelee said, waving the phone at us. "Says the bass are nesting this time of year, and should be ferocious."

"What?" she asked into the phone, then turned to us. "Mitch says the lake hasn't been fished yet this season." Shel was writing something down as she talked.

"I want to go," Fritz said.

"I'm in, too," I echoed.

"I noticed you didn't bring a pole," I said to Shelee when she hung up. "I'm sure you can borrow one if you want to go."

"No," Shel said, handing me the directions to Mitch's home, "I want to sleep in and have breakfast with Naomi and her cousin. Turns out the cousin is the girl who showed us to our room. I think she's quite the artist, must be in the genes up here."

"Better get some shuteye, child," she told Fritz, holding up the extra bedding. "Couch or hide-a-bed?"

"Couch."

Shel smiled. "Fine with me." We each gave the boy a goodnight pat on the head; Shel kissed him and I punched him lightly on the shoulder. We headed into the bedroom.

* * * * *

The alarm buzzed a few minutes before six. I leaned over and nuzzled Shelee, warm and sweet smelling. She reached up, patted my face, and wished us good fishing. I pulled on my fishing pants and went out to wake Fritz who was covered with a yellow blanket and sound asleep on the couch. "Wake up, bud, it's time to fish," I whispered, kissing him on the cheek.

"I don't think I want to go," he said groggily. "I'm going to hang out with Auntie Shel. There's lots of kids' stuff to do."

I sat next to him, running my fingers through his hair. "All right." I sighed and made a casting and fish-hooking motion with my arm. "Your Uncle Phil was looking forward to fishing with you." I reeled in a large, imaginary fish. "Are you sure you don't want to go? I'd enjoy your company." I held the fish up for Fritz to see.

He gave me a half-smile, sat up, and stretched. "Okay, I'll go."

We finished dressing and drove to Mitch's through the superb spring morning. The cottonwoods shed green light through their new leaves. The sun sifted through the foliage and cast filigreed emerald brilliance.

When we arrived at the Wallace's home, set back in the woods about a hundred yards off the main road, the enticing smells of breakfast greeted us. A thin Indian woman with long, graying hair greeted us at the door. She had a weathered, dark face with fine features, intense, almost black eyes, and a broad smile.

"Hi, I'm Melody Wallace," she said. "Mitchell's mother." She showed us into the house. "This is my husband, Frank," she continued as we entered the kitchen. We shook hands and I introduced Fritz just as Mitch came into the kitchen.

"Let's eat," Mitch said, "the bass are waiting." We sat down to a perfect fishing breakfast of fried perch and corncakes. Fritz ate a ton of food. We picked up our dishes, thanked Melody, and barged out the door. She patted Fritz on the shoulder as he passed her.

I walked over to the car and got our fishing gear. I also brought out a package of cheeses I'd picked up in town. Melody accepted the gift with a generous smile. "The way you enjoyed your food was thanks enough," she said. "Catch lots of fish, you guys."

Fritz and Mitch piled into the back of the family pickup and I rode in the cab with Frank. Unlike his wife, Mr. Wallace had light skin, dark brown hair pulled back in a ponytail, and a round face; he was somewhat on the plump side. He spoke in a matter-of-fact manner, without much enthusiasm. We arrived at the lake after a short ten-minute drive from the house.

Mitch took Fritz's hands and swung him down from the tailgate, talking excitedly about the fishing. "We don't get to fish this lake unless we have guests," Mitch said, "because it's reserved for the tourists. You're more welcome than you realize." He handed us the fishing gear as he talked.

Mitchell continued his mile-a-minute chatter, becoming more animated as the four of us put our poles together. We loaded our gear into two green rowboats equipped with small outboards. The boats were moored at a short pier, along with several similar-looking boats without motors. Mitch fired up the outboard on one boat, then motioned for Fritz to get in. Frank and I followed as their boat stitched a straight wake across the calm lake, and headed for a wooded shore about a half mile north of the pier.

"There are some beaver houses in the water along that shore," Frank said, as he pointed to some low piles of brush a few feet out from the bank. He handed me a top-water plug that looked like a frog. The back hook was removed and the remaining treble hook was trimmed to two prongs with the barbs flattened. "Let's use these plugs," he said. "We'll keep a few fish and release the rest. The females like to keep closer to home and guard the nest, so we should catch mostly males."

Frank cut the motor and put the oars in the water as we drifted toward one beaver house. The kids had arrived a few moments earlier and I watched Mitch wait for Fritz to make the first cast. Fritz, an experienced fisherman, was so excited that his first cast went into the middle of the brush and was immediately snagged up.

"We'll get it in a second," Mitch said, handing Fritz his pole. Here, catch a fish or two before we go after your plug."

Fritz laid his pole in the bottom of the boat and cast with Mitch's. He brought the plug back quickly to within a few feet of the beaver house and then started a slow reel-and-stop motion. The bait appeared to be swimming on the water. The water exploded underneath the plug as a five-pound large-mouth blasted free of the lake. Fritz set the hook while the bass was still airborne and reeled quickly to take up the slack.

"I can see you know what you're doing," Mitch said.

Fritz, for a change, was speechless while the bass made another jump and several runs before they netted it.

"Did you see that?" yelled Fritz. "Man, what a fish!" Then he grinned at Mitch. "Thanks for letting me catch the first one," he said, and handed him the pole.

We watched as this especially graceful kid climbed onto the unsteady brush pile and retrieved the plug.

"Pitch the plug into the boat," Mitch suggested. "A bass could take it right next to us. We'll come back here in a few minutes." Then he called out, "Dad, cast about ten feet off of that next brush pile and watch what happens." He pointed to a mound of sticks about fifty feet away.

"I was just going to make that suggestion," Frank said with a subtle nod. We both cast in the indicated direction, resting the plugs in the water for a moment before reeling. A ripple appeared next to the brush. The ripple became a fin extending above the water, then enlarged to a green-black hump charging directly at my plug. Frank had stopped reeling.

"Don't flinch," he said. It was good advice. The fish smashed into my plug and kept going, directly at our boat. I tried to set the hook while reeling frantically. The bass became a flying fish, leaving the confines of the lake and sailing directly at me. I had no chance to tighten my line, much less set the hook. The bass shook the plug off in midair, splashing water on me as he hit the surface and dove free. I stared at my plug bobbing a few feet from the boat.

"If they're charging like that, reel fast as hell just before they strike," Frank said, fighting a bass that had taken his plug shortly after mine hit. I netted his fish and looked over to see the boys both playing fish at the same time.

"You want a towel, Uncle Phil?" Fritz hollered. I ignored him and cast again, this time hooking a fish that jumped twice and threw the plug. Two casts later, I finally landed my first fish. Frank already had two and there were at least three in the kids' boat.

"This fishing is better than I've seen in years," Frank said. "You guys are good luck." We fished at a slower pace as he talked about his tribe's history. "Our tribe had an Indian name, Tekaot, before the settlers came," he said. "I think Rouland is a bastardized word for 'rolling butt' in French. The fur trappers called us 'Rouland,' and the name stuck."

"Did you consider going back to the original name?" I asked.

"The government blackmailed us when the reservation treaty was signed a hundred years ago. We requested a name change and they refused, promising we'd get more money if we stayed with Rouland. We never got the money and we've still got the name; I guess everyone's comfortable with it now."

"I hear your tourist activities have really paid off," I commented.

Frank gestured with a sweeping motion around the lake. "You know Quincy Anderson, Naomi's father?" I shook my head. "You'll meet him this afternoon. We're mostly responsible for this tourist development. I studied wildlife management in college and moved back here after school. Quincy studied business. It was sort of expected that graduates would return to help out, or at least send money. That's where I met Melody—at the university. She's Nez Perce. Man, has she got stories to tell."

We paused to watch Mitch boat a bass weighing close to eight pounds. Mitch held it up for a moment, then returned it to the water. Frank gave his boy thumbs-up. "Nice fish, son," he yelled.

"You've a great kid there," I said. "I understand he's near the top of his class. And I love the way he's interacting with Fritz."

"He is a good kid," Frank said. "You know, things were different when I went to college. The state legislature, in its infinite generosity, established an Indian scholarship program where one boy and one girl from each reservation were given full tuition to a state college. I got mine one year and Quincy got his the next. It was a four-year ride and a good deal for whoever got it. But it sure left a lot of talent back home here. Everyone was so poor in those days, no one else could afford to go to college."

Frank rowed toward another brush pile as he talked. "We advertised and developed a bunch of these fishing lakes; in the fall, we do guided hunts for grouse, pheasant, and whitetails, and things have just boomed. Next year we're going to start promoting cross-country skiing and ice fishing. Now, most of our kids can go on to college if they want to. And we've got our own scholarship fund. We're even thinking about starting a summer camp." He held up two fingers at the back of his head, smiled, and said, "Give them city kids a taste of Indian life."

"Ever consider a gambling casino?" I asked. "So many other reservations are doing the gambling thing."

"We've talked about it—a possibility, maybe," he answered. "We're doin' okay and almost everyone likes the rural atmosphere here. And that's tied into our cultural identity. Besides, it's a beautiful place—I'd hate to spoil it with a casino and crowds of people." He looked at his watch and called to the other boat. "Time to head back, gentlemen; we can fish again tomorrow."

Back at the pier, Mitch and his dad cleaned the fish while Fritz and I put the fishing stuff away. They locked the motors and boat gear in a metal shed on the shore-end of the pier.

It was almost ten-thirty, and Fritz was all smiles. "What a great morning," he said. "I bet Shel will want to come tomorrow." We loaded into the truck and headed back to the Wallaces'.

"There are some less-visible benefits from our economic success," he said. "We've been able to control the usual alcohol problems, and money has been the main factor. We've got our own chapter of AA here and a full-time social worker. Years ago, there was all the booze-related child and spouse abuse crap. It was terrible, but now the social worker handles those problems, too. Mitchell tells me you're an advocate for abused children."

"I've had a pretty good record of helping abuse victims," I said. "I become almost evangelical when I get involved on their side. But I refuse to treat perpetrators—can't develop the right empathy."

"We're tough on drunk drivers, throw 'em in jail," Frank said. "Drunks, too. Our reputation is tough enough that I hope you'll see real restraint in drinking this weekend. You know, I think psychiatry is the one form of Western medicine most like Indian shamanism. Do you prescribe drugs?"

I nodded.

"I've seen some of our people really fucked up on psychiatric drugs." He waved a finger at me, raising his eyebrows.

"I'm feeling slightly cornered," I said. "Psychotropic medications can be misused like any other; they need careful monitoring. Some of these drugs have miraculous results when used properly, though not all individuals respond. I'm really careful about giving out prescriptions. Less than a quarter of my patients are on meds."

He seemed satisfied with my explanation. We rode silently for the rest of the short trip back to his house.

Melody, Naomi, and Naomi's cousin were sitting at the kitchen table, drinking coffee with Shelee when we walked in. Fritz could hardly contain himself. "Aunt Shel, you've just got to go fishing with us. You'll never believe how great it is!" I walked over to Shel and kissed her on the cheek.

Shelee introduced Naomi's cousin, Kathy, then said, "Let me see your fish, then I might believe you." Mitch produced the cooler filled with bass. "Now I'm a believer," Shelee said. "When do we go?"

"Tomorrow morning," said Fritz. "We threw a bunch of big ones back!"

Shel smiled at Kathy and looked up at me. "Phil, I want you to see some of Kathy's paintings. I'm sure she can be considered for a scholarship at the art school. She graduates high school next spring."

"How 'bout we come visit before dinner this evening?" I suggested.

"Sounds fine," Kathy said.

Melody set out a plate of smoked northern pike and some of the cheese I'd given her. The fish was delicious, and I had to restrain myself from eating the whole plate. Fritz had no trouble; he crammed a big piece of fish into his mouth, then wandered outside to look around, giving a hint of the comic as he left, appearing to almost run into the screen door. After a while, most of us piled into the cars and headed for the opening ceremonies.

## Eight / Shelee

The ceremonies were held in the large field across from the Guest Lodge. Benches were set up facing a bandstand decorated with red, white, and blue streamers. Additional decorations included the American flag, the Minnesota state flag, and the flags of several nearby states. Indian coup sticks, festooned with feathers, wads of fur, and red, white, and blue streamers, flanked the flags. I could only speculate as to why our national colors were on the coup sticks. I nudged Phil. "Those fur wads aren't scalps, are they?" He shook his head without looking at me.

Behind the benches was a group of picnic tables. Farther back, smoke rose from several barbecues. I admired our glorious spring sky, which had sprouted some puffy clouds. A number of women were unloading goodies from cars and putting the food out next to the grills.

Naomi said she'd like us to sit at one of the tables in the front, just behind the benches. This first row of picnic tables had red-and-white tablecloths, the remaining ones were bare. Frank Wallace had donned an Indian tunic and had a large black feather in his hair. The feather hung from a short, beaded strand tied just above his ponytail. His tunic, a long, almost white, buckskin shirt, was decorated with red and yellow painted symbols.

Frank was showing people to the front tables, as were Naomi and her cousin. Kathy brought over an elderly Indian couple with two children in tow, and introduced the adults—dignitaries it seemed—from the Aplosa reservation in South Dakota. They in turn introduced their grandchildren. The little girl, Louise, who looked about ten, wore a white suede dress adorned with exquisite beadwork. She was slightly taller than Fritz and gave him a shy smile. "You want to play my video game?" she asked. Fritz nodded as she produced a hand-held computer game from the broad pocket of her dress. The other grandchild, a seven-year-old boy named Dell, joined in, and the three became immediately engrossed in the game. The device gave off tiny beeps and squeaks, and Mrs. Black Fox—no one had offered first names yet—reached over and turned off the game's sound.

"I've been doin' that for two days," she said to Phil and me.

"Grandma, the sound resets every time we turn the game off," Louise explained.

Grandma looked skyward. "Is that so?" she said as she offered me her hand. "My name's Martha and this is my husband, Bill. I'm in charge of video games; Bill's in charge of everything else."

I shook her hand. "I'm Shelee, and this is Phil and Fritz."

Soon, Quincy began his speech from the bandstand. Phil, who hadn't met him yet, whispered, "I didn't know Quincy was the tribal chairman."

Quincy Anderson looked very regal, dressed in yellow buckskin decorated with a profusion of white fur ropes along his sleeves and shoulders. A cascade of small-beaded, multicolored shell necklaces hung around his neck, and his two long braids were tied off into large bone medallions. It turned out the front tables were reserved for special guests, and looking around, I discovered, except for another couple a short distance away, we were the only non-Native Americans present. When the white woman at the other table—she looked familiar but I don't pay much attention to politics—was introduced as Minnesota's lieutenant governor, I began to feel really honored.

Next, I was introduced as professor and mentor to Naomi. Bill Black Fox was introduced as the chief of the Aplosa. There were representatives of several tribes and reservations here and, as Bill and the other tribal leaders were introduced, each walked up to the bandstand and took a seat next to Quincy.

While the introductions dragged on, the wind wafted the smell of barbecue to the crowd. My appetite responded. Louise was fiddling with the computer game when the sound came back on, and Martha looked at the kid and smiled with just a touch of fire in her eye. Louise turned off the game and handed it to her grandmother.

After everyone had been introduced, a large drum was brought out. The men on the bandstand gathered around it.

The older men pulled their chairs up to the drum; the younger ones squatted next to it. Chief Quincy requested that Mrs. Ormstead, the lieutenant governor, join the drummers. I decided it was a big deal to ask a woman to join what appeared to be an all-male club. She, of course, agreed—everyone was playing politics here. Someone pulled up a chair for her and handed her a drumstick.

Then Chief Quincy announced that the festival was officially open. "Now, our dance of welcome," he said. The drummers started drumming and chanting. Louise, along with a number of other kids, got up and began to dance in a loose circle to our left as Quincy joined the drummers. My stomach growled, the seat was hard, and I was bored. Then I noticed Phil Sloan.

Phil had moved to the grass in front of me. Even sitting, he looked taller than everyone else. I could see his shoulder muscles under his shirt as he reached to hand something to Fritz. Goddamn he looked good. I imagined running my hands under his shirt. Perhaps he sensed my look, because just then he turned and winked at me. Did he give a little flex? I forgot my hunger and the hard seat, wanting him then and there. Phil sported a hat that only he could wear—told me he bought it at the Salvation Army store, but I think it cost a small fortune from some catalog outfit. The thing looks like a western hat from the 1920s, tan felt with an off-center *v*-shaped crease in the crown, and a straight, six-inch brim with a modest downcast in front. Phil's blond hair stuck out all around. I was beginning a wonderful sexual fantasy when Quincy left the drummers and invited everyone to start enjoying the food, join the dancers, or both.

Martha sprang to life. "Lunchtime," she declared, as she motioned for Bill to come down off the stage. Bill stood up and pointed his drumstick in our direction. I thought for a minute he wanted Phil or me to be a drummer, but to my relief he was pointing to a young man behind us. The new drummer relieved

Bill Black Fox. "He's from our tribe," Martha said as Bill joined us. "Let's eat."

"So you're the chief," Phil said to Bill as we filed along the back tables, filling our paper plates. "I guess you *are* in charge of everything."

"Everything except Martha and the rest of the women in my family," Chief Black Fox said wearily. "They're all head-strong and mostly nuts. What do you do?"

"I'm a physician, a . . . a psychiatrist," Phil answered.

"No shit! Where do I sign up?" Bill asked. "You make house calls?" He looked behind him, concerned his grandchildren might have heard him, then patted Phil on the shoulder.

Nearby, we could hear a man talking to Mrs. Ormstead, complaining about some legislation, but couldn't make out the details.

"Bill, I bet you hear a lot of that," Phil said.

"That's all I ever hear," he replied. "I'd guess you get paid a bit more than I do for listening to all that bull."

Phil smiled. "Well, salaries in the city are somewhat higher than in the country."

We began to eat, but the Black Foxes hardly had a chance to enjoy their lunch—groups of people came by to say hello and chitchat. Sometimes we were introduced, and other times not. Everyone seemed to be enjoying themselves.

Fritz and Dell were almost finished eating by the time Louise joined us, her face and dress dusty from the dancing. She balanced a sizable plate of food and a couple of cans of pop. She might have dropped them if Fritz hadn't helped her. With the dancing completed, it was announced there would be various games in the field behind the bandstand. Quincy Anderson and his wife came over with their lunches and soon became involved in conversations with the people coming by to see Bill and Martha.

When Kathy and Naomi walked over with ice cream, the Black Foxes decided to move on.

"We're going for dessert and coffee," Martha said, picking up their plates. "I think we'll visit around. We enjoyed talking with you folks." She bent over and kissed each child on the head, including Fritz. Fritz gave Martha a sly smile. "Change your dress before you go to play," she reminded her granddaughter.

"I want to talk about the headshrinking business sometime," Bill said to Phil as they left.

"Dammit, I feel like painting and I didn't bring my paints," I said. "Guess I'll get my sketchbook and chalk."

"Please bring me my book," Phil asked as I got up to go to the car. When I returned with my stuff and Phil's book, I contemplated asking him if he wanted to go back to the room and take a nap, but the colors of the day were too inspiring, and I decided to draw—at least for now. His book was a Manny Weston mystery, a hardcover, and inside the flyleaf there was an inscription from Manny to Phil.

"Did Weston give you this?" I asked, handing him the book, flipping the cover shut.

"No, I bought it about a week ago," Phil said. "But he signed it when he saw I had the book."

"Signed with an author's personal message, now that's worth something," I said. We sat with our backs against the table's top, enjoying the sights and the sunshine, and I started to sketch. The kids headed for more dessert, offering to bring us something. We asked for coffee.

I drew the dancers from memory, using the children playing in the field for reference. A cloud of dust, partly hiding the drummers, provided the mood. I started over, this time putting drummers on the ground, the setting an ancient ritual, the dancers suspended in dust. On the next sheet, the dust became the focus, colors became the dancers—that was the effect I wanted, things alive in the dust cloud. What are they? Why are they there? I ran some black into the color shapes. They gesture to me as I move quickly to the next sheet. Same format, the color forms become signs, a space map for movement.

This is good work, I thought, and not really appreciated. I sat back, closed the sketchbook, then my eyes, taking in all the sounds of the day.

"Think I'll go play ball," Phil said softly, caressing my hand. I showed him my sketches and he nodded approvingly, studying the first drawing of the drummers, dust, and dancers. "Ever consider doing something like this, something representational?" he asked.

"I've considered it. Can't wait until I get these last two on canvas. Next time my paints come with us." Then I flipped the paper over, showing him the final two sketches again.

"Nice," Phil said. "Visually poetic." He kissed me and left for the ballfield.

I got a little choked up as I watched him walk away, feeling so much love for him. I wondered, what did he just do? Phil encourages and supports me—loves me—yet I never feel pushed or crowded.

On my way to the playground where the little kid games were going on, I took some things back to the car. I opened the mystery book and reread Manny's odd inscription: "Dr. Sloan," it said, "mysteries within mysteries."

## Nine / Phil

Later in the afternoon, we went to see Kathy's paintings, driving the ten miles or so to her cousin's house with Naomi as our guide. We stood around and talked with her parents, drank a beer, and looked at her artwork. I felt a little awkward, and didn't like the paintings, which were stark, weird, and amateurish. When I discussed my impressions with Shel, she explained the fine points of seeing beyond the work at hand.

"Consider the hidden psyche," she said. "It's like one of Manny's secret rooms, revealed only when one suspends common perceptions."

"Sounds like art BS to me."

"I tell you this girl has superior potential. Trust my judgment as a teacher of great artists."

"Good enough," I said.

The evening pig roast took place at a pavilion, next to a small lake, about a mile from the Guest Lodge. It was a beautiful setting, with ducks and geese swimming on the lake and weeping willows along the path leading to the pavilion. We sat under a cottonwood tree at a circular table built around the trunk.

"Can we run or something next week?" Shelee asked me as we munched on roast pork and trimmings. "This is turning into Fat Weekend."

"Let's jog Tuesday and Thursday mornings," I suggested. "The six A.M. thing. I've got racquetball on Monday and Wednesday."

Shel gestured with the last morsel of barbecue on her fork. "Sounds good to me. Okay with you, piggy?" she said, chomping down on the piece of pork. "That's it. No seconds for this girl. Coffee only, no ice cream, maybe a cookie." She pointed in the direction of Fritz, who sat with Louise, her brother, and their grandparents. The kids sat off to one side, away from the adults who shared the table. "I think he likes that cute girl," Shel said. "Takes after his Uncle Phil—sweet on slightly older women." She grabbed a handful of my shirt and pulled me forward. "*Slightly older,* right Phil?" A group we'd talked with earlier that day walked past us. Shel let go of my shirt and smiled at them.

"There's dancing after dinner," a woman said. "Save me a polka," one of the men said to Shelee.

"Ya, sure," Shel said.

Soon, the band took the stage and began tuning up. Judging by the band members' appearances—they had long hair and tie-dyed clothes—I figured we'd get a dose of bad rock and roll.

"Try to polka to those guys," I said to Shelee. She shrugged.

While the band tuned up, Chief Quincy gave a short speech, talking about the prairie potlatch, scheduled for tomorrow.

"We have borrowed this idea from our Northwest brothers, substituting our own good food for theirs," he explained. "Now enjoy the dancing, my friends, and thanks for being here."

We walked over to sit with the Black Fox family and Fritz. "Why're you two over there by yourselves?" Martha asked.

"We enjoy each other's company," Shel said. "We figured to get plenty of socializing once the dancing starts." About then the band fired up a strong country-western tune and people moved to the dance floor. The music was quite good, and Shel and I joined the dancers. A number of men asked Shel to dance, including Lester Ormstead, the lieutenant governor's husband.

I danced with Dorothy Ormstead, and afterward she and her husband sat with us. We talked briefly about some proposed legislation that dealt with child abuse. She knew I was due to consult with some folks in the governor's office on the topic. I danced with a few ladies, including Martha and some of the women I'd met in the afternoon. Naomi and her cousin were nowhere in sight. I was feeling tired, and Shel looked pooped from all the male attention. She suggested we leave, I agreed, and we said our goodnights.

On our way to the motel, we crossed the road to the potlatch site where a pit had been dug and lined with smooth stones. We stopped to chat with the fire crew who were setting wood into the pit, then headed across the street.

"God, the food's going to be good tomorrow," Shel said. "I'm still full from dinner but I bet I recover by morning."

When we got to the motel, Fritz was watching TV with several people in the lobby.

"I've been up since six o'clock," I told him. "We're going to bed."

"I'll be in as soon as the show's over," he said. A few minutes later he popped into the room.

"Why were you watching TV in the lobby?" Shel asked.

"I like what those Indians have to say about the TV shows," he said. "I can use some of their screwed views in my comic routines."

"Skewed, not screwed, Fritz," Shel corrected him. "Kinda off center like you, my boy. Why don't you play Little League like your friends?"

"What's Little League?" Fritz asked.

"I should have known better," Shelee said, shaking her head. "Here, let's make up your bed." She got the yellow blanket out of the closet.

"When you guys go to bed, are you going to do it?" Fritz asked, wrapping his arms around his head and standing on one foot.

Shel grabbed him from behind, digging her knuckles into his head. "Do what, Fritzie?" she asked as the kid squirmed and struggled.

"It!" he said.

"What's 'it,' you smart aleck twerp?" She continued her knuckle torture.

"You know, 'it,' 'the deed!' " Shelee picked Fritz up, held him upside down, and squeezed. His arms and legs stuck out in all directions.

Fritz gasped, "Please put me down, oh mighty aunt. You're killing me."

"I'll let you off easy, this time," she said, tossing him in the direction of the couch. He bounced against the back cushions and lay there, maybe wondering if he'd offended her. "What kind of question is that?" Shel asked. "You've stayed with us many times and never asked a question like that." Shelee smiled, and Fritz relaxed a bit.

"Yeah, I'm curious, too," I said, thinking about screwed and skewed.

"I'm getting more tuned in to adult relationships," he said, starting to look cheerful again. "Mom wonders how come you guys don't get married."

"I'll be damned!" Shel exclaimed, "I *just* discussed this with Abby!"

Fritz, surprised by her outburst, covered his face.

"I'm sorry, Fritz," Shel said, making a gesture of futility with her hands, "but I'm just irritated that your mom keeps bringing it up."

I looked at the kid. "Fritz, Shel gets just as mad when I ask her."

"Just so you're both aware," she said, "it's nobody's business except Phil's and mine." Then Shel struck her Carmen pose. "Besides, *Il matrimónio é tomba del amore!*"

"Carmen speaks Italian?" I asked.

"She speaks any language she wants to," Shel responded imperiously.

"What's that mean?" Fritz asked.

"It means, Marriage is the tomb of love," I said.

"What's *that* mean?" he asked. "Death to love?"

Shel sat next to Fritz and put her arm around him. She rearranged his hair affectionately. "This is one chick who doesn't want to find out, sweetheart. Now it's bedtime." Shelee spread the blanket on the couch and fluffed up Fritz's pillow. "Is anyone fishing in the morning?" she asked.

"I want to sleep in," I said. Fritz gave us his we-just-gotta-go-fishing look.

"Then let's call and see if we can fish after the potlatch tomorrow," Shel suggested. She hugged the kid, walked into the bedroom, and closed the door. I called Mitch's house and left a message.

"They're still at the dance" I said. "I'm sure we can fish in the afternoon. They'll be tired in the morning, too." Then I kissed the slightly confused nine-year-old on the forehead and said, "Goodnight."

Jonah Thornton drove to Stone Lake Saturday evening to meet Morton Lewis. Only a few days had passed since he'd been charged, and released on bail. He felt an overwhelming fury at having to pay advance lawyer fees, suffer the annoyance of people's stares, and pledge his farm for bail money. Pledging the farm was probably okay, he thought; that left available cash—just in case. He had to move quickly because there was a hearing in a week or two. Then the trial could start as early as July. He'd built his farm—his family's for over seventy years—into one of the showplaces of the county. The damn women in his household had sabotaged everything. Even stupid Mary blamed him for all the troubles.

But Jonah had a plan, one he could try out soon. He pulled up to the Stone-Rock Bar, parked his car, and went inside, then sat at the bar until Lewis showed up. They moved to a table near the back and talked while they watched three motorcycle girls shoot pool.

Morton Lewis smiled at Jonah. "I heard the brigade commander booted you out last month."

"No goddamn way," Jonah said. "I'm on probation. That's all."

"What did you do?"

Thornton guzzled from his beer bottle, set it down, and wiped his hand across his mouth. "Nothing. Just told those idiots what's really wrong with this country." He rubbed a napkin between his hands. "Troop practice is next Sunday. You want to ride out with me?"

"No," Lewis said. "My lawyer told me to quit. Bad for my image." He turned slightly and stared at the floor.

A pool shooter racked the balls, then broke them with a loud crack. Her companion dropped some change into the jukebox. The first shooter began to run the table.

"I'm thinking about pleading guilty," Morton Lewis said over the noise blasting from the jukebox. He stirred his drink despondently, then broke the plastic stir-stick into several pieces and dropped them into the ashtray.

Jonah glared and pointed at Lewis, his hand like a pistol. "What? You're a fucking chickenshit."

Lewis shrugged. "I won't have any chance with the court," he said. "Helen's decided she wants a divorce, and plans to testify against me."

"Wives can't do that!" Jonah hissed.

"My attorney said she can, since she knows what's been going on."

"I hate all them pussies!" Thornton raged. The pool players looked over at him.

"Goddamn, Jonah, pipe down, or they'll kick us out of here," Lewis said.

"Go to hell!" Jonah growled.

Morton Lewis pushed his chair back, stood, and dropped some money on the table. He headed for the side door.

"Do what you want," Jonah called after him. "but I'm damned if *I'll* plead guilty!" Thornton was left alone with his thoughts—the nidus swarmed in his brain.

I woke up to find Shel returning from the bathroom. She gave me a rather lingering snuggle, which got me thinking about lovemaking. Fritz appeared sound asleep on the couch when I looked out at him, but I decided to lock our door anyway. No luck, no lock.

I got into bed with about half a hard-on. Shelee moved lovingly next to me, then suddenly got face to face, pressing her nose against mine. With her eyes just a couple of inches away, she looked cross-eyed and strange.

"Let's do the *deed*," she said. "Is the Twerpoid asleep?"

"Yes."

She was wearing a pair of my pajamas and had unbuttoned the top; her breasts felt wonderful as she pressed against my chest. She reached inside my pajama bottoms—we were still nose to nose. "Why Phil," she said, "I believe you've been thinking about me."

"Nope, I was really thinking about the eight-pound bass Mitchell caught, loopy eyes." I rocked my head back and forth.

"Let me see if I can get you to pay better attention," she said. "How about this?" Shel snooped under the covers and kissed my penis—now that got my attention. I was trying to get her pajama bottoms off to repay the favor, when she surfaced. "I'm afraid Fritz is going to wake up," she said. "Time to bury the bologna."

"Have you ever considered writing romantic Minnesota poetry?" I asked. "You've missed your true calling."

We made love under the covers in case the kid peeked in. I loved the way she took my hand and pressed it against her mouth when she came. Then she let go of my hand and lay there giggling quietly, catching her breath. We rested in each other's arms.

"Now, wouldn't you rather make love with me than fish?" Shel asked.

"I'll have to think about it," I said, "the fishing's pretty good up here."

She again took my face in both her hands. "I can have you knocked off, white eyes. I have friends here on the reservation." Shelee pressed my cheeks together, moving my head from side to side. "They would understand, death to a nonhuman species. I am She-Eagle-Who-Humps."

I laughed. "I guess I knew that."

"I will have your butt stuffed to decorate my parlor," Shel continued. She released my face and shoved my head back against the pillow. Then she cuddled against me, her face touching my neck. "Oh, I love you, my Phil." We both drifted back to sleep.

The kid woke us up at about eight o'clock when he looked in. "Hey, get up you guys—I'm hungry."

Figuring he was still curious about us, I didn't mention that he'd forgotten to knock. "They're serving doughnuts and stuff by the potlatch fire if you can't wait," I said. "We'll be up in a few minutes."

"I'll wait." He shrugged and closed the door. Sounds of his television cartoons followed me into the shower with Shel.

After we'd dressed, the three of us went to find breakfast. A note at the front desk from Frank said they, too, preferred to fish in the afternoon. Food was still being served across the street, so we ate there. The fire pit was now covered with stones, and steam and food vapors rose from the mound. The smell was delightful. I walked over to feel the stones, which were slightly warm; the steam was quite hot.

"Can you believe the smell?" Fritz asked. We decided to take our sweet rolls and coffee, and walk to get away from the enticing aromas. We strolled around the pavilion lake with Fritz wondering about Louise, and Shelee wondering when we were going to eat. Fritz got his bicycle out of Shel's car and did bike racer imitations, working off some energy. Every now and then he'd join us, explaining his critical plays from yesterday's ballgame.

When we returned, the rocks had been removed from the top of the fire pit and tables brought up to receive the food. Several Roulands and friends removed the tangle of watercress and skunk cabbage leaves covering the food. Large screen baskets brimming with goodies were brought out next. The unexpected variety of foods for the potlatch included crawfish, freshwater mussels, and several baskets of catfish, bass, and walleye wrapped in leaves. There were also peeled cattail stalks, some sort of lake weed, potatoes, and several sides of pork. Everyone was in a jolly mood, the spring sun shone warmly, and we stuffed ourselves with food.

Naomi, Mitch, and Kathy came over to sit with us. Kathy brought her boyfriend, a quiet kid named Robert. There was much talk about the university, and Robert kept out of it, giving me the impression he wasn't planning on college. Fritz discovered crawfish for the first time and couldn't get enough of them—until Louise strolled over. He asked me if I'd finish his crawfish. I took his plate, and he took off, assuring us he'd be back by one o'clock for fishing.

I enjoyed the afternoon bass fishing just as much as yesterday's, watching Shelee catch the ferocious large-mouths. Mitch and Quincy fished with us, as Frank had to spend time with visiting relatives. We again used two boats, Mitch and Fritz in one, and the three grown-ups in the other. With the festival officially over, Chief Quincy was glad to unwind. He'd given a short speech after the potlatch to thank everyone for coming and to invite them back next year. There was a brief chant and dance to wish all a good year, good friends, and safe travels.

Around four o'clock, we headed for the dock. We kept some fish for Quincy's family and quite a few to take back to town. Mitch took some for his mother, as she had given most of the previous day's catch away. We loaded the bass into our cooler along with ice from the motel, said our thank-you's, and started for home.

"Can we come back next year?" Fritz asked.

"All we need is an invitation," I said.

Thirty minutes into the drive home, my little family conked out, leaving me disappointed that the banter from Fritz had ceased. A few miles farther, the Jefferson County road sign jarred me into speculation about the Lewis and Thornton families. A lump rose in my chest, and I reached behind me to give sleeping Fritz an assuring pat, then slid my hand under Shel's leg. By now Dena and the Thornton girls should be safe in Minneapolis . . . and that felt good.

## Ten / Shelee

We dropped Fritz at my sister's and left enough fish for her family and for my folks. I was still pissed about her shooting her mouth off to Fritz, and considered telling her to stuff a fish; instead, I said nothing. Because I had a new girl taking care of my cats and wanted to check on them, we drove to my house to sleep there Sunday night.

Before we went to bed, I called Lucky and told him I'd be over in the morning with some bass.

"Thanks," he said, "but I could really use one of them fur bass." I hung up right then, knowing that Rose had probably heard his rude comment. She's his current girlfriend, and I don't know how she stands him.

"You know," I said to Phil after I slammed the phone down, "everybody in my family has a mouth problem!"

Phil and I creaked out of bed around six, and by seven-thirty, I was driving over to Lucky's house near Sweeney Lake. Rose seemed to appreciate the bass more than my uncle did. She gave Lucky a rather cool goodbye and left for work, leaving me to sip coffee with Mr. Attitude. He had a four days' growth of beard, his hair wasn't combed, and he looked like hell.

"I wonder what's got into her?" Lucky asked after she left.

"Maybe she heard your stupid remark on the phone last night."

"Naw," he said, "she wasn't here."

"Don't bullshit me. I know she was here, it was Sunday night."

"Goddammit, she was over at her sister's! We had a fight an' that's why I made the remark. I'm more sensitive than you might think, Shel. Now, let's talk about somethin' more important."

He might have been lying to me, but choosing not to pursue it, I got up, rinsed out my coffee cup, and began to pick up a few things around the kitchen. "What could possibly be more important than your sensitivity?" I asked.

"Leave that shit," he said. "Can you and Phil go to Olie's with me 'round the end of October? We're goin' elk hunting. See, I'm filling out the form right here." He waved a partially completed Montana hunting application. I snatched it from his hand.

"It says there's a *drawing* for out-of-state hunters. What makes you so sure you're going to get a permit?"

He grabbed a paper towel roll from the counter behind him, pulled off a piece, and blew his nose. "Don't worry, Shelee girl, I'll get one. Olie says there's an overpopulation of elk in his district. An' he told me they got a hot poker game out there with some drunk Indians. I'll get that Philbert in a game and whip his ass," he said.

"Lucky, we might like to go," I said. "Ask us again when you get the permit. Drunk Indians and Phil getting his ass whipped sounds like our kind of vacation."

"Don't you think I can beat him?"

"You haven't since you taught him to play when he was fourteen. What makes you think you can start now?" This had become the typically stupid, Uncle Lucky conversation. I decided to disengage.

"Phil and I want to go up to the farm this weekend. Okay? We'll get the garden ready to plant if you want."

"Rose and I are going on Wednesday to plant the garden; she's got Wednesdays off. I'll be back by Friday night, so the place is all yours this weekend."

"Isn't Rose staying, too?" I asked.

"Hell no, gotta keep her workin'."

I was irritated, and wanted to ask who was bringing home the paycheck these days, then decided it wasn't my business. I love my Uncle Lucky, though he's a total pain in the ass most of the time. I kissed him on the whiskers and headed for the door.

"Well, I'm off to work," I said. "Is the shotgun at the farm? I may want to paint." He nodded. "Have a good week, enjoy the fish, and think about shaving." He swung his hand upward along the side of his face, his fingers directing me to the kitchen door—we call it his blow-it-out-your-ear wave.

I thought about Lucky's long history with my family as I drove downtown to school. The navy's where he got the name Lucky. Day and night, he hand-loaded ammunition onto airplanes, developing gigantic arm and shoulder muscles. He'd done some boxing back in the old country and he started boxing competitively on his ship. By the time the war ended, he'd become middle-weight boxing champion of the navy. His name came from the perception that he always won his matches with a lucky punch, and maybe, too, because none of his ammunition ever blew up on him.

Lucky's home in town by Sweeney Lake, where he's lived for the past five years, belonged to my grandparents, now both in their nineties and in a nursing home. My mom's folks moved back to Norway in the late '60s. My grandfather passed away several years ago, and my grandmother still lives there, surrounded by my family who stayed in the old country. There's been quite a bit of pressure on my parents to visit the homeland, particularly since they were active in the Resistance, hiding political fugitives during the occupation. My parents just saw it as the patriotic thing to do—the locals consider them war heroes. My folks are embarrassed by all the possible attention and I think that's why they've never gone back.

Lucky never married; the navy must have done something to him in the romance department, though he's always had plenty of women around—he's in his seventies and still attracts them. Phil told me he had so many women at his farm—when Phil worked there as a kid—the boys called him Uncle Fucky.

* * * * *

I parked in the garage next to the Creative Arts building and headed in to my week's work. There was a note on my desk from Naomi thanking Phil and me for coming to the reservation. The girl's got it all wrong, I thought—we're going to send her and her folks a card to thank *them*. The note also said she had a painting problem, and asked to see me. It was almost an hour before my first class, so I walked up to the student studio.

The studio is a large room with a high ceiling and skylight, located on the top floor of the building. It has excellent light, and I use it during the summer when most of the students are gone. Each graduate student has his own space, laid out with colored tape on the floor, and sometimes with a sign hung on one of the room's supporting columns. A few of the spaces are neat and tidy but most are a total mess, with Naomi's somewhere in between. Sculptors seem to be the messiest; I suppose that's the nature of their craft.

Naomi worked at her easel, refining a nearly completed, large oil landscape of a small lake—possibly from the west end of town. She used a photo for reference, clipped to her paint box lid. The snapshot displayed the lake and spring foliage on the surrounding trees, some of which were lavishly in bloom. The light, coming from behind the viewer, appeared to me to be the constructional problem.

"Good-looking painting and photograph," I said. "Something recent?"

"No, the picture's from last year. I did this painting at home and the light's driving me nuts," she said. "It's washing out all the reflections in the background water." She held the snapshot next to her painting. "See, it looks natural in the picture but it's not working in the painting. I can't seem to distinguish where the water stops and the lake bank starts—they're the same color and brightness in the photo."

"Before we talk about the painting," I said, "please know we all had a sensational time this weekend. Thanks so much."

"My pleasure," she said

"Okay . . . this beautiful painting does have a complicated light problem. I'm pleased you've taken it on. What's your solution?"

"I could move the light's emphasis, but that changes the whole painting," she said. "I want to keep the bright background."

"We've spent hours of class time on interfaces, Naomi. Use what you learned here."

The painting was lovely, with a foreground of dark shadows and reflections on the lake, interrupted by an angular patch of yellow sunlight on the water, pointing to more distinct reflections of flowering trees and light green spring foliage. The distant lakeshore was bathed in brilliant yellow sunlight that washed out the reflections and transitions between the lake and the bank. All the bright light values were close, and it took an expert's touch to bring definition to the similarly colored masses. Naomi had provided definition by using distinct, small color splashes to accentuate most of the larger features. The flowering trees were extraordinary. Except for the distant lake bank, washed out by the sun, she'd pulled off a fine painting.

"I'm stumped," Naomi said.

"Think in terms of the meniscus," I suggested. "I demonstrated it in class."

The meniscus, like the little cupped edge that water forms next to a vertical glass surface, operates in nature where water interfaces with anything, even itself. The curved water surface gives off the strongest reflection in the lightscape on that portion of the painting. Therefore it's the brightest feature; and it can be emphasized with some subtle, contrasting dark lines on one or both sides.

Naomi looked a little less puzzled. "Where should one see the brightest reflections in the painting?" I asked.

She reached to the canvas and put a thin slice of pure white along a short length of the far shore. With another brush she put an even thinner, dark purple diffused line above the white. Parts of the shore and the yellow water reflections sprang to life. Naomi jumped up from her chair and tried to hug me. I stepped back, avoiding the paint on her hands and smock.

"I really love you too, sweetie, but I don't want to get paint on this outfit."

She sat down in her chair, bouncing up and down while she painted. "Oowee, I love you, Dr. Osbornson," she said between bounces.

"You may call me Shelee," I said, patted her shoulder, and walked back down the stairs.

Around noon, I returned to my office. Trish looked up as I walked in. "How about lunch?" she said.

"Let's go," I answered, "didn't have time this morning to make my usual."

She got her purse and we headed over to the Student Union cafeteria. We foraged through the salad bar, and walked out to the courtyard with our iced teas sloshing onto our food trays. I launched into a tirade about my sister.

"Well, Abby's been blabbing to Fritz. This weekend he asked us why we haven't gotten married. Can't decide if I'm going to say anything to my dear sister or not. I just can't believe she discussed it with Fritz."

"Maybe everybody wonders the same thing," Trish said.

"I don't need to hear that, and *you* know how I feel about all this. We're never going to have kids, we have a great life together, so why get married? I can't believe the conventional shit I'm hearing from my family—well, mainly from Abby."

"Are you aware you're waving your hands all around while you're talking?"

"I'm sorry," I said, eating more of my salad.

"Does it matter that Phil really wants to marry you?" Trish asked.

"I think Phil's crazy in that department. When you think of all the people he sees with marital problems."

Trish just looked at me.

"Okay, I know . . . bullshit! Not the real issue at all. It's what I experienced when I was married before; I became an aberrant stranger. That's what worries me."

"Well don't you think it all would be different with Phil?"

"Why take the chance, Trish? When I was married to Mark, I lost interest in everything except grad school. I even lost interest in sex; it almost became a chore. Can you believe that?"

"Knowing you, I find it hard to believe."

"Me, too," I said, through a mouthful of spinach. "Why should I take a risk? Phil and I have thermonuclear sex. And our independence—I love how it works now. What's marriage going to do to that?"

We finished our salads and gathered up our dishes. "Enough of this crap," I said as we stopped to buy a couple of 25-cent cookies. "I want to tell you about our weekend."

We walked back to the office where I had nearly forty portfolios to review. Also, I hold office hours for students on Monday afternoons, so I left my door ajar and went to work. But after about thirty minutes of not being able to concentrate—I kept replaying the lunchtime marriage conversation—I got up from my desk, pulled the door shut, and kicked off my shoes. I sat in my overstuffed chair in the corner, curled up with my feet under me, and closed my eyes.

I must have fallen asleep, waking when my phone made its irritating ring; Trish announced there was a student waiting to see me.

"Please come in first," I said, feeling strangely sad.

Trish came in as I leaned against my desk, putting my shoes on. "What's wrong, girl?" She wore her concerned look.

I wiped my eyes. "I'm okay," I said, "just thinking about our talk at lunch. Do I look all right?"

"No, not really. Why don't you go to the ladies' room before you see Clark," Trish suggested.

I walked quickly through the outer office, telling my student I'd be back in a minute.

## Eleven / Phil

Sid just left the office—he stayed for the full hour—I see a glimmer of progress. Also, we played racquetball yesterday; we've got another game tomorrow. Playing me two times in one week is unusual for Sid—he suggested it. Manny Weston will be here in a few minutes—I wonder what I'm going to hear from him today. Working with interesting clients like Sid and Manny, people who are really bright, is fun and also challenging.

Weston may be the smartest person I have ever met. *He's quite enigmatic, and I guess one of the most successful American mystery writers. Several of his books have been made into hit movies. I've not been crazy about mysteries, and had read only a couple of his books before he came in two weeks ago. I just finished his third book—now I think his writing is truly fascinating. Manny's very prolific, and his novels' bulletproof, tightly crafted plots are convoluted and complicated; his villains are intelligently brutal, absolutely ruthless, and often escape justice. I've become most envious of his mental flexibility and his ability to consider so many sides of a subject at one time.

I watched Manny light a cigarette and roll it between his thumb and forefinger. "Tell me more about your latest project," I said. "Are you writing a mystery that has a character who's been abused?"

"Not a mystery. This is a whole new area for me. I'm writing—researching really—a book called *Mikie and Mike,* the story of a man who was abused as a child and who comes to terms with his past. It's a story of personal reconciliation."

I found his use of the word *personal* interesting, remembering to bring it up sometime, and recalling that his plots resemble computer games, full of turns, drop-offs, secret rooms with overwhelming demons, traps, and things impossible to reach.

"My new book is patterned after the *Homecoming* approach of John Bradshaw's," Manny explained. "My introduction gives him credit for his contribution." The sun had crept over the building and was now shining on our table. "It's going to get damn hot," Manny said, slipping on a pair of sunglasses. "Should have come in this morning; thanks for seeing me this afternoon."

"Not a problem," I said. "So why do you live here in Minneapolis?"

"I like the winters."

"You do? Perhaps you need psychiatric help."

"No, the terrible weather keeps me focused on my writing," he said and smiled.

"But you can find terrible weather in a lot of places."

"Well, I visited here about ten years ago from Seattle, and there was something about the surroundings I liked. Guess I was tired of the Northwest and ready for a move. The U has a great library for research, and I've got a pass. It's the same arrangement I had at the University of Washington. I give a couple of talks yearly in the English department, and they provide me with library privileges.

"Did you grow up around Port Angeles?" I asked.

"Yes, my mother's from a reservation near there; she's Indian, Kahama. She was working as a waitress in a hash-house when she met my father during World War II. He was in the Coast Guard, stationed in Port Angeles. Worked as a steward—pretty demeaning job." Though Manny recounted his personal history in a methodical, rehearsed manner, he winced when he said "steward." I was developing a keen interest in the stories that lay behind his words.

"My father was from Michigan—man was he out of place. He might have been the only black man west of Seattle, and he married my mom while he was still in the service. I was born in '44 and didn't fit in anywhere. There were few black people in our town, and the Indians hated me, and hated my mother for having a black kid. My father was a big guy and became a lumberjack after the war. He didn't spend much time at home. They're not together anymore, and I've no idea where my father is; my mother and I visit infrequently. Anyway, I grew up without any friends to speak of, so I read. When I was eight, I decided to read every book in the public library."

"*Every* book?"

"I did try," he said. "Started with the A's . . . was in the M's when I went off to college on a scholarship. One could say I read *half* the books in the Port Angeles library. I suppose I gobbled 'em up the way a puppy eats hamburger for the first time. I recall reading Erik Erikson's books when I was twelve." Manny smiled as he lit another cigarette.

I laughed. "All I thought about at twelve was basketball. Did you start writing in college?"

"Yeah, at U Dub. I met a professor of Indian history there named Billy Hathaway; he liked my work and helped get my writing career started. I was never interested in black or Indian stories but I liked mysteries from the start. I had to hide my race to get my first book published."

"Has that shaped your writing?" I asked.

"Probably. You may notice I write mostly about white people. I felt like an outsider in college, too, so I've developed the habit of being a good observer. This new book is my first venture beyond mysteries."

Our time was up and I had a patient coming at four. "Manny," I said, "this is fascinating, can't wait till our next session. I should be paying you."

Manny stubbed out his cigarette. "You can't imagine how much money I make," he said as he stood up and shook my hand. "I don't know what to do with it all, so my wife and I give to many charities. But I'll save some of it for you," he added and laughed. "I have the feeling I'm going to get more than my money's worth."

I looked again at my watch, amazed at how quickly the hour had gone. I had a few minutes before my next client, so I called Shelee.

"See you sometime after eight o'clock," I said. "That meeting with the attorney general has been called for this evening."

"Sorry, I'll miss you at dinner," Shel said, "but as long as you're home for dessert. Oh, we can leave for Lucky's tomorrow evening if you want."

"Fine with me. I love you, Shel. See you later."

It was nearly five-thirty when I closed up the office and walked out to my car. Driving east on 94 to St. Paul, I could see the university off to the left, across the river. Shel was probably somewhere in the crowded westbound lanes, heading home.

Our third date was at Lucky's. I'd found a house to rent but hadn't moved in yet, so I was still living at his place. Lucky was up at his farm until Friday, so Shel came over for dinner on a Thursday night, less than a week after our first date. Shel brought dessert and two outstanding wines, an Italian rosé called Zeni and a Spanish red, Vina Mayor.

"This Zeni is sensational," I said as we enjoyed Shel's wine with the baked oysters I'd fixed for an appetizer.

"What's for dinner?" she asked, peeking around the kitchen.

"Fried spinach with shrimp cakes, flavored with garlic and nutmeg," I responded. "I'm hoping to impress you with my culinary skills."

"Well, the oysters were a good start. And this?"

"Specialties of the house," I continued. "Roasted tomatoes spiced with chili powder, and a simple pasta of chopped garlic and pesto. I'll broil kasseri cheese into the top of the noodles just before I serve it."

We were sipping the last of the Vina Mayor, cleaning up the dishes, coffee brewing, and we started kissing. It didn't take many hungry kisses and pulling at each other's clothes before we were in a mad rush to get into the bedroom. I was thinking to myself while we were kissing, I'm in love with this woman, but instead I said this trite thing that psychiatrists hear all the time.

"I feel like I've known you all of my life, Shel." It broke the spell and I felt stupid.

Shelee put her fingers on my mouth, laughing playfully. "Actually you *have* known me most of your life, Philip. Let's have dessert and coffee; we've got all evening."

About halfway through dessert I kissed her on the neck. "I've wanted you from the first five minutes at the pub," I whispered.

"Of course you did." She smiled and sighed, giving a sexy stretch. "I'm a piece of work."

Our passion took over again as we joyously took off our clothes—this time on the couch—but then a key rattled in the lock and Uncle Lucky walked into the living room, grinning.

"Oh, for god sakes!" Shel exclaimed, pulling an afghan around her. "I thought you weren't coming home until tomorrow."

"Change of plans," Lucky said. "What's for dinner?"

My exit to I-35 came up; I headed north for a few miles, leaving the freeway a block from the L'Arpenteur Bistro where I was due for my dinner meeting.

## Twelve / Shelee

I drove to Phil's house about five P.M. Friday for a weekend trip to Lucky's. We're leaving this evening because I'm happier with the new kid who's caring for my cats—we usually drive there on Saturdays. I'm taking my painting stuff so I can blow up a couple of VØLMs. One or both will go in the institute show. Phil was almost ready to leave when I got there, so I put my things in his Blazer.

"I'm sorry I was so late last night," Phil said as he backed out of the drive.

"Yeah, you were one tired boy," I said. "But it was fun sleeping in an extra hour. Is that why you didn't run this morning?"

"No, I had an r-ball game with Sidney today. He wore me out."

We drove through his neighborhood and headed west, out of town. "So tell me about the dinner," I asked.

"Well the meeting pissed me off," he said. "It lasted four hours. We could have finished in two."

"You met the attorney general?"

"No, the assistant attorney general. We were supposed to review proposed legislation on criminal statutes—about child abuse. He had two attorneys from his office there, and all they talked about were legal implications. Instead, *I* wanted to review the content and intent of the new laws!"

"Did you get mad at them?"

"Damn right!" Phil said. "My interest is to ensure that the new laws are more comprehensive than the old ones. It's their problem to make the statutes work."

Phil pointed to my ice chest on the backseat. "So what's for dinner, Shel?"

"Just soda pop and wine in the cooler," I said. "Keep driving, there's a surprise for you at Wagonga."

"Oh, that sounds nice."

"You want a pop?" I asked. He shook his head. "So will the legislature have open hearings?"

"Probably."

"Will you have to testify this time?"

"I don't know. Maybe." Phil threw his sunglasses on the dashboard. "To hell with this crap!" he said, scowling. His outburst startled me. "I placed another very disturbed, mistreated kid in a group home this week, and I just don't want to think about sadness any more. There's an unending sea of hurting kids out there."

He sighed as we turned onto the freeway, then reached over and took my hand. "I'm sorry, Shel. Are we going to the floating restaurant?"

"Yup. And it's my treat."

An hour later, we turned off the interstate at Wagonga. We drove through the countryside to The Belle Floater restaurant, by the shore of Lake Minne Belle. It's one of my favorite places. Phil and I had lunch at the Belle the first weekend we spent together.

As soon as we were seated at a table next to the water, the waiter brought some bread to feed the various animals who begged for our attention. There were chubs swimming among the blue-green waterweeds, ducks, geese, and gulls on and above the lake, and a couple of hungry muskrats hunkered on a nearby log. A turtle, who shared the log with the muskrats, eyed all the critters but showed no interest in our offerings.

"So what wine did you bring?" Phil asked, eyeing my cooler after I asked the waiter for a wine bucket.

"My last bottle of Hinzerling '79 Riesling," I said proudly, handing the wine to Phil.

"By god, Shelee, you've outdone yourself this time," Phil said, smiling and fondling the bottle.

We ordered our meals, then entertained ourselves feeding the menagerie and savoring the fabulous wine.

"They've got lemon cake on the menu," Phil said. "What say we take a piece with us to Lucky's?"

"Marvelous idea," I answered as the salads were served.

We finished our salads, and began throwing more bread to the swarm of chubs. The muskrats swam into the middle of the melee. A few minutes passed and the waiter brought our dinners.

"Okay, we're going to share dinners," I said. "Your morels look incredible."

Phil spooned morels onto my salad plate, then scooped extra white sauce onto the chicken-stuffed morels, and red sauce onto the sausage-stuffed ones.

"Jesus," Phil said, washing down a morel with more Riesling, "this red sauce is astounding."

We took our time eating the superb meal, complimenting the chef who later wandered through the dining area. After dinner, we ordered lemon cake to go and headed for Lucky's.

"What are we doing at the farm this weekend?" Phil asked.

"Well, old Luck called yesterday," I said, "and he's bought a bunch of plastic pipe and stuff for an automatic watering system for the garden. He was wondering if you'd get started on it."

"An irrigation system, huh? It'll be a welcome change," Phil replied. "I need to do something with my hands after this week."

"You know my uncle—that farm is the one thing he really takes pride in," I said. Lucky has always kept the place in pristine condition. The lake on the southwest corner of the property is more than a half-mile long and several hundred yards wide, probably formed from an oxbow arm a long time ago. Now it's fed by a large spring creek at the north end and a smaller one from the cattle pasture. We think there's another fairly big spring somewhere along the lake bottom, because the outflow is about twice as large as the inlet flow.

The lake is ringed by a dense cottonwood forest. The cattle pasture and hay fields are upland, on the north side of the property. Lucky has fenced off the cottonwoods from the cropland and pasture, to keep the cattle out of the trees. He uses the spring in the pasture for the cattle and pipes water from the lake for irrigation. There's a cement watering tank and spillway for the pasture spring so the cattle won't muddy up the stream. He plants a few catfish from the lake in the cattle tank to eat the bugs and weeds and keep the tank clean, and they get positively gigantic. When the catfish are big enough, Lucky nets one for dinner. It's strange to look into the cattle trough and see these big, yellow-brown catfish darting around.

My uncle built sheds along the fenced-off portion of the woods; the cattle use the sheds for protection during the coldest weather. There are heaters in the stock watering system so the tank won't freeze. A local farmer, Ned Frazier, leases the farm these days—our families have been friends for years. Lucky still runs a few cattle with Ned's and gives beef quarters to friends, my folks, and my grandparents' nursing home. The house and lake feel nicely secluded from the farm activities.

The old farmhouse is rustically beautiful. We've always called it "the cabin." It's a one-story slab log house that was probably fifty years old when Dad and Lucky bought the place. They completely insulated and gradually remodeled the house. My whole family uses it; although in the past few years, it's been Lucky, Phil, and me who spend the most time up there and keep things running. Fritz comes up often; occasionally we'll bring my niece, Heidi—she's seven and not as charmed with the place as we are.

Phil and I go up to the farm year-round. In the winter we cross-country ski and cuddle by the fire; sometimes Phil reads or works, and I paint. Ice fishing is quite good, but the few times we tried it we froze our butts off. But we have plenty of fishing in the warm months, mostly walleye, plus some bass in the lily pads by the outlet—catfish and some crappies, too. We've got a wildlife population of deer, muskrat, fox, grouse, rabbits, and some transient coyotes. Sometimes we hear the 'yotes, as Fritz calls them, howling in the fall nights. There's pheasants, too, up in the hay fields.

"Did you know that Lucky tried planting some wild turkeys a few years ago?" I said. We rattled across the cattle guard that signaled our arrival at the lane leading to the farm.

"When was that?"

"Oh, before we met."

"So what happened to them?"

"They died off, and I don't miss them."

"You don't like turkeys?" Phil asked.

"Not those. They got too domesticated, developed an attitude."

"Yeah, right."

"Really. They turned into arrogant pea brains. They'd challenge us whenever they were in an ugly mood, which was most of the time. We were here on a picnic one time, and a tom even chased a little kid. I tried to kill the stupid turkey with a stick but it got away."

"I wish I'd seen that," Phil said, laughing. "So they just died off?"

"I don't know. Lucky might have shot 'em all. Anyway, the turkeys disappeared. Maybe they ate morels and Lucky caught them in the act," I added, trying to recall.

"Now that's a capital offense," Phil said, parking by the cabin. We carried our things inside and settled in.

"You want some dessert?" I asked as I put things in the refrigerator.

"No, let's save it; but I could use some decaf," Phil said.

I started the coffee and laid out my painting stuff for the morning. Phil sat at the kitchen table studying Lucky's garden watering plan.

"This is going to work great," Phil said. "The garden's on a slope and it's a natural for this scheme."

I put the rest of our things away, then sat on the sofa and looked for something to read—it was only about 9 o'clock, too early for bed. I picked up the photo album from the lamp table and restlessly turned the pages. About halfway through, I stopped and ran my hand over this great picture of my sister and me sitting by the lake. The snapshot had been taken the summer after I finished the eighth grade, when Abby was going into her junior year in high school. You could see our dad in the background, fishing.

Phil was standing behind me now, his hands resting gently on my shoulders. "Who's that?" Phil asked, pointing to another picture.

"Oh, that's Marlene. Poor kid—her parents were these religious freaks who wouldn't let their children take a bath. They even had 'em excused from P.E. so they couldn't shower there."

"Come on, Shel," Phil said, "what kind of religion? You're making this up."

"No, I'm not. Her clothes were dirty and she just smelled to high heaven. She was a big girl, too, and her stupid folks wouldn't let her wear a bra, so she walked around school with one arm slung under her boobs, holding them up." I reached up and held Phil's hands on my shoulders. "Most of us were trying to make a graceful transition into womanhood; Marlene was making a transition into hell."

"Well, she looks okay in the photo."

"That's because I brought it up at dinner one evening, and Abby suggested I bring Marlene home and let her bathe. She even wanted me to wash Marlene's clothes or lend her mine. Of course *my clothes* would have been too small."

"Looks like they'd fit quite nicely," Phil cut in.

"Ahem . . . maybe now. What is this, Trash Shelee Month?" I said, removing his hands from my shoulders. "You and Abby can be the chairpersons."

"Just kidding. Go on."

"Abby and I got into this big fight about it at dinner. Abby said Marlene could take her bath in my training bra. I thought my beanpole sister should mind her own business. Anyway, Dad, always champion of the underdog, sided with Abby."

Phil began rubbing my shoulders. "So what happened?"

"I invited Marlene to our house, and I think it absolutely blew her away; she started coming once a week. Pretty soon the other girls heard about it, and Marlene started taking baths at everyone's house. Her stupid parents finally let her bathe at home. I was astonished they even had a bathroom."

Phil kissed me on top of my head, breathing into my hair. "What happened to the religious belief about not bathing?"

"Who knows. Maybe they were just cheap."

"Maybe really poor?" Phil suggested.

"No way. Probably had more to do with what my mom said to Marlene's mother the first time she drove Marlene home."

"What did she say?"

"I don't remember for sure, but I think Inga told Mrs. Shithead which way was up."

He nuzzled my hair again. "No wonder you're so confident, Shel. It's that loving, supportive family of yours."

After pouring a sizable shot of Grand Marnier into a snifter, Phil sat down beside me on the sofa, took a sip, then offered it to me.

"Listen to this," he said. "When the sun shines, the grasshoppers all face one way because they are afraid of their shadows. On a cloudy day they have no concern, and face wherever they want."

"Where did you come up with that?" I asked.

"From Manny. It's African. And I think it has to do with self-determination but I'm still puzzling over it."

"You mean they can't choose which way they face when the sun's out?"

"I don't think they *can* choose," he said. "That may be the point."

"They choose what they eat. That's choosing."

"Perhaps not," Phil said. "They may just bumble around until they run into something that tastes good. I think that's what people do, only in a more complex way."

"Look," I said, "if they're afraid when the sun's out, then fear for them is just a subset of stupid. But it's probably a survival strategy, looking in the direction away from their shadow. Or how about, when one sees clearly, direction replaces creativity?"

"You're taking this literally," Phil said.

"No I'm not. Let's go to bed, Philhead."

"In a minute," he said, and sipped his drink. Phil leafed through the family photo album. "Is this the first card you gave me?" He pulled my ten-year-old missive from the back pocket, smiled, and shook his head as he reread my silly note.

"Sure is," I said, looking at the card. "There's more in here." I took the album from him and searched around in the pocket. "Have you ever seen this old picture Lucky found in a drawer up here?" I handed him a black-and-white photo of a little girl posing by the lilac trees.

"Where's this from?" Phil asked, turning the photo over, studying the inscription.

"My dad or Lucky found it when they renovated the cabin—probably back in the late '40s."

"It says, *Our little lilac girl, 1902–07*," Phil read aloud. He gave me the strangest look I'd ever seen. "She's about two in this photograph, does that mean she died in 1907?" he asked incredulously. "Do you know anything about her?"

"No. Why, what's wrong?"

". . . Years ago, I had a dream . . . about a girl who looked like this."

"You're not supposed to dream of anyone but me," I said, kissing his cheek. I put the album away, but Phil continued to stare at the picture.

## Thirteen / Phil

We slept in Saturday morning and didn't finish breakfast until after nine o'clock. Shel painted awhile, then set up to make a couple of VØLMs. I'd seen her do this a few times before, and it's always fun.

I watched as she got up on a stepladder and hung a canvas from a tree limb using wire hooks. Then she attached string to rubber bands stretched around the tops of her paint cans—paint cans that she lets warm in the oven!

"If one can blows, the whole house will go," I told her once.

"I know what I'm doing," she assured me.

Still, whenever there are cans in the oven, I move outside.

I continued watching as Shel suspended the warmed cans from a 2x6 wired to the limb above the canvas. The cans hung from nails in the board, which positioned each paint bomb about six inches in front of the precolored canvas. When everything was ready, she got Lucky's shotgun and loaded one shell in the magazine and one in the chamber.

"If you are going to make two VØLMs, may I do one?" I asked.

"First of all, I'm the artist, and only I can create *the* VØLM. Besides, you question my technique; I saw you move outside."

"I didn't question your technique," I said. "Just want you to be careful with paint cans that might explode. By the way, how do you decide how many shots to fire?"

"The gun only holds three shells, and the most I've ever shot is two. It's an artistic decision, Philip. Anyway, I will not have my methods questioned by a mattress-back boy like you."

With this pronouncement, Shelee turned and fired two quick shots into the cluster of cans. Paint went everywhere. The deranged painter pumped out the second cartridge, then picked up both shells, and threw them at the canvas.

"The master's touch!" she shouted and laid the shotgun on the front porch. Then Shel put on rubber gloves, and took her new masterpiece down, tilting the painting in various ways to make the paint run around the canvas.

"Quit laughing," I told her, "or you might drop it." Shel held the VØLM at arm's length while paint dripped through the pellet holes.

When the paint thickened enough to stop running, Shelee tipped it slightly on edge, and working at the back of the painting, used a pallet knife and gesso to close the holes. In a day or so, she'll finish the patching with more gesso and touch-up paint, including the holes in the wooden stretcher bars. Shel patches the shot holes in the wood, then sands and paints the stretcher bars so there's no evidence of repair. According to Shelee, even her framer doesn't know how VØLMs are made.

"If you didn't have rubber gloves on, you'd be a mess," I said. Her orange dishwashing gloves were a variety of paint colors. "Maybe you could use the gloves as artwork."

Shel held up both hands. "But of course," she said, furrowing her brow and sounding like Bela Lugosi. "I learned this technique from the Maharishi." Then laying the wet canvas faceup on newspapers spread on the picnic table, she studied the painting, trying to decide top from bottom. Her final artistic touch was to place a couple of twigs under the bottom edge of the canvas. The paint, which was still slightly fluid, pooled at the upper edges of the color patterns. When hung, these raised paint ridges give an interesting relief to her creation. The colors and relief are accentuated and made more vivid by an application of lacquer in about a week.

Still chuckling to herself, Shel took off her gloves, picked up the 12-gauge, and prepared for the day's second assault on the art world. I stuck around until the mad artist shot the second canvas. This time she had a slightly different ceremony. Before pulling the trigger she shouted, "TEN THOUSAND DOLLARS!" The gun went "BOOM!" and I went fishing.

In less than an hour, I had three nice walleye, which I cleaned and took back to the cabin. I was putting them in the fridge when my woman arrived with a small bag of morels. "Let's go mushroom hunting this afternoon," she suggested. "I'll fix some lunch."

We moved her paintings aside and ate our sandwiches at the picnic table. "Be back in a second," Shel said, partway through our shared piece of lemon cake. A minute later she returned with a few cottonwood buds, then rubbed them on her neck and shoulders. "Sniff your honey," she commanded, and I complied.

"I love you," I said, kissing her softly. Then whispered, "Your skin *always* has the scent of spring cottonwoods." I ran my hand under her T-shirt. She responded to my touch, and perhaps to some mysterious inner poetry that fashions her emotional life.

I picked Shel up and carried her into the cabin's bedroom. We helped each other out of our clothes, then knelt on the edge of the bed, each with one foot on the floor, kissing and touching.

My god Shelee's beautiful in the buff! And though I see her most every day—dressed and undressed—I always marvel at this delightful woman. Shel's unique Osbornson color scheme —her figure, red hair, head-to-toe freckles, and that marvelous skin—simply drives me wild.

And we made love at some level near insanity—so often like our first time—Shelee again revealing an intense and focused passion that I'd never experienced before I met her—part of the magic that fills our times together. Then sleep welcomed us both.

It was after two o'clock when we awoke. We lay close together and talked, our faces a few inches apart. As Shelee talked, I watched her eyes, confident, clear, and expressive. Those honest, brown eyes, large enough to take in the whole world, could become mere lines, to examine, assess, or condemn. Suddenly I better understood her love for me: it's in her own way, yet on my terms. She seems to understand that instinctively . . . maybe one of life's happy accidents.

"You're not really listening to me, are you?" she asked.

"I love your face."

"Well, in that case, I'll forgive you," she said, regarding me with her narrow cat-eyed love stare. She nudged me in the ribs. "I love you, too. Let's go find some mushrooms."

"Okay," I said, "but can you help me assemble the watering system piping before we go? I need to cut and glue the sections; then things will be ready for Lucky or me to install when we get the weir box."

"Weird box?" Shel joked.

We worked together on the plastic piping. I measured and cut pipe; Shel trimmed the ends and glued the pieces. We built the header and fitted the solenoid valve to it, carrying it over to the garden a few times to make sure the outlet pipes had the right spacing for the garden rills. Then we measured the length of the feeder line from the spring creek to the garden, cut the pipes for the feeder line, and glued a few together. I decided not to assemble the rest of the system until we knew the exact spot for the creek water supply. "I'll do the electrical part tomorrow," I said, and we took off for the woods.

"Whoop! Get your butt over here," Shelee called. "Here's some stump mushrooms; come help me cut these off the tree." I walked over to see her carving a bunch of oyster mushrooms off a dead cottonwood. I opened my knife, trimmed the oysters, and put them into my bucket. We find lots of oysters this time of year, but since they're not as good eating as morels, we mostly dry them; they're tasty in spaghetti sauce and stews.

"These are in such great shape," I said, "let's have 'em for dinner and breakfast."

"Okay by me."

We walked on through the woods, a few yards apart, stopping to pick the morels we found growing in the cottonwood litter. Shel moved ahead, eager to find more, often announcing a new mushroom patch with an enthusiastic yell.

"Come here," Shel called, "my sack won't hold another 'shroom."

"Okay."

"Watch where you step," Shel said as I approached her, "I'm surrounded. Can you believe all these?" We filled our buckets to overflowing and headed back to Lucky's.

I smiled, thinking about my favorite activity. "I'm still groggy from our nap," I said as we walked into the cabin. "Let's take a shower."

Shel set the mushrooms in the sink, then turned and gave me a lingering kiss, pulling her clothes off as her lips remained on mine. More cat eyes. "Absolutely shower time," she purred.

I finished my shower first, now feeling quite awake and refreshed. Shel washed and dried her hair as I scattered our mushrooms onto a bed sheet on the floor in the corner. They would be partly dried by the time we went home tomorrow, and we'd finish the job in town with our food drier. I set a few of the best morels and oysters aside for dinner.

The afternoon had been warm, and Shel's paintings had already dried. Since the VØLMs were now ready for more touch-up, Shel got involved with her artwork, and I started dinner.

We dined on walleye, broiled along with our mushrooms and some tomatoes. Dinner was topped off with a salad and sourdough bread, plus an Italian Chardonnay—an ancient Plozner—one of the wines I'd shipped from D.C. when I moved here. The wine was alive with flavors, and Shelee went a little nuts over it.

"So this is one of your D.C. wines," she said. "You've even topped last night's Riesling. I bet your Washington hump-mates would do almost anything for a drink of this. In fact, I might do *anything,* wine or no wine."

"Don't indulge me," I kidded, mopping up the last of my walleye with an oyster mushroom.

"I will not have my insincerity questioned!" Shel wise-cracked. "The dishes can wait. C'mon."

We walked down to the lakeshore where nighthawks darted and swirled through the fading light, beckoning darkness with their calls. A cloud-shaded moon drifted in the eastern sky, and thunder boomed a long way off—I felt its pulse in the humid air. Shel held my arm and snuggled playfully against me. We could see people fishing on the other side of the lake—Lucky shares the lake with the adjacent outfit and the far shore is theirs.

The ranch across the lake always had been owned by a local family, until *the famous* people bought it. They're reclusive locally but not nationally. Duncan Cole owns the Minneapolis Norse, newspapers, and several cable stations. His wife, Gloria Burns, a glamorous, ex-movie star, has become Wall Street's favorite guru of investments. It's rumored her fortune is larger than her husband's. She owns many corporations, and always hires competent, famous businesspeople to manage them. Gloria Burns, known as Glo Buns when she was acting, is frequently on the serious talk shows. I loved her misbehavior on *Charlie Rose,* when, in the middle of an important point, she got up, walked around his table, and hugged him from behind.

Duncan and Gloria are favorites of the tabloids, having been dubbed Dunk and Glo. After about a year of intense local gossip, people around this area seemed to forget about them. But their corporate headquarters is in Minneapolis, so they get plenty of publicity there.

Shelee and I often wondered about the Coles. We'd wave when we saw them, and the waves were always returned. Many times it was in fading light such as this. They appeared to be evening creatures, vague, unavailable, unknowable.

Shel squeezed my hand, "Why don't you call them up for a poker game?" she asked. "That'd be a way to get to know them." It was nearly dark now but I could see Shel roll her eyes. "Why maybe I could learn to act," Shelee mused.

"You're already actress enough," I ventured.

"I am not." She ran her hand inside my shirt. "A girl can never be actress enough."

"A poker game is a great idea," I said. We headed back to the cabin. "I've been toying with a way to get to meet them. I'll give 'em a call in the morning."

"Do you ever treat psychopaths?" Shel asked, her voice full of mischief as we walked inside.

"I try to avoid them," I responded.

"Would you recognize . . . say . . . a sexual psychopath if you ever saw one?"

"Would you?" I asked. "It's the water, right? There's something in the water up here. Okay, how would I recognize one?"

"She's got red hair, freckles, breathes hard, and drools," Shel said.

"Ya?"

"That's right," she said, leading the way to bed. "This is the 'anything' I talked about, Buster." She began pulling my clothes off—the result was quite splendid.

## Fourteen / Phil

The early sunlight flooded into the kitchen, illuminating lazy dust particles floating in the morning air. Shelee was still sleeping, so I got up quietly, started the coffee, scowled at the dinner dishes on the counter, and brought the picture of the Lilac Girl back to bed. I watched the specks of dust play slow-motion tag through the open bedroom door as sunlight crept into the room, all the while pondering the little girl smiling shyly at me from the photo. She was dressed and posed, perhaps part of a family photo session, I guessed, one most likely shot professionally. Also, that she was smiling impressed me—in those days, kids in photos didn't smile much.

When the coffee was ready, I carried a cup back to bed and nudged Shel, kissing her face until she opened her eyes. "Sweetheart, who might know something about this photograph?" I asked.

"Maybe Ned Frazier," Shel said, sitting up and tasting her coffee. "He's got an aunt who grew up on his farm. She's in a rest home over by Glenwood, and probably old enough to have known the girl's parents. I think she even published a pioneer history of this area about twenty years ago."

"Thanks," I said with a grin and took back the coffee cup.

"Come back here with that," she yelled.

"More in the kitchen," I said, walking out of the bedroom.

We fixed breakfast together, more mushrooms, scrambled eggs, and toasted leftover bread with raspberry jam from Lucky's berry patch. After we'd cleaned up the dishes, I started on the watering system wiring. Shel finished touching up her paintings. I called Ned Frazier and asked about the family who originally lived here.

"I remember those folks back in the thirties," he said. "You knew the farmhouse was abandoned when the Osbornsons bought it, didn't you? Maybe tax default." He had no recollection about the child in the photo, but offered to see what he could find out from the rest of his family.

"Well, are you going to call Dunk and Glo?" Shelee asked when I hung up. It was just after 9:00 A.M.

"It's a little early," I said. "Thought I'd wait a bit."

Shel looked eager. "No time like the present. I'd like to call them."

"Do it."

She looked up the ranch number and dialed Lucky's old rotary phone.

"May I speak to Gloria Burns, please?" She put her hand over the mouthpiece. "It's woman to woman," she told me.

"Please tell her it's Dr. Osbornson, her neighbor from across the lake." Again, Shel covered the receiver. "I think I'm actually going to talk with *her*. I've got her personal secretary," Shelee said, her sentences running together. "No one's in the office. It's the foreman's day off." She winked at me, then crossed her eyes. I got up and turned on the tap, sniffing the water.

Shelee spun back to the phone. "Hi, Ms. Burns," Shel said, smiling at me. "This is Shel Osbornson from across the lake.

We were mushroom hunting yesterday, found a bunch of morels. We saw you fishing and . . ."

"Yeah, that was us. We'd like to bring you some mushrooms.

"Well, you probably do," she said. "Uh-huh . . . uh-huh.

"We'd love to meet you. . . . Sure, we can show you what to look for.

"Twelve-thirty lunch? Sounds fine. Let me check with Phil." Shel looked over at me.

I shook my head, "No."

Shel raised her fist, narrowed her eyes, and turned back to the phone. "Sure, twelve-thirty will be fine.

"Yes, that's me. I'm pleased you like my work. The *Post Express* does a great job of covering the exhibits. Okay, we'll see you in a little while. Thanks."

Shelee hung up the phone, beaming. "We're invited for lunch!" she squealed. Then soberly, "Please don't embarrass me."

"Um, I'm not the one to worry about," I said. "Are you really going to give some of our mushrooms away?"

"Consider it an investment, Philip! You're kidding, right?"

"Yes," I said smiling. "This will be fun, another Sloan-Osbornson adventure."

I went back to the irrigation wiring and installed a timer box and transformer under the window bench in the kitchen. I left the rest of it for Lucky to finish. Then I changed out of my grubby clothes, decided not to shave, and we took off for Dunk's place. We drove out the farm gate, turned west for a short distance, and then south on the county road for about a mile. Finally, we turned up the lane to the newly named Norse Ranch.

We arrived at a formidable-looking gate with a call box. The electric fence on either side of the gate was eight feet high, like one you might see at a zoo—no doubt to hold the buffalo and exotic animals we'd heard about. "Hello, this is Phil Sloan and Shel Osbornson to see the Coles," I said to the call box. There was a muffled response on the other end and the gate went up.

We drove through and I watched the gate close behind us in the mirror. "Do you know the Coles tried to buy our farm for more than three times its real value?" Shel said. I shook my head.

"My family turned them down without a second thought. Then they sent us a letter saying they were happy to be our neighbors."

We traveled along a pasture for about a half mile, passing a herd of several dozen buffalo and a group of Irish deer, some with gigantic antlers. Next, we came to a double cattle guard that separated some ranch buildings from the pasture. The road branched in several directions; it wasn't clear which road to take until we saw a small sign that read "Residence."

"You may take the road to the residence," Shel said in the voice she uses when talking with art critics. "I'm sure it's where we'll find Duncan and my friend Gloria. Lunch should be scrumptious as usual," she concluded.

"Maybe I should have left you at home," I said. "They may not be prepared to meet Fritz's Auntie Shel." We passed through a grove of cottonwoods, and sure enough, a house and grounds appeared, covering several acres of Minnesota prairie. Duncan Cole, in the flesh, stepped off the porch as we got out of the car. Shel carried our morel offering.

"Gloria's in the house tending to lunch," Duncan said. "I'm happy to meet you two. We've seen you by the lake several times. Dr. Osbornson, I assume that's your relative, Lucky Osbornson, who owns your farm?" We paused just outside the entrance.

"Yes, he's my uncle," Shelee said. "He owns it jointly with my parents. Do you know him?"

"No, but we got a curious letter from him last year," Duncan said, opening a side door to an ample entryway. "Some of my bison got out and damaged about a hundred yards of our common fence. My ranch staff, along with your tenant, Mr. Frazier, fixed the fence. He leases your farm, right?"

Shel nodded, probably wondering what crazy Lucky story was about to surface.

"My foreman told me the matter was settled. Then a few weeks later we received a bill from your uncle for a thousand dollars. The letter was curious, because it said he'd forget about the bill if we would sit in on one of his poker games. I assumed it was a joke, and told the foreman to pitch it."

"My Uncle Lucky's type of joke, Duncan," Shel said. "He's one of the stranger members of my family."

*Strange* is only a relative matter, I thought, looking at Shel, who grinned at me. I knew what she was thinking, like me—there goes the Dunk and Glo poker game. We walked through the entryway, down a cobblestone hall, and into a spacious atrium breakfast room just as Glo Buns entered—wearing an apron over jeans and a sweater. Shelee handed her the bag of morels, and Duncan introduced us.

"I think we have these in our woods," Gloria said. "You have time to look with us after lunch?" We both nodded, and she led us to the table, where we sat down to a luncheon of cold salmon and pineapple salad with a cream horseradish dressing. "The watercress is from our spring creek," Gloria pointed out.

The Coles served an inexpensive '86 Vernaccia that complimented the salad beautifully. I had speculated they'd serve an expensive, white Bordeaux. We praised both food and drink, and our mutual love of wine gave us something to talk about.

"Are you a football fan?" Duncan asked me partway through lunch.

"Well, I watch the Norse occasionally," I said. "If they're in the playoffs and the Super Bowl again this year, I'll watch 'em for sure."

"Hell," Duncan said, "if our quarterback stays healthy, we'll *win* the damn Super Bowl this year."

I was completely at ease, and wondered if Shel felt the same way. It wasn't long until her degree of comfort spoke for itself

—the mention of Duncan's cable channel got her started. The mind of Fritz seemed to be hovering somewhere over Shelee as we walked into their cottonwood forest after lunch.

"Please tell us, Duncan," Shel said, doing her Sam Donaldson interview, "does your VISA card have a number of charges for $19.95, plus $4.00 shipping and handling?" I covered my eyes while Dr. Osbornson continued. "Can you sing the first two lines of 'Home on the Range'? Perhaps that stuff in the tabloids is all true. Does your wife advise you on which mutual funds to buy?"

"She did advise me the other day," Duncan said, grinning, "but I think I misunderstood her, because I bought the fund management company."

"Thank you, Duncan; all of us here hope it works out for you," Shelee said.

To my relief, Shel was soon distracted by some mushrooms. "Here's what they look like in the wild, folks." Shel pointed to a patch of several blond morels. Duncan knelt down and picked them. He cut the dirt off the stems, and put them into a canvas bag that Gloria held for him. We began to find a good number of morels, along with some oyster mushrooms. We spread out, continuing our chatter while we hunted, yelling back and forth to each other. Some of the trees were blackened from an old fire, and Shelee called to anyone who would listen. "This is a productive area because of an old burn. They always produce more mushrooms."

"They don't call this Burn's Burn for nothing," Gloria commented.

The mushroom hunt lasted almost two hours, and we talked more about the Norsemen, current events, politics, and finance. The women got into a conversation about cooking. It was revealing to hear Gloria Burns chatting about household subjects. Here we were, walking and talking with these very famous people, normally, easily, and with Shelee as charming as I've ever seen her. Shel and Duncan discussed art. Duncan said he can never decide between traditional and modern styles, so he buys both. He complimented Shel's work.

"We go to the institute's spring show each year," Duncan said.

"I may shock the art community one of these days by submitting a traditional painting to the spring show," Shel said as we walked back to the Coles' house. "People don't understand what goes into a good abstract. Most of the modern abstract masters can do a detailed illustration or representational painting at will. I don't think the general public knows that. People will pay big money for schlock; that hurts the modern art movement."

"I saw in the paper where one of your paintings resold in New York for over sixty thousand," Gloria said. "People are paying big money for *your* works now."

"That's the same auction where the pastel basketballs and yellow urinals sold for over $100K," Shel said with disdain. "If I had any control over resales, my piece never would have been with garage-sale trash."

"I've always suspected," Duncan said and smiled, *"The Emperor's Clothes?"*

"Exactly," Shel replied.

"I hope you'll like the broad range of artwork we have in our corporate collection," Duncan said.

"Shelee, dear," Gloria asked, "why would you submit a traditional piece, when you're famous for your special abstracts?"

"Because I can," my girlfriend answered confidently.

As we approached the house, Duncan pointed to the garage. "I want to show you something."

"Yes," Gloria said briskly, "you *have* to see this odd fish I caught. It's in the freezer—some kind of weird catfish." Duncan opened a freezer and pulled out a two-foot long eelpout.

"Did you catch him in our lake?" I asked.

Duncan waved off to the east. "No, Gloria caught it in a lake we have on the other side of the ranch. What is the damn thing?"

Shelee picked up the frozen fish. "Mr. Cole, this thing's an eelpout," she said, this time talking like Ray Goulding. "Folks 'round here just call 'em 'pouts." She waved the fish in our faces. "Breed all their own, you know, 'snot commonly found this far south. Best put them on the ol' B-B-Q. They're like old Philbert here, ugly but quite edible."

To emphasize her point, she rapped the fish on the workbench next to the freezer. Its head broke off and fell on the floor. "Oops," she said, picking it up and handing both parts to Duncan. "Sorry."

"Shel, darling," I asked, "did you forget to take your medicine this morning?" I turned to the Coles. "Duncan and Gloria, I'm truly sorry about Shel's behavior. She's been under my care for almost ten years now, and the poor girl hasn't made much progress. We've been able to keep her out of the bin, though." Then I smiled at Shelee. "Sweetheart, perhaps you should offer to repair the Coles' fish."

They both laughed. "You two are quite a team," Gloria said. The four of us walked into the house via the kitchen entrance and dumped a good five pounds of wild mushrooms into the sink. "Thanks for showing us what to look for," Gloria said. We explained how to dry them, exchanged Minneapolis phone numbers, thanked them for a great Sunday afternoon, and headed back to Lucky's.

"Can you believe my uncle screwed up the Dunk and Glo poker game?" Shel asked as we drove across the first set of cattle guards.

"Maybe they'll go for it sometime," I said. "Actually, I don't think they're interested in anything like that."

"Perhaps I could star in a made-for-TV porno movie," Shel purred. "Minnesota TeleNet presents Shell-O Bumptious in

*RetroPussy, The Boinking of Philbert Sloan.*" The car approached the entrance and the electric gate swung open.

"Literally, I can't take you anywhere," I said with a laugh. "Maybe it's a virus—infectious nutso."

"Well, the Coles were surprisingly subdued," Shel said. "So were you."

"Who could compete with the self-appointed mistress of entertainment?" I said. "And those corny jokes. They've probably heard them all before."

"I'm sure," she replied, "but not from me. I'm just a funny girl."

I glanced over at Shelee. She looked smug. I'd seen that look before.

Services had already started when Jonah and Mary Thornton arrived at the Stone Lake Christian Church. They stood in an empty back pew and sang the chorus of the opening hymn. Mary felt relieved when Reverend Iverson began a Scripture reading as soon as the hymn was finished. No one, except old Mr. Emory, the usher, had noticed the Thorntons come in.

Mary felt terrible embarrassment and shock after the first few lines of Reverend Iverson's sermon—revelations of family sexual abuse in the community. She stood up quietly and went out to the car, then sat and listened to the radio, crying, waiting for Jonah. When he finally came out, Mary still had tears in her eyes.

"How could you stay for that sermon?" she asked.

Jonah frowned at his wife. "I wanted to hear what that goddamn preacher had to say. Why are you cryin'?"

"Let's go," she said. "People will be leaving soon." Jonah took his time driving out of the lot. He began to turn toward the highway, then suddenly wheeled the car around and parked in front of the church.

"Oh, please don't do this!" Mary pleaded. "Can't we just go?"

"I want to look them sanctimonious bastards in the eye," he said defiantly. But when the first worshippers came out, Jonah drove off.

Mary dabbed at her eyes. "Thank you," she whispered. They drove home in silence.

That afternoon, Jonah sat in his red pickup in the parking area near the militia's training range. He sipped a beer as he watched the brigade members arrive and go through the check gate. Jonah fingered the two hat covers—one orange, one blue—on the seat beside him while he waited. A man he knew walked over to the truck.

"I'm glad to see you back, Jonah," he said, reaching through the window to shake Thornton's hand. "Just between you and me, I agree with what you said last time. But the word's been passed down; we got to be politically correct these days."

"Yeah, right," Jonah said. "As long as I get to shoot some of those government homos, I don't care what we have to do in the meantime."

The man gestured at the gate. "What are you waiting for?"

"Him." Jonah pointed to a camper just pulling into the lot.

"Well, I hope I'm on your team," the man said and turned to go. "See you inside."

Jonah picked up his olive drab bivouac cap and fitted the blue cover on it. J.C. Abell, the blue team captain, got out of his camper and walked over to Jonah's truck. Thornton opened the door and shook Abell's hand.

"I want you for my platoon leader if you can keep your goddamn mouth shut," J.C. said with a smile.

The two men walked through the gate and up the path to the brigade headquarters, an abandoned Grange hall. "Mouth or no mouth, I got the best kill score in the outfit," Jonah said. "That's why you want me."

Abell glanced sideways at Thornton. "Are those charges true?"

"Fuck, no," Jonah said. "The feds think I owe them money and they're out to discredit me. They even got to my kids somehow."

It was near five o'clock when they finished the last training exercise. Again, Jonah had the highest number of kills—seven opposing team members dead or out of action. Each time he'd shot an orange soldier with his paint ball gun, Thornton imagined blasting Sloan or Dena Lewis. A few times he even saw his children in the sights.

J.C. congratulated Jonah as the two men drank a beer at Abell's camper. "You're still the best shooter here," he said. "You probably won both exercises for us."

Jonah smiled. "Damn right." He drained his bottle and set it on the tailgate. "See you next month," he said. "Thanks for the beer." Jonah headed for his truck. A friend called out to him as he walked across the parking area.

"Hey, Thornton. How come no coons and queers speech today?"

Jonah waved at the man. "You left out the kikes," he said.

## Fifteen / Shelee

Every Sunday, at one o'clock throughout the summer, the St. Paul Consort, or some other string group, played in the art institute's central hall. When I was nine, I started going to the concerts—it was safe in those days for a kid to travel alone on a bus around Minneapolis. I'd grab my bus money, a sweater, and a book, and head for the cool halls of the institute. We didn't have air-conditioning at home, and the Sunday concerts gave me an afternoon away from the stifling Minnesota summer heat.

I would wander around the art displays, listening to the music piped through the museum, or sometimes sat in the rotunda, watching the musicians. The crowds of people began to bother me—I felt the concerts were mine and mine alone—and I'd wish for a private box in the vacant spiral staircase that graced the rotunda dome. So I began to explore, and soon found an entrance to the balcony above the concert floor via a freight elevator, hidden by a screen that stood behind the concert players.

The staircase—probably only for decoration—was blocked by a heavy metal grate; but the balcony suited me quite nicely if I lay, or sat, or stayed on my hands and knees. I even found a little grille where I could look down to the crowd below.

So using my carrybag as a pillow, I'd read or daydream on the cool marble floor to the music of Mozart and Vivaldi. Many wonderful Sunday afternoons passed this way. The music washed over me, crying Dvorak, meditating Chopin, pounding Schubert, and soul-shredding Elgar. All the while the instruments worked their magic on my young mind and body. Pianos conversed with my spine, licentious low notes resonated, making me blush, cellos tickled my feet—often kissed my toes—and violins had their way with my heart.

But oh the violas! It was their music I yearned to hear. Trapped as I saw it—their alto sweet songs ignored—between the pompous cellos and the haughty violins. I wanted to rescue them from the malaise of the middle ground, the connecting fields of the musical landscape. They needed my recognition, and *I* was their emotional champion.

"These things legal?"

"Yes sir," the salesman said, "pretty much so."

"I thought a telephone recordin' device ain't legal?" Jonah Thornton asked the well-dressed clerk at the North Central Spy Shop.

"Well sir, we sell 'em. And as long as people know you're using it, then they're supposed to be okay. Never had any problems, just plug into a phone jack."

"Who buys this stuff?" Jonah continued, amazed at the variety of electronic listening devices.

"Oh, folks who want to be sure their kids aren't using dope . . . you know."

"I've got tickets to the St. Paul Consort for Saturday night," I told Phil on Thursday as we sat down to dinner at his house. When you hear what's on the program, I think you'll want to go."

"The program better be good," he said, serving his leftover bass-tomato stew. "The last time they played Clang Concerto for Fart Pillow and Kazoo. I swore I'd never go back."

"Then how come you applauded?"

"Because they were finished." He frowned. "I like Duke Ellington's remark, 'If it sounds good, it is good.' "

"Poor Phil, doesn't understand avant-garde music," I said, pouring him a second glass of a recent Merlot, one of my $6.99 discoveries.

"What's to understand, Shel? I want to hear music that I enjoy, Baroque and Classicist—organized melodies, pleasing to the ear. Avant-garde music? A contradiction in terms."

"I pretty much have to agree with your taste," I said. "Years ago, I took music appreciation and I remember agonizing over the popular Romantic composers, listening through all the pathos while waiting for the few melodic passages. But I have a lesser problem with the Impressionists—they relate to my artwork in some way. Well, the program Saturday is all Classicist, except for the last piece. They're doing an instrumental of the trio from *Lakmé*."

"You're kidding! It's probably the duet in the first act, there's no trio."

"I think it's one of your favorites, done with two violins and a viola, probably a cello, too. You're sure it's not a trio?"

"I'll go willingly," Phil said. "Maybe they are using three strings for harmony, plus the viola as an echo. I'm hearing that aria all over the place these days."

"Do not insult the viola," I said. "By the way, you would have died at the concert Abby and I went to in New York one time."

"When was that?"

"About a year before I met you. We attended an 'opening' at a gallery in Manhattan."

"A show of your works?"

"Yeah, my first New York show, a strange mixture of fun and stupidity. Anyway, the gallery owner had season passes to the Philharmonic and gave us tickets for a Sunday afternoon concert. They were second-row balcony, and we were so excited to go we didn't check the program. It was all Modernist, and the music just made me gag."

"Sounds awful."

"Cute, Phil. The last two pieces were *the worst*—by some dork college professor from New Brunswick. Crapola for Electric Piano and Orchestra. And he had the gall to be the pianist! The first piece was terrible but short, the second not so short."

"I'm glad I missed it," Phil said, smiling.

"In the middle of the second piece, an old lady on crutches got up from an orchestra seat and slowly made her way up the aisle. It was a great protest.

"Oh, did I tell you that Saturday we're going with Trish and her new boyfriend? She wants us to go to dinner with them before the concert."

"You're really slipping this in a little at a time, aren't you?" Phil observed. "What's the new boyfriend like?"

"Don't know," I said, "haven't met him yet. You know I see Seth Cooper at the university all the time." Seth is Trish's ex-husband. "I'm sure Trish runs into him at school, too."

"Does he reach for his gun when you say hello?"

"Every time."

Seth is a strange case. He's a security guard at the University Medical Center, across the street from my building. He was married to Trish for about five years; they have a son named Will, same age as my niece, Heidi. Seth wears a sidearm when he's working; I believe he thinks he's a western gunslinger—Phil thinks it's because of his name. I can be walking down the hall and see him with one of his security buddies a mile away. I'm sure he sees me, too, but doesn't seem to know who I am. When I pass him and say "Hi, Seth," he puts his hand on his gun and looks at me as if I've threatened him.

We used to see Trish and Seth socially, once in a blue moon—when they were still married—and he'd do the same thing. At a university Christmas party, I tried talking with him four different times throughout the evening. Each time he groped around on his hip, feeling for his revolver. One time he even looked down, probably wondering why it wasn't there. I wish I'd turned back to him once—just as I walked away from him—to see if he'd already forgotten who I was.

"Well, any boyfriend is an improvement over Seth," Phil said. "You know, Trish is a captive of her own beauty. I should say her home environment and society made her so. And beautiful women do cloud the male mind, even briefly blot out our mothers."

"Do I cloud your mind?"

"Probably. My brain's been known to fizzle."

"You still think Trish is the most beautiful woman in the world?" I continued.

"She appears to be the most physically beautiful female I've ever seen," he said.

I put this long, high-pressure nonresponse on Philbert.

"Yes?" he prompted as I took both our plates into the kitchen for the last of the fish.

He's so good at not reacting, I decided to drop the subject. "To hell with your Trish theories," I yelled from the kitchen.

"Did you see Manny today?" I rejoined him at the table, setting his plate in front of him.

"I did see Manny, and I still think he's moving toward counseling and away from our current arrangement. I love talking with you about our sessions but it may be coming to a close. We had this interesting exchange this afternoon when I asked him about . . . how he comes up with such bizarre situations and settings. Manny said he tries to put his characters in plots so powerful that the stories simply invent themselves and find their own way. Then he said—listen to this—he thinks he's having so much trouble with the *Mikie* novel because the landscape in the book is so impoverished. I suggested the area where *Mikie* is not impoverished is his mind. I thought that totally obvious to both of us. Manny just went blank. It was as if his mind had left the room; then he changed the subject."

"And this makes you think he's going to open up about his personal life and history?"

"Yes, I think *Mikie and Mike* is really about Manny; the first letter, M, repeated twice is more than a coincidence. Another thing, have you noticed there are very few African-Americans in his books? Really, hardly any people of color in significant roles."

"He may be writing to the majority of his readers, who are probably white," I said.

"You could be right," Phil replied, "but I think there's more to it."

"Are you aware he wrote a great series of essays in *The New Yorker* about Martin Luther King?" I asked.

"No. When? I'd like to read them."

"It seems to me it was around 1980. He focused on the peaceful influence of King and how things might have been different if he had lived."

"Do you remember any specifics?"

"Uh-uh," I said and shook my head. We finished dinner and moved into the kitchen to clean up.

"All right, I'm ready to hear more of your theory about Trish, how she continues to get into trouble with the men she chooses."

"Manny and I were talking about this last week," Phil said, starting the coffee. "There's a stage in child development when a kid becomes aware that he belongs in his family; that's brought on by successful experiences around age five or six. Actually, the seeds for feeling competent are laid from birth. But at about five or six, the kid earnestly attempts new things that make him conscious of his ability to contribute to his family, then later to society. Female children are often corrupted by being told they are incompetent. And beautiful ones get the message that looks are their principal attribute, and thus the main reason they belong to their family. Often this later translates into 'sex is all I can contribute to a relationship.' "

"How is this at work in Trish?" I asked.

"I don't know what her folks are like," Phil said. "But somehow she got the antithesis of the worthiness message: 'I am incompetent, therefore I must be served, and that makes me feel I belong.' The only thing Trish feels confident about is her looks, and that's why she emphasizes her appearance. I see women like this in therapy all the time, but it's not exclusively a woman's club. These adults continue to collect bad experiences throughout their lives. That way they're always in a one-down position, i.e., they need service."

"It's interesting you put it in those terms," I said. "The truly liberated women I know never had to be liberated; they come from loving families that shrugged off cultural biases and gave their kids lots of support. I believe our Western culture currently makes that possible, don't you think?"

"Yeah, still it doesn't happen enough."

"But in so much of the world, women are the most abused underclass," I continued, getting wound up. "I love the quote: '*If men had babies, abortions would be the highest church sacrament, a sacred right.*' "

Phil dished up some cherry ice cream.

"I bet other cultures have similar stories like the dependent nonsense of women springing from Adam's rib. They must, when you see how women are treated elsewhere. Personally, I think Adam sprang from something Eve left in the grove."

"How interesting," Phil said, pouring coffee into two mugs, joining me at the table.

"Many women are *so* conditioned," I declared, savoring a spoon of ice cream. "Have you ever noticed in the supermarket, when you go by a woman who might be *even slightly* in the way, she invariably says, 'Sorry'? Bullshit! She's got as much right to take up space as the next person. Men rarely respond that way."

"Insightful, very insightful."

"Enough of this," I said. "What else have you and Manny talked about lately?" I loaded the last few dishes into the dishwasher. We took our coffee into the front room.

"You know I went up to school on Tuesday to hear this fellow from Cornell give a lecture on the special theory of relativity?"

"I guess I knew. What's so special about it?"

"It's special because it says we can never go outside our universe."

"Just remember, your universe is right here," I said, pointing down the front of my blouse.

"In your sex-crazed mind, you believe you're pointing to your wonderful breasts," Phil said, smiling, "but *I know* you're pointing to your heart. Anyway, Einstein's theory, which he thought up on the way to work one day, fits into my idea of the cosmos. Manny's come to the same conclusion."

I set my coffee aside, and lay down on the couch, my head in Phil's lap. "Oh tell me, my galactic honey."

"Shel," Phil said, "if I've lost your interest . . ."

"Shut up, Philip, and keep talking." I smiled, waggling my head.

"Well, the theory says that even traveling at the speed of light, one cannot leave the universe. It curves back on itself; we're stuck here, so to speak."

"How can that be?" I asked. What's beyond the stars?"

"There is no *beyond*," Phil said. "Here, I'll show you." He held his left hand in the air with his fingers slightly curved. "Let's say my left hand is the perimeter of the cosmos." He stuck his right index finger between the fingers of his left hand. "Now if my index finger is us, moving toward the edge of the universe at the speed of light, gravity would cause us to move along my left hand so we can't escape the curve." He bent his protruding finger to conform to the arch of his left hand.

"So now it's *us* at the limits of the universe," I said. "I like the idea." His lap was feeling more comfortable all the time. "But just because you can't get outside, doesn't mean there isn't an outside."

"You're at the limits of my understanding," Phil said. "I think there's no dimension outside the universe that can contain time, space, or anything else. Okay, let's come back to the Milky Way." He turned his empty dessert dish upside down on the newspaper. "It's no coincidence we're out here on the perimeter of our galaxy," he said, pointing to the dish's rim. "I think we're here for a reason."

I rolled over, face down. "Each woman to her own universe," I said, trying to warm up his lap. "Okay, why are we here?" I asked, my words muffled in his pants.

"The earth's in a good position to observe both the Milky Way and the rest of the heavens." He was stroking my hair.

I turned to look at him. "Hmmh, that feels good."

"See, if we were at the middle of the galaxy," he said, picking up the plate and touching its center, "we couldn't see what's outside because of the high density of stars. And think about it, there's trillions of stars out there and we haven't ever received a signal from another civilization. I mean, we should be hearing the evening news from somewhere."

"Wait a minute," I said, sitting up. "I know something about this. Who spoke at that lecture series we went to a couple of years ago? Remember that historical geographer? She talked about the unique nature of earth from the standpoint of its collection of minerals and the protection life gets from the structure of the atmosphere. She even said the earth is protected by the outer planets—they somehow shield us from collisions with asteroids and stuff."

"I think I finally have your attention."

"Go on," I said, "it's only temporary. Earth is the only place in the galaxy where food and sex are not interchangeable."

"Perhaps. So along with you, my love, that's another unique set of earthly features. I think our universe is some kid's high school science project. Sort of like a very complex ant farm. The glass in the ant farm is the edge of everything. We may be on a closet shelf somewhere, perhaps a discarded toy."

"Where the hell is all this leading, my Phil-Sloan sex toy? Our uniqueness may be a good argument for the existence of God." I lay down again and put my head in his lap.

"I like my ant farm theory better," Phil said. "Let me put it another way. Most of the cosmos is chaotic from a life-support view. So any sentient beings, such as we are, will try to ascribe order to it, projecting their need to justify existence. Perhaps our existence is just a beautiful anomaly."

"There's a Sons of Norway dinner Sunday afternoon," I said, changing the subject. "My family's going to be there, will you go with me?"

"Ya betcha," Phil said. He reached over and picked up his latest Manny Weston novel, turning his body slightly sideways so the book wasn't over my face.

Phil began weaving his fingers through my hair again, and I closed my eyes, trying to recall a conversation we had once about what he called diminished reality. It had to do with the compromises people make in relationships. He said that you become somewhat self-serving by loving unconditionally, if you are reasonably selective or lucky about choosing your partner. A relationship that functions becomes a reflection of your wishes.

"You still believe that?" I asked.

"Believe what?"

"Never mind," I answered drowsily, appreciating his fingers moving in my hair. I have these wonderful feelings about this man—I'm always learning from him. His intellect often seems far beyond his spoken thoughts. And he's never asked or implied that I should compromise on anything. Well, maybe on the marriage and family thing. . . . I drifted off to sleep, his beautiful face my last conscious image.

## Sixteen / Phil

The morning after the concert, Shel and I slept until seven, then went running.

"We're having a light breakfast today," Shel said, peeking her head into the shower.

I turned off the water, and Shelee handed me a towel. "Good and light," I said, anticipating enough food at the Sons of Norway to last me until midweek. I assume no one in Norway really eats like that, or most everyone would be dead by forty.

"Glad you liked the concert so much," she said, now sorting through the laundry.

"I said that?"

"Not exactly, but you've been humming the *Lakmé* aria all morning."

"You got me," I said. "The concert was good, dinner was very nice, and even Trish's new boyfriend was okay."

"Gimme that towel," Shel said, pulling it from around my waist. "Breakfast in five minutes." She disappeared with the dirty laundry.

After breakfast, I left for my place. When I got home, there was a message from Lucky on the answering machine. Shelee had told him about our visit with Dunk and Glo, and he was trying to twist my tail about the poker game. I figured I'd see him this afternoon and twist his tail right back—an old habit from long years of friendship.

I met Lucky the summer before I started high school, the summer that Teddy Granger and I got jobs at a wool factory. Ted, a neighbor kid, was two years older and could drive. His brother had given him a Model-A Ford that ran okay but had a totally rusted-out body. So Teddy stripped the old body off and replaced it with a wooden bench seat and a boxlike enclosure to sit in. The entire car was painted black. The damn thing only did about thirty-five miles per hour, so we had to use the surface streets. In this black, wooden car, putting along at a crawl in the early morning, Ted drove us to our new job—eight hours of shit-dipping.

Our job was to take large pieces of raw wool from a grading bin and pack them into seven-foot burlap bags that hung from a frame. When each sack was full, we had to tie the top off, mark the wool grade on the side of the bag, load it onto a handcart, and stack it on end for pickup.

But one of us had to get inside the sack to fill it. The kid outside would toss the wool into the bag, and the kid inside would then have to pull the wool past his face and body, stomp on it, and work his way to the top of the bag. The wool was greasy and full of sheep shit. We took turns inside the wool sacks, and by the end of the day, we both had this mixture of filth and lanolin nicely worked into our skin. Teddy's wooden car was well suited for two wretched teenagers. We were exhausted after work and would climb into his bizarre vehicle and, again at a crawl, drive home.

At home, no amount of washing helped, and I would emerge from the shower as dirty as when I started, still smelling like sheep. It promised to be a permanent skin condition that Teddy and I called dipped-in-shit syndrome. But then, one of my dad's patients, Lucky Osbornson, mentioned that he needed workers for his hay farm. When Dad told me the news, I immediately called Lucky and got jobs for both Teddy and me. Poor Mr. Shapiro at the wool factory was disappointed when we told him we were quitting. He said we were the best workers he'd ever had. No wonder, he usually hired transients from skid row who would quit as soon as they got saturated with lanolin and had booze money.

Lucky's farm job was ideal. We lived in wooden-floor tents by the lake, worked ten hours a day, got the weekends off, and were fed like kings. He even let us fish once in a while. That summer I learned to play poker, the hard way, using my $50 weekly pay. Lucky played poker with us during the evenings when he wasn't entertaining a "honey," as he called his women. He kept a lid on the game by allowing a single buy-in of five dollars per night. Sometimes we had bigger games on the weekends with the kids who didn't go home—I often stayed there for the card games and the fishing.

Lucky was a foul-mouthed, rough SOB, but he was fair. We knew about his boxing, so no one ever crossed him—he could have whipped the whole bunch of us. He chose to keep us in line with what we called the evil eye. He'd give us this squinty, sideways look, grunt slightly, and clench his fist, flexing one huge forearm. That's all it took.

I worked for Lucky four summers and we became close friends. Our friendship developed slowly—mostly we played cards and fished together. After my father died, we grew even closer. Poker seemed to come naturally to me, so I often cleaned out the games. Sometimes it'd be just Lucky and me, head-to-head at the end of the evening. Sometimes I would end up with all the money.

I played poker every chance I got over the next several years, even more in college. In my first few months of residency at Capitol Memorial, I played twice a week in a small game with several doctors, students, and a few businesspeople. It was a steady game, almost always full, and I could bring home $200 in an evening if I played well.

One night some of the players were smoking marijuana, and the betting got crazy. The game went on tilt—a couple of the doctors blew $1,000 or more. One of the players brought a guest, a lobbyist with a ton of money that he flashed around. I won about $3,000 and left the place at the same time as the lobbyist. When we walked out to the street, he said there was a game with lots of money and loose players every Friday night in a downtown hotel. He invited me to the next game, perhaps hoping I would bring the three grand and lose it. Because I had recently broken up with a girl I'd been dating from New York, and had too much time on my hands, I thought a second game might be a good diversion.

The new poker game turned out to be unlike any I had seen. It was located in a new apartment complex, not a hotel as the lobbyist had implied. The setup was quite plush, with three bedrooms, a full kitchen, and a part-time Korean housekeeper who lived there.

I identified myself through the intercom at the apartment's entrance before being allowed to go up. Kwo, the housekeeper, who was positively gigantic, let me in. He could have doubled as a bouncer if needed.

One night, after we were on friendly terms, I asked, "So what's your day job, Kwo?"

He gave a wry smile. "I work at a service station, Dr. Sloan, holding up cars while they're being repaired." Actually, Kwo was the lunch chef at one of D.C.'s best restaurants. He'd received his chef's training in Germany and spoke English with a German accent. He repaid his free room and board at the apartment with his Friday evening poker duties, and by cooking up fancy dinners for some of the players and their girlfriends. The apartment was a rendezvous spot every night except Friday.

The poker game appeared to be a real gold mine. I lost about $500 the first night and tried to appear somewhat awed by the game when I made a few dumb bets. Getting invited back was higher on my agenda than winning. I also decided to become friends with Kwo, if possible—his friendship could be an asset. The next four Fridays gave me time to adjust to the players' styles, and learn their weak and strong points. I always bought $4,000 in chips and never allowed my stack to vary by more than about $1,000. I quickly became a regular at the Friday games and on the fourth and fifth sessions, took home about $800 in profits.

Most of the players were serious drinkers and gorged themselves on Kwo's sensational food. About half of them smoked dope, which gave the game a surreal pace. Regular players included two senators and a House member, several lobbyists, and a couple of ambassadors. There were also several sleazy types, including the asshole I called Carp.

The game was awash with big money, and I seemed to be the only player using his own funds. We played with fancy, monogrammed chips and the minimum buy-in was $2,000. The smallest chip was worth $50. Most of the players bought in for $5,000, with many rebuys during the evening. The senators and the rest of them boasted about their cash sources and bashed constituents and employers alike. The worst was the Carp, a supplier of both dope and women to some of the players. He repeatedly bragged about his income from drugs and prostitutes.

There were times when the action would get completely out of control, with bets of several thousand coming down. I stayed out of most of those pots, watching and listening. The information I gathered served me well. After about six weeks, I was considered a regular, with a fairly predictable style. My efforts to befriend Kwo paid off, and sometimes I would come early to help him fix the food. Kwo soon expected me about an hour before each game. He usually knew who was playing that evening, and his review helped me get ready.

No one really liked Carp and his disgusting prattle. He was my first target and I started looking for an opportunity to take him down. I figured everyone would tolerate some big wins on my part if Mr. Raymond J. Starkey, aka Carp, was my main contributor. I called him Carp because he looked like the carp I'd seen back home sucking lake scum. He was fat, ugly, and continuously smoking a cigar. He pursed his lips and made kissing sounds on the cigar butt, reminiscent of feeding carp. His stagnant eye set, turned slightly downward, gave him a distinct fish face.

My tenth game, about two hours in, gave me the opportunity I had hoped for. There were often ten or more players at the table, so we usually played a poker game called hold'em. The game is well suited for a full table: Each player is dealt two cards down and there's a round of betting. Then three cards are "flopped" face up in the center followed by another betting round. Fourth and fifth center cards are dealt, face up, one at a time, with a betting round for each. A player uses the cards in his hand and the cards on the board, in any combination, to make a five-card poker hand.

The play revved up after Carp lost a $5,000 pot to Senator Paul Bradock. Carp got pissed off and bought $10,000 in chips. I had about $5,000 in front of me and decided to buy another five.

"Well, my god," one of the lobbyists said, "is Dr. Sloan finally going to swim with the big guys?"

"I can sail with the best of 'em," I replied, counting my new chips. Carp ran a big hand back at Bradock, trapping other players, and ended up with about $15,000 in front of him. A few hands later, I slow-played a hand and won a $2,000 pot from one of Carp's gangster buddies.

"Bet your goddamn hand!" the player shouted angrily at me.

"Why should I?" I said. "You were betting it for me."

"Oh, fuck you!" he said. I ignored him.

There was an advantage to my being big, young, and appearing in shape—no one was willing to confront me—and confrontations were rare. But whenever voices did become shrill, Kwo would stand in the kitchen entry. He'd cross his arms and stare icily at everyone; then the players would re-focus on the game. Fortunately, guns were forbidden.

A few hands later, Raymond Carpface announced he was going to buy another $25,000. Now he had about $40,000 in front of him. About half the other players made rebuys, including me. I put down my last $10,000 for more chips. If I got the right cards, my time was at hand.

The Carp made a gigantic bluff against the player on my left, the other senator in the game, Bill Malanda, from Florida. Malanda had three of a kind and Carp had a two-way straight to fill. Carp put the senator all-in for about $12,000. I couldn't believe Malanda called, since Carp could have held a pat straight based on the three flopped cards. The fourth card, a six, filled the straight, and Carp triumphantly turned his cards up before the fifth card hit the board. The fifth card was also a six, giving Malanda a full house. The loss sent the Carp into a frenzy of betting on the next series of hands. I was waiting for him to explode in a giant gusher of fat oil. He won a few hands—not enough for him. Soon the greedy bastard was twisting straight into hell.

While Carp was still cursing and slamming his cards and chips on the table I was dealt the king and ten of clubs. Malanda led off the betting with $200, and I called. Carp raised to $500 and two players on his left called; so did Malanda and I. The flop came nine of diamonds, and the ten and king of spades. Malanda, with a pair of nines in the hole, led off betting his trips with $300, having legitimate concern about the possible pat straight. Carp had a nut flush draw with the ace and nine of spades in his hand. He decided to call and play along, as did the one player on his left who did flop a straight. The player who slow-played the straight was a new man, and really didn't understand how to play no-limit poker. Also, he was the manager of the dairy lobby and probably had more money than anyone else in the room. The fifth caller before the flop round folded.

The fourth card made my hand—it was the king of diamonds. Bill had a full house and I had a bigger one. He decided to slow-play his hand, which helped me out immensely. I peeked at my king-ten hole cards and checked to the Carp. Old Carp passed, too, hoping for a free draw. The milkman opened up the betting, one card too late. He bet $2,000, and both Malanda and I called. Then Carp shoved $10,000 into the pot, an insane bluff in his position. The dairy lobby called, and Senator Malanda just couldn't wait. He called the $10,000 and raised all-in, another $17,300. I remember the exact amount because I was $5,700 short. I counted my chips out, generating a side pot. I didn't want to lose the Carp, figuring a mild needle might bring him in.

"Will you lend me bus fare home, Raymond?" I asked, smiling to my right.

The Carp ignored me and counted out his bet. Poor Bill Malanda did not look worried, brightening further when Raymond Carp said, "One of you cocksuckers has the nuts, right?" Raymond shoved the $17,300 into the pot. To everyone's surprise, the lobbyist called. He was holding the jack and queen of diamonds. So the king of diamonds on the fourth card gave him draws at a straight flush and a king flush. The fifth card hit the board, the five of spades. The reality of that card finally got Carp's attention, because he turned his hand up saying, "I've got a nut flush and I must be beat somewhere."

"Right here," Bill Malanda said, turning up his nines-over-kings full house and reaching for the pot.

"Sorry, guys," I said, showing my kings over tens. The milkman flashed his jack-queen briefly, assuring us he had a legitimate draw. I started pulling in an $80,000 pot, while Malanda collected the side pot. Apparently, when you make your money from pimping, dope, and government graft, it loses its value somewhere along the way, I decided.

That hand permanently changed the complexion of the Friday night game, and Carp vowed he'd never again bring less than $100,000. His ugly behavior increased in proportion to the amount of cash he brought to future games. He also said, and remained true to his word, that he would always buy in for $25,000, minimum. I was on my way to making a small fortune playing poker; if fame came later, so be it. I went home that evening with over $60,000 in winnings. I called Lucky the next morning to tell him he'd been a good teacher.

## Seventeen / Phil

It was poker night again and I was dragging in a $6,500 pot. The dairy lobby guy, who was now a regular player, looked at me and shook his head. "I'd sure like to have a pup out of you," he said.

"You'd have yourself a shit-eating dog," the Carp offered.

"Then you'll be my first meal, Raymond," I said to Carp.

The game's stakes had gone up after the $80,000 hand and pretty much stayed there. Both the government and gangster types made the adjustment quite comfortably. I made the adjustment with their money. "I have to play well," I told them. "I'm playing with my own money."

"No you're not," Senator Bradock said, "you're playing with my money."

"He's playing with everybody's money!" Carp whined. He was telling the truth. I had banked almost a quarter of a million dollars in the first three months. Bradock's beeper went off during the next hand. He folded his cards and went to the phone.

"Come on, Bill," he said to Senator Malanda, "we've got a quorum call." Malanda cashed in his chips, Bradock left his on the table. He asked Kwo to bring him the cash Monday if he did not return.

"I can't, Senator," the Korean said, "I'm going out of town tomorrow evening, and I'll be gone until Wednesday."

The Japanese ambassador had called earlier to say that he'd be late and was bringing another player. There were now only eight players at the table with the two senators out; we were a little short-handed.

"Phil, will you bring me my money if I don't make it back?" Bradock asked.

"Quit yakking and play cards!" Carpface interrupted. "Where the hell are those fucking Japs?"

I told Senator Bradock I'd be glad to bring him the money, then turned to Kwo, who was helping the senators with their coats. "What do you think of Raymond's language?" I asked.

"Word 'Jap' no problem," he said, lapsing from perfect English into pidgin. "I kill only when Kwo hears 'g' word." The two senators left and we returned to the game. Soon we heard the door-knocker, and Kwo let in the Japanese ambassador and another Oriental man who looked like an older, carbon copy of Kwo. Ambassador Yoto introduced his guest as the visiting Japanese ambassador to Turkey, the honorable Fujiami Nagatu. I figured the SOB was the killer-hat guy from the James Bond novels. Stupid Carp just licked his lips, hoping he was an easy mark.

Carp gouged a gray booger, the size of a large pea, out of his nose. Then he dapped it between his fingers, all the while playing with his chips. He popped it in his mouth and peeked at his cards. The two Japanese looked at him in horror, and Yoto said something in Japanese to Nagatu. I assumed he said the booger was simply a piece of rubber cement the Carp used to nauseate guests. I had a pair of surgical gloves in my pocket, reserved for Carp's guest welcome. I put them on and said, "I don't want to get hepatitis from you, Raymond. No telling what you do with your whores."

"Well, it's for sure I don't fuck 'em," he said, spitting into a napkin. "Only let 'em give me blow jobs." He continued, providing vivid details of what some of his heroin-addicted prostitutes do for a fix.

Nagatu appeared to understand some English but spoke little of it. When Kwo brought him a drink, he spoke to him in Japanese and Kwo answered him back. I made a mental note to ask Kwo where he had learned Japanese.

"I thought you two cultures don't talk to each other," Carp said. Kwo ignored him and Nagatu appeared to not understand—Nagatu appeared not to understand simple arithmetic, either. After winning a hand against both Japanese, Raymond was ecstatic. "This is turning into a regular bug-fucking contest," Carp snorted. "No wonder you people lost the war." Yoto stiffened, and again, Nagatu seemed unaware. "You must be a retired Kamikaze pilot," Raymond concluded.

Fujiami Nagatu looked genuinely confused. He spoke quietly with Yoto while watching the others play several hands. Their attention returned to the game as Fujiami bought $50,000 in chips; Yoto shook his head. I figured Fujiami was easy money and sat there hoping for some decent cards. Too many people were chasing him for a bluff to work. About then, a shoot-'em-up hand developed.

It was my turn to deal, and the two Japanese sat next to me on my left. With Nagatu, Carp, and the dairy lobby in for the flop, I dealt an eight and four of hearts, and the ace of clubs to the table. The milkman bet $2,000 and Carp raised it by $10,000. Nagatu put $12,000 in front of his stack of chips. Then he absent-mindedly elbowed his whole stack toward the pot.

Carp exploded. "Is that supposed to be a bet?" he shouted. "That's a fucking string bet! Not legitimate! What the fuck is going on?"

"Take it easy, Raymond," I said, hoping Nagatu had trapped the Carp. "He's a guest and may not understand what a string bet is." Turning to my left, I said, "Mr. Nagatu, you must put your entire bet in the pot at once or announce it." The chips were still in never-never land. "Do you intend to bet all of your chips?" I asked. He nodded.

The dairy man folded, saying, "That's the best goddamn stutter bet I've ever seen."

I turned to the Carp, "He's putting you all in. Do you call?"

"Of course I call," Raymond said. "I've got the bes' fuckin' hand." He turned over two eights, giving him trips for the round, and shoved all of his chips forward. I counted out $37,200 in chips, threw $200 back to Carp, and extracted $49,000 from Nagatu's stack. I gave Raymond his $200 back—it was the custom in this game to return parts of all-in calls under $500.

Nagatu stared at the Carp's hand. "Kamikaze bug fucker," he mumbled and turned over the ace and three of hearts. I didn't think much of his chances but I liked his style. "Two hundred dollars more, please," he said in perfect English, and put $200 in chips next to the pot.

Carp was so pumped up, he didn't mind the breach of etiquette. "So you speak our language," he said. "I can use the two extra hundred." He grinned and threw the chips in the pile. The next card I turned was the king of clubs, and the fifth was the two of hearts, giving killer-hat a winning flush.

The remainder of the evening was all downhill for Raymond Carp. He simply wallowed in his own avarice, trying to get even with Fujiami Nagatu. He lost his $100,000, giving at least $60,000 to the Asian contingent, and a gracious $4,000 to me. Senator Bradock did not return, so I cashed in his chips and took his money with me.

Monday was my half day off from the hospital, and I headed over to Bradock's office. My residency duties included two night shifts and three day shifts, each supposed to be twelve hours, but they usually stretched to about fourteen. Most evenings when I was at the hospital, I ate my meals in the patient cafeteria. I found that observing patients and taking meals with them was helpful to both the patients and me. The patients were the best teachers at this point in my training.

It was about ten-thirty in the morning when I walked into Bradock's outer office. He was the junior senator from South Carolina. One look around the office and I knew he had discovered the voting power of his black constituency. I assumed many of his staff were South Carolina transplants or appointees. A Southern senator's office staffed with a balance of whites and blacks was unheard of just a few years earlier.

"I'm Dr. Sloan to see Senator Bradock," I said to the receptionist.

She picked up the phone and announced me to someone. There was a pause, then she turned to me, "The senator said he'd like to chat with you if you could wait a few minutes. He's in a meeting just winding up. Would you like some coffee?"

"Thanks," I said, and sat down on one of the leather couches by the door. I flipped through a magazine and paused at an ad for Las Vegas, fancying a little poker with the big guys.

I felt her arrival before I heard her voice. Then I looked up into the exquisite, penetrating dark eyes of a tall, slender black woman. "Excuse me, are you Dr. Sloan?" she asked. Before I could answer, she smiled and extended her hand. "I'm Serena Martin, one of Senator Bradock's aids."

I stood and shook her hand. "Nice to meet you."

"Would you like to wait in my office?" she asked. Serena turned quickly—the full, loose curls of her black hair danced at the back of her neck. I followed Ms. Martin past the receptionist into a large office with three desks. She sat on the corner of one desk. Three coats hung on the coat rack; I assumed her office mates were elsewhere. "So you're one of the senator's poker buddies?" she asked with interest, flashing a smile that accentuated her elegant cheekbones.

I was bothered by Serena's question. Perhaps she expected me to hand her Paul's money—away from the front office—and she'd be on her way.

"That's right," I said, looking at her. *Really* looking at her.

Washington is full of beautiful, available women, supposedly the best ratio of women to men in the country—ideal from a bachelor's viewpoint. But I preferred having a steady girlfriend, and figured I'd meet someone sooner or later. I hadn't had a truly serious date since breaking off with a woman from New York four months before. And that relationship was limited to when she was in D.C. on business—she had made it clear that New York was off limits. In any case, I wasn't ready to see Serena Martin go without making a personal connection.

"May I sit there?" I asked, taking a step toward a small settee in the corner.

She nodded, and I sat on one of the broad leather arms, striking a pose similar to hers. "Are you from South Carolina, Ms. Martin?"

"Pennsylvania," she said. "But I received my law degree from the University of South Carolina."

"Then you decided to come to Washington?"

She smiled. "I received a two-year appointment to the senator's legal staff from the university. This is an ideal spot for me, since my specialty is international trade law. I have about another year to go on my appointment."

"So what after that?"

"I'll probably stay here in D.C." She paused. "What about you? What kind of doctor are you Mr. Sloan? Dr. Sloan," she corrected. But before I could answer, the phone on her desk rang. "Yes, Senator, he's right here," she said. "All right, I'll ask him." She hung up and turned back to me. "The senator said you might be returning his poker winnings. You may give them to me if you like."

"Did the senator really say they were winnings?" I asked with a chuckle. "Can I give you the money after lunch?"

Serena Martin looked mildly irritated. "Do you mean you wish to turn the money over after lunch—*after* you have eaten?" she asked. "Dr. Sloan," she continued as she walked to the coat rack and opened her purse, "I'd be happy to lend you what you might need for lunch. Would that make you more comfortable, so you could give Senator Bradock his poker money now?"

I was feeling idiotic but decided to keep the theme going. Perhaps she'd be impressed with my Jimmy Stewart approach. Looking at my watch, I said, "Well, lunchtime's in an hour and . . . and there's lots of places 'round here where a fella and his lady friend might find a good meal, ma'am."

Serena Martin ignored me. She took two twenty-dollar bills out of her purse and offered them to me. "This should be enough for a couple of drinks, a good lunch, a tip, and bus fare home."

I was in so deep, there was nothing I could do to get out of this one. I tried to take the money, but she held on to it.

"The envelope please, Dr. Sloan."

"Did you know I work at a mental hospital, Ms. Martin?" I asked, pulling on the bills.

"That would not surprise me in the least, Dr. Sloan. Does the hospital staff know you're visiting a United States senator's office today? Perhaps we could call the hospital and *they* could take you to lunch?"

Just then, with both of us still tugging at the money, Senator Bradock walked in. "Is this scoundrel giving you a rough time, Serena?" he asked. Paul Bradock beamed and put his arm around my shoulder. I smiled sheepishly. Then I let go of the greenbacks and shook the senator's hand.

"This is the best poker player in our game," he said. "He's getting rich at my expense."

Serena put the money in her purse, and I handed the senator his poker envelope. "He has to be a shrink. Right?" Serena said, shaking her head.

"That's what he's told us, but based on his poker playing, he's probably a proctologist."

"I'm a resident in psychiatry at Capitol Memorial," I said to Serena, "and I would enjoy having lunch with you today."

"He's a dangerous man, counselor Martin," Bradock moaned. "I do not know that he can be trusted. At best he's a shrewd thief; at his worst, who knows?"

Serena's demeanor changed as she extended her hand and grasped mine briefly. "Meet me in front of the building, north entrance at noon. I'd love to have lunch with any scoundrel who can filch our esteemed senator's hardly earned money," she said coolly, glancing sideways at Paul Bradock. I was startled by her deliberate response.

The senator headed for the door, putting the poker envelope inside his jacket. He waved and looked back at us. "Oh, I've surrounded myself with the glibbest of the glib," he said, leaving the room.

## Eighteen / Phil

Serena escorted me through the reception office. "I'm looking forward to lunch," she said. I smiled, then walked down the stairs into the chilly, fall day. I buttoned up my coat and quickly walked the long block to the Capitol, where I wandered around, thinking about the magnificence of the premises and the equivocal nature of most of the folks who legislate here. Soon it was time to meet Serena, so I walked back to her building, arriving just as she came through the entrance.

"I know of a great Chinese restaurant a block and a half from here on D Street," I said. "But it's pretty cold; maybe you'd rather get a cab and go . . ."

"No, no. I love Chinese. We'll just walk quickly." Serena took my arm. "It's such a pleasure to meet a nonpolitical, non-government man," she said and smiled, her eyes dancing. We chatted about hometowns as we hurried down First Street.

When we got to the restaurant, the host seated us next to a healthy blaze in a white brick fireplace. "Nice choice, Dr. Sloan," Serena said, turning her chair sideways by the hearth to warm her hands.

"So what's it like working in a senator's office?" I asked after the waitress took our order.

"In a minute," she replied. "I want to know what's it like to play high-stakes poker with Paul Bradock and his buddies. You *do know* about his connections with those cutthroats?"

"Not exactly," I said, "please tell me."

"Is that creep, Raymond Starkey, in the game?"

"Yes."

"I thought so," Serena said with disgust. "They're all in bed together, that bunch."

"I'm interested, if you can tell me more." The waitress brought our soup.

"I don't think anything is a secret in this town," Serena said quietly. "But take a guess: What does Bradock, from a Southern state, have to do with Bill Malanda from Florida, the dairy lobby, and a skunk like Starkey?" Serena asked, drinking her shark's-fin soup directly from the bowl.

"I haven't a clue," I said after thinking for a moment.

"Have you noticed Raymond's cigars? What kind they are?"

"No, they just stink."

Serena shook her head. "Those are $100 Havanas, Phil. Starkey pays off the crooks in Miami to hold down the traffic in smuggled Cuban cigars."

I was astonished. "You're kidding. Sounds like a lot of trouble for a few cigars." Our lunches were served.

"It's big business," Serena said, jabbing her chopsticks in the air. "Is there a dairy lobbyist in the game?"

"Yeah."

"See, they dumped the last guy because he started to complain about his duties."

"This is crazy," I said. "Complain about what duties?"

"You really *are* from the Midwest," Serena said with gentle exasperation. "Okay, I'll lay it out for you. Bradock can't get too close to the tobacco lobby, so the dairy guy brings in the tobacco money for the senator. He and Malanda dole it out to Starkey for the Cubans."

"Let me guess," I said. "Bill Malanda gets campaign support from the Miami crowd."

"Bingo! And campaign money, of course," Serena said. "That's the main thing this town's about—money."

"Amazing," I said. "Now tell me about you."

"Grew up in Pittsburgh. My father's an internist and my mother's a labor attorney, turned civil rights lawyer. So when I decided to follow in my mom's footsteps, my folks suggested I go to a college in the Deep South, to experience the reality of discrimination."

Any woman as elegant and attractive as Serena, I reflected, wouldn't experience discrimination except from other women who were jealous.

"But the whole civil rights thing just doesn't hold my interest," she said. "I majored in econ for prelaw—found it far more interesting than sociology. I started law school in Virginia, then transferred back to SC after a year. Sort of eased back into the South." She pointed again with her chopsticks, now decorated with a bean sprout. "Finally, I felt really at home in Columbia and missed it when I left, but now I love Washington. No more Southern towns for this girl."

The waitress cleared our table and Serena, now without her chopsticks, played with an empty water glass as she talked, making circles with her middle finger on the bottom of the glass. The circles started at the outer edge and wound inward, stopping at the center. Then she'd repeat it, starting her finger massage again at the edge. It dawned on me I'd made a connection with this lady, happily noting that this female circlemaking crossed ethnic lines—I'd seen it before when a woman indicated she wanted to spend more time with me. Her small circular motions were getting me quite excited, and I was beginning to feel a little giddy.

She looked at her watch. "I've got to get back to work," she said. "There's a briefing for some tobacco exporters at two, and I have to set up the handouts and give a presentation." She flashed her distinctive smile.

We helped each other with our coats and headed out the door.

"More tobacco stuff, huh?" I said as we walked down the block.

"Yes, and I love it when this Afro-woman gets to tell those good-old-boy farmers what's happening on the rest of the planet. Have to say that Senator P. Bradock gives me all the help I need. He may be part of the good-old-boys' club but he supports and encourages his staff. And I've never heard him imply anything racist," she said as we turned the corner and faced into the fall breeze.

"Well he's just some kind of modern, Southern boy," I said. She gave me a inquiring look. "He was a blatant racist ten years ago," I added.

"Time and voter demographics, Dr. Sloan, time and demographics."

The wind picked up as we walked back along First Street toward her office. She took my arm, leaning against me to block the cold. I sensed our connection was deepening. "There's a sensational Cantonese and Szechuan restaurant just a few blocks from my apartment," I said. "How about dinner and a movie on Saturday?"

"I can't Saturday," she said. "I'm going to Virginia Beach for the weekend. I'll be home Sunday afternoon, though. Can we do it then?"

"Sunday's fine." I said.

"I'd prefer to meet you," she said when we got to the Senate Office Building.

I held the door for Serena and said, "Okay, I'll look up the restaurant's address in your office."

Serena led me to the reception counter on the first floor. "You don't need to come up," she said. "We can get it right here." It seemed curious that she didn't want me back upstairs, but I followed her lead and looked up the address from a phone book supplied by a security guard. We exchanged home numbers and agreed to meet at five-thirty on Sunday. Unexpectedly, she gave my hand a squeeze, pulled me toward her, and kissed me on the cheek. "Thanks so much for lunch," Serena said, smiling. "Call me later and give me directions from the Key Bridge. See ya."

Though I'd met this woman only three hours earlier, I found myself wishing it was already Sunday afternoon. All a little confusing, I thought, attributing it to hormones. I walked out of the building and over to Second Street to find my car, thinking of the impression she'd left on me. She had a comfortably independent manner about her, one of the attributes I most admire in a woman. I had an idea her independence came from her parents—by professional example—because she told me that she and her brother didn't see much of them. Her brother, Serena said, was three years older and an architect in Boston. The two of them had really grown up on their own, she explained—big house, live-in help, intermittent parents.

Thursday, I called Serena from the hospital with directions to the Golden Lobster. "You're going to love their sweet-and-sour redfish," I told her. "Oh, there goes my pager. See ya Sunday," I said, realizing I sounded a little like her.

The poker game on Friday was slow and uninteresting. My cards were mediocre and I left early. Late afternoon Sunday, I walked over to the restaurant and found the damn place closed.

Impossible, I thought. Everything is open Sundays in Georgetown. No problem, I decided; we could go around the corner to the Imperial China Cafe, a place almost as good. I waited half an hour but no Serena.

My hunger got the best of me, so I walked across the street to a drugstore, wrote out a note, and left it on the front door of the restaurant. Then I strolled over to the Imperial and asked for a table for two, hoping I hadn't been stood up. I'd taken a few bites of my food when Serena came into the restaurant, out of breath and looking a little frazzled.

"I'm sorry I'm late," she said. "The traffic was impossible, and I didn't plan very well. Thanks for leaving the note." She kissed me on the cheek, then sat down next to me.

"Hungry?" I asked

"Yes, what's for dinner?" Serena began tasting my food. "Damn that's good!" She motioned the waitress over. "What shall I order?"

"Get their sampler," I suggested. "And a couple of Chinese beers," I said to the waitress. "Beer okay, Serena?" I asked in afterthought.

"Sure."

We combed through the paper for a local movie list while we shared my food. "That's what I want to see," Serena said, pointing to a listing for a show just down the street. "I missed it the first time around."

"*Hammersmith Is Out,* with Liz Taylor and Richard Burton," I read aloud. "Great cast; what's it about?"

"The movie's up your alley, Dr. Sloan—a lunatic tries to take over the world; Burton plays the nut, of course."

"Just my thing," I said as the waitress brought Serena's Imperial Cafe sampler.

After dinner, we got some espresso at a take-out counter near the restaurant. The movie was a short four blocks away, and we walked down M Street, sipping our coffee and blowing foggy breath clouds into the night air. The movie was totally enjoyable, and Serena had a delightful laugh. I found myself feeling almost blessed with her company.

In the cold Georgetown night after the movie, Serena took my arm and pushed against me in a way that was becoming pleasantly familiar.

"Did you walk to the restaurant?" she asked.

"I did."

"Then let's pick up my car and I'll drive you home."

Her car was parked just a few blocks from my apartment, but wanting the opportunity to ask her up, I accepted her offer.

"Would you like to come up for a drink?" I asked, as her car idled in the street in front of my apartment. "The guy across the way doesn't have a car and lets me park in his driveway. There's room for two cars if you let me out first."

"I'll come in on one condition," she said. She didn't wait for my response. "I'm grubby from the beach and I'd like to take a shower. I assume you have running water."

"Fine with me," I answered, getting out of her car, not quite believing my ears. She parked her car, locked it, and opened the trunk. Serena pulled out a small suitcase and handed it to me. I took her arm and we walked up the stairs.

"Make yourself at home," I told her and took her coat. "I'm into German wines these days," I said, offering her a glass of Riesling from an opened bottle in the fridge. She took the wine and kissed me on the cheek again. This time the kiss lingered a moment. My head was spinning.

"Where's the shower?" she asked cheerfully, picking up her suitcase.

"Through my room," I said, pointing to my half-opened bedroom door. "There's fresh towels in the cabinet."

"Thanks." Ms. Martin walked into my room, put the suitcase on the bed, and closed the door. I had just turned on the television when Serena emerged. She had on a white terry cloth bathrobe.

"Dinner and the show were really fun," she said with a serious air—but her eyes were dancing again. The look of Serena's white robe against her ebony skin was almost overwhelming. "Would you like to join me in the shower?" she asked.

"That's the best shower invitation I've ever heard," I said. Then I got up from the couch and took her hand, leading her into my room. Serena took off her robe and laid it on my bed; she watched me undress.

I reached out and put my hand on her shoulder, balancing myself as I removed the last of my clothes. Then I ran my hand down her arm and led the way into the bathroom. I turned on the shower, kissed Serena, and pulled her into the warm spray, marveling at her delightful woman smell and skin texture as we washed each other.

Serena and I were to spend more than a year together. After that first night, I quickly became immersed in our relationship. We became a hot item, seeing each other three or four nights each week. She was bright, witty, and almost always wore white underwear. It was a year when I fell quite in love with this cosmopolitan D.C. woman. She loved me, too, I guess, but in a different way.

## Nineteen / Shelee

I was in my studio when I heard Phil come into the house. "I'm up here," I yelled.

He walked up the stairs and into the room. "Ready for the Sons of Norway?" he asked, then kissed me on the back of the neck.

"Just about," I answered, placing a VØLM in a frame on my easel. "What do you think of this frame?" It was a spare I'd rejected before.

He studied it for a moment, then looked at the other VØLM—also in a recycled frame—propped by the window.

"I'm neutral," Phil said. "Neither one thrills me. Aren't these going in the institute show?"

"Yes, if they get accepted." I walked back and forth between the two pieces.

"Did you see the article about the show in the *Express* this morning?" he asked.

"Yeah," I said, "it sounds pretty elegant this year. You *will* be my date, won't you?"

Phil kissed me again. "Wouldn't miss it. So, are Abby and the kids joining us today?"

"Uh-uh. I called her but she had some lame excuse. She hates these 'old-folks get-togethers,' as she calls 'em." I removed the VØLMs from the frames and handed them to Phil. "Please take these downstairs. I'm going to call my framer."

"On Sunday?"

"Sure, she's used to me," I said, dialing. "I need to get these in first thing tomorrow. Maybe we can drop them by her house.

"Good news," I said to Phil as I headed down the stairs. "She's going into the shop and we can leave them there. It's not much out of the way."

When we arrived at West Side Gallery, Marion was restoring some antique frames. "Don't stop," I told her. "I'll just look around."

I left Marion and Phil in the workroom and meandered through the frame display. I had pastel lacquered wood in mind and found several samples that would complement my pieces. I took the samples back to the workroom, where Marion was taking apart an ornate gold-leaf frame.

"This one's French," she was telling Phil as I walked into her back-room shop. "It's about two hundred years old and worth almost as much as the painting that was in it. I've got three here from the Provincial Museum in Ottawa."

As I tried out the lacquered wood samples on my VØLMs, I asked Marion, "What's that dental X-ray machine doing in the frame room?"

"Oh, I use that to locate nails and fasteners in these old frames," Marion said. "It minimizes the damage when I take them apart."

She and Phil held my paintings as I tried out the various frame corners. After a few minutes of experimentation, we settled on a three-inch wide, rust-orange, oval-profile frame for my dark, moody VØLM, and a similarly shaped, deep blue frame for my bright one. "They're going to hang close together," I said, "so the frames have got to be complementary."

"Good choices," Phil said as I regarded both pieces one last time. "Let's go, I'm famished."

"Very nice," Marion said. "Fantastic. I'll call you when they're ready."

I took Phil's arm. "Thanks," I said.

Phil parked his Blazer in the lot behind the Sons' lodge, a row away from Lucky's red Suburban. Phil said, "I see Lucky's here. Wonder if he liked my piping job?" The smell of good Scandinavian food was in the air. Phil held my hand as we walked into the hall, waved to a few people, and then spotted Lucky. Phil and I both hugged him. "Was the irrigation setup okay?" Phil asked.

"Sure was, bub," Lucky said with his snaggle-toothed smile. "Thanks for not hookin' up the wiring. I moved the timer to the closet on the other side of the door. Ran the wires under the porch in a conduit so the skunks and mice'll leave 'em be." Phil beamed at Lucky.

I often forget that Phil and Lucky are really close buddies. Phil's dad, who was a cancer specialist, died of leukemia of all things, when Phil was seventeen. His mom remarried another doctor, an anesthesiologist and family friend, within a year. His mom's quick re-marriage didn't set well with Phil. At that time I don't think he was even close to being over the loss of his dad. Also, he's never cared for his stepfather—that surprises me, since Phil likes almost everybody. Anyway, as soon as Phil graduated from high school, he moved out to Lucky's farm. By that time he'd been offered scholarships to U of M and Ohio State, each one a full four-year academic ride. I guess his family was upset when he decided to go to Ohio State.

When he finished premed, he applied to Minnesota and was accepted. But maybe because of his stepfather—though he's never said—he decided instead to go to American Medical College in D.C. He also did his internship and residency in Washington. His mom and stepdad moved to Racine while Phil was a first-year intern. The stepfather works at a private clinic there, and Phil visits them only about once a year, even though it's an easy drive from Minneapolis. Lucky and Phil became really close that summer before college.

We piled our plates high with food and steered Lucky toward a side door leading to the ball field. A few tables were set up out there, and though it was a blustery day, the building sheltered us, and we could enjoy the warm sunshine. Just as we reached the door, the noisy hall fell silent, and I knew my parents had arrived. The brief silence was followed by cheers and applause.

Phil smiled. "Your folks are here." We put our food on a table and I went back in to greet Inga and Stewart. Lucky and Phil were both hungry, so they stayed outside to gab and eat.

By the time I got to my parents, they were surrounded by a crowd. I hugged them both and shook hands with a dozen people, practicing my Norwegian. "We're eating outside with Lucky," I told my dad and winked at him. My folks always receive a hero's welcome at these Norwegian affairs, and it embarrasses them; but I think it's exciting. I'm very proud—they risked their lives for several years during the war.

The Nazis had stupidly expected the Scandinavian countries to welcome them with open arms. After all, they reasoned, these were Aryan brothers. So for the first year, the German occupation in Norway was not militarily intense. That gave the underground resistance time to build and organize; and it was supported by the general population. After about a year, the

Nazis started rounding up and jailing politicians they suspected of not being sympathetic to the Third Reich.

My folks worked with my dad's parents on the family farm near a town called Tönsberg. They hid fugitives from the Nazis as part of an underground railroad to Great Britain. Their location, about seventy miles south of Oslo, was a way station on the freedom road to England. The fugitives left my parents' farm for either Kristiansand, or a town farther to the west, Egersund. Both of these towns had fishing fleets, and the boats helped smuggle people to British submarines in the North Sea. Many Norwegians, including my family, had people living under the floorboards in their houses and barns. Sometimes they lived underground for months at a time, until safe passage could be worked out. In my family home, they were fed and nursed by my parents and grandparents.

One thing my father did was to remove the human waste each day and mix it with the cow manure. Some German soldiers came by one early spring day with a truck and wanted some manure for their garden, even offered to pay for it. My dad was afraid to refuse, so he gave it to them. The farmers, who were really smart and planned ahead, had two piles of manure, one with, and one without, human sign. Sadly, the Germans got the one without. My dad will tell you he's always regretted not being able to put Norwegian shit on German food.

Things got really spooky when a neighbor was shipped off to a concentration camp for hiding a Russian refugee. The Russian looked quite Nordic, and was supposed to be a cousin living and working at the neighbor's farm. There must have been a German sympathizer in the area, because the man had lived at the farm for two years before being caught. The neighbor was shipped off and returned after six months—but no one knows what happened to the poor Russian. All the Osbornsons got through the war unscathed, and when the Germans withdrew from Norway, there were still refugees living under my parents' floorboards. When the Nazis left Tönsberg, my mom and dad slept through the night—their first full night's sleep since the war had started.

By the time my folks joined us at the table, we were finished eating, and Lucky was blathering about elk hunting and poker games. The first thing Lucky said to Mom and Dad was, "You know that huntin' trip I was tellin' you about? Well, old Philbert here wants to go to Montanee, too, and he promises not to play poker."

"Montanee? What are you drinking?" I quipped. "Even Lucky isn't going if he doesn't get a permit."

"Maybe I already have a permit," Lucky snarled.

"Maybe you'd better talk nice to us or I won't go. Which means 'Old Philbert here' might decide to stay home, too. It's too soon for you to get the permit; I read the form."

Lucky turned to Stewart. "You folks raised a smart-ass girl, you know that?"

Mom stood up and pulled on Lucky's arm. "Come help me round up some of this food for Mother and Dad. We're going to take it over to the rest home, and you're coming with us." We remained there, talking with my dad until they returned with the food. Then Phil and I said our goodbyes and headed to my house.

"What do you think of this Montana trip?" I asked Phil as we pulled out of the parking lot. "It's the last week in October, and I can get my classes covered."

"I think I can arrange to be gone for a week or so," he said. "I'd love to see Olie, and we can ski and goof off. It'll be super."

"Better bring your earplugs for nonstop Lucky chatter," I suggested.

When I returned to my office from lunch Monday afternoon, I found Trish excited about a phone call from the art critic at the *Post Express*, Elizabeth Carbonnader. "She wants to do a preview story on your submittals to the institute's show this year," Trish said. She handed me the message.

"The BS they write makes me gag," I said, aiming my finger down my throat. "I'll call her back, though. Please ring her up, will you Trish, dear? I'll take the call in my office." I hung up my cardigan just as the phone rang.

"Good afternoon, Elizabeth. What can I do for you today?" I asked in the slightly unctuous tone that signals her feeding time. Trish sat at her desk, pretending to do her nails, making faces.

"Shelee," she oozed, "I want to do an advance piece on the institute show for next Sunday's edition. May I do a review of your artwork? You *are* going to grace the show with your abstracts this year?"

"Yes, Liz, I am submitting two works as usual," I said. "I deliver the paintings on Wednesday, then they get juried, and I won't know if the works are accepted until Monday. The institute's quite secretive about the selection. You sure you want to review pieces that might not make the show? And will your review be favorable?"

"You're too modest, Dr. O.," Liz said, leaking into the phone like Plastic Man. "And of course my review will be favorable. After your latest New York sale, you *know* they'll make it in this year."

"Nothing's guaranteed," I said, "but you're welcome to do a critique. You can see them at the West Side Gallery. I'll call Marion and let her know you're coming in. Have a good week," I said and hung up.

I grabbed my lecture notes and headed out the door for class. "Trish, will you call Marion at the West Side Gallery? Please let her know that Liz from the *Post Express* will be in to look at my VØLMs."

"Sure thing, Shel," Trish said with a wave.

Next morning, Trish handed me a message to call the frame shop. "Marion says it's urgent."

"What could be so urgent?" I asked. "Did you call her yesterday?"

"Yes," Trish said, dialing the shop, "but she wasn't available, so I told one of her staff. Pick up the phone, it's ringing."

"Hi, Marion, what's up? Anything wrong with my paintings?"

"No, your paintings are fine, Shelee," Marion said. "They'll be framed today but . . . um, yesterday I was showing my new girl how to use the X-ray machine and I demonstrated with one of your paintings. You know, looking for the metal corner gussets in the stretcher bars."

"Oh?"

"Well, we saw several metal pellets imbedded in the wood," Marion said hesitantly.

I didn't know whether to be annoyed or amused. "How did you know what they were, Marion?"

"Oh, this is so embarrassing," Marion went on. "When I was out for lunch, a man brought in one of your original VØLMs. Remember the one you called *Tapestry,* the one with all the purple?"

"Yes."

"Well, he was going to have it reframed as a gift for his daughter, and the new girl, Suzie, told him we had two new VØLMs in the back. Unfortunately, she told him about the pellets, too."

"Terrific. But how do you know they were steel pellets?" I asked, beginning to get irritated. "The pellets, Marion!"

"Suzie offered to X-ray the man's VØLM," Marion said quickly. "Well, they took the frame off, discovered two pellets near the surface on the wood stretcher, and they dug them out. Then they noticed a strange pattern on the back of the canvas."

Of course, I thought. That was a painting I framed myself and had done a sloppy job repairing the stretcher bar holes. I didn't gesso the back of the canvas, just scraped off the extra paint that oozed through the shot holes. So the paint on the back of the canvas would naturally be raised in a clearly visible pattern. I figured no one would ever see the painting's back—I'd used a poster board backing.

"So anyway," Marion said, "he's decided to wait on the new frame, until he has a chance to find out more. Do we have a problem here?"

"No, no," I told her, not wanting to explain. "Did you get the message that Liz Carbonnader is coming in to look at the new VØLMs—or has she already been in?"

"Not yet," Marion said, "but I'll watch for her. *I'll* wait on her myself," she added, letting me know that her staff would not be blabbing to Ms. Carbonnader about the pellets.

"Thanks," I said. I clicked the receiver and called Phil to tell him the story, but he wasn't available.

Friday morning found Jonah watching Sloan's office building on Hennepin Avenue. It was just a one-story job, but there were several entrances, and he couldn't figure out how to identify the doctor or spot his car. He could have asked, but he guessed people might be suspicious.

He never should have made that phone call, he thought, it was too soon for it. The weather was hot and Jonah wiped the sweat off his forehead nervously. Something had to be figured out soon. He couldn't just hang around, someone would notice. Finally Jonah walked quickly through the clinic until he located Sloan's office. The door was closed, but he walked on, satisfied that he'd figured out the most likely building exit to watch. That could be done from across the street, he decided, sitting at the Fish'nBurger.

Jonah returned to the restaurant, ordered, and sat down. A table emptied and he moved to it, giving him a better view of the clinic's entrance. He spent three hours watching, reading a detective novel, and eating fast food, all the while mulling events over and coming to terms with his situation.

He was getting tired, and hoped no one noticed how long he'd been sitting there, but he needed to know what Sloan looked like, otherwise he knew his plan wouldn't work. And he had no intention of going to jail before . . .

Getting even made total sense to Jonah: goddamn city folk couldn't understand how hard he'd worked on that farm. Maybe what he'd done was wrong but it was over now. He hadn't touched that goddamned Carol for more'n three years. And Trudy'd been raising so much hell, he was going to quit with her, too. Now he'd probably go to jail and lose the farm because of those little cunts.

Well, he damn well knew where to find his own kids and the Lewis girl; now all he needed was to locate Dr. Know-It-All Sloan. He'd scare the hell out of the son of a bitch, if he could get his home phone number. The detective book had told him how to get the unlisted number, but he needed the doctor's home address to do it.

To hell with this, Jonah decided, and got up. I'm wasting my time, he thought, but at least he had a little time now. He had told his wife, Mary, that he was going to help out two afternoons a week at the county nursing home near Rawlings Creek. No one would question him at the nursing home, because they were used to seeing Jonah visit his mother there. He reasoned that he could stop by the home on his way to the city, and if Mary called to check on him, his halfwit mother was so out of it, she'd most likely tell his wife that he was around there somewhere.

Jonah Thornton drove back to Stone Lake. He desperately hoped to come up with something better next time.

## Twenty / Phil

My appointment schedule Friday said, "*2 p.m., Female, G. B. (would not leave name), no info.*" That's not an unusual entry, since many first-time clients prefer anonymity. But I was curious and kept an eye on the parking lot around two. I saw her in a beat-up sedan as she pulled in—I knew it was Glo even with her dark glasses and hat. My first thoughts were, shit! I want to be friends with these people, not Gloria's shrink First the poker game, now this. Maybe it's just a social visit. Then—*aren't we being a little self-serving Phil?*

My office door was open. Gloria blew into the room and started talking immediately.

"How'ja like my car?" she asked. Her thumb jerked toward the window. "I saw you check me out. I borrowed the car from one of my housekeepers."

"Oh, is your car in the shop?" I asked and smiled. "What brings you to visit?"

"Thanks so much for introducing us to mushroom hunting the other weekend," she said, ignoring the car prattle. "I'm inviting you and Ms. Osbornson to a gathering we're having next Saturday night." She handed me an envelope and removed her glasses. She was visibly discomposed.

"Gloria, it's really nice to see you," I said. "Most likely we can make the party, I need to check with Shelee first, and—"

Glo knew my next words and she interrupted skillfully. "I've been married about three years," she said, "and I think I'm going nuts. I told Duncan I was coming to see you—he said it was okay. Oh, I didn't need his approval, but we get so much unwanted publicity, I felt it was better to let him know. I'd like to see you on a regular basis."

"Thank you for your confidence in wanting to see me," I said. I was flattered she sought my help, also suspicious; but dealing with mixed motives is part of my profession. Gloria finally took a breath, and I stood up, made the time-out signal, and jammed into the conversation. "Your presence here, as well as all of our conversations, are completely confidential," I assured her. "Keep the G. B. initials for all communications with my office, if you wish. Would you like to sit down?" She ignored me, poking around the office. "I'll be pleased to see you professionally," I said, briefly thinking about Sid, "*and* that means that I cannot see you socially."

"Well, you may certainly tell your girlfriend," she said. "I'm sure she can keep a secret."

"I can tell her you phoned in the party invitation, if you wish," I answered, waving the envelope. "Uh . . . did you hear what I said just now?"

Gloria waved her hand. "No, that's all right," she said. "I'm sure I can trust you both."

"I will tell Shel you brought the invitation," I said. "That's all. If you are going to see me for counseling, then social is not possible. We need to agree on one or the other." When she didn't respond, I continued. "I have a female colleague who is very competent and will ensure your privacy. You may want to talk with her and then make a decision about whom you want to see."

Gloria Burns was annoyed. "Yes, Doctor."

"Please consider this, Gloria. Decide which will work best for you."

She bristled. "Phil, I'd prefer to see you. That's why I'm here, and I don't want to hear any ethical bullshit. Why can't we also be friends?"

"Gloria, it has to do with establishing and maintaining boundaries. Our interactions here would be compromised by social activities—it could even be damaging. But we can spend the rest of the hour talking, and later you can make a decision."

"Well my goodness, Phil, you're a tough one," she said and sat down.

I reflected that clients almost never give their real reasons why they first visit a psychiatrist. Quite often, stated needs are only slightly related to real issues. As frequently observed, the heart speaks with invisible languages.

We talked until the end of the hour, and when I saw Gloria to the door, she still had avoided deciding between social and therapy. From my window, I watched her leave. She donned her dark glasses as she backed her car out and gave me a perfunctory wave. By god, Gloria may be a perfect ARFVIN, I thought.

The flight attendant brought our second round of drinks as I continued to blather. "Serena, do you know what an ARFVIN is?" I asked, wondering why I'm engaged in a raving monologue about sensitive hospital stuff. Serena and I were flying off to Vegas for some sun and gambling.

"No, but I bet there's one flying this plane," Serena said indulgently.

"It's what Karl Grant defines as a perfect patient, an attractive, rich female who's verbal, intelligent, and neurotic. He actually said that in a lecture one day, and I bet he limits his practice to ARFVINs. Grant's a dangerous man."

"To danger," Serena said, lifting her glass in a toast, mild sarcasm in her tone—I found it irritating. "How so?" she continued.

"Karl's a strict Freudian and keeps his private clients hooked for years, including a number of high-profile folks who pay big fees to finance his cocaine habit."

"Your supervisor at the hospital is a coke addict?" Serena asked incredulously.

"Yeah," I said. "Now do I have your attention?" Serena nodded. "The U.S. Senate isn't the only place with scandalous situations. And I think Crazy Karl—that's what the staff calls him—is truly dangerous. He's got so much power, I don't dare challenge him. I don't know how to do it, but I'd love to put that S.O.B. under. He says his dope use is recreational, *and* he continues to treat addicts both at the hospital and in private practice."

Serena shook her head. "Now I've heard everything."

"I question if Karl actually helps anyone," I continued. "It's his scam. There's this joke at the hospital that he's so hooked on being in synch with Freud he's mimicked Freud's cocaine addiction. It may be projection on my part, but I think Dr. Grant sees Freud as a father incorporation in himself."

"You've had too much to drink," Serena said, her playful smile returned. "What the hell does that mean?"

"It means that old Sigmund lives inside his head," I said, "and tells him to take dope. Do you ever watch that buffoon, Lenny Young, the local news reporter on Channel Eight?"

"Occasionally."

"The two of them are friends and show up at hospital staff parties together. In fact Karl looks like Lenny Young—tall and skinny, the same CIA crew cut. The two of them put on this suave act—make complete fools out of themselves. At one of these parties, to test the level of Karl's recreational addiction, I told them that I play poker with several dope peddlers. Suddenly I was their best friend, couldn't get away from 'em. When I made it clear I wasn't going to help them score, they left me alone."

"Can't you request a different supervisor?" Serena asked.

Our dinners were set in front of us, and we ordered splits of wine. "It's not that simple," I said. "Psychiatric residents are required to complete a year or more of psychoanalysis. And I've been working with Karl Grant for almost a year now. I'm really looking forward to the end of these useless sessions. Hopefully, they'll wind up in January."

"Well, I can't see it's helped you much," Serena said, glancing sideways at me, then diving into her food.

I began to eat my dinner in silence. This is serious stuff, I thought. Perhaps Serena—even though she was kidding—didn't understand. I'd hoped to work on three things with Dr. Grant: unresolved sadness about my father's death, anger at my mom for remarrying, and my attitudes toward certain clients. But I found my personal analysis benefited more from brainstorming with other residents as we prepared to work with our hospital patients. The work with these patients was also therapeutic for me. I'm sure what I felt about my mother was traditional stuff, right up

Karl's alley. But I didn't make any progress with him on that issue, or any others; in Karl Grant's case, I just didn't trust him.

Another issue for me was friendships. I didn't have any close male friends in D.C., even after four years of school there. Though there were a number of potential friendships back home, I hadn't kept in touch with anyone. No close friends, missing friends, not motivated to make close friends—I found all this curious and had considered bringing it up in therapy. I could have used a few women buddies, too, but preferred a girlfriend if I had to choose. But should I have to choose? I had some acquaintances from the hospital staff who I spent an occasional evening with, though none of these associations developed into what I'd call a friendship. My fellow shrinks were simply too emotionally needy for close companionship.

If I were to count girlfriends, I'd had one and a half, the half being Sarah Andrews. And now I feared Serena was going to hit the street any day. I guessed that meeting women in D.C. and easy sex was simply too convenient, and maybe the reason I had few close ties. I kept busy enough with my hospital crazies, poker, and an occasional girlfriend.

I never did anything to get Karl Grant busted—things sort of took care of themselves. Two years after I left Washington, Dr. Grant blew his brains out. I heard Lenny Young broke down during the evening news when he reported the suicide. He was fired a few weeks later. Someone had connected the two as more than just friends.

## Twenty-one / Shelee

On Friday, I received a note from Liz Carbonnader saying she loved the VØLMs. She enclosed an advance copy of her article for Sunday. I smiled when I read it: "Dr. Shelee Osbornson's latest works, titled VØLM LX and LXI, are a rampage of vibrant pastels. The helplessly enraptured viewer experiences an exquisite representation of abstract reality, the evocative juxtapositions: desire and fulfillment.

"Ms. Osbornson, who is a professor of fine arts at the University of Minnesota's Minneapolis campus, has shown her work at the Twin Cities Art Institute Spring Show for the past twelve years. Her 'VØLMs,' as she calls them, have won best of show or similar high honors in four of these years. It is this writer's opinion that the latest two renderings by Dr. Osbornson will again garner high accolades for her. The technique she uses to produce these fine paintings of passionate, multidimensional color layers is still a mystery to the art world. One of her older VØLMs recently sold at Sotheby's auction house in New York for $62,000." —E. C.

I laughed. Evidently Liz hadn't heard about the pellet discoveries at the West Side. I gave the article to Trish, making a mental note to look for the write-up in the Sunday paper.

"This looks like standard art drivel, except it's about *your* work," Trish said. "Anyway, she called it evocative. Why object? It goes with the territory."

"It's evocative all right," I said, "and I'm probably overreacting, but so much of art reporting are these vapid, self-serving descriptions that take on a life of their own. If reporters didn't feed drivel to their readers, they'd have almost nothing to say. They rarely focus on serious art subjects, and their so-called sophisticated critiques are just elitist cluck-clucking. Like the fashion news," I added, "which I also try to avoid."

Trish stood up, patting her sun-yellow dress. "You're on dangerous ground, girl. I *am* the fashion news."

I went into my office and called Phil at work. I left a message to remind him about the weekend.

"Tell me more about this wedding tomorrow," Phil said at dinner Friday night.

"April Gresham is marrying this crazy guy, Laszlo Zeemann," I said. "April's a potter on our faculty, and Laszlo's a professor of contemporary Eastern European literature."

"Is that his title?" Phil asked.

"I don't think so. Although that's how April introduced him. We gave a little party for her a couple of weeks ago and he dropped by. He's both weird and sexy, looks and talks as if he were booted off the freak wagon. It's an outdoor wedding with a picnic and a dance. If I know April, it'll be lots of fun."

"Oh, that reminds me," he said, handing me an envelope.

"An invitation," I said in surprise. "To the Coles'!"

Phil grinned. "Next Saturday night."

"Where did you get this?"

"Hand delivered to my office," he said.

"Oh? Who delivered it?"

"Gloria herself."

"Ah, she came in for an appointment," I said, pointing at Phil. "You *scoundrel!*"

Phil shrugged with amusement. "I didn't say appointment."

The wedding was at a farm about fifteen miles south of town. When we arrived, we saw a large crowd had preceded us, many of them university people. The dress was everything from formal wear to Levi's and cut-offs. A pig roasted on a spit, and picnic tables were set under a canopy. A couple of tables were laden with snacks, wine, and soft drinks. Phil headed for the beer kegs and filled two paper cups with dark beer.

Laszlo ran around introducing people, trying to make everyone feel welcome. He was really quite charming and looked a little less crazy—he had combed his hair and beard. His attire set the tone for the wedding: a tuxedo jacket with tails, dress shirt, black tie, and cut-off blue jeans with cowboy boots. I knew at least half the people, and as usual, Phil seemed to automatically know everyone.

After about an hour of drinking, munching, and socializing, a member of the band got up on the altar, a flatbed trailer decorated with straw bales and flowers, and blew a fanfare. "My friends," he announced, "please prepare for the wedding ceremony." Which everyone took to mean, refill your drinks. So we filled our beer glasses and sat down on folding chairs as the wedding began.

Laszlo and the minister walked to the edge of the altar and looked out toward the graveled county road bordering the farm. We could see a carriage traveling along the road, drawn by a fine prancing horse. The trumpeter blew another fanfare. "The bride, Miss April Gresham, arrives," he proclaimed, just as the carriage came down the farm lane, along the hedgerow behind the altar. An older gentleman, the bride's father, stepped from the crowd. He helped April from the carriage and escorted her up the stairs. Laszlo, who had donned a cowboy hat for the ceremony, came forward, bowed to the father with a flourish of his hat, and took his bride's arm. April wore an elegantly beautiful, ankle-length bridal gown of ivory silk. She later told us it was her mother's.

The minister proceeded through the ceremony, and Laszlo and April recited self-composed vows that I found quite enchanting. I could see Phil out of the corner of my eye, his jaw set firmly. His slightly grim look prompted me to slide my hand into his and think of the several times he's proposed. We have often discussed marriage, and though I love him dearly, I'm *not* going to screw it up with what I regard as an artificial addition to the great friendship we already have.

The marriage vows were finished, the couple kissed, and Mr. and Mrs. Laszlo Zeemann were presented to the guests. We all stood and applauded. "Time to party," April shouted. "Drink, eat, and polka!"

"And watch the skies," Laszlo added. "Some of my friends are going to drop in." Soon lunch was served and everyone took drinks and filled their plates. Suddenly an airplane buzzed the gathering. "Here are my friends!" Laszlo shouted from somewhere in the crowd. The plane zoomed over the field and spiraled upward, making looping circles as it gained altitude, climbing in the blue spring sky. It soon became a small, humming dot, barely visible.

Someone gasped.

"Look!" someone else shouted. An even smaller dot hurtled from the plane; several more followed. Five skydivers fell toward the Minnesota plain, free-falling at incredible speed. Three parachutes opened and two divers continued to hurtle. One more opened but the last one did not. We could see something trailing behind his body. The wedding party held its collective breath. There was not a sound anywhere. The diver seemed frightfully close to the ground, but then the chute opened and everyone cheered. I looked at April and she was pale and shaken. I knew what she must have felt—near tragedy was no way to start a marriage.

The skydivers daringly stunted their way to the ground, landing in the field behind the altar as Laszlo trundled out to meet them with a tray of beers, shouting the name of each friend as they hit the ground. The divers, two women and three men, waved to the crowd, hugged the manic Zeemann, sipped beers, and folded chutes. Soon they were circulating with the guests, munching barbecued pig and talking skydiving, their goggles, badges of adventure, slung around their necks. But the crowd was subdued, relieved and recovering from fear.

The band finished eating and assaulted the stage. Laszlo introduced them as the Hell's Angels Polka Band. One of the band members handed Laszlo a shopping bag. The bag contained large, red wax lips in cellophane packages that he started throwing to the crowd. "You can't dance the polka without the proper garb," he yelled. Many people complied, putting the totally ridiculous lips into their mouths. Couples looked at each other, some tried to kiss, and almost everyone laughed.

The band ignited a wild polka tune, and Phil and I danced, lips and all. The crowd, now wholly recovered, began to let loose, ready to celebrate with abandon.

After about three-quarters of an hour of frenzied polka music, the band took a break. Some of the dancers still wore their red wax lips, looking beyond bizarre. An English lit professor named Greg Kaufman, a nut with a flair for comedy, took advantage of the intermission. Greg walked up the straw bales onto the flatbed stage wearing dark glasses and carrying a cane. He led the farm owner's large black dog on a leash, and turned the critter toward the audience. The dog, wearing cockeyed sun glasses, gazed stupidly at the crowd. Kaufman shoved a pair of wax lips into the animal's mouth, but he promptly let them drop. Everyone whooped with laughter. The professor held a piece of notebook paper off to one side and appeared to be scanning it with his fingers as he spoke to the crowd:

*Ode to April's Wedding, by Raphael Retriever*

Raphael told me you were here with another man,
Raphael is my seeing-eye dog
Unfortunately I am completely blind.

Raphael said the man was very handsome
Raphael's taste in men is questionable
Unfortunately I am only three feet tall.

You said your name is April
I would have preferred someone named May or June
Unfortunately April has been a cruel month for me.

I once loved a girl named Autumn in the late fall
It was an untimely choice, she turned cold in December
My darling became allergic to dreadful metaphors
Unfortunately she moved to Florida.

The dog sniffed the lips, then began to eat them, losing his glasses in the process. He chomped vigorously, slobbering large pieces of red wax. Our poet waited for the laughter to subside.

> Raphael will drive me home, even though
> he's had too much to drink.
> We will be stopped by the police
> Unfortunately he will not be able to talk
> his way out of it this time.
>
> I will hear the officer ask, "What seems to be
> the problem, Blubber Lips?"

The professor-turned-minstrel bowed to the crowd's applause, patted the dog, and turned him loose as they walked from the stage.

Phil and I ate, drank, danced, schmoozed, and had a joyous afternoon. We left the party in the early evening, after hugging the bride and groom and half the rowdy crowd. The festivities were still in high gear. We drove home feeling warm and close. I feared the subject of marriage might come up and felt relieved when it didn't.

"You got another call from Liz Carbonnader," Trish said as I walked into my office Wednesday morning. Trish sat at her desk, reading a copy of the *Post Express*. The assistant department head stood behind her, reading over her shoulder and probably leering down her dress. Trish passed the paper to Asshead, who pointed to an article in the *Lifestyles* section. He smiled and handed the folded newspaper to me. "You made a bigger headline this time," Trish said.

I glanced at the article, then rolled my eyes with exasperation. "Shit! I guess I'll call Marion," I grumbled. I ignored Asshead's smirk and went into my office. Screw him, I thought,

I've got two pieces in the institute's show, and he's only got one. I closed my door and dialed the West Side Gallery.

"Marion, here we go again," I said. "What happened this time?"

"What, what?"

"Look at page three of the *Post*'s *Lifestyles* section," I said.

Marion read the article while I waited on the phone. "I'm *sorry,* Shel. Liz was never out of my sight when she was here, so I don't know what happened. My girls are just coming in. I'll call you back."

I called Phil, who, as usual, wasn't available, then sorted through my morning's work and waited for Marion's call. The delay was beneficial—I began to see some humor in the situation. My phone rang.

"It seems the man who brought his VØLM into the shop called Liz after Sunday's *Post* article," Marion said. "Then Liz came back here at noon Monday and talked with Suzie, the girl who X-rayed the paintings. I'm a little suspicious about Liz's timing; she may know I'm gone at noon."

"Do tell," I said. "And the infamous Suzie strikes again."

"I may fire her," Marion continued, "but you know how Liz Carbonnader is. She intimidated the hell out of everyone, ran all over Suzie. She was afraid to tell me."

"Don't fire her on my behalf," I told her. "Art prospers on controversy."

## Twenty-two / Phil

Gloria Burns called on Tuesday to say she'd decided to see Sonja Goldfarb, the analyst I'd recommended at the end of our first meeting. "I'm going to try your friend Sonja next week," Gloria said, "but may I still see you this Friday? I promise it'll be my last professional visit with you, Phil." I reluctantly agreed.

When she arrived Friday afternoon, I watched as she pulled in next to the building in the same borrowed car. "Are you coming to our party tomorrow?" She asked breathlessly as she plopped onto the couch.

"You bet," I said, "we wouldn't miss it for the world. Tell me about your week."

"My week?"

I nodded and smiled. "It was fine," Gloria said. "Busy as hell. How was your girlfriend's week? Her paintings made a splash with the shotgun pellet mystery."

"Shelee's treating it like a joke," I said. "She's getting a ton of free publicity out of this. We'll test the waters tonight at the show opening. But so far Shelee's been quite flippant. She's been misquoting a critic of Matisse by saying, 'I throw paint pots in the face of the public!' "

Gloria laughed.

"Now tell me more 'bout what's going on with Gloria." I said.

"Well, *I* pay attention to details," Gloria responded. "There are *tons* of last-minute arrangements for the party, the food and all that. And the guest list keeps growing. Clifford Anthony wants to bring three associates from Atlanta, Wickers Riesen wants to bring his boyfriend, even though his wife is going to be there, and I've been in the middle of the Harmck Corporation buyout all week. This party is really a business, rather than a social gathering, but I think you'll find it exciting." Her monologue continued for almost five minutes while I sat in interested silence.

"Your Dr. Goldfarb comes highly recommended," Gloria said, changing the subject. "Have you thought about our conversations from last time?" she asked—an unusual question from a client.

"Yes, I have," I said. "Gloria, I wish you could be more specific about what's bothering you." Our first session had yielded little information and no emotion.

"This is my third marriage," Gloria said with a sigh. "I love Duncan dearly, but he complains that we don't have enough time together. I guess I'm a workaholic. My previous therapist thought that I struggle to stay insecure by appearing to struggle for security with all my business activities."

"Sounds pretty complicated to me," I said. "So what are these struggles supposed to do?"

"She said they insulate me, distract me from discovering my real self. Struggling keeps me occupied with things outside of me."

"Has this knowledge helped change your work habits or do you even want to change them?"

"I suppose I do, and I have a little," she said. "The social this weekend is a small example. It's mostly for our network and movie staff. I've formed a production company with Duncan. We're going to produce TV movies and show them on his network. So we're working together."

"Is that what you want?"

"You may not understand—a production company is small potatoes for Gloria Burns. Buying and running major companies here and overseas is my forte. And my love, too," Gloria added.

"Is Duncan happy with this joint venture?"

"I guess so. But I think he wants to do more recreational stuff with me—you know, vacations and things." Gloria went on talking, reciting minor complaints about Duncan, excusing each one as her problem or perception.

Often, the most consequential therapy takes place in the last few minutes of a session, and I tried to make that happen. But there was no getting past Gloria's surface conversation.

When our time was almost up, I said, "Gloria, I'm not perceiving that you are troubled. I may be missing something, but you seem neither depressed nor elated, and I'm not hearing complaints that sound important or debilitating."

"Perhaps you're right." She sighed, appearing slightly frustrated.

"Will you consider sending your previous analyst's records to Sonja Goldfarb?" I asked.

"Okay."

The hour ended and I asked Gloria to sign a release form and requested her permission to talk with Sonja. I wanted to nudge her along, aiming to ensure that therapy with Dr. Goldfarb was really going to happen.

"Consider making some notes before you see her," I advised. "Perhaps a definitive list of issues that have meaning for you." Out of the blue I added, "Please consider a question from one of the tabloids: Why do you want more money and corporate power? You and Duncan have enough to support a small European country. Gloria, take an inventory of your life. What's important?"

She stood up and put on her hat and dark glasses. "Good question, Doc. I'll ask the citizens of Burnsia about it. See ya at the party."

My next client, a woman with a history of collecting unhappy experiences, has flourished in a group program she joined after about a year's therapy with me. She's still in the group, even though I'm no longer professionally involved with it. Her visits to me are infrequent and usually pertain to something that she can't resolve on her own. I think of Pamela as one of my truly successful clients, one for whom therapy actually worked. Often, analysts are burdened with patients who simply become more skilled at being crazy.

It turned out Pam was forging a new relationship and found herself feeling and acting in ways reminiscent of her unsuccessful past. "I'm confident these concerns are telling you something important," I said after we had talked for some time.

"They're telling me I'm scared to death," she responded. "I still relate to my incredible insecurity when I started with you. If you remember, I was not very selective about my partners and would latch on to any man who showed interest in me. I was always in trouble of some sort." Pam sat on the edge of the couch, her manner both impatient and engaging. "So now I've got this special guy in my life and I'm reverting back. Why the hell do people act in ways that keep them from their goals?"

"I'll answer that in a minute," I said, hoping to stay focused on the real issues. "So, am I hearing that this man's a good selection and he's enriching your life?"

Undeterred, she rephrased her question. "Yes, but I want to know why we often behave in ways that sabotage what we really want. I hear that in group all the time."

"It's very subjective," I said. "There's all kinds of models and reasons, no cut-and-dried formulas; it depends on the individual. In school they taught us that people are usually not aware of their real goals—what they *truly* want. Then they bring in the Oedipal thing, our unconscious needs in conflict with expressed aims. That's old stuff and I don't think very useful. If I chose to look for those things, I could see them in myself and in most of my patients. So what?"

Pam nodded.

"But I think emotional health is supported by a resourceful curiosity about one's self," I said. "And you sound interested in your own behavior—that's the healthy process. Tell me about this new guy, how these problems seem to relate."

"He's terrific," Pamela said. "I want to know why I'm feeling threatened by the relationship, and why I'm doing things like calling him when I have nothing to talk about, or hugging him when he's busy and not really interested. Stuff like that. What you said doesn't seem to apply here."

"Does he resent these actions you feel might be excessive?" I asked.

"I think he might," Pamela responded. "I don't even want to get like this. I feel driven, and want to get out of that mode."

"Maybe some of it's your natural rhythm and temperament," I suggested. "And many things may be gender related. Most women and men have different tempos and needs. One of the ways people in a relationship thrive emotionally is by making adjustments to each other. Have you shared your personal history with him?" I was distracted, remembering how nonverbal Shelee is about our relationship.

"Yes," she said. "Now I wish I hadn't because I've alerted him to my desperate mannerisms. And I don't see how being curious about my behavior helps me in any way."

"Curious replaces judgmental," I said. That's helpful because the unfolding of a relationship is so imprecise, one can't help but perceive some of what happens as mistakes. But if you can accept the imprecision from the gentle viewpoint of curiosity . . .

"Much of genuine self-confidence is actually self-acceptance," I continued. "It's really self-awareness of how you are, your personal mixture of facts and mysteries. That is not exactly the same as knowing one's self. For example, when I'm openly curious about myself, the more reality expands to include my whole person. The accepting-and-questioning process provides options that encompass all of you, including the unrevealed. Perhaps even the never revealed."

"How's that supposed to modify how I feel and what I do?" she asked with a smile. "I mean, how does it apply to being compulsive?"

I smiled back. "Look, we've talked about this before. Trying to change a specific behavior may work temporarily, but it also narrows your focus. If your actions are truly destructive, then resolve to change them. I'm not convinced there's anything wrong with what you are doing."

"Yeah, but I don't want to burden him with all my dysfunctional crap. It's not my favorite topic of conversation."

"When will you share all of yourself with him?" I asked.

"Not the stuff we're talking about," she said. "That's reserved for my sessions with you and the therapy group. Run the curiosity thing by me once more."

Our time was almost up. "Choosing to reserve certain things for therapy is an example," I said. "Your good sense will evaluate subjects for your curiosity and make some decisions for you. Now go forth and imagine, gather your puzzles and fancies. Cherish them as living flowers, introduce them to one another, meld the blooms into sacred bouquets. . . . Change their arrangement daily."

Pam smiled, and we stood and hugged—as we had often done before. "Thank you, Phil, I guess," she said and shrugged. "I'll see you soon."

After Pam left, I went to my side table and took out one of Shel's photos. "Shelee, you are my sacred bouquet," I whispered, touching her picture.

## Twenty-three / Shelee

After the shotgun pellet story in Wednesday's paper, I received phone calls from a couple of reporters—in addition to Liz Carbonnader's call. Phil and I kicked around some possible responses, but I decided to stonewall it until the spring show opening on Friday, hoping to get some publicity from the story. Liz's article was pretty negative—but who cares! The art business is a negative.

Phil picked me up around six Friday night. As soon as we got there, Hal Bernare, a member of the prize jury, told me one VØLM had been up for an award, then dropped after the paper's article.

"The strange publicity made it difficult to be objective about your work," he said, probably being honest. "You're one of our favorites, and I'm sure you'll be in contention next year." I was really flattered, and told him so. The other jury members were not so open and seemed uncomfortable with the controversy. One avoided the subject while raving about the food—as if we were at some sort of museum picnic. Two others offered sympathy—one for my bad luck, the other for the gallery's situation. While I enjoyed the pellet controversy throughout the week, the damn topic became totally boring after the show's first hour.

Finally, Phil and I sat down to eat goodies on a settee in the center of the gallery where my VØLMs were hung. Soon a show toad came up and sat across from us. Every artist and gallery has their share of these groupies, and I'm glad I don't do many gallery shows, so I can avoid them. The toad, who's often a member of the art snob crowd, is conspicuous because he rarely buys anything. Toads hang around forever, asking and talking complete nonsense, and taking time away from friends and customers. Most toads are older women; however, this one was a man in his fifties.

Male or female, toads are always garish dressers—this one was no exception. His blue jeans, big enough to fit King Kong, were held up with green suspenders plus a belt with a gigantic silver-and-brass buckle. The buckle had a raised engraving of an eighteen-wheeler truck. Since the jeans were too long, he'd turned up the cuffs about ten inches, showing off his yellow cowboy boots. He sported a yellow western hat that matched his boots, a green neckerchief, and an orange silk shirt, too tight and paper thin. I guessed he had a lot of body hair because the shirt appeared to be stuffed with rice.

Amazingly, the toad's first name also happened to be Phil, and before I knew it, the Phils were deep in conversation. "I hope you know how pleased Ms. Ozx is with your interest in her artwork," Phil said loudly. I wanted to strangle him; he could converse with a stump. But Ozx, I wondered? Who the hell is Ozx? For the next hour, they chatted about sports, mass transit, and the best fast-food places. They even discussed all the folks they know named Phil, including a woman friend of toad's named Phil. At least the guy left me alone so I could eat and chat with passersby—toad hadn't heard about the pellet article. But when Phil asked, "Would you please get us some coffee, Ms. Ozx?" I was really annoyed.

"Your chance to escape," he whispered.

"Don't worry," I whispered back, "Miss Ozx is planning her revenge. You'll be known henceforth as Philbert Flat Nut." He ignored me.

"Be sure to drink all your coffee, Philip darling," I said when I returned. "It's a *very special* blend," I cooed in my most insinuating tone before walking off. But Crypto-Toad, M.D., was totally oblivious, still chatting with his new friend—kindred spirits, perhaps. I don't know how Phil does it, he's never bored.

By now, several people were around my artwork, and one of them turned out to be Walter Gladstone, owner of the notorious "Early VØLM with Pellets."

"Dr. Osbornson," he said after introducing himself, "I hope my phone call to Ms. Carbonnader hasn't caused you problems, but I was puzzled. Also, maybe I was a little upset at first, then a Houston collector called yesterday and offered me $25,000 for the painting."

"There's no accounting for Texans," I said. "Sell it to him, Mr. Gladstone. Then you can buy these at twelve thousand each. Kind of like a two-for sale," I said, pointing to my VØLMs.

He smiled.

"Did the collector give his name?" I asked. "I'm wondering if it's the same guy who paid sixty thou for my resale."

"Ah, your New York resale; I read about that. But no, this caller was a woman," Walter said. "I've got her name at home, and I don't think they're connected.

"You never know," I said.

"Would you sign this?" he asked, handing me Wednesday's *Post* folded to display Liz's article. I signed the paper above the headline: SHOTGUN PELLETS FOUND IN OSBORNSON ABSTRACTS, and handed him back the newspaper.

"Are you going to tell anyone what the shotgun pellets and holes have to do with your VØLMs?" he asked.

"I've given it some thought," I said and gave him my most winning smile. "Is it okay if I call you Walter?" He nodded and smiled back. Just then I saw the *Post*'s own Elizabeth C. approaching, and I stepped to one side, welcoming her to the conversation. I introduced her to Walter Gladstone.

"Liz, Mr. Gladstone wants to know if I'm going to reveal anything about the pellets, et cetera. But some things are best left a mystery." I turned to Walter and said, "You see the art press thrives on speculations about the local art loonies." Elizabeth took a small recorder from her purse.

"If you want to write something meaningful about my paintings," I said to her, "try quoting this: I believe my artwork has spirit—my conventional abstracts. And for years they didn't get the recognition they deserved. Fortunately, VØLMs were a hit, and for a while they carried my other work along. One of my early abstracts was selected for the permanent collection in this museum, though that didn't happen until these splashier paintings won some prizes," I said, gesturing like Babe Ruth to my works on the wall. "What does that say for the synthetic values people attribute to art?"

"Do you feel your splashier work has spirit, too, Dr. Osbornson?" Liz asked, unfazed.

"If it does to the viewer, then so be it," I intoned. "They don't feel that way to me. The economics of demand and sales doesn't make sense. I marked these up two thousand dollars this year and I expect them to sell, particularly with all the publicity. My other paintings, which I think are much better, struggle to sell at one-quarter this price."

Liz started to reply when Phil touched my arm; his friend, Phil, stood not far behind him. "Now here's a true piece of art," I said, winking at Phil. "We've got to be going. Nice seeing you, Elizabeth. I enjoy your thoughtful articles," I lied. "And it's a pleasure meeting you, Mr. Gladstone."

"Please, before you go, let me take some pictures." She beckoned to her photographer.

After the photos, I took Phil's arm and we walked through the museum, greeting people on the way out.

When we were finally at home in bed, I murmured to Phil sleepily, "I'm in love with a man who talks to toads."

"Talks *with* toads, Shel. And I don't quite remember," he said and sighed, "I may have asked Phil to come to dinner next week."

"I truly hope you two will be very happy, honey. Goodnight now." I slid my hand under his back.

We slept in Saturday morning, until a little after eight. Phil got up, went to the kitchen, and started the coffee, returning a few minutes later with a great-smelling brew.

"This is good stuff," he said, and handed me a steaming cup. "Beans from that espresso shop by the lake near Lucky's."

I took a sip. "This *is* good. Remember when we got the kids gelati there and they wouldn't eat it because they didn't like the name?"

Phil smiled. "Yeah, I remember. The same day we went fishing and Heidi caught that six-pound catfish."

That day, just as we prepared to head back to Abby's with a nice bunch of crappies, Heidi caught a big catfish. She was about five at the time, and so proud of her catch, we added it to the stringer and drove to my sister's, where we left most of the fish.

Two days later Abby called me. "What are we going to do with this stupid catfish?" she asked.

"Eat it," I told her.

"You don't understand," Abby continued. "It's still alive and Heidi wouldn't let me kill it. We put it in the downstairs bathtub, and it's been swimming around ever since. We've been feeding it soda crackers."

"What a hoot," I said.

"You mean, what a mess! And now it's a neighborhood celebrity."

Then Heidi got on the line. "Auntie Shel," she said, "I named it Catty, get it?"

"I got it, sweetheart. Maybe Catty needs to see his friends in the lake by your house."

"Uh-uh," Heidi said. "He says he wants to go back to the lake by Lucky's, where we caught him."

So Abby and I piled a bunch of kids into my station wagon—about half of Heidi's kindergarten class—and took Catty home. Heidi sat in the middle of the backseat, wearing her pink bathing suit. She held the catfish, wrapped like a baby in a wet towel, and cooed soothing fish talk to her homely child, giving it little kisses on the forehead. We had a bucket of water on the floor, and every once in a while she'd dip the fish's head in it. Catty, for his part, rolled his eyes as he opened and closed his mouth—as if talking with Heidi.

When we arrived at the lake, my little niece waded into the water, unwrapped the placid catfish, and put it gently into the lake. The fish lingered around her feet for a short time, then leisurely swam off.

"Everyone called goodbye to Catty, and we went for ice cream—not gelati," I told Phil.

"That's one of your most charming family stories," Phil said, getting out of bed. "How about something special for breakfast?"

"Your German pancakes?" I asked eagerly and got up. Phil makes these marvelous pancakes that look like a giant popover. They fill an entire twelve-inch pan. My mother calls them David Eyre pancakes—she's still pissed at anything German.

"German pancakes it is," he said and headed into the kitchen. I followed and helped with the cooking. Soon we sat down at the breakfast table to airy pancakes, maple syrup, fresh cantaloupe, orange juice, and broiled ham.

"I continue to be curious about your attitude toward marriage," Phil said, passing me the butter.

"And I continue to be curious about your curiosity, my darling," I answered. "Now leave the goddamn subject alone!"

Phil opened the morning paper and began to read while he ate, using silence better than any person I know—now applying it to me. I began to feel uncomfortable. "Okay Phil, what is it you want to know? What the hell haven't we covered?" I said, my discomfort rapidly turning to irritation.

"We both love children so much, Shel, and there's a variety of ways to have kids these days," he said. "We could adopt. Would you consider marriage then?"

I stared at him.

"Your eggs are likely viable. What about in vitro fertilization?"

"You're serious, aren't you?" I responded. "I'm being drawn into this even though I don't want to be."

"We can drop it if you wish."

"Oh, that's disingenuous bullshit. Let's air this out—air it out, Dr. Sloan. First of all, I have a great distrust of the unknown. And there're things going on in my life you don't know about—I haven't had time to tell you."

"What?"

"I'm getting a letter from Yale's art school. Asshead told me they were going to offer me a year's teaching chair."

"And?"

"I'm going to turn them down, even though the department's dying for me to go. It's a big deal for any professor."

"I'm impressed, Shel," Phil said. "I love our life together and would hate a separation."

"Me, too."

"Tell me about your distrust of the unknown," he asked gently.

"It's like cave exploring—and I have no desire to explore caves. I'll read about them, look at pictures or the Discovery Channel, but I'm not going in. Caves are for other folks—like Manny's heroes who inhabit all those dark chambers in his novels—that's because they're fictional and can afford to risk everything." I got up and took a large cookbook down from his kitchen shelf and opened it to stand on the table. "Here, I'll show you," I said. "You know how you say marriage releases the monster in some people? Well, I don't know if there's a monster in me— "

"What are you doing, 'Lee?" Phil said. He rarely calls me that. I was feeling really angry.

"You interrupted me!" I said and glared at him. "Let's say this book is marriage." Phil keeps a pewter-and-brass duck on his kitchen table, and I stuck it behind the cookbook where he couldn't see it. Then I grabbed a picture of me off the wall and waved it in his face. "Here's your loving girlfriend about to enter into god-knows-what." I put my picture behind the book and pushed the pewter duck out the other side. "And this is what you might get, sucker! That's what my first and last husband got: a lead duck! You want to take that chance? I don't."

Phil just shrugged, perhaps shocked by my outburst. I was bothered by it, too, but I wasn't finished.

"You have a great intuitive mind," I raved on. "But when it comes to the subject of you and me and marriage, you're stuck in therapeutic mode. Exploring the unknown is for people who need to find resolution for their emotional health, and this woman's not one of them. I feel resolved.

"I've thought long and hard about this," I said, starting to calm down a little. "It's my body that can't conceive, not yours."

"But the unknown— "

"See!" I interrupted, pointing at Phil and sitting down. "The unknown is one of *your* favorite themes, not mine. Can we just drop it? Please?" I was embarrassed by my outburst.

"Of course, Shel. I accept how you feel." He gave me a hug. "Lead duck, indeed," he said and smiled. Phil picked up the cookbook and picture and put them back in place.

## Twenty-four / Phil

Shelee stayed at my house for most of the morning, then went home in the early afternoon to get ready for the Coles' bash.

"Watch me turn every head at the Dunk-do," she said when we walked out to her car.

Dr. O. can look wonderfully glamorous, but when I picked her up at seven, she was simply dazzling. Shel wore a sleeveless, jade-green sheer lace dress with a cream-colored camisole. The bodice was revealing without being cut too low—a fascinating construction that I speculated about all evening. I'm sure I had good company with that speculation. She wore some modest emerald jewelry that she'd borrowed from her sister, including a teardrop pendant resting between her breasts.

Her hair was a masterpiece—Shelee said Abby helped her with it—all fluffed up and curly, topped off with a scalloped lace crown, the same color as the camisole, with small, beaded jade streamers radiating from the center of the crown, through the lace, and woven into her hair. Cream-colored pumps completed the ensemble. She also carried a small green satin evening purse. Shelee's blessed with an extraordinary personal color scheme, and her outfit set it off like fireworks.

I drove my car away from her house and headed for the freeway as Shel's perfume worked its magic on my libido. "You look sensational," I said. "You're going to cause a riot."

"That's my intention," she answered with a sexy smile. "Can't be helped if I stimulate a few wet dreams tonight. It's you I'll go home with." She rolled her eyes and picked up my right hand, pressing her mouth to my palm. "You're a marked man now, Phil, and don't forget it."

"My shorts are getting marked from the inside out," I said.

"Of course," Shel said and blew into my palm, "that's also my plan. I'm glad one of us is wearing underwear. . . ."

"Jesus!"

As we drove into the city, we could see the Cole-Burns Office Center towering over the Mississippi. The sun was lighting up the west side of the building, casting a shadow across the river for several blocks on the east shore. The Coles own one of the most impressive high-rises in downtown

Minneapolis, a full city block at the base and sixty-five stories high, constructed with alternating faces of white and black marble. Completed about six years ago, it houses the Norse offices, most of Duncan's television and publishing activities, and the headquarters for several of Gloria's many corporations. As rumor has it, the building's completely full and they're trying to buy the forty-five story complex across the street.

The party invitation had a map on the back that led us to the right parking entrance. "How's Gloria's therapy coming along?" Shel asked as we turned off the street and into the building.

"It isn't," I said. "I referred her to another therapist. Neither of us could figure out why she was seeing me. But that's all confidential."

"Okay."

Small "COLE-BURNS PARTY" signs pointed along one of the lanes in the well-lit parking garage. We arrived at a gate with two uniformed attendants. One of them asked to see our invitation, then let us pass to an upper level of the garage. A crowd of attendants met us in the parking area next to a bank of elevators. The elevator on the far right had a party sign over it and we waited with another uniformed dude until it arrived from somewhere above. He tipped his hat as we got in with another couple. "Have a pleasant evening, folks," he said.

I held Shel's hand and smiled at our elevator companions. Shelee suppressed giggles, trying to move my hand toward her crotch as the elevator rose. I assumed we were in the Coles' private elevator; it appeared to have only three possible stops: the garage, the building's main floor, and the sixty-fourth floor, which the man began to describe.

"It takes up an entire city block," he said, "and houses the Cole empire's corporate art collection as well as the executive offices."

"You don't say," Shel said, raising an eyebrow.

The looks Shel got from the man in the elevator and the male attendants indicated that this was going to be quite an evening. Trouble surfaced briefly when the door opened to a noisy crowd and a gigantic, two-story room covered by a skylight. The male half of the elevator couple stood by the door to let his wife out first, then smiled back at Shel, waiting for her to exit. His wife grabbed him by the arm and jerked him out into the crowd before Shelee reached the threshold.

"Well, I've seen quite enough rude behavior for one night," Shel said. "Where's our invitation? I want a refund!"

Shel was about to do more mouth-off when a familiar female voice called out, "Dr. and Mrs. Sloan, it's so nice you came. You two will brighten this dull affair." Gloria, sporting a bizarre hairstyle, moved between us and took our arms, leading us into a corner of the immense room. "I want to apologize for inviting you to this dreary business dinner. I promise to have you two up for a more intimate gathering soon." Then she turned to *Mrs. Sloan*. "Shelee, dear," she said, "you're just a knockout this evening. I love your jade ensemble."

"Oh, it's just something my sister and I threw together."

"Phil, I'd keep an eye on her," she said. "Dinner's in a little while and I have to check on things. The bar's right over there. See you in a bit."

"What do you think of her hair?" I asked Shel after Gloria left.

"It's on the money," Shel said with a laugh. "The style's called punk rich."

We looked around the room. Sure enough, numerous fine paintings were scattered on the walls and many sculptures decorated the floor and planters. But it was really too crowded to see them well. Then we walked over to the bar and ordered drinks.

"Last night Miss Ozx, now Mrs. Dr. Sloan," Shel complained. "It's because of that damn wedding ring you wear, Phil. Do you know how embarrassing it is to be seen with an apparently married man?"

"It's news to me that *anything* can embarrass you," I said. Shel pulled at my left hand where I wear my grandfather's ring—a three-quarter carat diamond in an old-fashioned setting, the stone set almost flush with the wide top on the gold band. My grandfather gave it to my dad when I was about twelve. But my father didn't like rings and never wore it. Then when he died, Mom gave it to me. I've worn it ever since, first on my right hand; then when I met Shel and started my medical practice, I moved it to my left hand. I'm no longer interested in other women, and wearing a wedding ring seemed to put my female patients more at ease. Shelee sometimes needles me about it. She says I'm pretending to be married to her.

"I suppose you're going to tell me you wear it so women won't hustle you," Shel said.

"It hasn't worked with the waitress at the Chinese restaurant near my office," I teased.

"Oh, the Chinese connection? Tell me about it."

"I think she has a crush on me."

"What makes you think so?" Shel asked.

"For one thing," I said, "she noticed I like sweet-and-sour sauce. So lately she brings it over as soon as I sit down."

"That's to annoy you when it turns solid before your lunch comes. What else?"

"Well, she chatters at me."

"What about?"

"Who knows? She doesn't speak a word of English."

Shelee laughed. "Maybe she's swearing at you."

"No way. She likes me. She even writes me notes in Chinese on the back of my bills."

"Listen, I know about those notes," Shel said. "'You are standing on my foot,' or 'Leave a bigger tip, Buster.' Chinese people are very polite, you know."

"I did know that."

"How often do you go to this restaurant?"

"About once a week."

"How cute is she?"

"Not as cute as you."

"I think you'd better stay away from your Oriental cutie for a while, honey." Shelee kissed my cheek. Just then dinner was announced.

When everyone was seated, Duncan stood and gave a brief welcome. He proposed a toast to the new Burns-Cole Production Company and its first project, a movie to be made in the Twin Cities. He promised more details from Gloria after dinner. The seating arrangement, round tables with ten settings each, provided good opportunities to get acquainted with other guests. Couples were seated at the same tables, but not next to each other. We'd located our table early and moved my seating card next to Shel's. No one seemed to notice when we sat down together.

Three appetizers were served: the first two, oysters Rockefeller and stuffed mushroom caps, were fairly standard but prepared well. Lightly smoked Atlantic salmon in a Choron sauce, the third appetizer, caused Shel to whisper, "This stuff's almost as good as our sex."

"Not quite," I said.

"Although it can't compare to how we'll make love tonight," she whispered again.

The waiters brought sorbet to punctuate the appetizers. A pheasant-and-ham barley soup came next, lightly spiced with curry. More sorbet was followed by entrées of Belgian hare with a plum sauce, and cubes of Chilean sea bass in a crisp orange-and-ginger crust; the fish was served with a hot peanut-and-lime sweet-and-sour sauce. I was in food heaven. Sensational side dishes were roasted red potato cubes tossed with green onions and Chinese pea pods, finished off with a forcemeat glaze, and a beet top soufflé with fresh mushrooms, all green and pink and delicious. Simple green salads complemented the dinner.

Duncan and Gloria know their wines; they served several whites and reds—impossible to get now, yet cost under seven or eight bucks back in the mid '80s. They must have quite an extensive cellar, I decided. Two exceptional wines, ones that Shel and I had once owned and finished years ago, were the Fetzer 1980 Zinfandel and the Broich '85 Idaho Riesling, the finest Riesling ever to visit this planet. The Fetzer Zin, full flavored and mellow, was old enough to settle, and had clarified slightly.

The wisdom of our sitting together became evident as we tasted the various wines and shared our dinners and desserts. The guests occupied about twenty of the round dining tables. The Coles sat at a straight table on a raised platform a couple of steps up from the main floor. Duncan and Gloria were flanked by about a dozen guests.

Shelee had glasses of several wines, alternating among them, occasionally chirping about the taste. I'm sure the woman sitting next to her assumed, correctly, that Shel was essentially nuts. Most of the party-goers were associated with the production company and movie activity, or were company executives and well-known broadcasters from Duncan's television enterprises. At least one celebrity was located at each of the dinner tables. Our table was graced with Clifford Anthony, the author of the novel selected for the movie project.

Anthony's novel, *SABOR*, had been a runaway bestseller, and he was on leave from his regular job as public affairs editor for the *Atlanta Clarion* so he could consult on his movie script. The Burns-Cole Company had paid him $2 million for the movie rights. I wondered how the two million had affected his lifestyle, that and the fortune he's making from the book sales. Perhaps he's like Manny, who lives modestly and comfortably and gives millions away to various Indian and African-American charities and universities.

Shelee read Clifford's book—*SABOR* stands for Sisters and Brothers of Revenge. I struggled through a hundred pages or so, became irritated at the vigilante premise, and quit. I felt he was taking a cheap shot at the public's fear of crime and desire for retribution—an overused theme.

"Could your book be trafficking in popular sentiments, namely revenge and the belief in easy solutions?" I asked Anthony as two extraordinary desserts were served, a tiramisu with the damnedest pastry crust and fondant filling I'd ever tasted, and an apricot cobbler with a brandy sauce.

"Hell, no!" Anthony said, his voice rising. "I'm trafficking only in *my* sentiments for revenge. I'm overwhelmed and sick about what's going on in our cities all over the country. I'm only too happy to share my feelings and opinions with the reading public, and now movie audiences. Trying to write objectively about this tragedy every day finally got to me. If I'm trafficking, then so be it!"

"Your movie will be a success if you bring the same passion to the script as you've just expressed," Shelee said. "I read your book and loved it," she added as two dessert wines, an ancient German Riesling and a fabulous, twenty-year-old port were served. The wines, plus several kinds of coffee provided a splendid finish.

I was pleased Shelee moved to check Clifford's strong reaction to my question; I realized that this book was quite an intellectual shift for Cliff Anthony, lettered Southern liberal.

"Thank you, Ms. Osbornson. Dr. Osbornson, is it?" Cliff said.

"Shelee will do just fine," she said and smiled.

"I've been vilified by many of my colleagues and others for my book," Clifford continued with obvious discomfort. "I see where you got some controversial press about your paintings lately."

"Yes, but certainly not to the extent that you did," Shel responded. "I don't yet know how it will affect my art sales. The test will be whether or not one of my paintings shows up in the Coles' collection." Shelee waved at the art wall across the room. Her comments moved the conversation on to lighter subjects, and the tension subsided.

I was aware that I'd become uncomfortable with what seemed to be an interesting and deeply felt conversation, and I wondered why. Usually I thrive on such discussions and don't mind taking a polar position. Maybe it was the affable nature of the dinner and surroundings. Or maybe it was the nagging concern I had about Jonah Thornton—something I still hadn't told Shelee. It took Deputy Hartung a month to finally get back to me about the phone call, and then all he could tell me was that it came from a pay phone in Stone Lake.

I felt a tap on my shoulder, and I turned to look up into the smiling countenance and towering bulk of Manny Weston.

"Dr. Philip Sloan," he said with newfound Weston eloquence, "how very nice to see you." He surveyed the table, seeming to connect with all who met his gaze. "And perhaps one of these remarkable women is Dr. Osbornson?"

It went through my mind that I was witnessing a very different Manny Weston as I contemplated introducing Shelee, the lady with her mouth wide open and perhaps no panties. Fortunately Shelee introduced herself, and stood to take his hand. I stood also, gave him a handshake, and presented him to the rest of the table.

Gloria borrowed a microphone from the band, which was setting up behind her, and introduced the people at her table and some guests throughout the room, including Manny, who was now sitting at our table.

"So as you can see from the abundance of talent here tonight," she said, "we feel the success of this project is practically guaranteed. But enough of that. In a short time," she continued, turning to the band, "we will have some of the finest dance music you have ever stepped to. I'm sure some of you already know the Twin Cities' premier swing band, the astounding Herringbones." Everyone clapped, and the band bowed and waved. The band continued to set up as people finished their desserts, and Gloria talked about the film project.

"Dance and enjoy yourselves," Gloria concluded. Some guests drifted off to the small tables around the dance floor, and the serving crew began clearing the dining area.

Manny whispered something to Shelee and stood, offering her his arm. "I see enough of you weekly, Dr. Sloan," he said. "May I borrow your lady for a few moments? I'd like to introduce her to my wife." They walked off without waiting for my answer. Where, I wondered, was the powerfully shy Weston of yesteryear?

After several minutes' discussion of Weston mysteries, I left the table and meandered through the crowd. I finally spotted Shel and Manny sitting with three other people. While I continued to ponder Manny's gregarious behavior, he introduced his wife and friends and invited me to sit. I listened as Manny told us he was consulting with Burns-Cole on two movie plots based on early novels.

The band began playing an upbeat swing tune, and I asked Connie Weston to dance. When I escorted Connie back to the table, I saw Shelee returning from the powder room. "Excuse me," I said, and led Shel to the dance floor. After our dance, we picked up a couple of drinks at the bar.

As we headed back to the Westons' table, Duncan and Gloria walked up with two very recognizable people in tow, Francine Billion and Tom Pierce. Francine is one of the lead anchors on BFN, the Burns Financial Network. She's a tall, good-looking blond with a keen intellect for business news—an interesting mixture of brains and allure.

Tom Pierce, the Minneapolis anchorman for the evening news on Duncan's Omnibus Channel, had recently elevated his ratings to second among all national news programs, including the networks; he's become quite a Twin Cities celebrity. And Pierce, according to Duncan Cole himself in various interviews, is the brains behind the success. Duncan credits Tom with the broadcast's four-part format with co-hosts in Washington, London, and Tokyo.

Gloria provided the introductions. The "face man," as Shel refers to Tom Pierce, asked Shelee to dance, and I asked Glo.

"Are you enjoying our little party?" Gloria asked once we were on the dance floor.

"Indeed," I said. "Thank you for inviting us; the dinner and wines were sensational." I looked over at Pierce and Shel. "You know," I said, "Shel and I admire the brilliant teams you and Duncan routinely assemble."

"That's all Duncan," she said. "The Midwest Marvel, they call him. When he announced he was going to provide network news without an anchor in New York, even the Minneapolis press was skeptical. 'If there's something going on in New York, I suppose we'll cover it,' he told them at the time."

I laughed. "That's a quote that's come back to haunt the broadcast establishment," I said.

"Yes," Gloria said, moving in close enough that it was suddenly awkward. Abruptly then—as though aware of her behavior—she distanced herself more appropriately. "I guess I shouldn't dance so close to my doctor," she said and sighed. I felt a little cornered but decided to say nothing. We chatted idly for the rest of the dance. The six of us reassembled after the dance number and made more small talk while the band played a few tunes.

Then Francine asked me to dance, and as we moved together, she snuggled close. I found myself promptly turned on. The world of big business and beautiful women, I guessed, and subtlety adjusted our position to a less exciting level. Part of the problem was her cologne; my brain was fogged with carnality. To my surprise, Francine asked some perceptive personal questions, quite in contrast with her seductive behavior. I answered her questions in a somewhat dazed state. My lustful response to her attentions caught me totally off guard. I had assumed no woman could do that to me but Shelee, and I felt relieved when the dance was over. We walked back to the rest of the group, and I immediately asked the She woman to dance.

"What did the Billion bitch do to you?" Shel asked as I took her in my arms. "You're all turned on. I'll kill her. She offered you money. . . . Right? It's curtains for Francine. Her demise at my hands will make the front page. No back-page art story this time."

"They'll have SABOR take you out," I admonished.

"Not a chance," Shel said. "I am the jealous lover from hell. They'll know they've met their match when my wrath descends on the scum."

"How do you know I'm turned on, Shel? It's not like I've got a hard-on or anything."

"Oh, my darling boy, Phil-Phil. There's so much you don't know about yourself. I, the master of your moods, don't need a simple erection to tell me you're sexually aroused. Poor dear, what has she done to you?" She gently raised her thigh, nudging my crotch as we danced. "Dancing," Shel said, "is the ultimate flirting platform, Doctor. You did know that, didn't you?"

"Well, she did come on to me," I said dreamily. "I'm kind of lightheaded."

"Honey," she purred, "you will be all right until I get you home. Then I want you to go straight to bed. You need the kind of therapy that only I can give you. Don't you want to check to see if I really forgot my panties?"

I ran my hand across the back of her dress, feeling for a waistband.

"That's not what I had in mind," Shel said, and smiled.

"It'll have to do for now," I answered, pushing back from her as we danced. I could see color rising at the hollow of her throat. "My god, Shel, I believe you're turned on."

I drew Shel to me, and she looked up. "*Very*," she said, "but I don't understand how you always seem to know."

## Twenty-five / Shelee

Phil and I stayed out on the dance floor; I kept my eye on the Coles and their big-shot TV friends. After a while, they drifted away.

"Is your therapy responsible for Manny Weston's suddenly outgoing personality?" I asked.

"Anything's possible," Phil said, looking across the dance floor. I turned to follow his gaze. He had spotted Harris Martinsdale, the symphony director, dancing with a rather large woman; the two were absorbed in spirited conversation. Phil, who knows Harris much better than I do, nodded to him as we danced closer, and Harris smiled back.

"Do you know who that woman is?" Phil asked. She looked familiar but I couldn't place her. "Katrine Meissonier! She's here to sing Leonora in *La Forza del Destino* next week. We saw her in another Verdi opera about four years ago. I really want to meet her. Let's go over."

"Why aren't we going to *The Forces*?" I asked quickly. "They're going to want to know."

"I'm not crazy about Verdi, and you're indifferent," Phil said.

"Maybe we'd better just keep dancing, Phil." But at the end of the set, the band leader announced a break, and Harris and Katrine headed our way. "Here they come," I said. "You know Martinsdale is going to ask you about your radio program. Oh, I want to see you get out of this one."

Harris shook our hands and introduced Katrine. "Phil is the psychiatrist who does the screwball opera program I was telling you about; you know, on the college radio station," he told Mme. Meissonier. Harris grinned at Phil. "Please tell Katrine about your 'Opera for Soap Lovers.' "

"This month I'm doing Tosca," Phil said. "I was able to borrow a sensational old recording from the university featuring

Callas, Di Stefano, and Gobbi at La Scala. The definitive Tosca, in my opinion," he added.

"I, too, have that recording," Katrine said, "and I agree with you. And it's not just the fabulous cast; it's the best pacing of any Tosca. Perhaps I'll listen to your program."

"Next Sunday evening at ten," Harris told her.

"You may want to reconsider," I cut in. "Phil calls Tosca a 'mall bunny.' "

"I don't get it," she said.

"I'm trying to educate people about the joys of opera and make it entertaining in the process," Phil said. "I talk about the story, read from the libretto, introduce some arias, and discuss the characters in pop psychology terms. Also, I joke around with the plots. I get quite a bit of mail from insulted traditionalists."

"I bet you do," Katrine said with a chuckle. "Now, I *really* want to hear your broadcast."

The band returned from its break, and Phil, bewitched for a second time this evening, asked the famous soprano for the next dance; Harris asked me.

"Say," Harris said, "I've seen two pieces at the Quintessence Gallery by one of your students, Naomi Anderson."

"She's one of my most capable protégés," I said proudly. "Naomi's going to be famous one day; her talent is blended with genius."

"Yes, I'm thinking of purchasing one of her pieces. I love her style."

"How did you know that she's one of my students?" I asked.

"She has a handout that mentions her studies with you," Harris said. "I continue to see many fine works from your art school. By students and faculty."

"Talented students and a great teaching staff," I said, feeling quite charmed. "Our curriculum is demanding—requires numerous illustration and design courses. By the time the students graduate, they have a thorough knowledge of drawing, architecture, graphics, and art history. Even photography. They become artistic craftsmen as well as fine artists."

Harris nodded. "Ms. Anderson is an older student, no doubt."

"She's in her early twenties."

"My, she's doing fine work for such a young artist."

"Some of the best French painters in the late 1800s were just teenagers," I said. The music ended, and we walked back to Phil and Katrine who were talking excitedly.

"The only tiramisu better than this evening's was at the Ristorante Adige in Verona," I heard Katrine say—flirtatiously, I thought. But I still liked her. She was unassuming and wonderfully charming for an international diva with a reputation for tempestuousness.

Phil smiled at us. "Katrine has invited us to hear *La Forza* from her personal box next Saturday. Her parents will be here from France, and we'll sit with them."

"What a treat," I said with a smile. "We'll be there, and I'll brush up on my French."

"Oh, they speak English," Mme. Meissonier said. "They also speak Spanish, Portuguese, and Italian."

"What an unusual coincidence," Phil said, "Dr. Osbornson here swears in all of those languages, and Swahili, too."

"It's time to head for home, Dr. Sloan," I said, giving him a look. "By the way," I said to Katrine as we shook hands, "are you related to Meissonier, the French artist?"

"Yes," she said, "Jean Louis is my great-great-grandfather on my mother's side. I took his name after I decided on an operatic career. It helps to sound famous if you want to be in the Paris Opera. How do you know of him?"

"Shelee's the artist who did the painting you liked so much in the museum collection," Harris explained.

"Ah, the *artiste* everyone is talking about," Katrine said, smiling at me.

We said goodbye and went to search for Dunk and Glo. We thanked them, and they hugged us both warmly. As we headed for the elevator to the garage we waved to the band and fortunately avoided the anchor-faces.

"Tom Pierce told me I'm 'The Beautiful Queen of Green,' " I cooed as we drove home.

"Pierce is right about that, Green Queen," Phil said, reaching for me. "This is one of those times I miss the old bench seats."

"Queen of Green," I corrected, turning my legs toward him. I stroked the inside of Phil's leg. He thoughtfully checked for my lack of underwear.

"You weren't kidding," he said, probing farther.

"Ummmh," I whispered. "No wonder Miss French Pastry wants you in her personal box. You're a sexy guy." I began to melt all over his hand. "What do you think?"

"I don't think," Phil said. "I know I love you."

When we arrived at my home—feeling our cozy best—I stripped off everything but my camisole. I crawled into bed with Phil and began to touch him in ways he enjoys, giving his unit special lollypop kisses—that makes him almost crazy. I reached over to turn off the light.

"Leave it on," he said as he stroked the back of my head. "I love to look at you and watch what you're doing. "You were so beautiful tonight," he continued, toying with my hair. "The way you touch me; it always overwhelms me."

I took him into my mouth until he was quite wet and hard. "I believe I'm ready for stiff-dick therapy," I said as I rolled over, took off my camisole, and lifted my legs so he could slide under me. With my legs bent over his body, I could feel him thrusting inside of me, all the while his hands caressing me.

Phil has these stunning muscles along his back that radiate across his shoulders. They were tense now, and I shoved my hand under his back to feel them work. He wets his finger with his tongue and begins to touch me. I'm close to coming, so I wrap my arm around his top leg and pull him against me so I won't lose him. I know by his breathing that he's close, too. And I move with him, squirm and wiggle, floating off into my room, sparkles in the air, sparkles in my body.

We lay there quietly for some time. Finally, he reached over and turned off the lamp. Phil kissed me and stroked my face. Then I undid my hair while Phil softly combed it through with his fingers. Fellini cat dozed at the edge of my pillow, his rumbling purrs mingled with my approaching sleep.

"You did come?" I asked, struggling to stay awake.

"Of course," he said. "Where were you?"

"Off somewhere. . . . But with you, Phil. It's getting more profound each time we make love. I'm discovering new things." I drowsily moved my feet under the covers, finding my camisole and idly spreading part of it under me to cover our love puddle. Phil turned over, his back pushing gently against my breasts; I snuggled into him, my arm across his chest.

Phil woke up about seven-thirty. "Let's go running," he said, kissing me awake. "I need the exercise after overeating the past two nights."

"Right, you need the exercise, I'll just go along for the company," I said, stretching. I fished some running clothes out of my dresser and went down to the kitchen to put on the coffee. Then I went into the downstairs bathroom. But before I got dressed, I stopped to examine my figure in the mirror. I look pretty damn good for forty-one, I thought, even if I am a little overweight. Still, Phil claims he likes me that way. For a moment, I speculated about the fate of my body if I had a baby or two. I'd be willing to pay my dues for kids like Fritz and Heidi.

I sipped coffee and orange juice while I waited for Phil. As we began our stretches, I said, "I'm still feeling embarrassed about my outburst yesterday."

"Aw, I pushed it." Phil smiled apologetically. "Part of good communication is knowing when to keep *my* mouth shut. It seemed you wanted to drop the subject, and I pressured you into talking. I don't fully understand your feelings, and they're quite different from mine," he said, lacing up his running shoes. "But I honor your feelings and I'm willing to leave the subject alone."

"Thanks," I said as I opened the front door.

We headed up the street on our basic running course—about thirty minutes and more than three miles, including several circuits around a lake that lies between our houses.

"Why do you think Duncan and Gloria are so friendly?" I asked, panting as we turned off the street and onto the path around the lake.

"I don't know; they're still a mystery to me. All I can figure is being democratic has paid off for them. They're noted for hiring the brightest and the best, then getting most of them to move to Minnesota."

"They're so rich and famous, they can be friends with almost anyone. Why us?"

"It's going to take more than a few weeks to establish a real friendship," Phil said. Several Canada geese waddled from the grass, crossed our path, and flounced into the lake. They were followed by a dozen half-grown goslings who plunged into the water after them, shaking their gray feathers into place.

"Those two have more than money working for them," Phil continued. "They have an attitude of success and it's compelling. You want to invite them over for dinner? I'd have fun cooking for them."

"Sounds okay. . . . So Gloria wasn't benefiting from your sessions?" I asked.

"Well that, and I gave her a choice—therapy or social, and she chose social. Figure that one. I have a theory about it, but I prefer social with her, anyway."

"Is she seeing anyone?"

"I recommended a psychologist, but whether Gloria is seeing her, I don't know."

"Well, I must say you're not an elitist, Dr. Sloan, sending her to a psychologist rather than an M.D. shrink. You'll never make it on *The Shrinks of the Rich and Famous*."

"Gloria needed a change," Phil said. Then he jabbed the air. "It just occurred to me, Shel, people near the absolute top of their professions, such as Gloria and Duncan, develop transparent honesty—they're not afraid of who they are—and that enhances their success. So perhaps for them, friendships are not based on elements of judgment and class."

We circled the lake twice without talking. I was starting to tire, so I concentrated on breathing and keeping up with Phil. About twenty minutes into the run, my wind returned. "Why do you call my heroine, Tosca, a mall bunny?" I asked.

"She's your hero?"

"Yes. Tosca's a great artist and dies for her man," I said. "So I identify with her."

"The boyfriend Mario's a twit just like Tosca," Phil said. "He won't deal with her jealousy. He's afraid to confront her, and they both die as a result."

"Give them a break, Dr. Sloan."

"I can't. I despair at people's stupidity. If a person's open to it, one can learn even in the most unusual circumstances. Yet most of us remain stuck, safe but destructive—or just dull."

"It was the nineteenth century; you're not supposed to take the story word for word."

"Why not? It isn't old enough to be symbolic. Only the oldest stories can be elevated to myth."

"I think you're baiting me," I said. We were making our last turn around the long shore of the lake. The path leading to the street and home lay a distant half mile ahead. When we finally reached the street, we began our walk to cool down.

"Sometimes I think I'm living some kind of parable, and you are my only true reality," Phil said wistfully. "I don't perceive that as a problem, just a peculiar connection with something."

I took Phil's hand and kissed the back of it. "I love you," I told him, "even if you are living a parable, whatever that means."

"For example, my office building has this janitorial service. The service's owner works along with everyone else, including his son who's mildly retarded."

"A Down's kid?"

"No, there's no evidence of that, and his motor skills are fine. The kid's good natured, about twenty, and works as hard as anyone. He loves the machinery, especially the floor polisher and a big vacuum. If I'm around there late afternoons, he tries telling me about the equipment he's using. But I can barely understand him; so I just nod and smile a lot."

We paused at Newley Boulevard, waiting for the crossing light. "Anyway," Phil said, "one day the father asks me if I can help the kid, so I told him to have the kid's school send me some test information. The data were in line with his physical skills, except for his speech. I made a couple of phone inquiries and then asked the father to drop by the office."

The light changed, and we crossed the street. "I asked the dad why all the employees had first and last names on their name tags; yet his son's tag had only a first name."

"What did he say?"

"He said, 'Hell, he knows who he is, and so does everyone else.' Then I asked if his son had ever had speech therapy, or been examined for the problem—there was no mention of it in his records."

"Had he?"

"Nope. As far as the man knew, his son had never been evaluated or helped with his speech. 'Why should he?' he says, 'I can understand him perfectly, and so can my wife.' "

"So what did you do?"

"I gave the father the name of a speech therapist and suggested he give the kid a new name tag. 'Let him decide what names he wants on it,' I told him. The guy looked suspicious, then began asking a bunch of questions. 'Trust me,' I said, 'and see how things work out.' That was six weeks ago, and I already see positive changes in the boy's speech and pride."

"Nice story," I said, "but what's it got to do with Tosca and parables?"

"I'm not sure," Phil said with a shrug. "But my point is that just because you love someone, it doesn't mean you know what's best for them. Or that if you *do know*, perhaps you do nothing.

"Here's a young man who's had years of special education, he lives with two parents who obviously love him, yet it appears no one has tried to help him with his speech. He's stayed isolated through benign conspiracy, neglected by parents and professional folks who should understand the problem!"

"You are in some mood, Phil Sloan."

When we reached the house, I fished the key out of my pocket and opened the door as Phil picked up the Sunday paper. We went straight into the bathroom to shower, shedding our clothes as we went. I adjusted the water and got in; Phil joined me a few moments later. I was shampooing my hair when Phil began to gently wash me in some wonderfully private places. "Is this gratuitous lavatio?" I asked, caressing him with a little soap of my own.

"Yes, I certainly hope so," he said, grabbing my hand and leading me dripping from the shower to the bed.

"Don't you want to dry off?" I asked, hurriedly wrapping my still-wet hair in a towel.

"No," he said.

"All that lovemaking, and you're still so serious," I told Phil through a mouthful of Cheerios.

"Well, since I've had a wonderful dose of reality with you, I don't feel so muddled."

"Sweetheart, you *look* muddled," I continued, cutting one of the first really good cantaloupes of the season.

"I was thinking about this dream," he said. "Are you up for it?"

"If I'm in it."

"I was on a log raft just beyond the surf," he said, staring out into my backyard. "And I'm looking at this strange beach. It's odd because there's a surf on the other side of the beach, too. There are three or four creatures—perhaps calling to me from the shore—but I can't hear what they're saying because the surf's too loud. They sort of looked like paper cutouts of people, two-dimensional, and they were standing sideways. Their mouths were crescent shaped and their skin was parchment-brown like a Polynesian's. I've thought about it for days, but I still don't have one insight into what this dream is telling me."

"Is the janitor's family Polynesian?" I said, trying to tease him.

"I don't know any Polynesians," Phil said seriously. "The figures all look exactly the same."

"Male or female?" I asked as we carried our coffee and the newspaper into the parlor. "Maybe it means we're going to Hawaii."

"And whatever they're saying, it's repeated," he said, ignoring me. "I get the idea that even without the surf, they still would not be audible. Maybe they're mute and can't sign because they don't have arms or hands. They're stationary, too, maybe a warning."

"Better ask your unconscious," I suggested, picking up the paper to see if the *Express* covered the institute opening. I soon found an article by Liz, along with a companion piece on the opposite page. The first article contained most of our interview, some gossip about Phil and me, and a photo of Phil with his arm around Ms. Ozx. Messrs. Gladstone and Toad stood with us, and my two VØLMs hung in the background.

"Take a look," I said, handing Phil the paper. "Here's a picture of you with your new friend."

"Liz actually quoted you," he said, scanning the article.

"I don't know why she's so nice to me; maybe she owns some of my stuff."

Phil smiled. "And both VØLMs sold."

"Must have happened after we left. See, I told you I'm rich. So rich, I'll even spring for Hawaii."

## Twenty-six / Phil

The phone rang as I was going out the door. Shelee answered it and motioned for me to wait. "It's Lucky," she said. "He wants you to play poker this afternoon—which is fine with me. I brought a bunch of work home." Shel gave me the phone.

Lucky never calls me for a poker game unless they're short players. I chatted with Lucky for a few minutes and volunteered to help start the game. "I might not stay very long," I warned him.

"I know, the smoke and my bad manners," he grumbled.

"Right," I said, and hung up. "Lucky got his Montana elk permit yesterday," I told Shel. "He wants to spend about a week in Montana, around the first of November. What do you think?"

"I think it'll be lots of fun," she answered. "But Lucky's compulsive about trip plans, so we better pick dates that'll work for our schedules before he gets involved."

"How about ten days beginning the last day in October?" I suggested, looking at the calendar. "That's a Friday."

"Oh boy," Shel said, "on the road with Uncle Nutso over Halloween."

I drove to my house to get some poker cash and check my phone messages. One of them, forwarded by my answering service, surprised the hell out of me. It was from Serena Martin; she and her husband would be visiting Minneapolis in mid-July. She left a number and asked that I call her back.

"I would enjoy seeing you," Serena said, warmly, softly. I wrote the number down, took $300 out of my dresser, and drove to Lucky's. I had no idea hearing Serena's gentle voice after all these years would affect me so strongly.

I parked my Blazer in Lucky's driveway behind his Suburban so his poker buddies couldn't block my retreat. I was early and let myself in when no one answered the door. Lucky was on the back porch working over some potted geraniums. "Hey bud, how are you doing?" I asked.

"Terrible," he said. "Goddamn Rose went over to her sister's for the night. Said she couldn't put up with the tobacco smoke. I need her to serve my guests."

"I don't know what the world's coming to," I observed. "Women are totally unreliable these days. I suppose you also wanted her to kiss your ass."

"You can fuckin' kiss my ass, too, funny boy. I called and told her I'm putting pussy on my shopping list if she didn't come home."

"I bet that'll bring her," I said. "Must have run out of gas or she'd be here by now."

Lucky frowned and finished propping up his flowers. "Is *Dr. Osbornson* goin' to Montana with us?" he asked bluntly, filling a watering can by the side of the house.

"She's planning on it. Why?"

"I just want to know," he said.

"Sounds like you're upset with your favorite niece. What's going on?"

"She's getting way too much publicity over those shotgun paintings—and too much money. You know they were my idea." He was watering the plants, his back to me. Lucky gets churlish when he thinks he's not in the family limelight, and this was one of those times.

"I thought your main contribution was your shotgun and goodwill," I said. "What are you pissed about?"

"I think she's too big for her bitches," he said, turning to me and smiling at his pun. "We need to get her out to Olie Volborg's so she can cook and tend to us men a little. She ever cook for you, sonny boy, or do you do it all?"

"Lucky, this conversation is verging on the absurd. You know Shel is a grand cook. What's the problem?" But he ignored me and began watering his flower beds. Then it occurred to me—he called me sonny boy. He missed spending time alone with me.

"Lucky, we'll have a great time on the trip," I said and gave him a sideways hug across the shoulders. "I'll go on a couple of hunts with you."

Lucky smiled. "Good," he said. "Olie and I need a boy like you, someone with a strong back and a weak mind. Hope you're still lifting them weights; maybe someday you'll have arms like mine." He set down the watering can, pulled up his sleeve, and made a fist. He had amazing muscle tone for a man in his seventies—his forearms were gigantic.

"I don't want arms like that. They'd scare off my patients."

He laughed. "We need you in the game, too. But I 'spect you'll keep a lid on your play; no professional shit, you know what I mean?"

"Don't win, that's what you mean."

"You're gettin' smarter all the time," he said.

I came to attention and gave him a quick salute. "Yes, sir!"

Lucky grinned and filled the watering can again. "Shelee girl will be an asset. She's a looker, so she'll dress up Olie's and keep them Indians distracted while I steal their money." He set the watering can by his flowers, motioned to me, and headed inside.

"Ol' Volborg's got some homemade hootch out there, and we'll get your Ph.D. girlfriend to fry up some elk guts when we kill 'em," he said, slamming the screen door. "Damned if I know when she turned into such an intellectual," he added, shaking his head.

"The Halloween trip's sounding better all the time," I told him as the doorbell rang.

I let two of his poker cronies in. The four of us set up his card table and put out two bags of potato chips and a big carton of Double Stuff Oreos. I started some coffee while Lucky moved beer and soft drink cans from the back of his refrigerator to the front. Lucky counted out chips as three more players arrived. We now had enough players to start the game and they didn't need me to keep it going. But I hadn't played poker in quite a while, so I decided to stay as long as I could stand the smoke.

Around eight o'clock, Lucky's doorbell rang, announcing the pizza man. I was down about $200 after four hours' play. More players had arrived, making us nine-handed. Any game with over eight players usually plays a lot of hold'em, which was fine with me. The game stopped while everyone crammed pizza into their faces. I ate three slices, thanked Lucky, and made my getaway.

The air outside had changed, and as I backed into the street, I detected a hint of summer humidity. I turned the Blazer and headed for home, thinking I'd stop and listen to Serena's message again. But when I parked in my driveway, I just sat there thinking. After a few minutes, I went inside, reset the machine without listening to Serena, and drove to Shel's. Nevertheless, Serena Martin was still on my mind.

"Eat your dinner," Serena said. "Two drinks and you're a babbling maniac. How much money are you taking to Vegas?"

"Ten thousand," I lied. I had $30,000 in my overnight bag. The idea of playing high-stakes poker in Las Vegas had me intrigued. I looked out the plane's window, down to the scattered lights on the now-darkening Texas plains below us.

"Now I know you're nuts," she said. "Those professionals are going to take your money. I'm glad *I've* got our tickets so we don't have to take the bus home." I shook my head. "Well I'm hanging on to these." Serena patted her purse on the empty seat between us.

"I'm going to start slowly," I said, stuffing airline broccoli into my mouth. "Maybe play in a limit game."

I had recently done some analysis with my undergrad statistics book to figure the odds for various drawing hands in hold'em poker. I was shocked when I found that many of my plays were bad, odds-off bets. It turned out I could boil the drawing and betting odds down to four or five simple rules, rules my own play often violated.

My next step had been a series of calculations to see how often I'd be dealt certain card combinations and how often they could expect help from the board. I also figured out the frequency of certain cards and combinations appearing on the board. Again, after many pages of computations, the results reduced to a few easily remembered rules. With fifty-two cards in a deck, which made each card worth about 2 percent, most calculations became simple multiples of two.

I was astonished when I discovered my personal run of cards were in the ninety-ninth percentile—far above average—and had to conclude that I was an average-to-competent poker player with magic cards. I would have preferred to be an expert poker player with above-average cards. The statistics had seriously bruised my ego.

Two things struck us when we got off the plane in Vegas. It was warm, a welcome change from the cold D.C. weather, and the gambling started right at the departure gates—slot machines clanged everywhere. We picked up our bags and caught a limo to the Golden Nugget. The Nugget was billed as having good poker action, and there were major games at Binion's casino across the street. The travel agent booked tickets for a couple of shows, though mainly I was interested in high-stakes poker.

"I'm content to eat good food and soak in the sun," Serena said as we checked in.

"No interest in watching me play poker?" I asked.

"Not much," she admitted, looking around the lobby.

"I'm turning into a goddamn racist," Serena said quietly while we waited for the elevator. "Every black brother or sister I see is decked out, and I can't help but wonder if they can afford it. I never think that about the white folks I see."

"I think you're a caring person, Serena, and I hope you care about me when this trip's over," I said with a smile, suddenly feeling vulnerable.

"I will as long as you're sweet to me," she replied, patting my butt so the bellman noticed.

"The weather's certainly nice and warm," I said, trying to divert the bellman's gaze. "Must be hot during the day, if it's this warm at night. I wonder where the pool is?"

"On the roof," he said as the elevator door opened.

Ten o'clock local time made it 1:00 A.M. back home. It was Friday and we had both worked most of the day. Serena and I agreed we were too tired to do anything but bathe and go to bed. So we took a bath together in the elegant bathroom, soaked luxuriously, and guzzled champagne. Soon we revived enough to make love. I had never told Serena how much I cared for her, and at that moment there in our bath, I longed to do so. Always I sensed that she didn't want to know, because whenever I hinted at my feelings, she seemed to ignore me. But later, as I gazed at her sleeping in my arms, I resolved to talk with her about it sometime during our trip.

The next morning, I woke up about six. Serena wanted to sleep in, so I pulled on my clothes, put on a beat-up baseball cap, placed the DO NOT DISTURB sign on the door, and headed down to the lobby.

A no-limit, hold'em game was under way on what looked like a small stage two steps above the poker floor. Two poker tables next to the game were vacant, as were the tables on the floor below. The rest of the casino was empty except for a few hard-core slot players on the other side of the cavernous room. A jackpot bell rang somewhere among the sea of machines.

There were seven players at the oval poker table, with a central dealer who worked for the casino. The dealer raked a few dollars out of each pot for the house. The game must have been going all night; the players looked gray and haggard. Several sprawled in their seats and appeared to pay little attention to the action. Each man had several thousand dollars in chips stacked on the table in front of him. A few had stacks of $100 bills mixed in with their chips.

I ordered an orange juice and coffee from the cocktail waitress. Then from an adjacent, empty poker table, I watched the players go through the motions.

"Come on, young fella," one of the players called to me, "we need a wide-awake guy like you in this game. It's only a hundred dollars' buy-in." The dealer wet his lips with his tongue and paused to look at me—bright ceiling lights reflected in a lizard's eye.

I smiled, knowing I had no intention of swimming with those sharks yet. "I gotta finish my juice first," I said. They ignored me after that brief exchange, and I observed the game for almost an hour. I tried out my statistics on the cards the dealer dealt to the board; my numbers were comfortably confirmed. The players handled their cards, play, and chips with a ruthless certainty that I found a little chilling. They chattered back and forth, fatigued but confident, then fell into a stupor while waiting for the next deal. The deals came quickly—more than thirty hands an hour—much faster than our game back home.

One of the players stood up abruptly after winning a big pot. "I've had enough of this crew for one night," he said to the table. "And enough of your money." Then he turned to the dealer. "I'm cashing out," he said to the dealer, throwing him a $25 toke. The dealer reached over and handed the player several yellow plastic chip trays from the table where I was sitting. The player began stacking his chips in the trays. This signaled the end of the game, and everyone started racking their chips. "See, young man," the player who quit said to me, "we needed your action to keep the game going."

"I'm an action kind of guy, but not just now," I said, thinking how much more careful these players were with their money than my D.C. crowd. I got up and walked through the casino, across the street, and into Binion's Horseshoe Club. Figuring a low-stakes game would be more comfortable for the time being, I looked for a $10/$20 hold'em game, and soon found one that had a few seats open. I bought $200 worth of $5 and $10 chips and settled in. I played conservatively, watching the other players bash away at each other. It was astounding to see the quality of the competition. Hole cards were rarely revealed except on called hands; and when shown, the players had usually bet to positive odds. There was little speculation or bluffing except for position bets.

No one paid much attention to me until Serena walked in and suggested we get some breakfast. She looked fresh and beautiful, wearing a turquoise, short-sleeved blouse and a full skirt with a red and black print. Her turquoise jewelry and hair comb matched the skirt colors. The dealer said I could leave my chips on the table for an hour, so I stacked them neatly and left the game. I was hungry, due for a break, and happy to walk through the maze of mostly empty poker tables with this gorgeous woman on my arm. Drool on, fuckheads, I thought, pleased with my own arrogance.

"You are this man's dream come true," I said when we reached the sidewalk.

"It's nice to get out of the D.C. weather and into spring," she said, looking up at the sky. "You like my outfit?"

"I love your outfit and I'm crazy about you." She stiffened slightly at my words. Who cares, I thought, no time like the present.

Half a block down the street, we turned into a gaudy café, the Lucky Draw. The sign in front advertised TWO EGGS,

MEAT, HASH BROWNS, TOAST, & COFFEE $1.99. We took seats next to each other in a high-backed booth. The moment the waitress left with our orders, Serena laid out her romantic plans. They didn't include me.

"Honey, I love you dearly," she said, holding my hand. "But I'm going to marry a black man someday. That's just how it is."

"How do you know?" I asked. "You have more white friends than black. And there are plenty of mixed couples in Washington."

"That's not the point, Phil," she said, taking a sip of coffee. "My family has a strong connection to our heritage and I want to preserve it. I don't make a big deal out of it now, but when I'm married with kids, heritage will be an important part of my life. Many black families don't have this kind of link to their history; my family does."

"But I honor your heritage, and marrying a white man won't destroy your history or break any links. For example, my family—"

"Phil," she said, "the connection you have with your family is almost nonexistent. I don't think you have any idea how close my brother and I are to my parents."

"And you're not going to give me an opportunity to find out or experience that, are you?" I said. "That was clear when your folks were in D.C. last month." We hadn't seen each other the whole time they were there. Serena didn't make any excuses about it either, simply said they were coming, and that she'd see me after they left. I still don't know why I didn't confront her about it, but guessed that her folks didn't approve of me—or maybe *she* didn't.

"You also have a heritage of scholarship in your family," I said, my frustration rising. "Certainly I have a similar commitment to—" I was struggling for something meaningful to say, but just then the waitress brought gigantic plates of food.

"Have you ever considered there's more to your behavior than preserving ethnicity?" I asked.

"Perhaps there is," she said, her lovely dark eyes fixed on me, "but I don't want to argue with you on our vacation. Besides, I'm enjoying your company." Serena glanced away, then picked at her breakfast.

I sighed. Her typical response to personal issues was matter-of-fact and protective, and I found it disturbing. Irritating. I was in love with Serena, but she had much less emotion invested in our relationship than I had, which shouldn't have been surprising—she had little emotion invested in anything. I even wondered if she was as committed to her family traditions as she claimed—I knew I might never find out.

"So I guess this means you won't move to Minneapolis with me when my residency is finished in April?" I asked half-heartedly. I had toyed with the idea of asking Serena to marry me at some point.

"Come on, Phil," she said shaking her head, "I'm not moving to lily-white Minnesota. Also, I've got another year to go with my appointment in Washington."

"You can move after your appointment, and Minneapolis is almost as cosmopolitan as D.C.," I said. "I'd consider staying in town for another six months if I believed we had a future." I was digging myself in deeper and didn't even want to continue the damn conversation.

"I'm flattered you care for me but I'm not ready to make these kinds of decisions. I'll think about what you've said. Please, let's drop this subject. I want to go read and sun, and I assume you want to get back to gambling."

We walked back down the street toward Binion's and our hotel. Serena had not lost her control for an instant. I felt a strong sense of loss, knowing she had dismissed our discussion and would not consider it further. But there was another feeling within me—acceptance. Serena wasn't going to change, and I knew it was all right. I gave the relationship only a few more months; then I would miss her terribly. That could be all right, too, I decided; there was someone important in my future. I kissed Serena goodbye in front of Binion's and agreed to meet her later for lunch.

My chips were still stacked where I had left them, and the table was full except for my seat. The dealer explained I'd been gone more than an hour, so I owed an extra blind bet. He said I could play it then and be in the hand, or wait until the button came around to me. I chose the latter and settled in to watch the play.

After about an hour, I was bored, missing the out-of-control action from my D.C. game. Most of the players here were cautious, thoughtful, and engaged in noisy chatter around the table. A couple of the players seemed to know almost everybody. It turned out the talkers were dealers from another club—a casino that was supposed to have big poker action in the evening. Most everyone's fingernails were manicured and finished with clear polish—idiosyncratic of dealers and regular players.

One of the manicures got up from the table and announced he was taking a break. A few minutes later I saw him walk from the back of the casino and sit down at the bar. "Deal me out," I said to the dealer and walked around the now busy poker tables and over to the bar. I sat down next to him. "This game's pretty calm," I said. "Tell me where's there more action."

"I deal tourist games on the Strip," he said. "Looser than this one. Where're you from?" Before I could answer, he said, "Are you the guy who left with that good-looking black lady? Where'd you meet her?" He had a New Jersey accent and the words tumbled out of his mouth.

"She's my girlfriend," I said.

"Geez, she's a looker. Ol' Stevie almost bit clear through his arm when he saw her."

"We're from Washington, D.C.," I said.

"Work for the government?" he asked, pronouncing the word like "gubbernut."

"She does. I like to think I'm a poker player."

"There's a lot of people in this town who think they're poker players," he said. By the way, my name's Charlie, Charles Johanson." He extended his hand and I shook it.

I smiled. "With a name like yours, you should be from Minnesota like I am."

"Close," he said. "I was born in Grand Forks. My folks moved to Jersey when I was a little kid. What are you doing in Washington?"

"Going to school, but I plan to move home when I'm finished."

Charlie pulled a business card out of his shirt pocket and handed it to me. The card read: **Charles Johanson—Poker and Blackjack Dealer—Desert $tars Casino**. It had a Strip address with a couple of phone numbers.

"I'm dealing poker tonight," he said. "Come out and see me. I think you'll like the game." He nodded over to our table. "That game'll get better as the day wears on. One or two of the locals will lose it and go on tilt. Some bus tours will come in, too, and those tourists will spice it up." I thanked him and walked back to the poker table.

The game plodded along for another two hours. I sat there hoping someone would arc out of control; where was Carp when I needed him?

I looked down at my cards when Charlie, who was sitting across the table from me, let out a low whistle. "Here comes your girlfriend." I turned to see Serena working her way toward the table. It was my bet, so I turned back to my cards.

"How're you doing?" she asked as she caressed my neck with her fingers.

She seduces to keep me silent and it works, I reflected. "Oh, so-so," I replied. "Ready for lunch? I am." I folded my hand after the flop, threw the dealer a $5 toke, and picked up my chips. "Thanks for the game, guys," I said. "See you later." There were no responses except for a smile from Charlie and a

"Thanks" from the dealer. Most poker games are that way—the remaining players resent anyone leaving the game.

"I'm ready to quit," I said to Serena. We waited while the cashier counted out my chips. "That game's too slow. I'll play after tonight's show."

We ate a light lunch in the Nugget's café—the dinner show was only a few hours away. Serena sat next to me while we ate, making little finger circles on the inside of my leg. Her program was simply too sweet to resist, and after lunch we went up to our room and made love.

## Twenty-seven / Phil

I woke in our sun-warmed hotel room. Serena was sleeping tranquilly with her arms wrapped around her pillow. I snuggled up against her back, thinking about how different life would be when I returned to Minneapolis in the spring. Serena stirred, made a little murmur, and pushed her smooth tush against me. She took my hand and pressed it between her breasts. Nestling my face into her sweet-smelling hair, I thought about how much Lucky would enjoy Serena. He would have a fit of male ecstasy if I brought her home with me. A bit of a racist, Lucky's always lusted for black women. Serena would be the queen of his household if we stayed with him—and my plan was to stay at Lucky's until we—*face it, Phil, the correct pronoun is I*—found a place to live.

Serena woke up and turned to kiss me, making a sound close to purring. "What time is it?" she whispered.

I raised on my elbow and looked at the clock on the night table. "Not quite five," I said.

"You want to try the shower this time? See if it's as nice as the bath?"

"You're on."

"I love the sexy bathroom setup," she said and got up. I loved, I decided, women who purred.

We went down to the lobby an hour later to catch a bus to the Strip. On the third stop, we got off with other tourists at the Oasis Sands Hotel and joined the end of the show queue that wound through the casino.

The travel agency in D.C. had indeed earned its fee by getting us tickets to see Elton John and a "mystery performer" who turned out to be an Elvis impersonator. Elvis had been dead for less than three years, and I first considered the act in questionable taste. Though the food was mediocre, we found a good bottle of wine on the menu, and the entertainment turned out to be remarkable. The Elvis act was a little corny but well done, and Elton John was terrific.

A dance band played in the casino bar after the show, and we danced and chattered for over an hour. We held hands as we walked back to our table. "Are you going to play poker tonight?" she asked.

"Yes, but I'm in no hurry. You're more fun."

After a few more dances, we walked to the Desert $tars Casino, two hotels down the Strip from the Oasis. The poker action seemed unexpectedly lively compared to the afternoon game. I looked around for Charlie Johanson but couldn't spot him. Two $15/$30 hold'em games were going full tilt, with both tables full. I located the pit boss, signed up for a seat, and then left on the shuttle with Serena to accompany her back to the hotel. The round-trip took almost an hour.

When I returned, I found that my name had been called and dropped from the list. I put my name back on and waited. The ensuing wait was beneficial, because I discovered why the casino had a reputation for its poker action.

What drives action in a hold'em game is many players in each pot, along with flops containing face cards and no aces—aces make players cautious. While I waited for a seat, I watched a high-action game and was amazed to see all of the face cards dealt to the board. I started keeping track of the ratio of aces to kings—in a random deal, the ratio should be equal. In this game, the board showed three times as many kings as aces.

Card decks are changed frequently in casino games and after each deck change the cards stayed random for a few rounds—until the dealer set up a "face mel," a loose group of face cards the dealer assembled as he collected the discards He then "shuffled-up the deck" by keeping the mel together. When the cards are cut, often near the center, the mel is dealt to the players and the board.

I wondered if any of the players knew what was going on. Finally a seat opened, and I sat down, eager to apply my new knowledge. Within ninety minutes I had won over $4,500. I had chips stacked twenty high in a neat little triangle-shaped armory of $5, $10, $25, and black $100 chips. I placed two stacks of the hundreds on top of my triangle to needle the other players.

Near midnight, a new dealer came on shift, giving me an opportunity to stretch while he prepared a fresh deck. Just when I decided to look for a no-limit game, Charlie Johanson appeared and patted me on the shoulder.

"Looks like you've got the game figured out, Sloan," he said and grinned.

"Thanks for telling me about this casino," I said quietly, as we moved a few yards away from the table. "The action is unbelievable! Can I buy you a drink?"

"No thanks," he said. "My shift's over, an' I'm moonlighting at a casino downtown. I start there in an hour."

"The downtown games as active as these?" I asked, figuring he'd shut down if I revealed any knowledge about the face card shuffle. His look told me he was slightly suspicious.

Charlie smiled. "We've got a $100/$200 and a no-limit game. They're both as lively as these but I can't solicit you in this casino." He looked at his watch. "I'm taking the twelve-thirty shuttle out front. Don't acknowledge me. Just get off where I do." He shook my hand and moved off.

After playing a few more rounds, I cashed in. I heard the shuttle announcement in the lobby, so I played a slot machine close to the front entrance. From the door, I could see Johanson waiting with three other people at the bus stop. A couple of minutes later the shuttle pulled up, and I got in just as the door closed.

I rode in the front of the bus. It made various stops around the Strip at grand and not-so-grand hotels, then turned north on the freeway for the short trip downtown. At the Fremont Street exit, a few blocks from our hotel, I moved to a spot behind Charlie so I would know when he got off. A weekend crowd filled the bus, and people were standing in the aisle. Charlie got up a few seconds before his stop so I could see him. He went out the side door, and I followed him down the street and into the Paradise Club.

Once inside the casino, I saw several active poker games in a roped-off area. I stopped to watch a crap game in the center of the gaming floor, then wandered over to the poker area. Charlie was just settling into the dealer's seat at a full $10/$20 game. I found the $100/$200 game sputtering along with five players; the no-limit table was vacant. I bought $2,000 in chips and then noticed two players from the big morning game at the Nugget. They were an odd pair. One wore a cowboy hat and a frayed western shirt covered with food stains—the same shirt from this morning. The other man, who looked Mediterranean, appeared quite dapper in an immaculate, white linen suit.

"When's the no-limit game start?" I asked, pointing at the empty table.

"That game waits for Crazy Ray," the guy in the white suit said, speaking in a thick Spanish accent. The dealer prepared a fresh deck, listlessly spreading and mixing the cards face up on the table, then shuffling them several times.

"Crazy's been on a streak the last few days," the dirty shirt said. "He usually gets here about now. There'll be some gamblers following that little fuck like flies on shit." Both players smiled.

"Crazy sounds like my kind of guy," I said, hoping it wasn't Raymond Scumsucker from D.C. I put my chips on the table and sat down, nodding to the dealer. "I'll wait for the button," I told him.

"Ray's no fun when he's winning," the man in the cowboy hat continued, lighting a cigarette. "He's ripped a few new assholes in this bunch since his streak began. But he'll crash and burn sometime."

The man in the suit suddenly looked up. "Soon, I hope. He has already won over a hundred thousand," he said. Then he turned back to his cards, silent again.

"Speak of the devil," the dealer said with a subtle grin.

"That's him," someone else mumbled.

A small man swaggered up to the table with a beautiful, stoned woman on his arm. Out of nowhere, several more players materialized.

Crazy Ray glared at the crowd that now filled up the $100/ $200 table. "I'll show you fuckin' pussies how to play poker," he sneered, then sat down at a seat apparently left vacant for him. "Let's make this a no-limit game!" he shouted, flashing a roll of bills. "I'll buy thirty thou if you take the fuckin' limit off." His brunette sat behind him, dragging on a cigarette. Her mouth sagged open between puffs, and one eyelid closed, making that side of her face appear paralyzed. She watched Crazy out of the open eye, though it appeared lifeless.

"No-limit all right with everyone?" the dealer asked, addressing the table. One player objected and was directed to a lower-limit game. The dealer put the HOLD'EM – NO-LIMIT sign from the adjacent table into the slot by his chip tray.

Crazy bought $30,000 as promised. Most of the other players bought between $5,000 and $10,000. Several mingled folded $100 bills with their chips.

"Cash plays in this game, gentlemen," the dealer announced, and I added $4,000 in $100s to my stack. The cards slipped around the table, and the game became insane from the first deal. The shuffle-up was on, Crazy crashed, and the crowd got most of their week's investment back. Ray distributed about $80,000 to the table in the next two hours. I was fortunate to get almost a third of it. Ray's girlfriend disappeared about the time he put his last $20,000 in the game. She patted him on top of the head and told him she was going to the ladies' room, leaving a burning cigarette in the ashtray.

"The cunt's not comin' back, Ray," one of the players taunted. Ray solemnly shook his head and kept on betting. He stubbed out his girlfriend's burning cigarette filter on the table behind him as he lost his last pot. I seemed to be the only tourist in the game and Ray assumed I was an easy touch. He stood up and threw the dealer a $10 chip from his pocket.

"Loan me a thousand from your stack, big guy," he said to me. "You're the big winner here, and it's mostly my money."

"Don't give the little cocksucker a dime!" one of the players shouted. "He's borrowed from everybody and never paid us back."

"What'd you do with the other twenty thou, Ray?" another player asked hatefully. "Buy horse for the whore?"

He wagged his middle finger at the players, his face a knot of anger. "I just paid you shitbags back tonight, and he's got the biggest part of it," he said pointing at me.

"Sorry," I said. "I'm just a poor struggling student. Need the money for tuition."

"Student? Bullshit! What kind of student?"

"Medical student."

"A pig docker! That's what kind of fuckin' doctor you're going to be!" He was right in my face, so I stood up. I was twice his size but he didn't back off. I moved sideways, my left hand covering my right, resting both slightly forward of my hip, the stance we were trained to use at the hospital when confronted by a potentially assaultive patient. It was a relaxed, nonthreatening posture that allowed a staff member to protect his face, genitals, or whatever, by using both his hands and the leg closest to the patient. As I stood there, pondering Ray's emotional history—probably a tale of horrors—two security guards arrived.

"Security's here, Ray," the dealer said quietly. "Settle down."

He glanced at the guards and backed away. "What kind of doctor you gonna be?" he asked sheepishly.

"I'm studying to be a psychiatrist," I said, "but meeting you tonight has made me change my mind." The table roared, and the tension relaxed a little.

Crazy Ray persisted, his pleadings accented with a brown-toothed grimace. "Then loan me a hundred, Doc, so I can get into one of them limit games. I'll pay you back double."

"Sorry," I said again, raising both hands. Ray's scowl deepened and he left, followed by the two burly security men. He immediately tried to badger a loan from a player at the next table but the player pushed him away. One guard leaned over, said something privately to Ray, and Crazy made a beeline out of the casino. The game broke up, and on my way out, I saw Charlie busy dealing at another table. I figured I'd thank him in the morning and walked the two blocks back to the Nugget.

Serena had the door bolted when I got to the room. She let me in, half asleep and complained about my smoky clothes. She went back to bed; I joined her after a shower. I didnt play much poker after that—mostly hung out with Serena. We saw a great magic show and musical review Sunday night and left for D.C. Monday morning. I knew the days with my beautiful companion were numbered and resolved to make the best of it. I went looking for Charlie twice before we left but never found him.

## Twenty-eight / Phil

"Good morning, Molly," I said as I walked into the office that morning. My secretary, who comes in two or three mornings a week, smiled at me from her desk. Molly takes care of mountains of medical paperwork, insurance forms, and so forth. She also sets up appointments, then leaves the information on my desk or faxes it to me at home. She calls when something needs to be scheduled outside our usual hours, but I've learned to avoid most emergencies by not treating crazy people. I have her make morning appointments for potentially assaultive, emotionally fragile, or underage clients. Her presence helps calm these patients and provides extra security. Even though my practice is low-keyed, out-of-control situations can develop.

Once several years ago, an amazingly strong teenage boy—another abuse victim—attacked me. I held him and called for Molly. She rushed in from the outer office as the kid screamed he was being raped. I relaxed my hold for a second while Molly called the police, and the boy elbowed me in the eye, broke loose, and gave me a roundhouse kick in the ribs. Molly joined in the struggle, and he knocked her down. As he tried to rush out of the office, she grabbed his foot, tripping him. I jumped the kid and pinned him to the floor until the cops got there. We both took a medical self-defense course after that incident.

"Please tell Mr. Weston to come right in when he gets here," I told Molly.

She nodded and I closed my door. I had just finished Manny's latest mystery, written a few notes about it, and put them in his folder. Manny's writing could not be put strictly in the mystery genre. Though mystery buffs love his meticulous detail, in my opinion his books are more mystery and adventure with a good dose of horror. His stories definitely seize readers at the outset and hold their interest; plots unfold like several spirals, spinning in multiple directions. Characters, events, and scenery intertwine, as of course they must—but then brilliantly spiral outward. Elements, brought to the forefront one moment, fade to the background the next; yet at some level they are always present, urging the reader to interpret them—or misinterpret them. And, though a plot might seem clear—even transparent—it never is.

One character in several of his novels is an anti-hero detective named Gunther Bruno. Bruno, who's like a dimwitted Columbo, is unimaginative, plodding, and often distracted by events outside the mystery. At times you want to grab the son of a bitch by the lapels and say, "Here, Bruno, can't you see the goddamn clues?" Gunther shambles along, hoping to run into the villain at any time other than during meals or after bedtime.

But Bruno becomes this linear, slowly moving, yet unrelenting force that shatters each puzzling spiral despite its spin or direction. And as the plot evolves, he becomes a malevolent tar baby who draws the villain to him. Why Bruno's intellect and ferocity grow as he appears to feed on the evidence intrigues me. And why, I wondered, had Manny chosen such a stereotypical character.

Then, too, a Manny Weston setting is dreamlike, the surroundings strange, and unlike the predictable Bruno, most of his characters are bizarre. I suspect there is much that is unexplored in Manny's personal history. Often I feel an intense discomfort when I read his books, particularly in some of the peculiar rooms and landscapes that become so real.

Molly buzzed to let me know Manny had arrived.

"Nice to see you," I said. "Come on in." He plopped down in his favorite chair, and I sat on the couch. My eagerness to ask him about his Cole-Burns party persona evaporated—Manny looked more disheveled than usual.

"How's everything going?" I asked.

"I'm obsessed with this *Mikie* book," he said, his eyes bleary. Manny rubbed his face with both hands and put his smudged glasses on top of his head where they disappeared into his tangled hair.

"It's completely taken over my life. I can't sleep, I'm depressed all the time, and my wife is pissed off at me. And though I'm writing eighteen hours a day, the writing is lousy."

"So what's that about?" I said. He frowned as he handed me two sheets of paper stapled together at the top.

"Here," Manny said.

"The introduction to *Mikie*?"

"My *proposed* introduction," he said. "Please read it."

I read it carefully. It was a short, heartbreaking chronicle of his own abusive childhood. I finished it and looked over at him. "Mikie is you," I said.

Manny put his head in his hands. "Yes, he is," he said. He looked up then, vulnerable, almost childlike. "I've got to talk about it. That's okay, isn't it?"

"Of course."

He paused, then began to elaborate on the events of his childhood. It was familiar stuff—a mostly absent father, beatings when his father was home, a mother who couldn't protect her son, and a son who couldn't protect his mother from a raging husband.

"The welfare folks became involved a few times," Manny said. "You know, halfheartedly. It was pretty much what they expected of 'coloreds or Indians,' " he added bitterly.

"So the library was more than a learning place for you," I said

"Yes, it became a physical refuge."

"And now books are your community."

"And so is my writing, but I *don't* want to get into therapy; I just want to finish the damn book!"

"Why not do both? They may be closely linked."

Manny was silent for a moment. "Mikie and Manny?"

"Uh-huh. Why not use the book to come to terms with your own history? If you can gain some objectivity and work through some of this, your activities may become more tractable. You understand how therapy is supposed to work?"

"I guess," he said. "But we've talked so much about the dynamics of children, I'm overloaded with information. I can't sort out what I've learned from our talks and what applies to me. Does that make sense?"

"Yes. In fact, I'd like you to put as much of that aside as you can. The concepts we've discussed can interfere—the process is not an exercise in knowledge. More important, you may be much further along in healing than you realize."

"At least with *Mikie,* I've quit repeating myself," Manny said. "I'm beginning to find my novels redundant. Do you?"

"Personally, I find the mystery format somewhat redundant. But your books aren't strictly mysteries; your settings, however, seem somewhat repetitious, yes."

"Several reviewers who I respect have said similar things, and I agree. Maybe a child's need to repeat? I remember you said children repeat to learn and some adults repeat because they have to. Are my readers also trained to repeat?"

"Hup! There you go with your own psychoanalysis," I said, smiling.

"But isn't that why I write—to investigate myself, so to speak? And because I'm stuck, I repeat myself, for instance with Bruno."

"Yes, though only from the periphery. You keep Bruno outside."

Manny looked at me, puzzled. "Consider your cityscapes," I said. "They are a recurring metaphor, too terrifying to look beyond. Bruno, who might not be sensitive enough to frighten, goes after the villain, but never peers behind those walls. Perhaps you don't either."

"What do you mean?"

Gunther Bruno is a white man," I said. "At least I've always assumed he's white."

Manny shrugged. "White people buy my books and they identify with a white detective. So you're wondering why he's an idiot?" He laughed with a sudden sense of fun. "I'd hate to write about a man of color who's so blundering," he added.

"Yet you've made him effective despite his flaws," I said.

"Well, he can't be all bad."

"Why not write about an African-American or Native American detective who's bright and capable?" I asked.

Manny ran both hands through his hair, bumping his eyeglasses loose. "Because no one would believe a character like that," he said, pulling a handkerchief from his pocket. He began to clean his glasses. "And I chose to make Mikie white. I'm definitely catering to my readers."

"Interesting," I said. "You have a detective who's heavyset like you; he often loses his man and even fades out of some plots. He's somewhat ineffectual but is never replaced by a better detective." Manny nodded.

"Could Mikie grow up to be a better Gunther?" I asked.

"What are you getting at?"

"You have legitimate complaints against your parents, the Indian community, the white power base—even that there was no black community in the town where you grew up. Did I leave anyone out?"

"Yes, you left out Manny Weston," he said, blinking. "So you're suggesting I should let white folks read about my pain?"

"I'm suggesting that you write about what you know best, about who you know best. And that's what you're doing in *Mikie and Mike*; you go beyond those personal barriers that Bruno can't break through."

"To a global fantasy?"

"What's your view of global fantasy?" I asked.

"Mike triumphs in my book. Maybe he's just Superman, the comic book version. Because I fear I can't save myself, do I invent outlandish fiction to solve?"

"People like Manny and Mikie heal and triumph all the time," I answered. "I think the global fantasy is a different phenomenon. Shelee and I have talked about this, how disturbed children, though often skilled in art, particularly graphic illustration, may have to *learn* to be truly creative rather than repeating global themes. You're way beyond that with *Mikie*. Now you are exploring the greatest mystery of all: the human mind and spirit. Whenever one explores, the cycle of discovery—which often reveals more mystery—beckons us on."

Manny stared at a picture on the wall, then turned back to me. "Here's a mystery for you. I respect my mother, and I hate my father; so why do I identify much more with being black than Indian?"

"It's not unusual for an abuse victim to identify with his abuser," I said.

Manny stared at me now; he had tears in his eyes. "You know I've written essays about African-Americans," he said finally. "Including a series about Martin Luther King."

"I know. In *The New Yorker*; I've read them. Shelee told me about them."

"Oh, I *like* that girlfriend of yours."

"She likes you, too. Matter of fact, she's been after me to ask you and Connie over for dinner," I said. "And she loved seeing you at the Cole-Burns party."

"So when's dinner?"

"Ah, that was when I was your consultant. Now I hope we're doing therapy—at least I think that's where we're headed." I looked at him quizzically and he smiled.

"You can't socialize with clients?"

"No, it's not a good idea."

"Too bad," he said, looking at his watch. He got up. "I once wrote that Martin Luther King was the voice of reason in a time of unreasonable circumstances. Maybe that's what you are for me, emotionally that is."

I also stood up. "I'm honored," I said, and shook Manny's hand. He smiled and we hugged each other.

"Come in before next week if you need to, and I'm available at home, too." I wrote my home number down and handed it to him.

"Thanks, Doc," he said. He went toward the door, then paused. "You know," he said, turning back to me, "I want *Mikie* to sell, but not for the money. For the first time, I want people to read *me*."

"My feeling is the book will do quite well," I said. "I know it's written from the heart."

Tears came to Manny's eyes again, and without another word, he nodded and went out the door.

Jonah was working in the machinery shed when he saw the mail truck pull up at the side of the road. Though it was not his practice to fetch the mail, he walked out to the box. Among the usual stuff, just as he'd suspected, was a letter from Carol and Trudy—the one they'd promised his wife when they called home. He left everything in the mailbox except the letter, and that he took into the shed.

Thornton slit the envelope open and read the letter carefully. On the second reading, so he would never forget, he read aloud: "Mama, we fear for your safety and we think Daddy is dangerous. Please leave there and come to Minneapolis. Dr. Sloan can help you."

There was a newspaper photo, too—of Sloan and his famous artist friend. "She's a professor at the university," Carol had written in the margin with an arrow. Jonah folded the photo and put it in his pocket. He tore up the letter and dropped the pieces into the smoldering trash barrel by the side of the building.

Then he made plans to go to Minneapolis.

## Twenty-nine / Shelee

"You old sweetie," I said, when I saw Phil coming into my office with flowers. "I know, you just want me to be cooperative when your girlfriend gets here."

"You see right through me," he said and kissed my cheek. Then he sat down across from me, serious as hell. "Look, I'll just go to lunch with them," Phil said. "I understand you might feel uncomfortable around her. Her husband probably feels the same about me."

"Oh, give me a couple of weeks. Maybe I'll be too curious to pass on it."

"Okay," he said with a smile. "You about ready?"

"Let me put these gorgeous flowers in water."

"They're from the supermarket," I heard Phil say as I headed down the hall. Ah, but such an arrangement; someone at the store knows poetry of form and composition. The thought of Phil picking out flowers in that busy supermarket near campus was nice. I wondered, had he ever brought *her* flowers? I suddenly felt the same jealousy as when I found a picture of them eating ice cream cones in front of the Capitol. She looked so stunningly self-assured.

"The water's taking an awfully long time," Phil said from the doorway of the janitor's closet. "Tears? What's wrong?"

"Nothing," I said, turning away from him. "I broke half the stems and now the arrangement is all . . ."

"Come here," he said and held me. "I'll buy a thousand bouquets if you want." He stroked my hair. "But this isn't about the flowers."

"No, it's just that she's so worldly, so successful. I can't imagine being a partner in a D.C. law firm, or working for a senator, or . . ."

"You're comparing yourself?" Phil asked, kissing my forehead. "I'm surprised. You're a university professor and an accomplished artist. My favorite artist."

"I feel so silly."

"Hummm," Phil said, still holding me. Then he took the flowers and wiped off the wet vase. "These look great."

"I'll be all right about Serena," I said with a sigh. We walked back to my office. "I'll probably end up liking her, or throwing a party for them. Who knows."

Phil smiled. "Whatever you decide is fine." He squeezed my hand, then looked at his watch. "Let's go eat. I'm due at the hospital in less than an hour."

"Another abused kid?"

"Yeah, another evaluation."

I left work midafternoon and went to the grocery store for things to take to Abby's for the potluck tonight. When I passed the University Hospital, I noticed Phil's car parked on the street about a half a block from the front entrance. I double-parked and wrote him a quick note: *For a good time, any time, call me. Be prepared for the score of your life. P.S. Don't forget the wine. Love, ?* I put it under his windshield wiper and drove on.

That night after dinner, Abby and I sat on her back porch watching Phil, Tim, and the kids playing ball.

"Now that school's out," Abby said, "why don't we take the kids up to Lucky's for a week or two? The men can come up on weekends."

"Oh, I'd love to," I said, "but I have that master class starting Tuesday."

Abby groaned. "Let someone else do it; you've done it for the last five years. Enough."

"Three years," I corrected, "and I'm running it." Besides, though I didn't say it to Abby, it was a real plum—sponsored by the Minnesota Arts Council with funds from the Chicago Arts Committee and an NEA grant. Chicago pays for an artist from Illinois and I get to select another artist from anywhere in the country. And since I paint abstracts, and the Chicago group's pick is usually a contemporary expressionist, I try to get a traditional-style painter. This year I chose Marguerite Kampino from UCLA, a big name in California landscapes as well as portraiture.

"You know, out of more than fifty students from all over the world, Naomi Anderson qualified for this year's class," I told Abby. I even wondered if I hadn't chosen Kampino because I thought she'd be good for Naomi.

"Hmnnn," Abby said, unimpressed. "Does that mean you're going to host another blowout at Lucky's?"

"No, that was too much work last year; we'll stay in town. I think they'd just as soon paint in the courtyard next to the Student Union; it's colorful and the light's terrific. Besides, summer semester doesn't start for three weeks, so they'll have the run of the art school."

"I don't know how that can beat a week or two at Lucky's," Abby said and yawned. "Maybe after your class." She got up and began poking around her flower beds. I watched the ball-playing absentmindedly, my mind on the master class and Serena and her husband. Phil said they had two kids—girls, a couple years younger than Fritz and Heidi.

"Look out, Dad!" Fritz yelled.

Tim backed up to catch the ball and fell into one of the flower beds. The kids shouted with laughter and Phil, suppressing a grin, helped him up. Tim brushed bark and dirt from his pants.

"Time out," Tim said, and the two men came over to the porch. "You want a beer?" Tim asked Phil. Phil nodded and Tim went inside.

"Honey," I said, suddenly deciding, "I'm going to throw a party for Serena."

"What?"

"Yeah, a party at my place. We'll have it there because my backyard is better if the weather's nice. My air conditioner works better, too, and—"

"Wait a minute," he said. "That's a hell of a lot of work, and I don't want you to feel like you—"

"No, listen. We could invite the Coles, Trish, Abby, and Tim. How about Naomi and Mitchell? Maybe the Westons—make it a real eclectic bunch."

"We can't invite Manny," he said. Then he sat down on the porch steps and looked directly at me. "When did you decide this?"

"I'm not sure. Tonight. Maybe just now. I don't know."

He shook his head. "Hey, looks like Abby's going to play. C'mon."

I was feeling lazy. "No, I'm going to sit right here and finish my party plans."

The kids were calling to him and he waved to me. "We'll talk about it later," he said.

"You're just worried it'll be a disaster like last summer," I yelled after him.

"What disaster?" Tim asked, coming out onto the porch with two beers.

"That barbecue I had last summer," I said. "I'll take that." I held out my hand for Phil's beer.

"Oh, yeah," Tim said, "I remember: thunder and lightning—the power went out. One hell of a party."

"You forgot the rain and wind," I said as he went back into the house for another beer. And Uncle Lucky—more foul than the weather.

When first invited, Lucky accepted the invitation but, predictably, he called the day before to say he'd decided to have a poker game instead.

"A poker game!" I was furious. Everyone was coming, even my grandparents.

"There's some big gamblers in town and . . ."

I didn't want to hear it and I hung up on him. This kind of bullshit was his way of getting attention from the family. The day of the party—after the storm hit—we opened up the garage and moved the barbecue in there. In the midst of all the hubbub, Lucky called to ask Phil if he could move his poker game to Phil's because his power was off, too. It wasn't any of my business, but I was still pissed. So I picked up the other phone and told Lucky to shove it.

Phil loves my uncle and he puts up with a lot more of his obnoxious behavior than I do. Our power was back on, so Phil called his own house and got the answering machine and assumed the power was on there. He phoned Lucky back and told him to stop by for the key. "But you can't smoke in the house," he told him. Then Lucky blew up and hung up on Phil. Hanging up is a genetic trait in my family, I've decided. Not long after that, Lucky shows up with Rose to eat burgers with us. He said the game broke up because they couldn't heat up the pizza. I knew the pizza part was probably a lie because Lucky always sends out for it.

"What's going on with you two?" my mother had asked. I merely shook my head. Just the usual downside of my two-tier relationship with my uncle. So much of the time his family and personal behavior is completely odious. Other times, Lucky has been very loving and supportive when I needed him. Years before, when I separated from Mark, I moved back home with my parents. Abby was happily married—we'd had a double ceremony—but my traditionalist parents simply couldn't understand the breakup or deal with my gloom. So when it became obvious that I was getting them down, I decided to go up to Lucky's and spend some time alone. But as it turned out, Lucky was working at the farm that month, so I hung out with him a lot. He was amazingly understanding, putting up with my funk and patiently listening to all my complaints.

Lucky has always been partial to me, even though Abby was the firstborn. I speculate it has something to do with our coloring: Lucky and I are the only two in our family who have red hair, freckles, and brown eyes. Though my mother is fair with brown eyes, everyone else is blond and blue-eyed. Sometime during my stay, I pointed this out. Lucky got this twinkle in his eye and said, "You know I courted your mom in the old country before Stewart took a liking to her."

This was news to me. "What happened? Did you and dad fight over her?"

"Oh, no. I had lots of girlfriends, and your dad was kind of shy; old Stewart was serious about her right from the start. Courtin' in Norway was a family affair then. Our folks knew your ma's folks and liked her; all of us grew up together. I loved Inga, too, but not enough to get married."

We were eating dinner and Lucky sighed and stared at his plate. "When your dad wanted to marry her, it was okay by me; everyone figured she'd be a fine addition to the family." Lucky pushed back from the table and got another beer from the fridge. He still had a half-full bottle on the table. "About then I realized I wasn't the marryin' type," he said. "That's sure proved true, hasn't it?"

I didn't answer him, surprised by what I thought was regret in his voice.

"Bein' in the navy during the war really brought that home," he said, "not marryin'. We were a rough bunch and there was always lots of women whenever we put into port. An' for some reason, I got to worrying about all them people I killed."

"You killed people?" I asked as he sat back down.

"Well, when you think about all them munitions I loaded. Hell, those bombs and stuff killed all kinds of people I never knew. Now don't get me wrong; we had to win the war, no question 'bout it." Lucky paused for food and beer. "But looking back, I guess that loading ammunitions is what got me into boxing and made me tough."

"Tough? I heard you were pretty tough before you left Norway."

"I was ornery as hell and damn headstrong," he admitted. "The Krauts would have shot me for sure. I couldn't have waited for the underground. I wanted to kill them Germans right where they stood. But I was no hero," he concluded, cutting up the third steak and offering me half.

"I disagree," I said. "In your own way, you were as heroic as all the other Osbornsons."

"No, not like them, Shelee girl. Your folks and my folks risked their lives day-in and day-out for several years, helping people they didn't even know. I was safe on a carrier. Hell, we never saw much direct action."

It was a beautiful June morning and I was cutting lilacs from the bushes out front. Phil came out to the porch and down the steps.

He patted my butt. "Beautiful," he said.

"Me or the lilacs?" I asked. He got his briefcase and computer out of his car.

Phil smiled. "Um, both."

I followed Phil inside, my arms full of lilacs. "You're going to work on such a beautiful day?"

"For a little while," he said. "I've got an evaluation to write by Monday." He sat down on the divan and stacked papers from his briefcase on the coffee table. I went to the kitchen, put the lilacs into a couple of vases, and brought one vase back to the living room. Phil looked up from his reading.

"Thanks for the cute note you left on my car yesterday," he said. "It was a nice surprise—from my secret admirer." Phil looked back to his work.

"Is that the evaluation from the hospital yesterday?" I asked. "How did it go?"

"Actually, really upsetting. The county attorney asked me to review the testimony in an abuse case." Phil pointed to the court transcript he was reading. "So I had to go over the psychologist's report and visit the little boy in the hospital. Talked with his doctor, too. Horrible case. I may have to testify at the trial. The county really wants to nail this guy."

"So you're the backup opinion?" I said. I put the lilacs on the dining table and sat down in a chair across from Phil.

"Yeah, I agreed with the assessment. By the way, I ran into the infamous Homer Gustafson the other day; he's joined a physicians' advocacy group. He wants me to volunteer one afternoon a week at an in-patient children's clinic. Like the D.C. clinic where I trained."

"What'd you say?"

"I told him I'd think about it. You know, I was so burned out with all that in D.C., I don't know if I want to get involved again."

"How many abused children are you treating now?"

"Um, four out of five of my clients are abused kids."

"Okay, how many under the age of sixteen?"

"Four, I guess. The youngest is eight. Are you suggesting I already do enough of that kind of work?"

"You read my mind, honey." I stood and took his hand. "Come upstairs and talk with me; graduation's this afternoon and I've got to get ready. Can you finish your work after I leave?"

"Yes, and thanks for not inviting me to graduation," Phil said as he followed me up the stairs. "Remember, we're going to the opera to see Katrine tonight."

"Oh, I'll be back in plenty of time," I said. I searched through my closet for my cap and gown and a lightweight dress to wear.

Phil sat down on my bed as I laid out my clothes. He reached for my hand. "You know," he said with a smile, "this room has a warm, fresh smell like nowhere else on earth—it almost always puts me in a lustful mood."

"And I hope that lasts forever," I said, brushing my hair. "But changes scare me sometimes. I heard that Dr. Gustafson's first wife was *quite* overweight for years; then she slimmed down, got to looking great, and he left her! What do you make of that?"

"Well," Phil said, getting up and looking out the window, "it's pretty much an axiom in marriage therapy that relationships often fail after one or both partners get major issues resolved. And shrinks are not immune to that failing."

"You mean the relationship exists to solve their emotional problems and they no longer need it when things get solved?"

"Exactly. Or one spouse leaves because the other is resolved and quits stimulating the neurotic agenda. People also have affairs for those reasons—conflicted sex, money, power, or whatever is a tool to keep the emotional pot boiling. Like raising the stakes in a poker game."

"You're telling me that people use sex to serve their neuroses?" I asked.

"Of course. All the time," Phil said with mild surprise. He followed me into the bathroom and sat on the tub while I did my hair and makeup. "Or they quit sex to serve that same purpose."

"Damn, that's confusing," I said. "What do they accomplish with all that crap?"

"They compulsively play out their unresolved childhood issues."

"Relationships that evolve painfully might be a challenge to you therapists and your patients," I said, plaiting my hair into a loose braid and fixing it with a silver barrette. "But they don't sound fun to me. And who wants to live in a constant state of analysis? What a dreary emotional climate!"

"That's true. However, couples do stay together when they can make adjustments to new emotional structures in the relationship," Phil said. "People and circumstances change. That's when temporary analytical relationships are healthy. Where are you going with this? You don't look too happy."

"What if what we have—love and passion—is an artifice for unresolved problems? And since we're not in pain—in fact what we have enriches our lives—then why mess with it?"

"But we're not messing—"

I looked at my watch. "Sorry to interrupt. Let's fix some lunch; I've got to leave soon." We went downstairs. "Toasted cheese sandwiches okay?"

"Sure," he said. "When do we mess with our relationship?"

"Well, being analytical about having a family bothers me. I love you so. . . . I don't want to do anything to change our relationship. And we've got Abby's kids anytime we want them." Phil came over and hugged me. "My life is so full. I've got you, my family, my home. I've got my painting and my students," I said, turning to kiss him. I put the sandwiches in the broiler and set the table.

"The other day at lunch," I continued, "Trish asked why I don't quit teaching and just paint. She said I could get rich being a full-time artist."

"I bet," Phil said, giving me a knowing smile, "and you gave her the same answer: If it works, don't mess with it. Right?"

I nodded.

"You are an accomplished artist because you see things differently than other people," he said. "You see *life* differently, and that's to your credit. And I love you," Phil added. He kissed me again and we sat down for lunch.

## Thirty / Phil

Sidney began speaking the moment he entered my office. It was his regular Tuesday appointment. "I've been thinking about some of the things you've said over the past few sessions." He pushed the door closed with his foot. "So I decided to observe my own behavior."

I was pleased. Unless a person is in grave crisis, therapy often works best when the client leads. When the patient provides the direction and content of the discussions, the doctor can listen and observe, offering but without pushing, some possible interpretations. Recently, Sid's been reading some scholarly books about psychology, and he has consistently distrusted his feelings and chosen an intellectual view. So I was eager to see where he was going with this.

He stepped across the office and bounced down on the couch. "One thing came through quite clearly. I really do tend to keep people at a distance, and I'm pretty clever at it."

Sid leaned forward, passionately frowning as he continued. "Sunday morning I did something I *did not* like! When I came home from my girlfriend's and turned on the television—I was looking for one of the Sunday morning news programs—one of those Mormon commercials came on. It was supposed to be a real tear jerker, where the little kid keeps trying to do something and the father puts aside his work and helps the little kid. I started crying; I must have sniffled along for about five minutes. I turned off the set and then, whenever I turned it on . . . the news program was on then, not the commercial . . . I started bawling again. I did it about three times."

"What made you cry?" I asked.

"I don't know. All I could think of was these people care about kids. That's absurd—all they want is money; and these aren't real people, they're actors. I mean, these commercials are only about money."

"What's important is what you felt when you saw it," I said. "Why did people caring make you cry?"

"I said I don't know!"

"Was it a sad crying?"

"Of course it was sad! What other kinds of crying are there?"

I pressed on. "How does this relate to you?"

"Maybe I'm an actor like the kid," he said. "The little shit cried when he was frustrated. He's a good actor."

"How do you know he was acting?"

"Oh come on, Phil! What a stupid question."

"It may not be stupid. Because at some level you believed the child, Sid—at your feeling level. That's what connected. What you *thought* apparently didn't affect how you *felt*."

He was silent, thinking.

"I'd like to discuss how thinking and feeling can work together rather than in opposition. If you're open to that."

"I guess I am," he said, sloping back on the sofa.

I believe that bright people like Sid have an edge when it comes to creative change. Almost anyone can grasp new ways in the therapist's office or in an ideal milieu. The challenge comes when life's crises entice us back to the old ways. Perceptive and creative intelligence can come into play at these times, holding unwanted behaviors at bay. Lasting change takes considerable time, but it can be hastened, often by something as simple as modeling the desired behavior—by acting as if the change were already a reality.

"Sid," I said, "understanding your own feelings can help you change. Intellectualizing about them, however, does not necessarily lead to understanding. Curiosity about them can be helpful."

"Why's that?"

"Maybe because of the ambiguous nature of feelings."

"Well, you've just put two of my most aggravating concepts into one short sentence: feelings and ambiguity."

"Why take uncertainty as a hard concept?" I asked. "Why not see it as an unfinished fabric—parts of it not yet woven together—to be finished with the threads of understanding?"

"Now I know I'm smarter than you," he said, slightly mystified. "I know baloney when I hear it."

"Maybe this concept is simply too esoteric for you," I kidded. "I'm saying that as long as we're uncertain, that leaves us open to the realm of unlimited possibilities. And ambiguity provides a window for projecting our feelings. When we acknowledge our feelings and honor them, we personalize our reality, and that enables us to make better choices."

"I might have to give up being cynical," Sid said.

"Remember, cynicism is cheap."

"But priceless when precise," Sid responded with a smile.

I laughed. "Perhaps."

Sid was thoughtful about his next words. "Like weaving the patches before I have the self-understanding? Correct?"

"Yes! And diminished self-understanding is a priceless loss," I said.

"So beautiful in words, Philip. Now give me a practical example." Sid's eyes misted slightly.

"Okay, you offered family leave to your employees long before it was required by law. Why?"

"It works," he replied. "The result has been loyal, happy employees."

"You have it because it works? Or because you care about your staff?" Sid frowned but said nothing.

"Think about it. Isn't family leave something that can be abused? And what would happen if lots of employees used it at the same time? Your work is too technical to turn it over to a bunch of temps. You also have flextime. Think about that—the ambiguities of flextime and family leave."

"One thing at a time, Phil. The— "

"No," I said, interrupting, "All that and more. I'm saying that your company, and all that it means—loyal employees, profits, growth, et cetera—is whole, partly because you embraced uncertainty; you've allowed for the ambiguous nature of certain work rules."

"Okay, I get it in terms of business. But how does this translate to my personal life? My relationship with both my sons is strained, and I don't feel connected to my girlfriend except sexually. And though we have great sex, if she broke up with me tomorrow, I'd probably just shrug it off and find a new one."

"Think about how all this might apply to the personal. How does ambiguity make you feel? We'll talk about it next time."

Sid got up and stared out the window. Then suddenly he turned to me. "Why the *hell* am I here!" Sid asked angrily. "I was happy as a clam before I met you—happy and angry. Blissfully fucking angry!" he yelled. "Look at all the other people—rich, successful, and supposedly happy, but all hurting like hell!"

"I guess hurting rich is preferred to hurting poor," I said with a shrug.

Sid pointed at me, squinting. "Well aren't you a caring SOB."

We were at the end of our session and I wanted to get him focused in a more positive way. "I care about you, Sidney," I said, "and as you do your self-observations, be transparent to your feelings. Let them shine through.

"Since you're doing all this reading, pick one or two of these." I handed him an annotated list of self-therapy books for people with pernicious family histories.

"Thanks," he said, and sighed. "Got time for a game tomorrow?"

"Sure." I glanced at my schedule. "Two o'clock?"

He nodded and shook my hand. I watched him go out the door. Yesterday he beat me two games out of three. He played aggressively and with great zeal. I was enjoying his company more these days and saw some clear changes in him; he was warmer and more connected to his feelings. And his anger was moderating.

Jonah Thornton absentmindedly tossed his food wrappers and newspaper into the garbage at the Fish'nBurger. He ordered a coffee and continued to watch the clinic across the street. He watched as a couple come out of the clinic, then saw a woman with a child enter. All the while he thumbed through the two detective novels he'd bought at the spy shop. He was pleased with the purchase he'd made there that first day. The telephone recording device for Mary's conversations with Trudy and Carol was proving invaluable.

He glanced again at the clinic, then opened one of the mysteries at his dog-ear and began reading. The salesman at the spy shop had told him this author was "the best" when it came to details. His attention was diverted by a commotion at the entrance of the restaurant. An elderly man, escorted by a teenage boy, had fallen as he came inside. The boy and two employees helped the old man to a table. The accident made Jonah smile. Thornton looked back at the clinic.

By god, there he is! Jonah almost said aloud. He'd spotted Sloan standing on the median, waiting for the traffic to clear. Could he be heading over here? Jonah asked himself. To his surprise, Sloan entered the Fish'nBurger, walked within touching distance of him, and bought coffee and a sweet roll. He was a much bigger man than Thornton had expected, and Jonah let out his breath. Sloan went over to a seat by the window, in clear view, and appeared to be watching the clinic. Maybe Sloan was the one now waiting for prey, Jonah thought, staring at him.

## Thirty-one / Phil

I waited for Manny over coffee at the burger joint across the street from my office. Summer was starting to make itself felt—the temperature heading into the high eighties—but hot coffee's one of my favorites, regardless of the weather. Had Manny been just a friend, or another psychiatrist, I would have liked to discuss something I'd been reading. It was a book on spirituality by an American author who had studied in Japan, China, and in India for many years. A number of his concepts seemed faulty to me, intellectual folly.

But each time I was tempted to put the book aside, I'd stumble across a true gem of insight. I scanned ahead to the last chapter and discovered it was sensational; so now I'm reading the book backwards.

One of his concepts that I wanted to run by Manny was the author's belief that the congruently resolved person—one who is truly at peace with himself—doesn't have the need for physical connections to friends and lovers. The writer says that's an option for the self-actualized.

I'd discussed it briefly with Shelee a few nights before. "What do you make of this?" I said. We were reading in bed.

"Sounds like malarkey to me," she said, yawning.

"Yeah, I feel I've resolved most of my shit; yet I am dependent on our physical love and companionship."

"Of course," she said. "You may be resolved with the ordinary universe; however, that's only a shadow introduction to your relationship with me."

"Such clear logic."

"Also correct," Shelee said. She smiled and closed her book. "You just don't understand the nature of your woman—she is the most powerful love force on this planet and beyond," she explained calmly and nestled in my arms.

I gulped the rest of my coffee when I saw Manny getting out of a brand-new Lincoln in the parking lot across Hennepin, and I hurried over to meet him. I called out to him, and he turned and waited for me. He crushed out a smoke under his foot as I approached; we shook hands.

"Inside or outside?" I said, pointing at the picnic table.

"Inside. It's getting too damn hot out here," Manny said.

"Nice limo."

"I indulge myself with a new car each year," he said. "You probably wouldn't believe it's my only extravagance."

"Yes I would," I answered, looking at his rumpled jacket. And I had read about his generous donations. "Heard you were giving a couple of mil to the Center for Ethnic Writing at UW," I said as I unlocked the office door.

"I guess you think that's a joke." He shrugged. "I do so little ethnic writing."

"Still, it sounds like a fine project," I said, and motioned him inside.

"I've heard a few people were upset that I didn't give it to Minnesota." We walked into my office.

"So what? Washington's your alma mater, and you deserve lots of credit for your generosity. Have a seat," I said. I closed the door and sat down.

"That's exactly what my wife says. Now she wants me to be more visible, less reclusive." Manny sat back in his chair and crossed his legs. "Coming out of the closet with my personal tale of abuse ought to do it." He sighed.

"I noticed you were pretty outgoing at the Burns-Cole party a few weeks ago," I said, still wanting to explore that subject.

"Hell, I don't know what got into me." Manny sat quietly for a moment, then put his hands behind his neck and looked at the ceiling. "You know, I've become rich writing the white man's literature. So why do I feel trapped in it?"

"Why do you call it white man's literature?" I asked. He looked at me thoughtfully.

"I believe *Mikie and Mike* is a universal story," I said. "He could be any color. Your readers may be more ethnically diverse than you realize. I know we've been over this before, but what would happen if you made *Mikie* black or Indian?" I asked. "If you were to tell *your* story through Mikie?"

"*That*," he said, "would issue an indictment of my personal history too severe for me to deal with. I know literature is full of cruel stories of all colors; but my introduction, which I may not use anyway, is as far as I can go. . . . Is that a peripheral exploration again?"

I couldn't help smiling at that. "Remember," I said, "if you can separate your writing from some of what goes on here, your book would be less of a personal burden. Take Toni Morrison's writing, for instance."

"She's got more courage than I do," Manny said. He leaned back now, hesitating. "I keep having this dream. . . ."

"Go on."

"We've got three cats and an outside dog, and though we take good care of them in real life, in the dream they're neglected. I'm out on the road by myself, my wife's not home, and I realize I've made no arrangements for the pets. They're locked in the house or backyard without food or water. I've been away for a long time, and angry at myself because I haven't provided for them. I keep wondering how I could have forgotten them. But when I arrive home, the pets have made it okay and they're happy to see me. I'm glad they're fine, but I feel terrible guilt. Any ideas?"

"Tell me what you see when you get home. Anything changed in the house?"

"Well, the animals have food and water," Manny said, "but it's old. Someone has sort of cared for them. The backyard grass is long and overgrown. Come to think of it, it's always spring or summer, feels more like spring."

"What do your pets do when they see you?"

"They're happy," Manny said. "The dog's all over me and the cats just act like cats. They don't seem to mind I've neglected them. This bothers me, too, even though that's the way pets act—you know, they don't complain. I'm very upset by the dream because it's so contrary to how we treat our animals. I get this sick feeling whenever I wake from it."

"If you could speak for your pets, or compose a letter from them, what would you say?"

"Christ!" Manny exclaimed, leaning forward. "The poor things can't complain. Just as I couldn't complain as a child. That's what the dream's about!"

"But now you can," I said. "In your book. And millions of people of many colors will read it, and feel your pain and your triumph."

"Okay, Dr. Phil," he said, pleased but suddenly very serious, "I guess the connection between Mikie, Mike, and Manny is pretty obvious."

"What's your given name?" I asked.

"Emmanuel. Pretty biblical, huh?"

"I like it. Emmanuel Weston," I said slowly, emphasizing each syllable. "Now that's a writer's name."

"Oh, I can't change my name; people buy my books because Manny Weston is the author."

"Perhaps you could mystify your readers with two names. Or just put Manny in quotes."

He slumped back in his chair. "You know what's really bothering me? My depression," he said. "The more I write, the more depressed I get. Shouldn't it be the other way around?"

"It has been in the past, hasn't it?"

"Yeah, my writing has always been a release for me. Usually, I've felt at my best when I write. But with *this* book, there's an empty feeling in my gut. And I can't write as fast as the story evolves in my head. Sometimes I switch to just writing notes; other times I describe one sequence into the recorder while typing another on the computer." Manny got up and began to pace. "The more horrific the shit that pours out, the worse I feel, until I have to stop because of the pain in my belly. And I have this fear."

"Tell me about it."

"I think that I'm afraid that when I get to the healthy part of the book, I won't be able to write it. It's as if I don't want to recover. And the more my Mike in the book heals, the less I want to write about him."

"Is the healing part of the book the only healthy part?" I asked. "Writing the pain is also healthy."

"No, I want to quit hurting!" he protested. "I want to recapture some joy in my life!" Manny sat down, this time on the couch.

"You want to quit hurting, *and* you worry about recovering. Yet one leads to the other. What does that mean?"

Manny just looked at me, doubtfully.

"As for the depression," I said, "at least it's productive, a rare combination. Most depressed people are simply stuck with inaction. Let me ask you this: If Mikie were not white, would you feel better about his healing?"

Manny bolted off of the couch. "Goddammit, Sloan," he yelled in my face, "*why do you keep bringing up race?*"

"Because I truly care for you, my friend, and I hear great conflict in your perception about *who you are.*"

Manny sat back down and tears welled in his eyes. "I'm sorry, Phil," he said. Manny shook his head and tried to speak, but no words came. Finally, he put his head in his hands and quietly sobbed. I knew he had broken through some very old barriers. In a few minutes he took the tissues that I had set on the couch beside him.

"Some weeks back," I said gently, "we discussed how patients often want to become healers themselves. The psychiatrist in your book tells Mike that this response is a recognition that he can heal. I'm willing to bet that your combination of depression and hyperproductivity is the dam starting to break for you."

"What dam?"

"Healing," I said. "The self-therapy you've been doing through your writing. I predict a flood of innovative works from Emmanuel Weston."

Manny stood and tossed the tissue box on my desk. "But I'm *not* changing my name," he said with a grin.

Thornton watched the clinic from his car parked on the street near the parking lot. Shortly after one, he spotted Sloan leave the building with a gym bag and drive off. Jonah pulled into traffic, two cars behind the doctor's light blue Chevy Blazer, and followed him to the Pike Street Racquet Club. Jonah glanced at his watch as Dr. Sloan walked into the club. Jesus, Sloan's big, he noticed again.

Finally, around half past four, Sloan returned to his car, and Jonah followed him through the light, early evening commute. This time he stayed a half block behind the doctor's easy-to-spot Blazer. Be careful, he reminded himself; there was plenty of time. His lawyer, needing more time to prepare his defense, had asked for a continuance; the trial had been moved back to September.

Sloan led him through a residential area on the west side of the city, parked in front of a two-story house, and went inside. The mailbox had the name "Osbornson" across one side. Jonah figured that was the girlfriend's house, the same woman with Sloan in the *Post* photo. He also noticed the green station wagon parked in the driveway. The car had a University of Minnesota parking sticker on the back bumper. Satisfied, yet somewhat unsettled that he still didn't know Sloan's home address, Jonah drove on. Did Dr. Sloan live with Professor Osbornson, he wondered.

Thornton pulled into the first gas station with a phone booth. "Mary," he said when his wife answered, "make me some supper." He looked at his watch. "I'll be home by seven."

## Thirty-two / Shelee

Phil helped me plan the party for Serena and her husband. The night of the party, we trotted out our best wines and cooked up some great appetizers. For dinner, Phil made his sensational chippino, and we served it pickup style along with garlic bread and a green salad. We had flaming cherries jubilee for dessert, made with fresh Queen Anne cherries that I stewed just so. Other guests included Naomi and Mitch, my sister and Tim, Trish and her boyfriend, the Coles, and Marguerite Kampino, who happened to be in town for a show she was working on with the Twin Cities Art Institute.

All the guests, except Serena and Wayne, who hadn't arrived yet, seemed a bit uncomfortable when the Coles showed up. So Phil and I took Duncan and Gloria around and introduced them as our neighbors from up at Lucky's farm. The two were as charming as could be and put everyone at ease. I mean, what does one say to the couple who has six billion dollars?

I felt somewhat anxious about meeting Serena and wanted to get it over with. Meanwhile, I made the rounds. Duncan was talking football with Tim and Trish; Phil was with a group discussing current events; and Marguerite Kampino and Glo Burns were deep in conversation. Gloria's the newest member on the art institute's board of directors and was interested in Marguerite's upcoming show.

Finally Serena and her husband arrived. She was stunning, though according to Phil she'd put on a few pounds. What did he expect after ten years and two kids? Phil probably found her even more attractive now, since he likes plumpers. As soon as she walked in, Serena hugged Phil. I was standing behind them with her husband, Wayne.

"Oh, Phil," Serena simpered, looking across the room at Marguerite, "you've invited another African-American to make us feel at home." Wayne Neal stiffened at his wife's remark, but I wanted to laugh. With that comment, Serena had won my heart. I figured anyone who could nail Phil Sloan, even a little bit, belonged on my list of dearest friends.

Phil was taken aback for a second but quickly recovered. "Oh, Ms. Kampino?" he said. She's from the Rent-A-Black Agency; Twin Cities has everything, don't you know."

At that point I thought old Wayne was going to lose it. He looked really embarrassed by Phil and Serena's exchange, but then he grabbed Serena by the arm. "Good lord," he said to her, "there's Duncan Cole and Gloria Burns."

"Come on," I said, "I'll introduce you."

Soon the Neals and Coles were talking about some legal case they had all been involved in. Evidently, a few years before, the Neals had represented clients opposed to one of Gloria's corporate activities; Wayne had headed the domestic team and Serena managed the international side in what sounded like big-bucks litigation. My god, I thought, and excused myself, wondering whose side had won, the Coles or the Neals.

"I guess the cocktail circuit doesn't get any better than this," Naomi said to me when I approached her and Marguerite.

"No, it doesn't," Marguerite agreed. "Do you know that Gloria is commissioning me to do a portrait of her and Duncan for their anniversary?"

"Good for you," I said. "I'd do portraits and landscapes, too, if I could paint them as well as you do." Her work at my master class turned out to be an absolute treasure. The students had all benefited from her expertise, and Marguerite had developed an important connection with our best art museum. I liked Marguerite and hoped to see a lot more of her in the future.

After dinner we talked everyone but the Neals, who had to leave early, into a poker game. "We left the girls with the hotel's baby-sitting service," Serena explained to Tim and me, "and I'm not comfortable leaving them too long."

"I understand," I told her.

"Say, why don't you bring the kids over tomorrow?" Tim said. "They can play or go fishing with Fritz and Heidi."

"The girls would love that," Serena said. "But I'll let you know in the morning."

"Great, maybe we can all barbecue," Tim said, looking at me. Ah, well, I thought. I had mixed feelings about seeing them again. A picture of Phil and Serena making love under the Capitol dome kept occurring to me.

"Damn, the party was fun," I said to Phil as we cleaned up Sunday morning. I was loading the dishwasher when the phone rang.

"I'll get it," Phil said from the living room.

"Serena," I heard him say. "Yes, so did I. . . . Of course not." Of course not what? I wondered. Phil laughed several times and seemed to be doing most of the listening. The dishwasher was running and I couldn't hear without going into the other room. I felt irritated, yet how could I be jealous? It was obvious that Serena really loves her husband.

"Shel," Phil said, bringing me the phone, "it's Serena."

I stuck my tongue out at him and snatched the phone out of his hand. "Shelee," Serena said, "I want to thank you so much for the super party. Everything was great—the food, the company, your home."

"You're welcome," I said, sticking out my foot to trip Phil as he walked through the kitchen. He stepped around it and patted me on the butt, then grabbed my arm and pulled me into the living room.

"We're going back today. We received a call from some business friends who live near Chicago," she said. "They're about to go to Europe on a six-months' assignment and we need to spend some time with them before they leave."

Phil dragged me onto the couch. "Ah, too bad you can't stay longer," I said, trying to push Phil away.

"May I have your sister's number so I can let her know?"

"I'll call her if you'd like," I said. "I'm just glad you could make it last night."

"So are we," Serena said. "We had a wonderful time and so enjoyed meeting you and your friends. Very impressive, all of them." Phil had me pinned now. "We have some exciting news," she went on, "but I'll let Phil tell you about it. Please tell Abby and Tim we'll visit them next time. Thanks again."

"You're welcome. Have a safe trip," I said. I clicked the phone off and dropped it on the floor. Then I tried to squirm out from under Phil. "So what's the big news, Philip? You certainly talked long enough."

"Say *uncle*," he said, "and I'll let you up."

"Phil Sloan, you better let me up or I'll say a lot more than uncle," I warned him.

"Meaningless threats will get you everything," he said, laughing. He moved and I pulled myself up on his arm.

"So what's the news?"

"Remember that litigation Serena and Wayne were discussing with the Coles?"

"Yeah, it sounded like a big deal."

"Well, apparently Gloria had been very impressed with Wayne and Serena at the time, because she's offered each of them senior positions in the Burns legal department." Phil got off the couch and headed for the kitchen. I followed, plotting my revenge.

"Serena might become manager of their international law team," he said. "Where's the toast I left here?" Phil pointed to an empty dish on the counter.

"I ate it," I said. "Gloria offered her the manager's position?"

"I guess the current manager is retiring."

"That'll be right cozy," I said with a sneer, now stalking him with a butter knife. Phil grabbed me and kissed me hard on the lips, holding my arm as I tried to slash him. I relaxed and my weapon clattered to the floor.

"So they're taking the jobs for sure?" I asked.

"Looks like it," he said, holding me, stroking my hair. "Serena said they've already moved twice to get away from the crime in Washington. This would be a big step for them; she's a partner in her law firm, and Wayne's in line for partnership. They think that Gloria is counting on their D.C. contacts to help her companies."

I sighed. "We should give more parties." I picked up the butter knife and dropped it into the sink. "Between Marguerite and the Neals, we've promoted some valuable business."

"I hope you feel better about Serena now," Phil said, looking around the kitchen. "Any more of that bread?"

"I'll make you some toast," I offered and went to the refrigerator. "By the way, your friend, Ms. Neal, confirmed my humanist views about ethnic perspective."

"Oh?"

"Yup. Said she'd never considered an all-black university because she feels she's a citizen of America, not simply a black citizen."

"I'm not following you," he said.

"Serena said she had plenty of support and didn't need an extended family, like an ethnically focused college."

"Shel, ethnic fellowship is more than extended family," Phil said. "Everyone needs community, and racial association is one form. Perhaps Serena simply selected a larger community for her needs. I remember her complaining that her parents were hardly available, too busy with careers." Phil began buttering his toast.

"She acknowledged that. But she figures that since both she and her brother have the same attitude, her folks must have somehow enabled them to connect with the broader society."

"Maybe," Phil speculated, "but I also recall they were very upper crust, and the kids were mostly raised by white housekeepers." Phil smiled. "You really got to know Serena, didn't you?"

"Tell me," I said, putting more bread in the toaster, "have you always gone with self-actualized women . . . such as *moi*?"

"It's mostly illusion. All my women are self-actualized around their neuroses."

"*Oh,* that's not funny! My university's full of them . . . of *both* genders."

"Full of self-actualized neurotics?" Phil said, grinning.

I shook my head. "You get the coffee."

We took our toast and coffee out to the back porch and sat in the shade. "That poker game worked okay last night," Phil said.

"Selling $10,000 in chips for a dollar really leveled the field," I said. "But you just made up that American Bird game as you went along, right?"

"What makes you think so? You've played seven-card high-low before."

"Not by your rules. And you *changed* the rules each time you dealt it," I said, noticing the falling Virginia creeper vines along the side of the porch.

"Everyone seemed to like it."

"Yeah, the pots got enormous." I got up and began winding the new vines back into the leafy tangle on the porch arbor. "Don't you wish Manny and his wife had been here?" I asked.

"One ex-client and one current is enough," Phil said.

"Current? Who's current?"

"That's right; you're not in treatment, you're just nuts," he said. "But seriously, I like all my patients. I'd love to be friends with them if that were possible."

I could see weeds in the flower beds and went down the porch steps for a closer look. "What do you think of Trish's new flame?" I asked. It was the second time we'd been around him; I knew Phil had an opinion.

"He's in a state of utter FUBAR," Phil said. "Trish affects most men that way. Even Duncan appeared taken with her."

"No kidding," I said, pulling weeds and tossing them onto the lawn. My two cats followed us to the yard, first chasing around, then wrestling in the grass. Both are showing their age, so such an infrequent frolic was a pleasure to see.

Phil pulled weeds in the flower bed next to me. "Incredibly beautiful women in everyday life simply don't fit in," he said. "That's why we have the glamor professions, so gorgeous women can be themselves in environments that are reasonable for them."

"You mean outside of reality?"

"Exactly," Phil said. "I'll pick up the weeds," He walked back to the porch. "Trish and Terry, what an insipid combination.

It's possible Trish is simply too beautiful for her own emotional health since she settles for men like Terry."

"I did notice they sort of feed off each other."

"Yeah, and Terry thinks having a glamorous girlfriend will help his self-image, but all it does is heighten his insecurity."

"How do you know that?"

"You saw it," Phil said. "Terry did that subtle posturing all evening. He's a dead man; all his circuits have been fried, and he'll take Trish with him if she's not careful." Phil brought the five-gallon bucket that I use for yard trash from the side of the house.

"Jesus, Phil, you don't give them any slack at all. I remember you once said Trish must have eaten the books when she went to school. That was really harsh."

"Sorry," he said. "I guess you did ask me about Terry, not Trish."

"In my opinion, Trish never gets a chance to be herself around men. She's great when she's with me or other women—when it's just us girls. I'm enriched by our friendship."

"She's chosen reality for her friendship with you," Phil said. "I'm saying that she has plenty of opportunities to meet men, so she could be very discriminating and careful—and she elects not to. So we're back to self-image. If she doesn't feel worthy, then she will select unworthy companions. And it will keep happening until she decides to change." Phil picked up the rest of the weeds and dumped them on my trash pile.

"Maybe she's not aware that she makes bad choices in men," I said, heading for the garden.

"All she has to do is look at the outcome," Phil said. "No one makes meaningful changes because someone points out our errors. We only change when we are forced to."

"You mean until we hurt enough to look at what we're doing?" I began harvesting peas and handing them to Phil.

"That's right. Sometimes we use relationships to distract us from what's going on in ourselves. So if the Terrys and Seths of this world don't hurt Trish too badly, she probably won't change." He was opening pea pods, running the peas against his lower teeth, eating them as fast as I picked.

"I want those for dinner," I said, now tossing pea pods over his head and onto the lawn.

Phil began to help me pick. "A more usual scenario for men or women like Trish is to keep selecting more harmful partners until they find themselves face down in their own stuff—a variant of 'we love what may kill us.' When Trish exhibits wisdom about others in your conversations, perhaps you can get her to use it for herself." We picked the peas off the lawn. "So far she's selected only slightly destructive men," Phil said. "That's an interesting piece, and I'm not sure what it means."

When we went into the house, Phil unloaded the dishwasher and put the clean dishes away while I shelled peas. We worked silently. I was still thinking about Trish. "Another thing," Phil said, as if he could read my mind, "Trish really has an uphill battle against her little-princess affliction."

"So now we're gender bashing, Doctor?"

"You decide for yourself, Shel. But children get the message that they are worthy or not first from family and then from society. Within a functioning family, a kid develops the essential feelings of belonging that support his ability to contribute to his own life, his family's, and beyond." Phil finished putting the dishes away and stood next to me, shelling peas. "Unfortunately," he continued, "pretty little girls often get the lopsided message that the only way *they* can belong is through their beauty. So they learn to feel: 'to belong means I must remain beautiful—serve my beauty so I can feel worthy.' I think if Trish didn't have her son to keep her grounded in some reality, she would be keenly unhappy."

"Okay, Phil. Enough," I said and put the peas in the fridge. "Let's get some exercise."

"Subscriber Services—which magazine, please?"

This was Jonah Thornton's ninth, and last, call on the list. His library research had provided him with the 800 phone numbers for medical psychiatric journals. And Dr. Sloan subscribed to one—so far—but it was delivered to his office.

"*The United States–Canada Journal of Child Psychiatry*," Jonah said.

"Zip code, followed by last name?"

"55407, Sloan."

"Dr. Philip R. Sloan?"

"Correct, that's me," Jonah answered cheerfully.

"The phone number at your mailing address, area code first, please."

"612-24—. Oh, that's my office number. I recently changed my home number; what do you see on your screen?"

"612-586-4873."

"Okay, you've got my new number," Jonah said, scribbling it down.

"4923 Blaircross Road for the mailing address, Dr. Sloan?"

"That's right."

"What can we do for you today, Doctor?"

"I received a renewal notice from you folks, but, according to my mailing label, I've got another eighteen months to go."

"It must have been sent in error, Dr. Sloan. Our records don't show eighteen months. However, your subscription is paid up through next April."

"Well, thanks. It never hurts to check."

"You're welcome. Is there anything else we can help you with?"

"No, that's all I needed," Jonah said. "Thanks again. Bye."

## Thirty-three / Phil

I was convinced Shelee still had my relationship with Serena on her mind. Sure enough, a few nights later she brought it up.

"Were you over Serena when you met me?" Shel asked.

"I think so. If not, you soon made me forget her." But I didn't tell Shelee there was a time when I could not escape my memories of Serena—when I would wake in the night remembering her beautiful face next to me—those nights at her place, in a four-poster bed draped with ivory lace. Serena lived in an elegantly decorated apartment with delicate curtains and antiques.

"So she broke up with you?" Shelee asked.

"Yeah." I had grown irritated by Serena Martin's overbearing manner, and my suspicions that she was seeing someone else was working its quiet sabotage. Things had boiled over one night as we left the Kennedy Center. We'd just seen the Met perform *Adriana Lecouvreur,* and the plaza in front of the center was full of elegant-looking couples, a number of them interracial.

"Serena," I said, "I'll be leaving D.C. in about three months and I don't want to be in a funk about us when I go back to Minnesota. Maybe we should start seeing less of each other."

"So you called it off?" Shel asked.

"Not really. I just did what she wanted, I think." Serena had seemed relieved. "I've been feeling the same way," she responded much too quickly. "I'm going to miss you, too, Phil," she went on. "And I'm damned sorry for being so narrow, insisting that my personal image shape my future," she added—or something to that effect. She had snuggled against me then, in a way all too familiar. "Please stay with me tonight," she asked, expertly mixing plaintive and seductive. This I omitted in my story to Shel.

"That evening marked the end of my affair with Serena," I told Shel. "We saw each other once more for dinner, had a couple of lunches together, and returned the few things we'd loaned each other."

"So then you played the field, huh?"

"So then I played poker."

"Lucky said with the big boys."

"I'd say the dangerous big boys, now that I look back on it."

I remember that even though my last month in D.C. was hectic enough without anything extracurricular, I was obsessed with poker. I wanted some big wins in those last few games. Several days before the weekend I was to leave Washington for Minnesota, things were frantic. I was running late at the hospital the day of my last poker game with those slimeballs. Concerned that the game might be filled without me, I called Kwo and asked him to set out my chips to reserve a seat.

"Something told me not to tell Kwo I was leaving town," I explained to Shel.

"Why not?"

"I don't really know. I just didn't get to know him well enough to be sure I could trust him." I didn't think any of the players had kept a tally of my winnings. My two-year income from the game, almost $1.5 million, was an adequate student wage.

"Where's the Monkey Man?" I had asked when I got there —almost an hour late. Everyone was drinking and talking; the game had not yet started.

"I guess the stupid shit decided not to come back," Carp said.

"Too bad, I'm going to miss his action," I said. "I assume he's one of your guys, Ray."

"Fuck you, Sloan!" Carp scowled. "I'd never have anyone that stupid working for me."

"I thought he was your *boss,* Raymond," I said, scowling back at him. "Sort of the Main Mobster." The Carp was not amused.

Monkey Man, as everyone called him, was this hairy little guy who looked and played cards like a chimpanzee. He played out of control, was halfwitted, and seemingly had an unlimited supply of money. I figured he peddled dope. He'd been a heavy hitter for the past two or three months and had dumped a ton of cash.

"We ain't waiting," Carp said, and the game started. But by the third hand or so, Monkey came in and hung his jacket on the coat rack. The sports jacket, in plain view, sagged open, revealing a gun's wood and steel handle in a holster that was part of the lining. I don't know who all noticed, but the holster was sewn into the inside of the jacket and supported with several straps that were also part of the lining.

"He must have had some tailor," I told Shelee. "You'd never know he was carrying a gun unless you bumped him." Anyway, someone probably alerted Kwo, because while Monkey Man was involved in a hand, Kwo walked in and took the pistol out of his jacket.

"We do not allow firearms," Kwo said. "You may have the gun when you leave."

The Monkey waved his hand. "Whatever," he said and kept on playing. But within an amazing twenty minutes, Monkey ran out of money and grumbled that he had to leave. Kwo, who had removed the shells from the pistol, gave him the gun at the door. Monkey demanded his ammunition.

"Give me your address, please, and I'll send you the cartridges," Kwo said. But instead of an address, Kwo got the finger, and Monkey left with an empty gun. I was dying to know if there had been a shell in the chamber, and the next time Kwo came in, I asked him.

"What did he say?" Shelee wanted to know.

"He wouldn't tell me. Just said, 'Hairy little turd bad business, Dr. Sloan.' "

"So you never found out?"

"Nope."

As usual, Carp was irritated that someone had left the game. "Fuck that Monkey asshole!" he had snorted. "Nobody'll miss him 'cept his money." The game began again and quickly accelerated out of control. "The cops burned my main drug setup, an' I need a big win tonight," Carp said. "So you ladies better watch out."

I hated that son of a bitch, Carp, and I planned to mail anonymous letters to the Capitol Police and FBI from somewhere on the road back to Minneapolis, detailing what I knew about him. I had hopes he'd go down, dope pushers, pimps, whores, and all.

What a great night it turned out to be! My cards were simply bulletproof. One memorable hand came shortly after Raymond made a reckless play and won a big pot with three nines. I started with an ace and jack of diamonds. I called raises against Bradock and the Carp. I figured them both for low pairs. There was another player in the hand, a money launderer who had been with us for almost a year—no telling what he might be holding.

The flop came queen and eight of diamonds and a black nine. I tried to look distracted, eating a sandwich and hoping I wouldn't have to call a big bet. I had eyed their stacks earlier, and they each had about $20,000. I made a point to scratch my nose, a body language signal that said I had passed them up, hoping they were concerned I had a straight.

The laundry man had a king, three of diamonds, and Bradock held a jack, ten off-suit—he'd flopped a queen-high straight and decided to slow play it—a stupid idea with two diamonds on the board. The fourth card was the four of diamonds, giving Carp three fours. He pushed about $20,000 to the edge of the pot and announced he was going all-in. I was surprised when everyone called.

The game had been going for less than an hour and I was looking at a pot worth close to $75,000. I prayed that the fifth card didn't pair the board, remembering this hand was similar to the big one the Japanese ambassador ran into the Carp a year earlier. Raymond was just a sucker for a made flush against his full-house draw. Mercifully, the fifth card was the ace of clubs, and I had the nut flush.

Carp started to whine when I stacked my new chips. "Jesus Christ, do you always hold the fuckin' Brazils, Sloan?"

Before I could answer, Bert Milligan, the money launderer, put in his two-cents' worth. "My heart pumps piss for you, Raymond! The senator and I had you beat; your hand was fourth out of four."

Carp bought $40,000 in chips, and Bradock and Milligan each bought $25,000. I had at least $60,000 in winnings in my stack and was hoping for a $100,000 night—and the night was still young. What a fitting end that would be to my District of Columbia poker career, I decided. The game proceeded at a somewhat slower pace after that big hand, but I continued to get good cards, and ended up with an $88,000 win when the game broke up around two in the morning.

"Good god!" Shel said. "That was the last time you ever saw those people?"

"Yes. I think it must have been on a Thursday night, because I'd planned to go to the bank the next day." The poker night had been changed from Friday to accommodate one of the senator's girlfriends who had Fridays off. No one complained; the U.S. Congress paid the rent.

"Then the next morning, on my way to the bank, this crazy idea hit me." Because I was pretty sure the teller who usually waited on me figured I was in the rackets—since I never had a cash transaction less than $20,000—I decided to skip the bank. Instead I turned around and went home.

I got this beat-up old soft-side briefcase that I'd purchased at a Salvation Army store a couple years before. The leather flap cover was cracked and frayed and the clasp was broken. A red-white-and-blue bungee cord wrapped around the case kept it from flying open. The perfect container for big money, I decided, recalling that the case cost 75 cents and the bungee cost $1.25. I stuffed most of the poker cash in it—a total of $113,000, including the $25,000 I'd taken to the game. I threw it on the rear seat of the car when I left D.C. I wanted to feel what it was like to travel with $100,000 in cash.

I spent the rest of that day clearing out my desk and saying goodbye to colleagues and patients. Now I was ready to leave Washington to settle into the less hectic pace of the Midwest.

My setup in Minneapolis was ideal. Earlier, I'd answered an ad in *The American Psychiatric Journal* from a Dr. Glen Lovelace, an older physician who wanted someone to take over his practice as he planned to retire. I had met with Dr. Lovelace the previous summer, and we'd hit it off, talking mostly about treatment philosophies—I guess he liked what he heard. He knew my dad and stepfather, and liked them both. His office had an extra suite of rooms, so I was walking into a ready-made practice.

Minneapolis is an easy drive from D.C., and I arrived there at night, two days later. I wasn't expected at Glen's office until the following Monday, so I had about a week to look for a place to live and get settled. Meanwhile, I stayed with Lucky. I always stayed with him whenever I visited Minneapolis. Usually, he'd let me sit in on his poker games, or we'd just hang out together, and I didn't expect this time to be any different.

My headlights illuminated the back of Lucky's pickup truck when I pulled in. The truck was parked along the curb in front of his house. I noticed a large object covered with a tarp in the back. I grabbed one suitcase and the satchel full of money and headed up the walk.

I gave him a big hug when I walked into his house. The first thing he did was to offer me some three-day-old coffee, which I declined. Old coffee meant he didn't currently have a woman in his life. Knowing Lucky, that situation could change at any moment.

"What's in the briefcase?" he wanted to know.

Take a look," I said, and tossed it to him.

"Holy shit almighty! Where'd you get all this money, boy?" I told him about the poker games. "How much you got here?" he asked, his eyes wide.

"One-hundred-and-twenty-three thousand," I said, deciding to play with his head a little.

"Well, I want you to remember, you're my fa-vor-ite relative, even if we ain't blood related. And you know I can beat you at poker any time I want to," he added, walking out to the car with me to help bring in the rest of my stuff.

"What's in the back of your truck?" I asked.

"That's my goddamn big tele-vision," he said. "It quit on me 'bout a week ago, and I was plannin' to haul it to the dump. But the fuckin' city wants five dollars to let me dump it. Figure if I leave it outside in the truck, someone'll steal it." We walked back to the house with more luggage and made additional trips for the six cases of wine I'd hauled from D.C. I finished unloading, then locked a couple boxes of books in the trunk.

Lucky returned to the briefcase, hefting packages of $100 bills. I punched him in the shoulder. "Goodnight, bub," I said. "It's nice to be home." Then I headed to the spare bedroom, leaving him to riffle through the money. He was going to count it sometime in the next few minutes. I figured he would go half nuts trying to figure out why the total always came up $10,000 short.

"Did he?" Shel asked.

"Hell, yes. He still rags me about that one."

"Did you peek to see if he was counting it?"

"No. I didn't find out until morning. I just went to bed."

"I wouldn't have been able to sleep a wink," Shel said, "wondering what Lucky was thinking out there."

"Actually, I did have trouble sleeping that night," I said, "but not because of Lucky." I'd doze off briefly, then wake suddenly with jarring speculations about my medical career, or with Serena careening through my mind.

"In one weird dream," I told Shel, "Serena was there visiting Dr. Lovelace, concerned about her problems with me. I listened while he told Serena he was so upset with my functional disorders that he'd decided not to quit his practice. 'Serena,' he said, 'I could earn a decent living just treating the patients Phil's made crazy.'

"That dream helped me decide to focus on adult patients for the time being. I realized I was burned out with adolescents—I'd spent most of the past two years treating disturbed young people. The dream also turned out to be prophetic: Glen Lovelace decided not to retire completely, and worked a limited schedule for three more years."

"Some dream," Shel said.

"Yeah. So then next morning Lucky was in a bizarre mood. He insisted I drive his truck somewhere so someone could steal his TV—my punishment, I guess, for misleading him about the cash in the briefcase." Shelee laughed.

"But some thief had let me off the hook. 'Cause when I walked out front to take his truck into town, both the television and the tarp were gone. So then your uncle's mood improved and he told me about you."

"What did he say?"

"He said, 'You know that good-looking redhead niece of mine? Well, she was over here and I told her you were comin' back home. Between boyfriends, she is, and said she'd like you to call.' Then he told me about the professor you had just dumped. Lucky sure didn't like *him*."

"He was very protective in those days. What else did he tell you?" Shel asked tentatively.

I smiled. "Nothing about your boyfriend. But he did say, 'I'd jump on it if I were you, boy—you know what I mean?' "

"Oh, come on. He said that?"

"I think so. Then he showed me a couple of your pictures and I was sold."

"Hard sell?"

"Nope, I remember saying, 'She's a fine-looking woman, Uncle. I'll call her tomorrow.' "

"So how do you feel about Serena now, after all these years?" Shel asked.

I took Shel's hand. "I love you far more than I ever cared for Serena. And we have a much fuller relationship. You know, Wayne appears to be an intelligent and kind man, they're both successful lawyers, and they seem happily married. So I'm happy for her." Also, maybe I'm a little jealous, I thought, that they have two kids—daughters she said—Samia, and I forget the other's name. . . . "Of course, Lucky didn't tell me you'd be so ornery."

"Hell with you, Dr. Sloan, you ain't seen anything ornery yet!"

The Minneapolis July weather was in full swing by the weekend. We slept in late Saturday morning and had a leisurely breakfast. "It's too damn hot to run outside," I said. "Do you want to run at the club this afternoon?"

"No," Shel said, turning on the air-conditioning. "I've got to work here all day. Let's just go for a walk before it gets any hotter."

"One of our faculty asked about you the other day," Shel said as we headed out the door. "You know Tanna Lesterman—she does those airy impressionistic paintings that you like so much. She wants to get back into therapy."

"She's interested in me as a therapist?" I asked. "Isn't she lesbian?"

"Oh, I'm sure she is," Shel answered. "I think she lives with her lover, and I know they've both been involved in gay rights activities up at school. Why do you ask?"

"You know I try to avoid treating gays. You did know that, didn't you?"

Shelee looked astonished. "You're kidding!" she said. "We've never had this conversation. Are you serious?"

"Absolutely I'm serious."

"You're prejudiced!"

"I don't know if you'd call it prejudice," I said cautiously. "It's being honest with myself—I have objections to parts of the gay lifestyle that I've never been able to come to terms with. That's just the way I am. So, I've elected not to treat homosexuals."

We waited at an intersection for traffic to pass and Shel persisted. "A number of our professors are gay. I've never noticed you avoiding anyone at the college functions. Don't they cure you of homophobia in shrink school?"

Her off-the-mark question was more than a little snotty, but I wanted to keep the discussion focused. "They tried to, and I tried to. But it didn't work, and I'm not going to treat patients I might damage. So much of my practice is intuitive and spiritual; if I don't feel empathy with my patients, I may unwittingly hurt them.

Shelee glared at me.

"I'm simply acknowledging my limitations," I said.

"Outside of your practice, how do you feel about homosexuals?"

"This is really sensitive, private stuff, Shel. And just between you and me, okay?"

"Of course, Phil," she said. "I value your views, even if your head's fucked up."

"Well you certainly know how to end a conversation," I shot back. We crossed another street, still holding hands but not talking.

Finally, Shelee squeezed my hand. Sensing she was squirming uncomfortably, I gave her cheek a kiss.

"I apologize," she said. "I can't believe we've never talked about this."

"Could be I've avoided it," I said. "You know I support everyone's right to live their own lifestyle. However, when it comes to my clients, I have to do what I feel is best for each patient."

"But if a patient specifically wants counseling with you?"

"Well, I still try to be selective," I said. "I don't believe therapists have to be universalists when it comes to treating patients. Perhaps the great masters of psychology and psychiatry were universalists, but not me."

"Why not you?"

"Because I don't think it works. As a teacher, fine; as a practitioner, I have reservations. I don't want to use my clients as a learning tool, though I'm devoted to learning from those who I think I can truly help."

"I don't really see the difference," Shel said, letting go of my hand and moving in front of me to let two sweaty joggers run by. "So your feelings about gays are not moralistic?"

"I hope not," I said. "I've thought long and hard about it. It's a tricky piece, having strong opinions about things. I know moralism limits the intellect."

"I guess we both have strong likes and dislikes," she said. "But the spirit of openness provides amazing gifts. So what about your opinions limiting your perceptions?"

"Some of my opinions can permeate my practice if I'm not careful," I said. We moved single file again, this time making room for a grizzled, mumbling old man who rattled by, shoving a junk-heaped shopping cart.

"Don't you want to get over this mild prejudice about homosexuals?" Shel asked as she strode back beside me, taking my hand.

"My preference *is* to get over it," I said. "And that is an impetus for change. If I try to understand everything I do, then it gets in my way. Things reveal their true nature when they are ready to do so." We circled a block of shops about a mile from Shel's house, and started back.

"Maybe you don't want to look at your own dark side," Shel said, "the specter of your concealed nature."

"Challenging my perceptions doesn't work for me," I said. "I have to value them objectively and hope my understanding grows."

"Has it?"

"Sure, in some instances; in others it's narrowed. But I won't label a narrow view as faulty. So I honor my views, and in this instance use my mild homophobia to keep from possibly mistreating Professor Lesterman."

" 'To thine own self be true,' " Shel remarked. "Or more like: be true to your known self and beware of your unknown self, and don't mess with perceived perfection." A warm smile lit her lovely face as she gave me a passing kiss.

"You know how I feel about child abusers," I said. "I can't treat them, either." Her eyes narrowed.

"Before you blow your stack—I'm not in my way linking gays with child abuse. Some analysts can treat the abusers of this world, and more power to those folks. Someone has to try to help them."

Shel sighed. "But all this seems so judgmental. Weren't most abusers mistreated as children?"

"Yes, and I've treated kids who are abusive to other children."

"So you say tough shit to child abusers? No acting out allowed?"

"I wish it worked that way. Unfortunately, molested and abused children can't set aside their hurt without help, even as adults."

"But you won't help them?"

"I've tried . . . just can't develop empathy for adult abusers."

## Thirty-four / **Phil**

Our summer hummed along. Shel and I spent several weekends at Lucky's, the Symphony's '50s ball was a hoot, and Shelee dragged me off to one of her art shows in Toronto. Both Manny and Sid made important emotional discoveries, and Glo Burns kept in strange contact by referring an actress friend of hers, Willow McLendon. Willow's the female lead in

Burns-Cole's second Minneapolis movie project and currently has a supporting role in *SABOR*.

I continue to admire Gloria's business and creative skills, particularly her film expertise on the *SABOR* production. Her management style is often described enthusiastically by the business press. Though in a position to completely dominate the movie project, Gloria's not only made significant contributions to the activity herself but also let everyone else do their jobs.

Her *SABOR* production company gave a *Post Express* reporter unrestricted access to the project; a move that turned into a great public relations coup. It seems the whole Twin Cities feels like it's part of the moviemaking. There are usually a couple of articles, along with several photos, in the paper each week, and several other newspapers around the country have picked up the *SABOR* stories, too. So Gloria's project is getting all kinds of free publicity.

Sidney Simons is now seriously invested in therapy. The books he's reading, along with our sessions, have enabled him to be less compulsive and intense and to experience pleasure without feeling guilty. I decided to suggest a therapy group to him, the same one that Pam's in.

"What's a group supposed to do for me?" Sid asked skeptically. "I'm just getting comfortable with *our* conversations."

"That's why it may be time for you to move on," I said. "Consider the group a family where you can play out the past and present in a supportive environment."

"A family, huh?"

"Yeah, one that won't let you distance yourself all the time. And we can keep, drop, or schedule our sessions less frequently. You can just come in when you feel like it."

"All right. That'll get me out of this dreary office," Sid said and smiled. "I was struck by something in one of your books," he continued, "how people like me *intellectually* set themselves apart from others."

"Don't be too hard on yourself. Everyone has their distancing strategies. Again, I think the group will allow you to try out getting closer to people."

"But I don't know if I want to hear everyone's troubles," he commented. "I'm already a conflict junkie, Phil; why get further involved?"

"Ah, there's where you can help Sid-The-Rescuer. Learn to interact without getting immersed in crapola. Be selective concerning involvement."

Sid and I talked racquetball and kidded about some of the people at the sports club. I gave him the phone number of the doctor running the program and promised I'd call to recommend Sid. We agreed to meet two weeks later to review things.

"It's not like we're strangers, Sloan," Sid pointed out. "And you know you're in big racquetball trouble."

"We'll see who's in trouble on Friday," I said. I had this notion as Sid left my office—Manny, aka Emmanuel Weston, occupying the right side of my brain and Sidney the left.

I followed Sid into my outer office where a very large man, wearing dark glasses and a baseball cap, hid behind *The Sporting News.* This new client had come to me after a bizarre phone call from Duncan Cole.

"Phil, I have an unusual request," Duncan had said. "We have a player on our team who's had an unfortunate episode with one of his coaches, and we're requiring that he get counseling. I was hoping you'd see him." Duncan went on to recount the "Nate Thayer Incident," as the newspapers were calling it.

"Me?"

"You're the guy to handle him," Duncan said. "He's a big dude, and I think he needs a therapist who can stand up to him, not one of those skinny cerebromorphs."

"Cerebromorphs?"

"Oh you know, the kind of morph who thinks a lot." Duncan laughed. "Seriously, this is a big deal, Phil. Thayer's our best defensive tackle but he's suspended until the head coach is satisfied that his anger is under control. He's out of the preseason game this weekend and could miss more if he doesn't shape up. It'll affect our performance until we get him back in our lineup."

So now Nate Thayer, all 310 pounds of his six-foot-six frame, was crushing the cushions on my waiting room sofa. "You must be Nate Thayer," I said, extending my hand. "I'm Phil Sloan. How're you doing?"

"Hey, what's your program?" Nate said, getting up to shake my hand. "I expected some owl-eyed, bearded spook. You look like you might've played football."

"I did, on the freshman squad at Ohio State," I said. "Linebacker."

"You didn't play varsity?" Nate asked, settling into my overstuffed chair.

"No, there was a short-circuit in my brain," I said. "I just couldn't kill the quarterbacks. The coach got in my face—wanted me to smash everybody I hit. Tackling them seemed enough for me; so my lack of aggression got me moved to tight end, offense."

"Hey, you're supposed to stomp those suckers," Nate said. "Didn't they teach you that in high school? That's how you knock the ball loose."

"Never played in high school," I said. "I didn't get my size until my senior year when I started lifting weights."

"You made the frosh squad at OSU and you'd never played football?" Nate asked with genuine interest. "How'd you manage that?"

"I won my weight class in a bench press contest and some of my lifting buddies dared me to try out. And I ran track, played b-ball, and skied cross-country in high school when I was lighter."

"The tight end position work out?"

"I did all right. Football was a way of life at Ohio State, and I had a different agenda."

"Are you still lifting?"

"Fuckin-A, man!" I stood up, pulled my shirt off, and made the biggest biceps I could.

"I'm underwhelmed," Nate Thayer said, a little astonished at my behavior. "How much can you press?"

"Four hundred," I answered.

"Oh, bullshit! I can barely do four-twenty. Next you're going to tell me you do multiple reps."

"Three reps," I said, striking a pose. "I've got the muscle density of a Labrador retriever. I drink a quart of dog blood a day."

"Three reps? Then you're some kind of doper!" He shook his head. "Dog blood? That's all I need, a shrink who does dog." Nate got up and looked into the waiting room. "You've probably killed and eaten the doctor."

"I am a doctor and not a doper," I said, using my best Richard Nixon voice. I put my shirt back on. "I'll make you a deal: We'll arm wrestle, and the winner gets to give the other guy his one best shot. Between the belt and the neck, of course."

"No way!" Nate said, looking at me as if I were completely psychotic. "You're probably some kind of arm-wrestling geek. It's like our trainer at the Norse. He's this little Oriental guy, and he's stronger than most anyone there. He's got dog cells, too. Like a chimp—the little shit can pump unbelievable iron. Says a ninety-pound chimpanzee's stronger than the world's strongest man."

Thayer began to wave his hands around. "Wait a minute! What the hell's going on here?" he protested, taking the cap off his clean-shaven head. "I'm paying for this visit, I've been fined ten thousand dollars, my career's at stake, and we're talkin' animal crackers. Let's get on with the goddamn therapy!"

"Tell me about the fight with your coach," I said, sitting back down. I decided Thayer was an agreeable and pleasant fellow, quite unlike the newspapers' archvillain portrayal.

"You *are* a shrink?" Nate said, half smiling. "Did you read the accounts in the paper?"

"I did, yes, but I'd like to hear the original from you."

"The line coach shoved me, so I popped him . . . during scrimmage drills."

"Isn't there a lot of pushing going on during practice?" I asked.

"Yeah—don't know why I hit him."

"Were you upset?"

"I've thought about it," he said apologetically. "Henderson was demonstrating which way to move, and I guess he just pushed too hard. So I got in his face about it. Then he got right back in my face, and I slugged him. I think he overreacted—called it a brawl. It wasn't. Do you know I got a reprimand from the commissioner? He formally backed up the suspension." Nate stroked his short beard.

"The newspaper said Coach Henderson is your friend."

"Yes, we're friends," Nate said, leaning forward, elbows on his knees, face in his hands, looking at the floor. "I was an usher at his grand-niece's wedding. Can't believe he's threatened to press charges if I didn't agree to see you. I called his wife—you know—and apologized. He went home with a shiner."

"Henderson's about sixty-five, I understand."

"Oh, I've heard all this shit for a week!" Thayer flopped back in the chair. "Henderson's a big SOB. We're surrounded by violent action all the time. He can take it. You can add that I outweigh him by ninety pounds—I've heard *that* all week, too.

"The team doctor gave me a book on football violence that says I'm supposed to be this bone-crushing monster, get all kinds of perks and praise for smashing the other team, and yet be a sweet little boy the rest of the time. Maybe I can't do both. We've scuffled before—there's always scuffles. Anyway, the whole thing's been exaggerated. I'm getting the shaft!"

"Punching a sixty-five-year-old in the face may or may not be an exaggeration," I offered. "But I think Henderson cares about you." Nate Thayer eyed me seriously.

"Well he *better* care about me, and my contribution to the team."

"Do you take steroids?" I asked.

"I did in college," he said. "Haven't used them in six or eight years—turned out to be too dangerous."

We talked about his feelings during the incident with Henderson. Nate could only identify irritation.

"What about your marital history?" I asked.

Nate shifted his position, suddenly looking quite uncomfortable. "The papers picked that up too, didn't they?" He sighed. "My wife's almost as combative as I am. We've had our tiffs and she threatened to claim battering a couple of times. We worked it out. Never got counseling, though."

"Is there a pattern here?" I suggested. "Sounds like you're often in conflict with people smaller than you."

Thayer nodded.

"Do you ever take on anyone your size or larger?"

"I try to avoid fights during a game," he said. "It hurts the team. Off the field, everyone's smaller than me. Even you," he said in a joking but still threatening manner. "What would you've done if I'd taken you up on your stupid arm-wrestling challenge?"

"I'll tell you at the end of our session," I said. "Have you ever heard of 'Big Man Syndrome?' "

"Maybe . . . I don't know, what is it?"

"Society gives big people the message that says our shoulders are broad enough to take anything and everything. And big people are not allowed to have feelings of vulnerability."

"Now that's for sure," Nate said, brightening slightly. "Been told that all my life. I was always larger and more athletic than the other kids. My father used to whip me, then tell me I was too big to cry."

"How old's your father?"

"Mid-sixties," he said, looking at the floor again, shaking his head. "Sweet Jesus, so's Norm Henderson."

Nate Thayer, superstar and Pro Bowl left tackle stumbled through the next twenty minutes, telling chilling tales of a dreadful upbringing and hideous rituals of family combat. Nate was in tears by the time he finished. He described several members of his family still involved in violent conflict.

"They fight like kids," he said. "Then pretty soon we all do."

"Give me an example," I asked.

"My sister is such a bitch. For instance, she starts in on her husband and kids—you know, just ragging on them for no reason. I just want to punch her out. My father sort of orchestrates these fights. He seems to get everybody involved, including me. I mean things get so crazy sometimes. My father and brother had a fistfight at my mom's birthday last year. I had to break it up. My oldest brother's been in jail for assault."

"What happened after you broke up the fight?"

"Same thing that always happens," Nate said. "My father says we should be ashamed for fighting. Even though he was part of it. You know. We all blame each other then—until the next fight explodes."

"Is your father telling you how you should feel? Ashamed?"

"Maybe. I don't feel ashamed, just angry. But I'm not always part of the fights."

"When your father told you, Nate, that you were too big to cry after a whipping, how did you feel?"

"Angry."

"No one can say how each of us is supposed to feel," I said. "I suggest that when you see a family fight starting, leave. Not just the room, the house. Stay away for a while."

"Just get the hell out?"

"Yes. You are not responsible for their fights or for settling them. There's no rule that says you have to take everything."

"I never thought of that," Nate said. "Is this stuff going to turn me into a pussy?" he asked quite seriously, blowing his nose.

"Yes," I said, "everywhere but on the field. You'll still enjoy stomping quarterbacks. Now about the book from the team physician—I'm familiar with it, and it nails the sport. Football gives one of the worst messages of all: It supports the notion that someone can take what they want if they're big enough, and it reinforces the idea that your feelings don't count, nor do the feelings of others. Nate, if you can reserve the violence for the playing field, and be a complete pussy off the field, you might be a happier man." He frowned.

"So here's what I'd like you to do." He leaned forward in his chair, again stroking his beard. "I want you to see me every other week for a few months. I also want you to volunteer an eight-hour shift each week at the St. Paul Youth Inpatient Facility. You choose the shift, but I'd prefer it be day or swing."

"Phil, I've done volunteer work with kids before," he complained. "How's this going to be any different?"

"Because this time you'll be talking with me about your experiences," I said. "And you will be learning to have feelings as broad as your shoulders. Listen, Nate," I added, "if you'll go along with this, I'll let the coach know you're on the mend, and suggest lifting your suspension."

Giving his characteristic half-smile, Nate shrugged. "Okay, Dogdrinker, you're the man. Whatever you say."

"By the way," I said as he rose to leave, "you can come in more often if you wish. It's my feeling that you might benefit from more frequent visits. Oh, one more thing. Do you always feel like a large man, Nate?"

"No," he choked. . . . "No, not always."

"When you have those feelings—ones that don't fit with who *you are*—please pay attention to them. I'd like to hear about those next time."

**Jonah took his .357 magnum revolver along on his latest trip to town, just to see how it felt. Today would be a run-through. Now, with his trial a little more than a month away, he wanted to make some plans. He thought he'd just as well kill the lady art professor, too; wouldn't the bitch deserve**

whatever the boyfriend got? It would happen in mid-September, right after school began, before his trial.

It was almost noon when he got to the city, and he was hungry. He pulled into a café for lunch and, afterward, stopped at a phone booth on the corner. He called the homes of both Sloan and Osbornson and listened to their recordings—just to check things out. By now he knew everyone's routine, at least enough to get them all within an hour or so some night. He'd followed each person around during a day and an early evening. Trudy lived with her sister and Dena—the girls had an apartment near the university. They had day jobs and summer classes, but were usually home on weekdays by six. He'd spotted the professor lady's car twice in the parking garage across from the art school but guessed that when the university was back in full session, it would be much harder to locate. It didn't matter now, the woman spent most of her evenings with Sloan—he would just take them both at home one night.

As a little test, he drove past the girls' apartment and then west on the freeway to the Sloan and Osbornson houses. It was less than a thirty-five-minute drive in midafternoon, and traffic would be even lighter at night. Taking them all in less than an hour should not be a problem, he concluded.

There was only one thing more he wanted to do today and then he would head home. He would take a few minutes to spread a little terror.

"Alarm them, but don't overdo it," he told himself aloud. He stopped again, this time at a convenience store. He called Phil Sloan first and left a message. Then he dialed the girlfriend. To his surprise, she was home, and he delivered as much of the message as he could before she hung up on him. He laughed and went inside the store to use the can. He would not call the girls, though—that would be just too fucking obvious.

## Thirty-five / Phil

It was Tuesday afternoon, the last full week in August. When my three o'clock appointment left just before four, I noticed the message light on the phone in the outer office. It was from Shel and she sounded upset. "Please call me as soon as you're free," she said.

I called her immediately. "What's up?"

"You won't believe this! Some guy called here and said, 'You and your boyfriend are as good as dead.' He was creepy and Phil, I don't know . . . I feel sick and . . ."

"Sweetheart, listen to me. Lock the doors and windows. I'll call the police and be over in a few minutes. Okay?"

"Okay."

"Will you be all right until I get there?"

"Yes."

On a hunch, since there were no other messages on my office phone, I called home and listened to my machine. There were three calls, and one of them, at 3:19, was similar to the one Shel had just described. Next I called Deputy Hartung.

"The voice sounds very similar to the call my office got this spring," I told him. "I'm sure it's the same guy."

Hartung promised to look into it and check the phone records. He would call back, he said, and I gave him Shelee's number.

Then I went directly to Shel's.

Hartung still hadn't called by morning, so I phoned him from Shel's house—before we left for work. After holding for five minutes and getting cut off once, he finally answered. "The calls did not come from a pay phone in the 218 area code," he said.

"Then from where?" I asked.

"They could have been direct-dialed from anywhere, including Minneapolis," he said calmly. "But you have an unlisted number so . . ."

"That's right. So how did he get it? And how does he know who my girlfriend is?"

"I don't know. Are you sure it's not somebody who knows you?" He asked.

"Hell no," I said, feeling frustrated. "Carol Thornton listened to it and she thought it was her father." Shelee looked thoroughly distressed as I continued the unproductive conversation. "Have you questioned Lewis and Thornton?" I demanded.

"Yes, both Mr. Thornton and his wife said he was at the local nursing home visiting his mother all afternoon. A deputy checked with the home. The staff saw him around noon, and again in the lobby at five o'clock. We asked his mother, too," Matt Hartung went on, "but she's almost ninety and mostly out of it. Said he was there but she probably doesn't really know. Maybe you should call the metro police."

"As soon as we finish," I said. "I received a subpoena for a presentence deposition on Morton Lewis. So why wasn't I called for the trial?"

"Morton Lewis pleaded guilty," Hartung replied.

"So what about Thornton?"

"He hasn't gone to trial yet. His lawyer's working all the angles. I have a subpoena for you, for depositions for both the county prosecutor and Sveen Dunlap, Thornton's attorney."

I looked at my watch; I had an appointment at nine. "Terrific," I said. "But I'm not coming unless you put a lid on Thornton."

Matt Hartung ignored me and said, "Thornton's trial is in five weeks. If you could schedule a visit early next week, you could do both depositions in a morning or afternoon. Then you might not have to testify at the trial."

"What about the gynecologist's testimony?" I asked. "And Susan Tucker, the social worker?"

"Ms. Tucker isn't on either witness list," Hartung said, "and Dr. Brandt's testimony has been videotaped, including interrogatories—she may still have to testify at the trial if her deposition testimony is challenged.

"Dr. Sloan, if you'll come up, we can spend some time going over these threats. And I can show you pictures of Thornton and some photos of his car—off the record, of course. Personally, I can't believe he'd risk leaving the county. If he's caught, it can go against him, and then he's looking at waiting for his trial from jail. He might also have to forfeit bail."

"I'll be there Monday morning," I said. "Get those damn lawyers lined up. I hope the court throws the book at Thornton, then maybe he'll go after Sveen and leave me alone.

"Oh, Matthew," I added, "as far as Jonah Thornton taking risks, crazy people do that all the time!" I slammed the phone down.

Shelee gave me a tearful hug when I hung up and said she was going in to work. She also offered to call the metro police. Shel took the answering machine cassette I had picked up from my house the night before and gave me a kiss.

"What time will you be back *here*?" she asked—we had decided to stay at her house because she had deadbolts on both doors.

"Sometime between five-thirty and six," I said.

"I'll be home right at six," Shel said. "If you're going to be later, let me know at school. Okay?"

"I will, sweetheart. We'll get this figured out."

I called Shelee from my office shortly after eleven and we decided to have lunch together. She sounded frustrated by her morning conversations with the cops. I drove to the university and met Shel at noon in her office. It was one of those days when the city air feels and smells hot enough to burst into flame at any moment.

We walked to the Mexican café located in the cool, garden basement of Merriman Resident Hall. The place was packed with the summer-session lunch crowd. Shel and I ordered iced teas and sat out in the lobby, waiting for our table.

"I guess the local police response was as good as can be expected," Shel said wearily. "They offered to call Hartung and get Thornton's description, his car license, and so forth. They're going to look out for him in our neighborhoods and around our offices. But I'll believe the patrols when I see them. I talked with an officer named Kathleen Murell— "

"Your table is ready," the hostess said, interrupting from the doorway. We got up and followed her.

A college kid took our orders as soon as we were seated. "Anyway," Shel said, "Officer Murell listened to the recording, then asked me to send it to her. I suggested that they drop by and pick it up this evening when they were on patrol." Shelee began waving her fork around, her voice rising. I gently took her wrist and smiled. "But guess what?" Shel said, setting the fork down. "Kathy bitch declined; she said the cops could cover more ground by patrolling, rather than stopping to chat with us. See, that's why I think it's bullshit."

The following Monday morning I left home and headed for Stone Lake to meet with Matt Hartung. The depositions were scheduled for 9:00 and 10:30. I arrived in Stone Lake at 7:45 and went directly to the sheriff's department. Deputy Hartung, who seemed fairly intelligent, met me in his office. He was in his early thirties, slightly under six feet tall, with thickset shoulders; he had curly black hair, a neat mustache, and glasses.

"Dr. Sloan," he said as we carried coffee and doughnuts into a small conference room, "I'm impressed that you were able to keep Trudy Thornton in Minneapolis. I didn't think it was possible."

"You can thank Susan Tucker for that. If you ever met her, you'd understand. She makes the system work for kids."

"Trudy's better off away from here," he said quietly. Then Hartung showed me Jonah Thornton's mug shots and pictures of his white Buick and a beat-up, red Chevy pickup. Matt handed me the photos; license numbers and brief descriptions were penned on the bottom of the photos. Jonah Thornton looked rather ordinary: thinning dark hair and a lean, apathetic face. He was clean-shaven, with a detached, perhaps shrewd look in his eyes—a look which gave me the chills.

"Thanks," I said, putting the photos in my folder.

"You bet," he said. "Just don't say where you got them. Technically, Thornton's still just a suspect."

"What's this guy's state of mind?" I asked, thinking out loud.

Hartung scratched his head and took off his silver, wire-rim glasses. "You know, I've talked with Thornton in person only once since we arrested him," he said. "He behaves like most other defendants charged with their first serious crime. He's cooperative, but holding something back. I really can't read him. He and his father—the father's dead now—have always been on-again/off-again tax protesters. He's got some kind of long-term IRS hassle going with the feds."

I tapped the folder with the pictures. "Have you given these to the city cops?"

"No. In fact I haven't heard from them."

"They didn't contact you? Are you sure?" I asked incredulously.

"I'm in charge of both cases," he said. "I'd know if they tried."

"You'll be hearing from an officer . . . uh, Kathleen Murell or someone in her department. I'm calling her as soon as I get back to town."

The depositions took less time than I'd expected. When I arrived back in my office shortly after one, I picked up the phone to call Shel, then remembered she was working at a junior high school until after two. Instead, I called the police.

After a few false tries, the operator finally connected me to Officer Murell. I identified myself and recounted my discussion with Hartung. "So why no follow-through here?" I asked.

"Well, to be quite honest, Dr. Sloan—"

I interrupted. "Whenever I hear that phrase, Ms. Murell, I wonder if it means that most of the time you are not honest! For example, when you told Dr. Osbornson that you would check out the situation. You can't do that if you don't know who and what to look for! Right?"

There was a pause. "I want to apologize, Dr. Sloan, both to you and Ms. Osbornson. I have your tape right here, and I will phone Detective Hartung as soon as we're through. We've just been swamped; there're two large conventions in town and all the tourists . . ."

She rambled on for another few minutes, basically covering the same stuff. "Is there anyone else who might be threatening you or joking with you?"

I was ready to blow my stack. "That's the second time I've been asked that question! And the answer is no. Perhaps *you* and Detective Hartung might want to discuss that as part of *your* ongoing investigation," I said. "There will be one, won't there?" I asked coldly.

"If you're serious about waiving your right to a speedy trial, you'd be helping me out a bunch," Sveen Dunlap told Jonah. "The prosecutor's busy as hell, and so's the court. They'll go along with a continuance if I hint at a plea change. Most clients want to get these things out of the way."

"Well, I've got one more hay cuttin', and the corn won't dry out till almost November, so any delay helps me at the farm," Jonah said. "I've always done my own harvesting, and I'd like to do this year's, too."

"The trial might be put off until January; that all right?"

"No problem. What kind of pickle you get yourself into, Sveen?"

"A long, interstate land fraud trial. Hell of a mess."

Just what the doctor ordered, Jonah decided, when he left his attorney's office. He wanted to celebrate, so he drove to Minneapolis to look for a woman. As Thornton wove through the midday city traffic, he thought about the last time at Krystol's Bar, when he watched a couple of girls working the lunch crowd of construction workers and tradesmen. Now he found a table and sipped a beer, trying to decide which of the noontime ladies—there were three this time—would give him the best ride. The trial delay will help me complete my harvest in Minneapolis, too, he thought as he studied the crowd.

Of the three bar girls, he was attracted most by the dark, Mexican-looking woman. She wasn't much older than Carol for one thing. But it was her long-sleeved blouse in the hot bar that most interested him; the other two girls wore tank tops. I bet she's got needle tracks, he ventured. If she was into the expensive dope, maybe she could help him find what he needed right there in town.

"Hey, Sugarspoon," he called to her. "You had lunch yet? There's a Mexican joint just down the street."

## Thirty-six / Shelee

Phil's trip to Stone Lake and our phone calls to the authorities did little to help us feel safer. At first I was angry at Phil for not telling me about the threatening phone call in April, though his reasoning seemed sound. There was nothing I could have done then except worry. But now things had really changed; the pictures of Thornton and his vehicles made us uncomfortably paranoid. We saw white sedans everywhere. Though I doubted Thornton would drive his old pickup to Minneapolis, it didn't keep me from being suspicious of every older, red truck I saw. We talked about it until we were both exhausted, wanting to believe that they were one-time crank calls from someone other than Jonah Thornton. Finally, we decided there was nothing else to do but stay alert and put the rest out of our minds. And because I had volunteered for an art project at the nearby junior high, it was easy to do—I was frustrated even after the first day.

"I'm not connecting with these kids," I complained to Phil. "These students were the ones who had to make up work before they could move to the next grade when school started—the word 'student' may be a misnomer. Most of them missed school because of truancy; only a few had legitimate reasons.

"My schedule goes from eleven to noon, and then again for an hour after lunch. Most of them don't want to take art and are irritated about being in my class. I ate lunch with them today and tried to get acquainted. They're absolute slobs; they threw french fries at each other and made a big mess. Why am I doing this? I'm facing two weeks of this crap!"

"Put a bouquet of flowers on the lunch table and tell the kids art is part of everyday life," Phil suggested. "See what happens."

What a dumb idea, I thought—junior high kids and flowers? But I was willing to try anything. So for the rest of the week, I took in a fresh bouquet every day. "So it's working?" Phil asked.

"Like a charm," I said and smiled.

"Most of the kids are really involved in the class now, working on a wide variety of art projects—ones that specifically interest them," I said. It was Saturday and we were in my kitchen, sipping our morning coffee, watching heavy rain splash down on my driveway. "And *they're* bringing the flowers next week," I said. Someone even brought in a red-and-white checkered tablecloth for lunch on Friday. The kids who were going down the street for burgers are bringing them back to sit with us. Of course, now there's competition to see who can make the best vase for the flowers. Several teachers asked me what was going on. I gave you the credit, sweetie."

Phil walked over to the window and watched the downpour. "I wonder if the principal is bright enough to keep these kids engaged?" Phil said. "For instance, why not encourage these students to decorate tables throughout the school year? Maybe their interest in art will develop into something personal. Perhaps someone may want to work with a florist during the winter. No telling where this might go. Thanks for trying my idea."

"Thanks for suggesting it. I didn't think kids that age would respond to flowers."

"Kids are amazing when you stimulate their creativity. I read where this phone company in Georgia was frustrated with customer complaints about their phone bills. So they asked some seventh graders to come up with improved billing forms. Their customers apparently love the new ones and it put a bunch of MBAs out of jobs."

I laughed. "What are we going to do about this weather and the kids?" I asked as I joined Phil at the window. We'd planned on taking Heidi and Fritz fishing for the day.

"Let's take them to lunch, and then over to my house; they can play computer games," Phil proposed. "We'll fix dinner with 'em, go to a movie or watch a video."

I called Abby to tell her about the new plans. "That's great," my sister said. "Thanks for taking them; we've made plans for this afternoon. You really want them this evening, too?"

"Sure," I said, "they can stay overnight, and I'll bring them back in the morning, 'bout ten o'clock or so. I'm going over to Trish's tomorrow to help her paint her living room and kitchen."

We had a typically enjoyable afternoon and evening with the two kids. Fritz and Heidi loved playing a space travel game on Phil's computer, zapping and zooming around space all afternoon. Just before dinner, Heidi asked me a question about gravity.

"It's what keeps me off the ceiling, sweetheart," I said. "Also it may be a gender issue: it's my opinion that gravity treats women more unkindly than it does men. But ask Uncle Phil, he's the gravity expert around here." My niece gave me a strange look, walked over, and pulled at Phil's sleeve.

"What's gravity?" she asked as Fritz roamed through the kitchen.

"Gravity is the force exerted by mass that warps the time-space continuum," Phil said.

"You're not serious, Philbert," I said. "Give the kids a straight answer."

"It's the straightest answer I know." He smiled. "That's directly from Albert Einstein's general theory of relativity."

"Did he also think this one up on the way to work?" I asked.

"Probably. If you guys give me a minute, I'll demonstrate." Phil rummaged through his junk drawer and pulled out an orange balloon sporting the words HAPPY BIRTHDAY. He chuckled and then blew it up, stopping when the balloon was about half full.

"Okay, girls and boys," Phil said, "let's say this balloon is space, and the words, HAPPY BIRTHDAY, are time. Notice that the words are spread evenly across the balloon; we'll call this balloon time-space. Gravity warps time and space like this." He held out the balloon to Fritz.

"Try pushing your fingers into words on the balloon," he said.

"Notice how the words stretch out when you poke the balloon," he continued. "That's what happens to time; gravity distorts time-space and time gets longer, just as HAPPY BIRTHDAY does." He held the balloon while Heidi tried it.

"Cute," I said. "You had this planned out ahead of time."

"I swear, Shel, I didn't. Haven't you noticed that when you spend time with young people, it stimulates the reckless nature of your imagination? Their innate curiosity is infectious. This balloon thing just occurred to me."

"Now he's really putting us on, don't you think?" I said to the kids.

"Dr. Philbrain," Heidi asked, "can you prove this?"

"Can't prove it personally, but there's several proofs around. For instance, scientists have put these very accurate atomic clocks in orbit, and they run slightly faster than the same ones on earth."

"Why?"

"Because there's less gravity in space."

"Is that true?" she asked.

"Yes," Phil answered. "And the difference in time rate is exactly what Einstein predicted. There's other, more complicated examples, one with the planet Mercury, and another with radioactive decay. One more point: Did you guys know a black hole has so much gravity that light can't get out?"

"No way, Philbrain," Fritz said.

"Yep, in black holes, gravity is so strong, and space-time is so distorted, that time does not pass. It actually stands still."

Both kids looked doubtful.

Phil popped the balloon with his next demonstration, claiming it was the Big Bang. "Look up the planet Mercury in the space game program; they might show how its time in orbit is changed by *way* too much gravity from the sun," he suggested, "or try a black hole." Phil poured me a glass of wine. "You kids go planet hopping, we'll fix dinner."

I could hear the children playing as Phil and I made dinner. Their laughter drew me from the kitchen and I went to Phil's office and looked in on them. They both gave me little finger waves, then went back to their game. I watched them for a moment.

"Dinner's in about ten—," I said, unable to finish my sentence. God, I love those kids, I thought wistfully.

Next morning after breakfast, I stopped by my house, fed the cats, and changed into a painting shirt and an old pair of shorts for the project at Trish's. Then I drove the kids to my sister's. The night before, Phil had found more balloons—the kids had inked PHIL SLOAN TIME ZONE on them with a laundry marker, along with a few choice illustrations. They were in the backseat blowing up the balloons, both eager to demonstrate advanced physics to Abby and Tim.

Tim came out to the car when we pulled into the driveway.

"What have you got?" he asked the kids.

"Space balloons," Heidi said.

"Dad, guess what?" Fritz said. "Einstein's theory of relativity has become crystal clear to me. I'll show you."

Tim smiled broadly and winked at me. "Okay," he said to both kids, "let's see what you've got."

Trish was painting her front room when I arrived. "Wow, are you ambitious," I said. "How long have you been working?"

"Since five-thirty—I couldn't sleep. Will's over at Seth's until tonight after dinner," she explained, rolling Subtle Peach over the remaining white walls. "Terry and I had a fight Friday, and I stewed about it all yesterday. I guess that's why I couldn't sleep."

I picked up some masking tape and began covering the polished wood baseboards below the two walls next in line for painting. Trish's home is a beautiful old two-story with sloping twelve-foot ceilings, built around 1915.

"I'll get the baseboards, Dr. O.," Trish said, climbing down from her ladder. "Will you do the touch-up along the cornices? You're the artist, and I'm afraid to touch them."

We yakked on through the morning and early afternoon, and finished painting her kitchen in a warm, almond white. By then, all the windows were open and the temperature in the house was above eighty-five degrees. The humidity was way up, too, from all the rain the day before. While we cleaned up, Trish got a bottle of white wine out of the fridge and poured us each a glass. We snacked on crackers and day-old fried chicken.

Though I had wrapped my hair up, I still got paint in it, mainly from dabbing the sweat off of my forehead and neck. I tried combing the paint out. "The goddamn paint's almost dry," I said. "I better wash it before we have to cut it out." We were starting to get pretty silly after finishing the wine, including a half-empty bottle of red. Then we switched to beer.

"I think I'm drunk," I said as I cleaned the kitchen sink so I could wash my hair. "You know, my hair is driving me nuts," I continued. "I probably should get it cut, but Phil fancies it long. Oh, well, the cool weather will be here soon—guess I like it long, too."

"Why don't you let me give you a perm?" Trish asked. "I've got one."

"I don't know."

"It'll give your hair more body," she said, "and keep it off your neck and shoulders."

I finished washing my hair, trying to decide. Trish handed me a towel and waved the perm at me. "Why not?" I said. So Trish wrapped my hair and applied the perm solution.

I called Phil to tell him I was going to be late. Trish and I ate macaroni and cheese and a green salad for dinner. "I've had enough alcohol for any Sunday I can remember," I told Trish.

"Me, too," she said, and went to answer the door. It was about seven o'clock now and old Slinger Seth came in with Will. Seth said hello to Trish and nodded to me. He fondled his holsterless hip, said goodbye to Will, and left.

"We'd better check the curl," Trish said and unwound a few curlers. "Oh *yes,* lots of it," she said and led me to the sink. She rinsed out the solution and put on the neutralizer. "C'mon," she said several minutes later, motioning again to the sink. She removed all the curlers and washed my hair. Next, I sat at the table while Trish combed out the curls and blew my hair dry.

"You guys are screwing up the television," Will yelled from the other room. Then he walked into the kitchen. "Can you turn off the—" There was a strange light in his eyes when he looked at me, amazed. "Shelee," he said, "do you really want your hair to look like that?"

"Like what?" I demanded.

Trish began to laugh. "Oh, it's not so bad—I think there's an antidote in the package."

"Antidote?" I yelled, heading for the bathroom. "My hair needs an antidote?" I should have known something was wrong when I could see curls in my peripheral vision—without moving my eyes.

"Come back here," Trish said, as she and Will followed me, laughing.

I ran through the living room and was just to the hall when my hair snagged in the doorway. Will and Trish really laughed now.

I stepped sideways into the bathroom and held back my hair so I could see myself. "Oh, my god!" I shouted. "I've got hair from hell!" I wrapped my arms around my head and charged back to confront my friend and her child. They were both choking with laughter.

"You people need CPR?" I said, but it only made them laugh harder.

We looked in the perm kit—sure enough there was a straightener for overcurled results. "Just pin it back so I can see," I said. "I'll use this stuff tomorrow. I don't work until Tuesday, and Phil has to see this; that is if I can get my head in the car."

"Thanks a lot," I told Trish, and drove to Phil's, hoping I wouldn't get stopped by the cops. Phil whooped when he saw me.

"You look like Little Orphan Annie with a neck and eyes," he said.

"I also have these," I said, squeezing my upper arms together to accentuate my breasts. Then it hit me! Time was right for Boob Attack. I briefly struck my Mrs. Mussolini/Floria Ducé pose before becoming the Portuguese street woman of my twisted imagination. I ripped my shirt open and undid my bra as the shirt buttons rolled across the floor. Phil just falls apart when I do this.

"Aw, jeez," Phil said. "Is this what I think it is?"

"You like these *melones,* huh, Yankee boy?" I asked, hoisting my breasts. "Maybe you like do a little ficky-fick? Hmm?" I strutted my stuff.

"Ficky-fick?" Phil said. "You must suffer from a rare form of geographic schizophrenia. I suppose you've forgotten your underwear again?"

Phil backed into the living room while I pushed against his chest; he was now putty in my hands. "I will not have my profession maligned!" I said, shoving him with both hands. "Of course no underwear. In my line of business a girl has to work fast." By now Phil was laughing and could only sputter. I gave him one last shove onto the couch.

Now I had him where I wanted him! I grabbed his hair, shoved his face into my breasts as I straddled his legs, and pinned him to the back of the couch. "My *melones* will turn you into a jelly-brain!" I shouted, squishing his head between my breasts. "Take this Yankee boy! THUPP, THUPP-THUPP," I said, and tipped him sideways onto his back. I kicked off my pants and lay on top of him. "Oh, Doctor Tiny-Butt Sloan," I cooed in my best Carmen voice, "This señorita needs you." He tried to reply, but I muffled his words with my kisses.

## Thirty-seven / Phil

Shelee Red-Mop and I went running Monday morning at six-thirty. Shel wore a tight bandana, trying to hide her frizzy hair. I fixed breakfast after our shower while she messed with her perm. When I kissed her goodbye a little before nine o'clock, she was still trying to comb her hair out. It was Labor

Day and I headed back to my place for some paperwork and a few chores, like installing a deadbolt on my front door.

There was a message from Lucky waiting for me when I got home. He wanted to talk about our Montana plans, which reminded me that the trip was less than two months away. I didn't return the call, but went downstairs to get my tools.

I was getting irritated as I drilled holes in my front door for the deadbolt. The inaction by the sheriff and police wasn't acceptable, yet it seemed there was nothing we could do about it. The additional lock was a good idea, though—now I'd have deadbolts on both doors.

Suddenly, the end of October couldn't come fast enough. Feeling really burned out with city life, I wished the three of us were leaving for Olie Volborg's place tomorrow. Although I'd seen him a few times in the Twin Cities when he visited Lucky, it had been over a dozen years since I had visited his home near Lodgepole, Montana. At that time, I'd just finished med school and needed a vacation from D.C., so I flew out to Billings to see Olie and spend some time in the mountains backpacking by myself. Olie was a friend from years before, when Lucky took me there when I was fifteen to do some horse packing and fishing in the high lakes that dot the Rocky Mountain highlands.

I was feeling relieved after finishing my internship and had a fresh attitude about life. My residency at a D.C. hospital was due to start in early September. In the meantime, I had a little more than a week to play. There's a high plateau in the mountains above Lodgepole. The area has at least a hundred lakes, around timberline, above 9,000 feet.

The trail starts a few miles up the road from Olie's, at 6,000 feet elevation, and climbs the next 3,000 feet to the plateau in about five miles. Once you get to the 9,000-foot level, it's a fairly flat hike to a great number of lakes. The scenery's beautiful, and there are different kinds of trout in the various lake systems. I was going to fly-fish for rainbow trout, cutthroat, brookies, and goldens. Some of the lakes are also stocked with grayling, a magnificent fish, but not great eating.

The first part of the hike would be an ugly experience for an out-of-shape medical student from sea level. The intern programs—well, poker, too—gave me little time for my usual activities of racquetball and weightlifting.

I'd been at Olie's for a couple of days, and planned to leave early the next morning for the high country. He offered to let me use his horses and pack setup, but walking and carrying a backpack was my way of getting back into shape.

A car pulled into Olie's driveway around midafternoon. Sarah Andrews sat in the passenger seat, the first in my series of ladies whose names started with the letter *S*. And it was Sarah who got out of the car and came knocking at our door. Seems that she and her friend were looking for the plateau trail and decided to stop for directions. I could see Olie off to one side when I opened the door for her.

"Can I help you?" I said. Sarah spoke with an English accent that added additional interest to the situation—I love accents. I glanced in Olie's direction to see his reaction. He exhaled a low whistle.

"The plateau trail's at the end of this road," I said. "About six miles west. Where are you headed?"

Sarah gestured toward the car. "My girlfriend and I are going to Lightning Lake for a few days. We'll probably hike around some."

"I'm going that way tomorrow," I said. "Sounds like you're from England."

She gave a lively smile. "I am. So's Annie," she said, pointing to the car again. "I work for the British Consulate in New York. My friend works for British Air—she lives in San Francisco. We usually spend our vacations together. This'll be the first time we've backpacked in the Rockies."

"Well, Lightning Lake is a cinch to find," I said, "the trail's well marked. I'll be ready to go first thing in the morning if you two would like a companion who knows the territory. I'm going to fish several lakes in the next few days, and Lightning would be a good base camp—planned to fish there, too. Actually, I was going to camp at Cathedral Lake. It's just a little farther and gets much less foot traffic than Lightning. I can show it to you on the map."

Ms. Andrews began to fidget, and I realized my brain was short-circuiting into motor-mouth syndrome. So I concluded, saying, "I can go with you tomorrow morning. It'll be cooler to hike then, too . . . uh, also."

"I'll go ask Annie," Sarah said. She smiled as she turned, sashaying to the car, tossing her long brown hair, "All right if we camp in your backyard for the night?"

Olie grinned and I called, "Affirmative!"

Sarah chatted with her friend for a minute, then stepped back as Annie, crunching fir cones beneath the rental car's tires, pulled in next to Olie's truck. Olie, the perfect host, offered to let the women sleep inside; but they declined and set up their tent behind the house. Fortunately, Olie was between dogs that summer and, for a change, his yard was clean of animal carcasses and dog crap.

After they got their stuff set up, the ladies were quite sociable—we sat around in the late afternoon, drinking some of Olie's single malt Scotch and getting acquainted. They pitched in, helping with dinner and the cleanup.

The two Englishwomen seemed pleased to find some good conversation in the wilds of Montana and were particularly interested in Olie's stories about Great Britain during World War II.

"Well, girls, I first met Phil's uncle when we left Norway together on a boat for England," Olie said, his Scotch-oiled manner a little too familiar. "Stayed in Britain, I did, and old Lucky Osbornson moved on to America—he picked up the name, Lucky, in the Pacific. In the navy, you know." Olie poured us all more Scotch.

"We kept in touch through all the hostilities. An' after the war, he wrote me from Minneapolis, so I moved there and stayed with him. But I didn't stay long. He and I took a car trip out here, playin' cards and chasin' women. Well, I owed that damn fool so much money by the time we got to Lodgepole, I sent him back to Minnesota without me. Took me six months to pay him back." Olie laughed as he went to the kitchen for some ice, then returned and freshened our drinks.

Sarah and Annie, who were experienced canoeists and backpackers, talked about their outdoor adventures—vacations mostly in the northern Midwest, including the Boundary Waters. "We've both been running, trying to get in shape for this altitude," Annie explained. "If this is fun, we're going to try Colorado or the Sierra next year."

"I come to Washington about twice a month for business at the embassy," Sarah said. "Perhaps we could tour around some."

"That would be fun," I said. "I'd welcome a break from work at the hospital."

It was about nine-thirty as the evening light began to fade. "We're exhausted," Annie said. "We flew in from New York and San Francisco this morning, then drove down from Billings. . . . Thanks for letting us stay here."

They both got up. "Guess we'll turn in," Sarah said.

The next morning, we loaded our stuff into the back of Olie's truck; I rode with him, and the Brits followed us up the road. The massif of the plateau rose ahead—above the forest—as we rattled into the parking area. Off to the northwest and a full three thousand feet higher, Le Pic Roux towered above the plateau. That morning, the peak lived up to its name, standing red in the morning sky, the sunlight creeping down its northeast face.

"What's with these grizzly bear warning signs?" Sarah asked, pointing at a Forest Service poster of a ferocious-looking bear standing on its hind legs.

"The closest grizzly is a hundred miles away in Yellowstone," Olie explained. "The Forest Service puts these signs up all over—they want to con campers into keeping a clean camp. Then, pointing to me, he said, "Sonny boy here can handle any bear situations. He'll just ask the motherfucker to lay down and explain his problems."

"My, you do have a way with words, Mr. Volborg," Sarah said and smiled too broadly, her eyes flashing irritation.

Because Olie had become a little stupid the evening before —trying to get too close to the ladies—I had the feeling things might erupt between him and Sarah. So I climbed into the back of the pickup and began handing down gear faster than they could handle it. Soon everything was stacked around the truck, and I jumped down. We loaded our food, then attached the sleeping bags and other loose gear to our backpacks.

I believe Olie got the message, because he accepted the girls' thanks and headed down the road. "See you guys in a few days," he called.

"Your friend's quite a character," Sarah remarked as Olie departed.

"You don't know the half of it," I said. "If you ever met my Uncle Lucky . . . well, Olie would sound like Winston Churchill in comparison."

"You mean you're *actually* related to some of these people?" Annie asked.

Mildly irritated at what I perceived as a snobbish question, I said, "Perhaps," and left it at that.

We headed up the trail in an air of interesting tension, the women leading the way. Soon the only thing on my mind was getting up the three thousand vertical feet that lay ahead of us. The ladies each wore fine hiking shorts. Two beautiful butts and four long, feminine legs walking up the trail ahead of me was some inspiration, but as the sweat began running through my headband, the inspiration faded in importance. After three-quarters of an hour, the women decided it was time for a break. We'd been talking along the way, and I hadn't paid much attention to anyone's condition except my own. When we stopped, they were as tired as I was.

"Running doesn't come close to preparing one for this kind of hike," Annie said. "How far do you think we've come?"

I got my map out and estimated that we were less than a fourth of the way. When we finished gasping, our talk turned to the scenery, and we started up the trail again. Two hours later, at the 9,000-foot level, I was in a red Zen of pain. The last thousand vertical feet was accomplished one hundred steps at a time, with a rest after each hundred. We each took turns counting.

The three of us flopped down in the grass next to the outlet stream of the first lake and rested, then ate our lunches and blessed Olie for the good food he'd sent. I took off my boots and stuck my burning feet into the creek—goddamn, it felt good! The women did the same.

## Thirty-eight / Phil

"Okay, Dr. Sloan, where the hell is Cathedral Lake?" Annie asked. "It better be close, or I'm going to die."

"It's two miles or so," Sarah offered. "I looked at the map during lunch. And only about three hundred feet elevation gain, and we're there. We just head toward the red peak. Right, Phil?"

I nodded, saving my strength. We packed up our stuff and headed for Pic Roux, traversing a difficult two miles of broken moraine. After about an hour's hike, we reached Cathedral, then walked around the shore, through grassy meadows filled with wildflowers, and found a good campsite near the inlet. The camping spot, next to one of three streams that feed the lake, was about fifty yards from the shore, in a small grove of alpine fir.

Trout rose in the lake's inlet swirl as we set up our camp; all of us were so tired that hardly anyone talked for the first half hour. The women erected a roomy, two-person dome tent, and I set up my smaller tent a short distance away. As we got our sleeping bags, air mattresses, food, and cook gear, the conversation picked up—our strength was returning.

We arranged the cooking area and gathered wood; it became obvious to me that Sarah and Annie knew their way around a wilderness camp. I noticed the women's superior camping equipment and decided this was quite an improvement over camping by myself. Neither of them did any "poor me" bullshit that I'd expected from city women. Rather than being pleasantly surprised, I asked my psychiatrist self, Mr. Chauvinist, why don't you quit prejudging?

I blew up my air mattress, laid it next to my tent, and put my sleeping bag on it. Then I put my extra shirt and down vest in the stuffing bag for a pillow and lay down for a nap. Sarah came over to sit on a rock a few feet away, but first took the leather gloves she used for wood gathering and lay them on the rock for a cushion.

"Easier on my bum," she said adjusting the gloves. "I can see how the lake got its name. My god this is beautiful—it *is* like a cathedral—a good choice, Phil. We've got the whole place to ourselves." I managed a smile. My eyelids were half closed, my cap partly over my face. Sarah paused for a moment, then said, "I can see you want to snooze. Visit with you later."

I'm not sure how long I slept, but the tree shadows had moved a bit, and I felt refreshed. The two women laughed and chatted somewhere down near the lake, the trees blocking my view. I picked up my pack rod and fishing gear and headed down the inlet stream to the lake. The two of them were sitting close together on a log that was partly in the water. They had changed clothes, and their hair was up in towels. "How did you guys wash your hair?" I asked. "The water's got to be freezing."

"Very quickly," Sarah replied. "We actually went swimming—skinny-dipping I believe it's called." She paused and let her hair loose, shaking it in the sunlight. "We thought about asking you to join us, but you were dozing. Would you have?"

"Perhaps," I said, feeling manipulated in spite of the invitation's appeal. I think they expected a further response, but I was silent. Then I put my fishing rod together carefully, deliberately. I felt the same tension I'd sensed at the start of the hike, but would not feel that way again on this trip—the next time I would experience it was in D.C., more than six months later—the advent of the Sarah Andrews sexual dilemma.

Fish were still working in the inlet water, so I plopped my fly in the feeding dimples. A fish immediately took it, and I reeled in a short, chunky cutthroat. "Let's have trout for dinner," I called. They agreed, so I kept the fish and caught a few more. I was using Olie's special trout fly, the Guza bug, and the fish went crazy for it. I asked the women if they wanted to try fishing. Neither was interested, so I fished until I had enough for dinner. I was pleased when Sarah and Annie took my stringer and cleaned the fish.

Our first dinner was damned tasty, including the fish which we wrapped in foil, along with some spices, and put in the fire for about ten minutes. The trout had bright orange flesh and tasted like salmon.

"This fish is absolutely delicious," Annie said. Sarah nodded in agreement, spitting trout bones into the fire. "Are they always this good and this color?" she asked.

"When there's freshwater shrimp in a lake, the fish are usually pink or orange like these," I said. "Cutthroat's the best eating, although golden trout can be slightly better—if you can catch them."

"I vote for trout every night, Dr. Phil Fisher," Sarah Andrews said. I passed my plastic bottle full of wine over to the girls.

The wine was supposed to last me for four days, but the three of us finished it off then and there. Our meal was completed with chocolate bars, dried fruit, and coffee.

The air became quite chilly after the sun went down, and it was almost dark by the time we finished dinner and the dishes. We put on our warmest clothes, stoked up the fire, and laid out our sleeping bags on a plastic ground cloth. The right thing to do was to sleep under the stars, even though it was cold—the night too beautiful to miss, the tents handy if it rained. . . . Our fire died down, we drank hot chocolate and talked.

A full moon rose in the eastern sky as we got into chilly sleeping bags. We were still now and watched the moon work its magic on the scenery. The four mountains that form the cathedral cirque were bathed in cool, pale cream. First, the peak of the tallest mountain, Pic Roux, was illuminated. As the moonlight worked its way down Pic Roux, the faces of the three nearby peaks became visible, the mystery of their still jet-black western faces only slightly revealed. The south end of Cathedral Lake, now rippled by a light wind, sparkled with the moon's reflection.

We woke to a sun dimmed by thin cloud cover and a pine squirrel who'd taken a disliking to our location. It was cold and frost covered the grass and our sleeping bags. The squirrel showed its displeasure by running up and down a nearby tree, raising all kinds of chittery hell. Annie, as it turned out, was into throwing things at the wildlife.

"Get out of here, you bloody rodent," she yelled, throwing a stick at the streaking squirrel, who obliged and left for friendlier parts. We ate breakfast and I got ready for my first fishing foray. The Brits decided not to accompany me, instead choosing to stay in camp and take it easy.

So I struck out alone, carrying my daypack and fishing gear, and hiked over a nearby ridge, down into a shallow, boulder-filled valley to Five Point Lakes. The upper three lakes are barren, not deep enough to keep from freezing solid in the winter. The two lower lakes are small, but quite deep, and I caught some good-sized rainbows in both. The cutthroats back at Cathedral were better eating than these 'bows, so I released the fish. After lunch, I realized how tired I was from the previous day's hike, so I lay down on the grass, behind some stunted pines for wind protection, and slept for over an hour. There were thunderheads building over the peaks when I woke up, and I decided to head back to camp. It was a good decision.

The wind picked up and the weather threatened by the time I arrived at camp. The women had gathered up all the gear and stowed it in my tent. "You can move in with us for the storm," Sarah said. "How was fishing?" I looked into their tent and saw my sleeping bag and air mattress already laid out.

"Fishing was fine," I said as I put my equipment away. The first thunderclap echoed on our side of the peaks. I managed a weak smile. "Thanks for the invitation. Could use some company—I hate these mountain storms."

The rain rushed across the lake, burst into our camp, and pounded on the tent, amplifying the storm. The noise made talk impossible. Lightning crashed close by, the thunder almost simultaneous with the flash—too close for anything but fear. We lay on our sleeping bags, occasionally exchanging smiles for reassurance. The rain turned to hail and the din intensified.

"Make sure you're completely on your air mattresses, in case of a lightning strike!" I yelled to the women.

"This is terrible!" one of them hollered.

"I'm scared shitless of lightning!" I shouted.

No one heard me, the furious noise overwhelmed us. I lay there with my eyes closed for most of the storm's forty minutes of hell, opening them only to check my watch. The shattering lightning flashes escalated to a point where they seemed continuous, and concerned about getting sick, I concentrated on keeping my lunch down. It seems funny now, but that helped the storm pass more quickly.

The rain finally quit, and we emerged from the tent to watch the storm boiling into the northeast. A few inches of hail lay on the ground and we had a mock snowball fight to celebrate our relief. We threw hail at one another's feet, splattering our shoes and pants. Our spirits rose even higher when the sun came out.

Sarah ducked behind a tree to avoid a speeding ice ball. "Let's call a truce!" Annie suggested, dropping her load of hail and knocking ice off her pants.

A pika beeped at us from the boulder slide above the camp. The small gray critter scurried across the grass at the base of the slide. It dug frantically in the hail, then stood on its hind feet and munched shoots.

"Is that a chinchilla?" Sarah asked, charmed by the pika's behavior.

"They might be related," I said.

The urge to write something struck me unexpectedly as I walked toward my tent to get my fishing tackle. Not quite sure what I wanted to put down, I decided to write a list so I put pencil and paper in my shirt pocket. Sometimes ideas seemed to only flutter on the edge of my thoughts, but I'd learned to respond to them anyway, no matter how vague, for I hoped this would lead me to a better understanding of myself.

I headed down to the lake to catch some dinner, crunching through the hail as I walked. There was no dry place to sit—slush still covered everything. I cleaned off a log that lay next to the lake and sat on my gloves, leaning the rod against my knee. After I finished tying on a fly, I remembered my idea about a list, so I took the paper out of my pocket and wrote three names on it. I read each name aloud and experienced a moment of utter sadness, but the feeling passed as I began to fish.

Sarah was starting the Primus stove when I returned with the fish. Meanwhile, Annie was in another conflict with the local fauna. A dipper worked the stream, bobbing up and down, leaving a dollop of poop on an occasional downstroke. Annie threw rocks at the bird, but it completely ignored her.

"I kinda like that bird," I said. "Glad you're a bad shot."

"The little fucker shit right where we have the food stored!" she said, pitching another rock at the bird. A moment later it buzzed off downstream.

The stove sputtered to life, and Sarah looked up at her friend. "Annie, all you had to do was swear at it; it's a very perceptive bird. Sticks and stones, Dearie."

"I'll stone the son of a bitch if he comes back," Annie replied.

I asked Annie to help me find some dry wood. "You have superior command of the English language," I told her as she picked up her gloves. We went foraging while Sarah started dinner. The damp wood made a smoky fire, and the fish cooked slowly—it became our second course. The sun had warmed the surroundings a little, so we again decided to sleep out. A few patches of hail lingered in the shaded places.

I slept well, but got up once in the middle of the night to take a leak. The moon had now moved low behind the mountains, revealing a sky full of stars. As I gazed at the constellations arrayed across the sky, I could see traces of the storm a long way off, somewhere to the northeast. It flashed occasional silent lightning, illuminating the peaks for a split second. The peaks then became invisible again, and I lay down to contemplate *massive* and *invisible* as I fell back to sleep.

The morning's view of the lake and mountains was one of the most beautiful I've ever seen. A thin fog floated over the lake and surrounding valley. The fog's transparency allowed me to see the dark lake and some indefinite shapes in the veiled countryside. The fog below the peaks made them appear suspended above the valley. A few wisps of mist swam in the clear air around the summits. The sun, rising in front of the mountains, played tag with the mists, coloring them yellow, then pink as the mist moved between the alpine shadows and sunlight. The mountains themselves seemed to be moving slowly forward through the fog as the sun brightened their flanks. The women continued to sleep soundly while I watched the spectacle. After a while, I got up and started the coffee.

The next three days were filled with good fishing, pleasant hikes, adequate food, and great scenery. On the afternoon of our fourth day, it was warm and humid. When we returned from our hike and fishing excursion, a solid bank of clouds moved slowly in from the south. We sat by the stream, talking about the hike out and how to deal with the rain if it came. Since it was so warm, we decided to risk sleeping out.

The cloud cover stayed but the rain didn't come, and the hike out the next morning was uneventful. We left the camp and walked around to the trail, then paused for several minutes to look back at Cathedral Lake. Finally we headed down the moraine and onto the main trail. The trek down from the mountains, in our greatly improved physical condition and with gravity's help, took less than three hours. After a short week in the hills, I found myself having trouble adjusting to the modern world again. But a hot shower at Olie's brought me back to reality.

The women stayed the evening, this time accepting the offer to sleep in the house. We exchanged addresses the next morning and hugged goodbye. Olie was still beaming from the kisses the Brits gave him before they left.

"I'll call you when I'm coming to Washington," Sarah said, giving me the impression she'd rather not have me phone her in New York—she'd offered only her office address and phone number.

"You're just one magic boy!" Olie said as the two women drove off, beeping their horn.

"Hope I get to see Sarah again," I confessed, kicking fir cones off the driveway as we walked back to the house.

"I suppose you're just lucky with pussy," Olie said.

"Sometimes."

"From what I've heard about school and poker playing, you're more than just lucky. What say we go to Billings tomorrow?" he suggested, knowing I needed to head for D.C. in the next day or so. "We'll find some women and play a little poker."

I finished installing my deadbolt and cleaned the shavings off the floor. My phone rang while I was putting stuff away. I picked it up downstairs; it was Shelee.

"I'll be over soon with my apricot-rhubarb surprise," she said.

Jonah grinned to himself. Little Sugarspoon—more like Sugarscrew—really came across. Not only did she have moves he'd never imagined but she seemed nice, so he gave her some extra cash. He also confided part of his little problem to her.

"That's easy," she said. "Let me introduce you around." They went back to the bar and Jonah met some folks. One of them was Ferris Olsen, a practiced burglar who shared Sugarspoon's dope habit. Olsen, of course, needed extra money and willingly agreed to help Jonah.

Later, as they toured Sloan's neighborhood, then the professor's, in Ferris's car, Jonah explained part of his plan. "I've checked these two out," he said. "They usually spend the night together, so one of the houses is always empty. I want to fix it so's I can get into either house without them knowing it."

"Should be damn easy," Ferris said, squinting at the Victorian homes. "These old houses with the alleys give you good cover to the back door or a window." He checked both homes with binoculars. "No evidence of any burglar alarm," he said. "Whadda you care if they know you've broken in?" he asked. "When they miss their stuff, they're going to know someone's been there."

"I ain't robbin' the place," Jonah said, annoyed by Ferris's prattle. "I want to get in when they're sleeping."

"In the house *where* they're sleeping?" Sugarspoon asked.

"That's right, sugar," Jonah said. "That's exactly right."

## Thirty-nine / Shelee

"Professor Osbornson? Hi, I'm Carol Thornton—a vet student from Dr. Arnott's medical illustration class."

"Okay, I'll be with you in a minute, Carol. Come on in." I stood to shake her hand. "Please sit down," I said, and looked for her portfolio on my side table.

It was six weeks into the fall semester, halfway through October, and I was subbing for Theon Arnott's graphic design and medical illustration classes. Theon, who had agreed to take my classes for a week in November, was off to a wedding in Newark. That morning, I was meeting individually with his students, reviewing comments on their portfolios for the illustration class.

When Carol Thornton looked at my photos of Phil, I felt a chill, suddenly realizing who she might be. Carol appeared astonished when she said, "Excuse me, but aren't those pictures of Dr. Sloan?"

"You're not going to believe—I met Carol Thornton today," I told Phil as we jogged around the indoor running track. It was about five-thirty Thursday evening and Phil and I were putting in our obligatory thirty minutes of agony at his sports club.

"Did she say anything about her father or the phone calls?"

"Nothing about the phone calls. She's as much afraid of him as we are, but says he's never tried to contact her or her sister. She thinks he's just blowing hot air."

"What happened at the trial?" Phil asked.

"It's incredible, the trial's been delayed again."

"What? Until when?"

"She doesn't know. She seems to be a really nice young woman, Phil. I can't imagine what she's been through."

The windows on the outside of the running track looked down on the parking lot, and Minneapolis's October weather was living up to its reputation. Sleet blew through the ebbing light, coating the cars with wet snow. I'd arrived a few minutes before Phil, changed, and stretched out, and now could see both our cars parked a short distance apart as we padded around the track's oval crowded with runners driven inside by the weather.

It became impossible to talk because we kept moving to single file so runners could pass. Finally we gave up. Phil's gait told me he was frustrated by the news he'd just heard, and when one of his friends ran by with a brief hello, Phil passed me, touching my shoulder.

"I'm going to run with Craig for a while," he said. "Need to work harder. I'll run till five after. Talk later." He quickened his pace and sprinted ahead, catching his friend in a quarter-circuit, Phil's blond, unruly hair bouncing with each stride.

Fine with me, I thought—just more opportunities to regard your tiny butt when you pass. We quit our runs at the agreed-upon time and walked a few cool-off rounds together.

"Are we going to do anything about this Jonah Thornton business?" I asked as we did our stretches in the balcony outside the weight room.

"Beats me," Phil said, "can't get shit from the authorities. I'll call the Stone Lake sheriff again and get an update. You know, they've only called me back once. Every other time I've had to call them, and they've never called you."

"I know," I said, "and neither have the damn city cops. There hasn't been an incident for about six week; maybe it's behind us."

"Let's hope," Phil said, wiping the sweat off his face, neck, and arms with a towel from his gym bag. Phil continued talking as we descended the stairs to the locker rooms. "I'm going home for a few minutes after my shower. I'll see you at your place. All right if we don't wait for each other?"

"That'll work," I said, grabbing his sweaty head and kissing him on the cheek just as Craig walked by. Craig smiled and shook his head. "See ya, Pussy Whipped," I said, patting his buns.

Wet sleet still drenched the parking lot when I walked to my car. I brushed an inch of slush off the door, threw my coat and stuff inside, and started the engine. I turned on the wipers to see a vacant-eyed, jack-o'-lantern card whacking back and forth on the windshield. I switched the wipers off, wondering why Phil would leave a card outside with snow coming down—we have keys to each other's cars.

Well it's the thought that counts, I supposed, recovering the soaked card from the wiper. I shook the water off and pitched it onto the dash to dry.

By the time I got home, Phil was already there. It was good to see my house lights through the heavy snow—giant, wet flakes, now falling at a furious pace. I reached into the backseat for an armful of school stuff and, concerned it might get wet, I wrapped it in my heavy coat. Phil met me at the door. I handed him my bundle.

"Can't let these portfolios get wet," I said, grabbing my coat for another load. I went back to the car and pulled it into the garage. I had one more bunch of portfolios.

"Is that it?" Phil asked, taking the stack of folders from me.

"Yes," I said. "I'll get my jogging stuff after dinner." Then I brushed the wet snow off my clothes onto the flagstone floor in the entrance to the kitchen. My cats sniffed and pawed, investigating the season's first snowy footprints.

After a quick dinner, Phil and I went to work at my kitchen table, doing our various evening projects. "This is Carol Thornton's portfolio," I said, handing her sheaf of drawings to Phil. "She's pretty talented with these biology illustrations."

"So many disturbed people are talented detail artists," Phil muttered, turning the pages. He moved his laptop computer aside and studied Carol's drawing of a dissected dog's head. "I bet if I had her father's picture here . . . the dog's eye and lashes . . . that's her father's eye."

"Do you still see any of those girls?" I asked.

"No," Phil answered. "They're all in a support group. Apparently doing okay—no one's called me. I'd expect little Trudy would be the one who shatters first." He stood up and paced around the kitchen.

"Shatter?"

"Yes—as in break down, fall apart," Phil said, now pacing quietly. I knew he was upset.

"You said yourself how strong these particular kids are. That the college girls have jobs and seem to be doing well in school. Don't you think that's amazing when you consider how their families have let them down?"

"Sure, but the scars from this kind of abuse—violations by family members—can last a lifetime. Maybe they'll get past it; maybe they won't."

"Do they have any family here?" I asked.

"I don't think so," Phil said, sitting back down. "There's the support group, and they've formed their own family, the three girls. Trudy moved out of the group home and lives with Carol and Dena now."

"Carol Thornton's an interesting kid," I said. "What are the other two like?"

"They're neat kids, too—all three are."

"Is there anything we can do to help them through this?"

"What did you have in mind?" Phil asked.

"Perhaps have them up for dinner, or a movie, some family activity."

"I don't know; I haven't seen them in months. I talked with Carol when we got the phone calls, and a few times with Susan Tucker—she's their social worker." Phil went to the fridge, searched around, and found a can of Squirt. He snapped it open. "Yeah . . . some kind of activity, that might be helpful. Let me think about it," he said, stretching. "Maybe after our trip."

Phil closed Carol's portfolio and pushed it back to me. Now his computer chattered softly, beeping to life as he focused his attention. We worked quietly while the season's last fly buzzed near the ceiling. My cats watched wide-eyed, prancing and chortling at the fly's every move.

Just before nine o'clock, I moved into the living room to watch *Frontline*, leaving Phil to his computer. He finished about ten-fifteen, and we wearily headed for bed. I snuggled up against him and was starting to fall asleep when I remembered my sweaty gym stuff in the car. That's all right, I thought, it's cold outside, and it'll keep till morning.

"Thanks, honey, for the Halloween card," I whispered. But he was already asleep and didn't hear me.

When Jonah returned home on Thursday evening, he ate the dinner Mary had left warming for him in the oven, then listened to the day's telephone conversations. He tapped the little phone recorder with his finger, smiling as he played, for a second time, an exchange between Carol and Mary. Professor Osbornson was going to be out of town the first week of November with Dr. Sloan. . . . Jonah dialed Ferris Olsen's apartment in St. Paul.

## Forty / Shelee

"Which way we headed, Uncle L?" Phil asked from the driver's seat as I slid into the backseat behind Lucky.

"South, bub." Lucky squinted into the just-risen, 7:30 A.M. sun slanting through the Suburban's window. "Interstate 35 to I-90," he directed, buckling his seat belt, waving to Rose as we pulled away from the curb. "I checked the weather an' there's a cold front comin' down from Manitoba. We'll probably miss that sucker if we go south. Gotta go south anyways, sooner or later."

Phil raised his hand, attempting to get a word in, but Lucky ignored him. "Ain't goin' through Billings," my uncle said, waving a map that he grabbed from the dashboard. "Ol' Volborg's sent me this here faster route. We just head west from Sheridan and hit Frannie, then into Montanee on a new road they got from Belfry to Roscoe." Phil looked back at me, smiling as we turned south onto SR-100.

"That's it, sonny boy," Lucky cackled. "We'll miss all them morning commuters this way."

"Drop me off when we get to Belfry," I said, stretching out along the seat. "Sounds like my— "

"That new road goes 'crost Elk Basin," Lucky cut in, slapping the dash. "An' when we come back, we're gonna have *us* a hemungo frackin' elk on top of this v-hicle!"

"On second thought, give him a tranquilizer, or drop me at school," I said, pulling a magazine out of my gym bag, recently converted to my cross-country ski bag. But Phil and Lucky were either not listening or ignoring me. I put the magazine aside, pulled the cleanest-looking hat from the gun rack, and put it over my eyes to take a nap.

I awoke about an hour later, stretched, and suggested a rest stop. Lucky was snoring softly, slumped against the passenger door. Phil nudged him as he pulled off I-35 into a truck stop just south of Owatonna. We parked in the busy lot, and the three of us trooped into Steele's Cafe for some quick relief. Phil met me at the counter and sprung for coffee-to-go.

"You going to pay for these here doughnuts, sonny boy?" Lucky asked, waving a package of fat grenades.

"Sure, if you'll drive."

Lucky smiled. " 'At's a deal," he said.

"Lucky, they put powdered sugar on those so the grease won't make 'em stick to the cellophane," I said.

"Womago du gogo-umph," Lucky replied, talking crumbs and sugar dust as we walked to the Suburban.

I got in front with my uncle and, as we pulled onto the freeway, I said, "I brought an adventure novel, a book on tape. Okay with you two if we start it?" This was my ploy to put a lid on Lucky's chatter and keep my sanity.

"What's a book on tape?" my uncle asked.

"It's a narration of a book. You'll like this one," I said. "I selected it especially for you. A political mystery about the first woman president; she sells Yellowstone Park to the Chinese."

"Tol'ja a woman should never be the president," Lucky said, smirking.

"You're not getting off that easy," Phil broke in. "I read the reviews, and she's a Republican."

"That only explains half of it," Lucky said. "Yeah, let's give it a shot."

I turned to Phil. "Could you get the cassettes from my sports bag?"

"Hey, it's Halloween," Lucky said, pointing to a patch of pumpkins beside the road.

"Oh, yeah, happy Halloween, Philip. And thanks for the card. Sorry I forgot about it."

"What card?"

"The one you left on my windshield. It's in the bottom of my bag. It's dried out and stuck—"

"I didn't give you a card, Shel," he said, searching in the bag. "You must have a secret admirer."

"Phil, it was on my window—the night of the sleet storm—at the club. Is it in there?" I asked, curious about the card.

"Here it is," he said, holding up the faded paper pumpkin. He tried to separate it, but it was stuck tight. So as not to tear it, he got out his pocket knife, slit the card at the seam, and pulled it apart.

"I would have put something like this *in* your car," he said. He frowned.

"What does it say?" I asked.

"It says: 'All nightmares will come true for you and your doctor friend.' That's an ominous piece of shit. Who would write that?"

"What the hell's going on here?" Lucky demanded.

"Maybe your friend Craig?" I said.

"Boy, I don't think so. . . . Hope it's not goddamn Thornton."

"What's this all about?" Lucky asked again.

"Did you ever call the sheriff?" I asked. "I didn't."

"No." Phil shook his head.

"Sheriff? Isn't anyone going to tell me what's going on?"

"There's been some threatening phone calls," Phil said, giving Lucky a rundown on everything.

"Why didn't one of you egghead squid-brains tell me about this Thornton fella?" Lucky said, waving a finger at us. "I'll kill the bastard."

Phil shrugged. "What's to tell. You heard the story—no one's sure it's even him."

Forty minutes had passed since we'd turned at the junction onto I-90, heading west through the late fall, Minnesota countryside. I was getting weary of Jonah Thornton speculations.

"I've got friends 'round Stone Lake," Lucky said scratching his head. "Maybe there's something I can do."

"Fine," I said. "Let's drop it and listen to the tape." I punched the first cassette into the slot on the dashboard.

"Audio-Discovery Books presents . . . read by Mr. Emmit R. Harris."

*YellowStone,* by William Nathan: Book I, *Treachery*.

> It was the year 2006. Crisis Millennia, the world insanity that preceded the Anniversary-of-the-Two-Thousand had continued unabated since 1998. Humans now realized: Few would ever see the turn of another century.
>
> Sol Chandler was trapped in the midst of the dread pervading the nation. When Interior's VIP-1 touched down at the Cody, Wyoming, municipal airport, Chandler, special presidential advisor for domestic affairs, had never imagined that any top secret activity might include Yellowstone National Park.

Three days later, when the plane left Cody, Sol's shock was just settling over him. He felt the wheels spin clear and the landing gear latch into the belly of the vintage DC-9 as it left the runway. The pilot jammed the engines, cutting a high climbing curve into the blue afternoon sky, heading east, back to Washington. The mountains of Yellowstone faded off the left wing

It's all a bad dream, he thought. No president would ever do such a thing. But this president was different. She had turned her staff and cabinet into worker bees, and she was the queen. Still, Sol thought, I've got to talk to her. She'll listen to me.

Sol did talk with the president the night he returned to Washington. And he was punished for his unfortunate response to the Yellowstone plan. Now Sol Chandler was no longer a worker bee, but a drone faking at nectar sucking. If he returned to the hive, the workers would kill him. If he contacted the queen—now mated to the Chinese—she'd renounce him, summoning the workers. He could not eat, could not sting, could not copulate, feebly buzzing—half housefly, half dead.

Six weeks had passed and Sol was now on a government jet headed for Cambodia. He hoped this East Asia special assignment—a welcome reprieve from his current White House inner-circle exile—might restore him to the president's favor. Yet this impossible thing in Yellowstone continued, and the queen's larva wriggled behind his eyes.

The Suburban's tires slapped and thumped along an uneven stretch of highway as we approached the South Dakota border, an endless landscape of farms and hills stretching to the horizon. It was just after noon.

"Let's eat in Sioux Falls," Lucky suggested from the seat next to me. "I know a good rib place. Just north of town, so it ain't too far."

"Long as I can get the diet plate," I said, "then it's fine with me."

"Look'it those crazy fools a-runnin'," Lucky exclaimed as we passed a group of lunchtime joggers, several in shorts, trooping along an adjacent frontage road. "They must be nuts—there's ice all over that field where the sprinkler's been goin'."

"Hell, I see people running in shorts all winter long at the university," I said, turning south toward Sioux Falls. "Mountain bikers, too. Either nuts, tough, or both."

"Speakin' of nuts," Lucky said over his shoulder to Phil, "I hope you brought plenty of money. 'Cause what I hear from Olie, those Indian friends of his are nutty poker players. I figure we should have ourselves quite a game." Phil smiled and patted Lucky on the shoulder.

"Can I play?" I asked. "This lady's brought money."

"If you think you can hold your own in a wild-ass, drunk Indian poker contest, then you come on in, sister," Lucky snorted. "Turn off here for the rib place. See it off there to the right? You'd likely be a goddamn distraction in the game, though."

I turned off the road, mushing through the dusty, loose gravel in the parking lot, and pulled in next to the Great Northern Barbecue Depot. The delectable fragrance of lunch smoked into the car. Phil and I shared a rib plate, finishing ten minutes before Lucky; then we sat and watched my uncle devour half a hog.

"Did I tell you about the David Mamet play that I watched the other day when you were at Trish's?" Phil asked me.

"The one from the Civic Auditorium?"

"Yeah, it was about sexual exploitation, and the theater-goers were interviewed by Tom Pierce after the performance—on Cole's KCB. Anyway, the play's notorious for the arguments it stimulates among the audience. And this audience was out-of-control angry."

"Amazing," I said. "What were they arguing about?"

"Most of the arguments were from people projecting their own emotions—often fears—onto the plot."

Lucky waved a partly eaten rib at us. "What the hell are you two geniuses jabbering about—projections?"

"More accurately, I'd say, what they felt about themselves influenced what they heard."

"Can you make all that malarkey a little more clear, Doc?" Lucky asked, wiping sauce from his chin.

"Okay," Phil replied, "Let's take the character of the president, for example, in the *YellowStone* tape: Her behavior is shaped by her own fear, so she instills it in others. When she surrounds herself with a regal presidency, she hopes that will somehow conceal her past—the fact that she was a prostitute in college."

"Hell, *I* could have told you that," Lucky said, soaking his mustache in beer.

"All right, smart guy," I cut in, "explain the rest of her behavior."

"I didn't ask you, I asked Dr. Sloan here."

"Oh?" I was about to pop him, but then the waiter brought my blueberry pie.

"She embraces the Chinese, one of the most powerful nations on earth," Phil said, "again selling part of herself symbolically—the park—to buy protection."

"May I please get a word in edgewise?" I said, prompting a scowl from Lucky. "A much simpler example," I said to Lucky, "when we're in a poker game in Montana, and you fear I might have you out-held, you ask me if the stakes are too high—that's projection of your anxieties."

"Tell that stupid waiter to bring my coffee to go," Lucky said, standing up. "The only thing I'm anxious about is hitting the road. Back in a minute!" he snarled, heading for the rest room.

"Why do you do that?" Phil asked. "Take it easy on the old guy."

"Baloney! He's the total know-it-all," I said, pulling the check out of Phil's hand. "I'll pay the bill; you leave the tip. Okay?"

At the cash register, I hugged my uncle, kissed him on the cheek, and whispered, "I love you, Uncle Smart-Ass." He beamed at the smiling cashier. We carried our coffees to the car as light snow swirled from an ash gray sky. We hit the road west.

I drove for the rest of the afternoon as the two men chatted. Then Lucky began to snooze in the backseat, and Phil—sitting next to me—read a book.

"I'll drive anytime you want me to," Phil said, looking up from his reading.

"Naw, I'm enjoying this," I said, reaching to caress his face. "Mind if I listen to the news?"

"No, go ahead."

I turned the dial for a few minutes but found only cowboy music, Paul Harvey, and Rush Limbaugh. "Well, so much for a world where vignettists explain reality," I said. "You thought any more about doing some family thing with Dena Lewis and the Thornton girls?"

Phil slipped his bookmark into the paperback and closed it. "Yeah, and I'm in favor of it. Did you have something in mind?"

"Thanksgiving."

"Sure. It's at your folks' this year. Will that work?"

"Abby's going over there early to start the turkey," I said. We can meet at my house, 'cause I'm bringing most of the side dishes. The girls can help me with the cooking and we'll all go over to Mom's in the afternoon."

I glanced back to see Lucky sleeping soundly. "Can I ask you something?"

"Uh-huh."

"Are you so passionate about understanding our relationship because you're purposely dispassionate in your practice?"

Phil nodded. "You're right about both, but I don't believe they're connected. There's at least three things going on in my practice relative to my emotional involvement. Modeling boundaries: That's one reason I don't get involved. The other two are therapy works best without emotional involvement, and I *must* stay uninvolved through self-discipline, because I'd go nuts wringing my hands over all the sorrow I hear. Often the best I can do is just listen. My being involved emotionally would bias the therapy." Phil finished his coffee and set the empty cup on the floor.

"But I am emotionally involved with those three girls. Because I'm not currently treating them, and they may still be in danger, I think a family activity would be healthy for them and enjoyable for us. You know, they're truly beyond survivor status when you figure the older two are in college, have jobs, and have made a home in Minneapolis.

"Anyway, I'm hoping that our activities with those kids won't violate the personal boundaries I try to set in my practice," Phil added, first pointing to a state trooper who zoomed by in the eastbound lane, then to the speedometer—I was doing over 75 mph, having just passed two large trucks.

I let the Suburban coast back to under seventy, eased into the right lane, and sipped my cold coffee. "What's your view of personal boundaries?" I asked. "I'm not sure I know what you mean."

"I know why," Phil said. "Bet you hardly ever think about them."

"True. Why not?"

"Because your grandparents and parents instinctively respect personal boundaries; you were raised that way. Respect is second nature in your family. I'll give you an opposite example: the genuine flap about your favorite movie director's family troubles. I mean, out of all the available women, he violates every family boundary by having an invidious affair with his in-effect stepdaughter. Bet he was raised in an environment where personal boundaries were regularly violated."

"Think how insightful his films are," I said. "So why is he so creative?"

"My guess is that he's very unresolved," Phil said, "and that's frequently the engine of creativity."

I yawned. "Wish Lucky were awake. I'm ready for more *YellowStone*."

Phil glanced out the window at a milepost, then to his watch. "We'll be at Wall Drug soon. Lucky wants to stop there to get something for Olie, I think."

## Forty-one / Phil

The light snow had stopped, but broken clouds remained, shielding our eyes as we drove into the sun, now nearing the western horizon. We arrived at Wall, South Dakota, with my stomach grumbling for dinner. The three of us bustled into Wall Drug with the tourist crowd. We were confronted with a profusion of Halloween decorations and sale items.

"Lucky, you really think there's anything Olie wants here?" Shelee chided. "Maybe one of those simulated mastodon skulls?"

"For once, girlie, you're right," Lucky said. "I'll take him a bottle of Scotch. Get it in Wyoming, cheaper I think. How much wine did you bring?"

"An assorted case," I told Lucky. "We'll drink well, that's for sure."

"Better pick up some Night Train or Ripple for them Injuns," Lucky said a little too loudly.

Shel blanched, half-glancing at an Indian family near us. "I'm out of here," she said, shaking her head. "See you at the car."

"That niece of mine's sure touchy." Lucky's eyes narrowed and he lowered his voice. "Those folks never heard us."

"Check it out with Shelee, my friend," I said. "You want to eat at the Prickly Pear Diner across the street?"

"Fine with me, if Ms. Highpockets has settled down. I'll drive after dinner; let's get a little farther west tonight."

Shelee maintained her angry mood through dinner and during the drive afterward, even though we listened to tapes most of the way. Later, we said goodnight to Lucky and settled into our room at the Box Elder Manor. Now Shel blew off steam.

"You heard him! I was totally embarrassed. Do they have the death penalty in Montana? I may kill him before this trip's through."

"If it makes you feel any better, I was embarrassed, too," I said, rubbing her shoulders. "Thanks for doing so much of the driving today."

"First, he sort of sucks me in—in spite of his 'girlie' phrase—then he unloads with the wine comment. I'm sure that Indian family heard him. And he knew it would irritate me!"

"I understand you're angry with him and I'll listen. But the best thing to do is to talk with him tomorrow. Tell him how you're feeling."

"I don't think I can," Shel said. "Why do I find him so aggravating?"

"I don't know," I said. "Wanna take a shower?"

Shel gave her first smile since before dinner. "You bet."

We were listening to Nathan's paleo-history in YellowStone—the second part of his book—and it was getting close to lunchtime.

Book II, *The Starveling*.

> The dire wolf trotted easily beside her as she ran the summit ridge, the snow wind spreading through the trees. Turning now, descending swiftly along the game trails, splattering the thin, recently fallen snow,

> bounding over and around the many trees brought down by last week's earth-shaking, she headed for her meadow—the one where the stream ran over yellow-metal stones. Next spring, she thought, that is where I want the child—

"Let's go to that burger joint," Lucky said, turning the stereo off and pointing to a billboard along the freeway. "Enough of them Neanderthal women running around the hills." The snow-capped Bighorn Mountains appeared to soar across the western horizon as we drove off the interstate into Buffalo, Wyoming.

"McBison's to the left; go under the freeway," Lucky instructed. "The sign said they had buffalo burgers. I'm goin' to get me one of those."

"Yummy!" Shel said sarcastically from the rear seat. She'd been sullen with Lucky all morning—unwilling to discuss yesterday's incident at Wall's. Lucky, for the most part, just ignored her. Fortunately, listening to the tape kept a damper on their acrimony.

"Either we get a truce at lunch," I said, "or I'm sitting separately."

Shelee lunged forward, wrapping her arms around Lucky's neck, and yelled, "Truce!" She pinned him to the seat's headrest, planting a noisy raspberry in his thinning hair.

"Okay, truce," Lucky wheezed, raising both hands. I eased the car into a parking spot.

"This way, miss," Lucky said to Shel with a flourish as he held the restaurant's door for her. "Welcome to *Buffo's*," he said, giving her back a quick Italian salute.

"I saw that," she said, gesturing backward, eyebrows raised. "And, for now, I'm choosing to ignore it." We had a leisurely lunch, spent some time at a local museum, and bought a couple bottles of Scotch for Olie.

Once back in the car, Lucky sought to catch up on lost time. But soon heavy snow hit us on the icy Montana highway south from Roscoe to Lodgepole. Driving through the dusk with visibility deteriorating, I regretted our delay. I sat next to Lucky listening to gravel from the thinly sanded, rutted road ticking against the car's underside.

"You doing okay with this snow?" I asked as we bumped along.

"Four-wheel drive and no problem, bub. We're less than thirty miles from Lodgepole and I'll keep takin' it slow. Let's eat there—it's a little early, but we've got almost an hour's drive to Volborg's sou'west of town. He's expectin' us, but I'll call from dinner to make sure he's home." We were quiet now, almost mesmerized by the steady fall of the snow in the headlights.

"Look at this fool comin' in the mirror!" Lucky said suddenly. An orange pickup sped by us, fishtailing up the road. A buck deer's head, illuminated through the snow-dust by a single red taillight, wagged over the rear bumper. "I bet he's doin' over sixty. . . . Nice rack, though," Lucky added, slowing down. The highway was obliterated by truck-blown snow.

Five minutes later, we saw headlights on the left side of the road pointing up through the snow-filled air. Lucky coasted to about 20 mph and passed the orange truck. Its two male occupants, attempting to free their high-centered pickup, paused from their frantic digging.

"Pull us out!" one of them yelled. He waved a shovel at our partly rolled-down window.

"Slow down, boys," Lucky yelled back, not slowing further. "Stupid idiots," he muttered, gaining speed and heading to Lodgepole.

We parked near a restaurant, then walked around Lodgepole before dinner, looking into the mostly closed storefronts. Shel spent some time in an expensive-looking art gallery, then caught up with us.

"There's some amazingly fine work in that gallery," she said breathlessly. "But more amazing, there's two small Kampino landscapes—can you imagine that, way out here in Montana—and they're each priced at $2,500. I think she comes out here—somewhere—in the summer to paint." Shel shook the snow out of her hair and batted her jacket with her gloves. "If I win enough money at poker, I may buy one of those on the way out of town."

"This here's the Lodgepole Cafe," Lucky said to me. "You and I ate here about twenty-five years ago—that summer when we went horse campin'. Remember that?"

"Sure do, my friend," I said, patting him on the back as we walked into the steamy-warm restaurant. We ordered our food and, just as the waitress brought us a bottle of '91 Rosemont Shiraz, the crew from the stranded pickup blustered inside.

"Who belongs to that red Suburban with the Minnesota plates?" one of them yelled, jerking his thumb over his shoulder.

"Fight time," Lucky hissed. "I'll take the big one."

"No fights!" Shel hissed back, grabbing Lucky's arm across the table.

"You just gave us away, sister," Lucky said. "Now they got us spotted. You don't know nothin' about layin' low, do you?"

The hostess, a small woman in her forties, wearing a full-skirted gingham dress confronted both men. "What's the problem, Warren?" she asked the smaller one.

"We were stuck, north out on 78, and those folks wouldn't stop to help us," he whined, pointing to our table. The larger man faded from angry to uncomfortable, nudging melting snow lumps with his foot. I got up and ambled over, trying to look simultaneously large and nonthreatening.

"Gentlemen," I said, "I'm apologizing for our not stopping, but you were in such a hurry when you passed us—driving pretty fast, guys—we thought maybe you'd been drinking, and we just didn't want to mess with the situation."

"We weren't drinking," the larger man said directly. "Warren here shot a big buck, and—"

The hostess turned to me, interrupting. "This isn't the first time Norbert and Warren have overstepped their welcome here.

I'll take care of this, and *you're* welcome to return to your table," she declared, totally in charge.

"Thanks." I retraced my steps to Shel and Lucky—the wine was two-thirds gone.

"This vino's delicious," Shel said to me, "and you've been appointed designated driver. We're the designated drinkers." She poured me a glass of wine and toasted. "Here's to a successful elk hunt, Uncle Buffo," Shel said with a smile. "By the way, when was the last time you threw a punch?"

"Not to worry, Shelee dear," Lucky said cheerily. "Punchin's just like riding a bicycle or makin' love—something you never forget how to do. Let's order another bottle of this stuff."

Lucky was expansive throughout dinner and, when he offered to pay the check, we happily accepted. The cold hit us as we left the warm café and stepped out into the clear night. The sky, now absent of snow, was full of bright stars. Shivering, we piled into the car, then scraped frost off the inside windshield. Lucky disappeared into the back, Shelee sat next to me, and I pointed our vehicle in Olie's direction.

A few blocks south of the Lodgepole, I turned west on a county road, heading toward the mountains. Soon the road and country were completely deserted—fields and hills of snow stretched into the darkness—and the love of my life sat next to me doing a little drum number on my leg. But her finger serenade didn't last long. The warm car and the wine took its toll; Shel dozed off.

Lucky stirred and leaned against the seat back. "How long since you been to Olie's?" he asked.

"A dozen years or so, I guess." I'd seen him a few times in the Twin Cities when he visited Lucky and we got together for poker.

"Olie told me you met some real dandy women out here when you were in school," he said quietly.

"Yeah, I spent almost a week with them camping at Cathedral Lake."

"Olie said they were English. Did one of them work in New York?"

I chuckled. "Yes, and she found her way to Washington." In fact, about a month after my mountain camping expedition with the English ladies, Sarah and Annie—two weeks into my D.C. residency—I received a call from Ms. Andrews.

"I'm coming to town next week on embassy business," she said. "Maybe we could get together."

We made a date for dinner, and my suspicions about a New York boyfriend were reawakened when Sarah volunteered that she was calling from the consulate to save on her phone bill.

But I was ready for some womanly company—perhaps someone more sophisticated than the girls I'd recently dated in Washington. The more I speculated about Sarah, the more I relished seeing her, remembering the discreet sexual hints she gave when we were camping. Although my psychiatric training warned me that my interpretation of her secret messages were probably projections of my own cravings for her luscious English body, I ignored them. What the hell was I to do with that useless bit of insight?

"Well tell me boy, did you see her?" Lucky asked.

"A few times, when she was in D.C. on business." A week after her call, Sarah, attributes and all, met me in the lobby of her hotel. We had drinks in the bar, then went across the street to one of the best East Indian restaurants in town. Why wasn't I astonished when she said the Indian food was better in New York, and better yet in London? She was a control freak, but I was so eager to see if she'd give up some control in bed, I didn't care. We sat next to each other in the restaurant's plush surroundings and Sarah flirted deliciously throughout dinner.

"Tell me about the rest of your trip," I said. "Didn't you plan to drive back to Billings and see the Bighorn battlefield? Do some Wild West stuff?"

Sarah leaned into me as she reached for the salt. She momentarily rested her hand on my leg. "Yes. Both Annie and I are American history buffs, but when we got to the highway junction, we drove south over the Beartooth Pass to Jackson Hole. Then when we got to Jackson, we changed our minds again and decided to go to Lake Tahoe." The waiter refilled our wine, and Sarah turned slightly to clink glasses, this time leaving her leg pressed against mine.

"So we skipped Teton Park," she continued, "and drove straight through to Tahoe. We suntanned, gambled, and went to a couple of shows. I drove to San Francisco with Annie, stayed for two days, and then went back to New York." She paused as the waiter cleared the table and brought us coffee.

Sarah unwrapped a chocolate mint and eased it into her mouth. Then she looked at her watch and said, "You want to see a movie? There's a super one in ten minutes on the hotel telly. Let's go to my room and watch it." She smiled. "I brought us some champagne from New York."

We headed across the street to her hotel. Once inside the room, she went to the bar refrigerator and extracted a bottle of fine-looking champagne and two glasses from the freezer. Sarah had planned all this quite well, I thought. I grabbed the ice bucket and went to the machine down the hall. When I returned, she excused herself to the bathroom. I put the champagne in the bucket, then looked through the hotel TV listing.

There were no movies starting at ten o'clock, but then I hadn't expected one. She emerged from the bathroom, her glossy brown hair undone—cascading to the middle of her back and over the top of her breasts. She'd removed her makeup, reminding me how beautiful she'd looked in the mountains a few weeks earlier.

"Which movie shall we watch?" I asked, waving the TV list to tease her.

"Not those, silly," she said. "Here, there's a goodie on right now." She tossed the hotel's X-rated movie guide to me from the side table. "This dirty movie called *Secretive Intentions*—I'm dying to see it. We're all adults here, right?"

Sarah disappeared into the bedroom and returned in a few minutes wearing a pin-striped, longish man's dress shirt—her "dressing gown," she called it. The champagne was open and I offered her a glass. And so we tippled, watching the first ten minutes of the X-flick. Then I was introduced to the Sarah Andrews world of mindless fucking.

It may have been the best physical experience of my sexual history—up to that time. And for the next several months we screwed our brains out everytime we saw each other. She was completely over the top when it came to sex. Sarah could have three orgasms in a row. I discovered the best place to make love was on the floor, because she'd knock us both out of bed almost every time she came.

One evening at my apartment, I tried pinning her against the wall along one side of my bed. But with the passionate strength of Hercules, she shoved the bed away, and we tumbled to the floor. Sarah didn't even notice and we kept on screwing in those narrow quarters, her head thumping under the bed, dust bunnies in her hair. Thus the floor became the only place I could really stay with Sarah. Even then I'd have to hold her down, or else wrap my arms and legs around her.

Her physical strength and total involvement during our lovemaking was amazing. Sometimes she'd grunt like a pig, humping me with consuming intensity. When she came, she'd rave incomprehensibly, speaking in tongues—a religious experience perhaps? I tried talking to Sarah about it when we were making love, but I don't think she heard me. When I later asked about her orgasmic blathering, she had no memory of it.

The romance even changed my rhythms for a while—I found our twice-monthly lovemaking quite sufficient for me, and stopped dating other women. I concentrated, instead, on the hospital and poker. But about three months into our affair, after I'd become Sarah's co-opted sex stooge, I began to chafe at the situation. And with absolutely nothing spiritual going on, plus some pretty negative stuff lurking behind the scenes, I was getting burned out. Participating in this "nutso-screw," as I called it, made me vulnerable to her control. I could not call her at home, but only at the English consulate. Nor could I ask about her life in New York or any other personal questions. Sometimes she would volunteer personal stuff, but it was fairly shallow, and if I pushed, she clammed up. She'd occasionally talk about Annie or her family in Great Britain.

I had met a rather interesting woman social worker at one of the hospital's inpatient clinics where I'd been working with adolescents. We went on two or three dates and I decided I could have a friendly, healthy connection with her. But as it turned out, she went back to an old boyfriend, though not before I had pulled the plug on my affair with Sarah.

One evening at dinner, I tried to talk to Sarah about what I was feeling. "Sarah," I said, "there are several things bothering me about our relationship." She continued eating, displaying no emotion.

"First of all, I know nothing about your life in New York City, but I'm assuming you have a boyfriend there you haven't told me about."

"Of course I have a boyfriend," she replied calmly. She had finished dinner and now arranged her silverware across her plate. "Don't you have a lady friend here? Or two or three?"

"No girlfriends," I replied. "I've had a few dates, but several years ago I decided to sleep with only one woman at a time." I knew where this conversation was leading, and I had this panicky, regretful feeling. Most men would kill to have sex like this, I reflected. Yet I needed to protect myself from falling for Sarah, becoming addicted to her. And I had no illusions about her, felt she couldn't be trusted—also I really didn't like her personality all that much. Still, there I was, under her spell.

"Do you think this is fair to your boyfriend in NYC?" I asked.

"He probably has another woman friend," she said, sipping her coffee. "I'm not going to break it off with him, if that's what you're implying. I don't ask questions, and I'm enjoying myself—that works for me."

"But sadly, not for me," I said.

"Well, if this is our last night together, we'd better make the best of it," she said deliberately. We did make the best of it, and I never saw or talked with Sarah after that. I picked up a Valentine card for her the following February, wrote something trivial on it, then let it lie around until mid-March before mailing it off.

We rattled over a snowy cattle guard and Shelee woke up. "Here's the turn to Olie's," Lucky said from behind me.

I made a left, heading the Suburban farther into the dark countryside. Snowy evergreens now lined the sides of the road; a ranch house and corral looked slightly familiar. Three miles farther, I turned into Olie Volborg's. The lights from the house illuminated the driveway, reflecting off the snowbank in his front yard.

Olie, wearing a decrepit, fur stocking hat, came tramping through the newly fallen snow. He hugged the three of us while a giant dog that looked like a husky rampaged around. The dog was a blizzard of animal motion.

"Beautiful dog," I said and pulled two suitcases from the Suburban's rear door, stepping aside so Shelee could grab her painting stuff.

"Slooper not dog . . . wolf!" Olie said, punching Lucky in the shoulder, dancing away boxer style.

"Welcome to Cartoon, Montana," Shel quipped. "I should have guessed."

## Forty-two / Shelee

"Olie, thanks for letting us use your bedroom," I said at breakfast.

"I don't mind bunking with Lucky," Olie said, "reminds me of the old days."

"How come you guys didn't go hunting, too much wind?"

"Yeah, we'll go if this blow dies down. No sense freezing our butts off. Anyway, we're going to have a poker game tonight."

I looked outside, marveling at the gusts that carried billows of snow across the yard. The lee side of the Suburban and Olie's truck were drifted to their tops. "Just like Minneapolis," I said. "Hey, there's ducks in your driveway."

"Lemme see," Olie said, coming over to stand next to me at his front window. He put an arm around my shoulder. "There's a warm springs up the road, but when the wind's blowing like this, they come roost in my drive. You want duck for dinner?"

"Is it duck season?" Phil asked as he and Lucky joined us at the window.

"It's always duck season in my driveway." Olie smiled and went to the back door to call Slooper. The dog was busy chewing a frozen, half-eaten deer carcass hanging from a fir tree. The big dog whined, growled, and wagged his tail violently when he saw the four mallards huddled against the wind. Olie grabbed his collar and led him back to the door. Then holding the dog's muzzle, shoving four fingers in his face, he said, "Four ducks!" and let him out.

We watched as Slooper made a mad dash across the backyard, bounded over his snow-drifted doghouse, and disappeared behind a snowbank near the road. He reappeared at the drive's entrance and rushed the ducks, smashing into a large mallard. Slooper then leaped into the air and caught a second duck fully three feet off the ground. He proudly picked up the two flapping birds and brought them to the back door.

Olie shrugged, walked through the kitchen, and picked up a dog biscuit from an open box by the door. Breaking the biscuit in two, he took the ducks from the dog, gave him the half-biscuit, and shoved him out the door.

"I told you *four* ducks," he grumbled at the dog. He closed the door and wrung the bird's necks.

I just couldn't resist asking, "How the hell is he supposed to get all four ducks?"

"Ol' Sloop's done it before," Olie replied. "He just clobbers the whole flock, breaks wings or something, then fetches all of 'em."

"Maybe you should have told him a*ll* the ducks," I said.

He ignored me and went to the freezer on the porch; he returned with five more ducks. "There's seven for dinner tonight," he said. "Who'll volunteer to fix it?"

"I'll do most of it," I offered, "if we can get Dr. Sloan to fix his famous drop-dead-duck."

"Why do you call it that?" my uncle asked.

"You'll find out when you taste it," Phil said, stretching, now parroting Lucky: "I ain't gonna clean 'em, though."

"Consider it done," Olie said, tossing a duck to Lucky. Soon the two older men were feathering the birds on the back porch while the wolf-dog chased feathers through the blowing snow.

"Save the giblets," Phil said when Olie came back inside to clean the birds.

It was early evening, the snow still blowing, and dinner, blessing Olie's house with delightful aromas, was almost ready. Our three guests arrived in a brand-new van and parked near our snowed-in vehicles. Monte DiPine, about six feet tall, with a slight build and a thin, calm face, smiled as he shook hands, his soft ocelot eyes accentuated by his ragged black-and-gray hair. The two scruffy-looking men contrasted sharply with the woman's neat appearance.

Rosebud Absarokee was a substantial woman in her mid-twenties who displayed a close family resemblance to her father, Joe. She had round, pleasant features and short black hair.

"Which one of you is the medical doctor?" she asked, explaining that she was a med tech at a clinic in Lodgepole.

"Dr. Phil here," Lucky cut in, smiling, "if you consider a headshrinker a real doctor."

"I'm thinking about going back to college—medical school this time—and could use any advice you might have," Rosebud said to Phil.

"We can talk at dinner," Phil said. "Right now I've got to get ducks in the broiler."

"This is the best damn duck I've ever tasted," Monte DiPine said, taking a drink of Chardonnay. Both a red and a white were open on the table. "How'd you fix this?" he asked.

"I poach the birds in white wine with the vegetables and spices," Phil said. "Then I split them and broil both ducks and vegetables, with a honey glaze on the birds. I boiled down the liquid to make the gravy. It's even better if you add anchovies to the glaze, but we didn't have any."

"Man, I'll buy you all the anchovies you want if you'll fix this again," Olie said. "Can you do it with grouse? I'm about out of ducks."

"I don't think so," Phil said. "But Shel and Lucky have a grouse recipe with roasted green peppers. It's a knockout."

"I hope you're coming again tomorrow night," Olie said to our Native American guests.

Joe glanced at the poker table. "Damn right, if your money holds out."

"I'll bring the grouse and green peppers and anything else you might need," Monte proposed.

"What the hell do you guys do?" Lucky asked obnoxiously.

"I manage oil and mineral operations for three Montana reservations, and Monte's the accountant for the Hehakra tribal council," Joe answered, gnawing on duck bones.

"Sounds like educated folks to me," Lucky said, scratching his head.

Joe smiled. "We both have degrees from Montana State."

"Well, you probably don't get to do much huntin' with all that going on," Lucky said as though he'd heard enough.

"No," Monte said, "but we still find time to do some big-game outfitting in the early season. I take care of Olie's horses in the winter."

Lucky shut up now and pushed back his plate.

After dinner, Rosebud and I finished up the dishes while the men began their poker game. She moved into the front room to read, and, as I put the last few dishes away, Lucky wandered into the kitchen, looking for a beer.

"Well, so much for your drunk Indian poker game," I said quietly. "I wonder if they won that new van playing cards. They both look like pros."

"Yeah, I know," he said, frowning as he snapped open a beer can. "You gonna play? We're short-handed, and that girl's not a poker player."

"I'm going to paint; maybe I'll play some, too."

Rosebud arrived in the afternoon with the groceries, explaining that the medical clinic was closed on Mondays. I was messing with my artwork.

"I *love* both these paintings," she said, admiring the work I'd started the previous evening.

"Thanks," I said with a smile. "I got so inspired painting last night, I didn't feel like playing cards." I'd started two pieces at once. One was a small field study, 9x12 inches, of the men playing poker. The second was a large 36x48-inch painting of noblemen and monks playing a board game in a monastery. I used the poker setting for a model. In the smaller painting, the men play cards in a room lit by a dim lantern, hung near the ceiling. Partial ghosts of frontiersmen and Indians, defined by light graduations, sit next to the players in rafter-cast shadows.

For the larger painting, I have spirits looking on from their shadowed places, watching my medieval gamesmen. Both paintings have warm background bright spots—roaring fires in each hearth, some candles on the mantels. Wolf-dog Slooper sleeps by the fire in the smaller work; but tonight, for the larger piece, I will turn him into an outsized monastery beast. I was still astonished by my sudden inspiration to try something representational.

"Keep on painting if you like," Rosebud said. "I brought some work from my office. I wanted to talk more with Dr. Sloan."

"He should be up soon," I said, putting the dinner fixings away, leaving the grouse out to thaw.

Just then, Phil wandered into the room, still sleepy from his nap. "Hi, Rosebud," he said, kissing me on the cheek. He shuffled into the kitchen and returned moments later with a microwaved cup of coffee.

"You bring that dinner stuff?" he asked, reposing in Olie's recliner.

"Uh-huh."

"Thanks. Can't believe you found Anaheim peppers in town—wait till you taste this recipe. It works for pheasant, too," Phil said.

"That's one reason I came early," Rosebud said, "can always use another grouse recipe." Then she turned to me. "Shelee, is Lucky your uncle or Phil's?"

"Can't you tell—we look alike, don't we?"

"But you called him 'Uncle,' too, Dr. Sloan."

"Phil."

"Okay . . . Phil."

"No blood relation, but we've been close friends since I was a kid," Phil said. "He may be the reason I went into psychiatry."

"You've never told me that," I said. "Drove you nuts?"

Phil laughed. "Not exactly. It's what he said to me when I was fourteen. He used to say it to all the kids who worked at his farm. At times, he has amazing insight into human nature."

"Rare, but true," I said.

Phil paused, sipping carefully at his too-hot coffee. "He told us: 'You teenagers are taking your personalities apart—the ones you got from your parents—and putting 'em back together to suit yourselves. That turns most kids into rebellious nitwits about now.' That sounded so true—no one had ever said anything like that to me before—and it really got my attention. I remember he asked me, 'How would you like to grow up to be one of the smartest men in the world?' That sounded pretty interesting, so I asked him. 'Here's the secret,' he said, doing one of his typical dramatic pauses before the punch line."

"What?"

Phil took a drink of his coffee. "Here's what he said: 'Part of your rebellion includes rejecting grown-ups' knowledge. But I guaran-damn-tee it, grown-ups know lots more than you pea-brains do. So if you can listen to their ideas—okay to ignore what don't work for you now, and *keep* those things that might work—you'll be smarter than just about anyone else.' "

"How interesting," Rosebud and I said almost together. "Like a tribal wise man," she concluded.

"More like the family wise-ass," I said. "So where does psychiatry come in?"

"Well, I wanted to be a doctor," Phil answered, "and those simple and powerful words of his pushed me in that direction. I've come to realize he's an important component of who I am."

"Much as I hate to admit it," I said, "the old fart's an important part of my person, too. And that gives me some discomfort, Phil; I've always loved you as a man who's separate from a common past."

Rosebud leaned forward. "Why discomfort?" she asked. "From my perspective, it's like our tribal experience—the wisdom of the elders—the historical connection that unifies our thoughts and feelings."

"Well there you have it," I said. "Ol' Phil and I are joined at the soul. But why does it have to be Lucky's brand of glue?"

Phil stood up. "Olie asked me to bring in some wood. Might as well do it now." He labored by the front door, stacking firewood from the pile in the yard. He roughly swept snow off the logs, then brought some of the wood into the house.

I moved back to my paintings and studied the larger one. The completed vision suddenly sparked to awareness. *I would make this a major work—an art studio in a monastery—Dutch and Flemish masters my ghosts, French Impressionists the active gamesters. Then mix their paintings agonistically; hang them on the stone and wood walls, except for a window, where an Osbornson landscape would appear—wild summer blooms along the prairie rim. . . . And an open door, a hallway's end—or beginning—a fusion of styles.*

"Damn! it's chilly out there," Phil said with a huff, standing the firewood on end—wood so cold the pieces clunked with a metallic sound as he dumped them into the bin by the hearth.

## Forty-three / Phil

"Shit-oh-dear, this hunting's slow," Lucky complained as he and Olie, back from the hunt, warmed themselves by the fire.

"We'll leave before dawn tomorrow," Olie said, stomping his feet, the last snow melting from his boots. "I know where the elk will be—they'll be on the move."

"By god, let's hope," Lucky said.

"Yes, sir," Olie said. "A day after a big blow, the elk start to move." He sat on the raised hearth, loosening his bootlaces. "That's why we left midmorning today, figured there wouldn't be much movement."

"*No* movement!" Lucky scowled. He'd lost almost $1,000 at poker last night.

"Shel and I are going to fix dinner tonight," Rosebud announced. "You guys rest up for the poker action. We'll eat soon as Dad and Monte get here."

"You okay with all this cooking?" I asked Shelee as I helped her wrap the grouse in bacon and roasted green chilies.

"Sure am," Shel said. She was munching on a piece of raw carrot and sipping leftover wine. "This is very relaxing. I'm showing Ms. Absarokee here how to make our sweet-and-sour curried carrots."

"Perfect menu selection. Maybe you've missed your true calling. . . . Artistry in the kitchen," I said, finishing with the last grouse.

Monte, Joe, and I gratefully cleaned up after our grouse dinner; Shel proceeded with her painting, and our poker game started a short time later.

"You gonna play cards or paint?" Lucky snarled at Shel. She'd folded almost every hand.

"I'm doing both," she said. "You're short-handed; I'll play a hand when I get one. I'm making a living with these paintings, so every time I fold my cards, it's more paint on the canvas and more money in my bank account."

I knew what Shelee was doing—I'd seen this act before. By participating in the game, she was helping our short-table situation, and her thorough understanding of poker and table strategy could be deadly. She'd work at her two easels, glancing at her cards, folding quickly in most instances, neither delaying nor really participating in the game. We were playing $25/$50 hold'em and she'd dropped about $300 in the game so far.

Lucky, who was perhaps most vulnerable to her play, continued to be irritated by Shel's behavior.

"You know it's bad luck to count your chips," Lucky said irritably.

"I'm not counting mine," Shel said, mildly sullen, "I'm counting yours." Then addressing the remaining three players—Olie and I had folded—Shel called a second raise. "If it'll make you feel better, I'll play this hand."

The flop put a red ace and two clubs, the six and nine, on the board. Shel, who was last in line, cold-called a re-raise, then called another raise. The turn card was the five of clubs, and action was checked around to Lucky who bet $50. Shel raised to $100. Lucky and Shel put in all raises, with Monte and Joe calling the whole way. Lucky shit a brick when a second red ace—the last up card—hit the board. He had a nut flush, he said, and would call anyone down. Shelee calmly raised each time the bet came her way, enticing competitive raises from both Indians. Lucky stupidly called, staring longingly at the pot, now approaching $2,500.

"Son of a bitch!" Lucky shouted when he saw Shelee's straight flush. "I should have known it!"

Joe and Monte, who both held full houses, groaned as Shel began stacking her gigantic pot. "White freckle-woman beat mighty poker drum," Joe Absarokee grunted.

"I haven't seen a straight flush for more than five years," Lucky complained, dealing Shelee out of the next hand.

"Misdeal," Olie said, pointing to Shel's lack of cards.

"Next time," Shel said with a smile, waving the deal on. "My money's resting."

"Your new paintings are impressive," I said to Shel who was sitting by the front window, drinking her morning brew. She looked intently at the scene before her—so intently that I joined her. I rested my arm around her shoulder as we watched the first sunlight scatter through the fir trees. Bright gems glittered in the snow. Then I wandered back to her paintings. "The faces in the European scene look vaguely familiar," I said. "Who are they?"

"They're a secret—until I check my references back home. I'm pretty sure I'll submit the big one to the institute's show next year. My god, Phil, look at this! They've killed a damn moose or something." I walked back quickly to the window and saw our hunters—who'd left less than two hours earlier—returning with an imposing brown animal that filled the back of Olie's truck.

"Gotta be an enormous elk," I said. "See, there's an antler sticking up by the cab."

Lucky came barging diagonally across the yard, through the snow, carrying his rifle, not bothering with the snow-packed walk. "They don't call me Lucky for nothing," he said, stomping into the house. "Shot that sucker right next to the road. Had to delay traffic when we winched it in."

"Hell," Olie said, catching his breath as he followed the great hunter inside, "we didn't even get to our hunting spot. We just saw this bull by the road at first light and Lucky shot him. We haven't even cleaned the sucker yet."

He smiled at Lucky. "Come on, you lucky SOB, let's get him hung up and dressed. Old Slooper will love some fresh elk." Then he turned to me. "You want to help us with an autopsy, Doc?"

"Only if you absolutely need me, " I said.

Olie drove his pickup to the back of the house, while his dog—maybe a wolf—danced around the vehicle. He backed the truck under the Douglas fir that held Slooper's deer carcass, pulled his winch cable from the truck's front bumper, and tossed it over a tree limb. Lucky looped the cable around the elk's antlers, then jumped down while Olie levitated the animal. Less than an hour later, the blood-splattered hunters were in the house washing up. The elk, headless, legless, and expertly dressed, now hung by its rear hocks. Slooper lay on top of the steaming gut pile, surrounded by carnage, gnashing gore.

* * * * *

The two older men continued to jabber excitedly as they ate a second breakfast that included a fry of elk kidneys. Shel and I joined in, agreeing that this delicacy was probably not one fully appreciated by the general public.

After we'd finished eating, Lucky excused himself to the back porch and returned with a washtub full of now-cooled elk liver. He shoved it at Dr. Osbornson. "You'll cook this up for dinner tonight, Miss Straight Flush," he said, "if you know what's good for you."

Shel bowed and took the tub. She smiled in good humor. "Yes, Son Excellence, Shithead Uncle for Life, I am your nitwit slave and I will do as I am told."

"That's better," Lucky said, heading for the shower.

The thermometer hovered near ten above, and after an early afternoon snack, Shelee and I skied up the road. We glided in long easy strides through the dazzling sunlight. "I hope Lucky's mood improves, now that he's got an elk," Shel said, skating ahead of me. Her single braid, tied with an emerald ribbon, swung like a pendulum charm across her back.

"Lucky's playing poker like an idiot," I said. "Won't lay down a hand; perhaps he's getting old. Who knows?" We passed an abandoned logging road on our right where three ski tracks emerged from it onto our road. "I think that lane loops off from this one, about two miles up," I called. "It'll make a good circuit, and we'll get some powder—maybe we can glide on part of it, too."

Shelee continued to set the pace. As I watched her lively strides ahead of me, I began thinking about lovemaking.

"Are you watching my butt, boy?" she asked.

"I *am*, and enjoying every minute of it," I said, wondering if there was somewhere I could drape that lovely butt over a log.

"Why don't you ski next to me?"

"I'm concerned a car might come along."

"Well, I'm picking up the pace," she said, skating harder as the road sloped upward at a demanding pitch. "I've gained weight on this trip. And we've been really lazy, Philbert. Got to work harder."

We skied up the hilly road in silence, alternating between skating and striding, regaining a little breath during the infrequent flats and downslopes. When we reached the start of the logging loop that curved off to our right and down the mountain, I looked ahead to a summit on the road above us. "I'm not ready to head back yet," I said, out of breath. "Race you to that hilltop."

"Deal," she said, and took off.

I can outrun Shel, but I can't out-ski her, particularly when she's skating. She reached the summit about twenty-five yards ahead of me, flopped against the snow on the road's side cut, unlatched her skis, and kicked them loose. "I am a Valkyrie," she said with a wheeze. "All I need is a steel brassiere. Please give me some water."

I shrugged off my daypack and handed it to her. She unzipped the top, pulled out the water bottle, guzzled eagerly, then handed the bottle to me. "Thanks, Phil. That's why I beat you," she said charitably, "you were carrying the pack."

I took my skis off and lay in the snow next to her. Though still breathing hard, I gave her the most lingering kiss I could manage.

"Mmm, that's nice."

"Hand me my pack, Shel, there's something I want to show you." I opened the small front pocket and took out my list of names, inscribed on a piece of cloth scavenged from a discarded, blue-and-white hiking shirt. "I've never shown this to anyone before," I told her. I pointed west to the mountains. "See that reddish peak—it's called Pic Roux—camped near there many years ago. I made this list after a frightful thunderstorm. Now I read it aloud whenever I'm out somewhere like this . . . that is, when I remember to."

"A list?"

"Yes. Of names."

"Whose, sweetheart?"

"My dad's . . . a few others . . . friends who have died." Shelee kissed me on the cheek and put her hands over mine. "People I've cared about," I said. "Even a stranger, Raoul Wallenberg."

"It's a fine tradition," she said, "honoring and remembering. Would you like me to read the list?"

"Yes."

"Look, the snow's melting on my pants," Shel said. "Feel how warm it's getting?" Indeed, a warm breeze picked up from the south, blowing snow off the trees. "Let's head down."

We latched into our skis and did shaky telemarks down the road, then turned onto the logging road. Because it was colder at the lower elevation and sheltered from the wind, the trail had ideal snow. Ten inches of powder covered the old road, undisturbed except for the three previous tracks. Most of our run back to Olie's was delightful, but about a mile from his house, the wind caught us. We finished our outing in a howling ground blizzard.

"You know, this weather stinks," I said as we put our ski gear on the porch. "And the funny thing is, I don't mind—it's just like home. We must be true people of the north."

Snow clouds moved in quickly, and by the time we'd changed out of our ski outfits, it was snowing hard.

## Forty-four / Shelee

"Yes, Oh Celestial Omnificence, Most Galactic Phallus, how can I assist you further?" I asked Lucky as I served him a plate of elk liver and fried potatoes.

"You know," my uncle said, addressing the table as I seated myself next to him, "I believe this Montana trip has been good for my niece. She's learnin' some manners. Pass the ketchup."

* * * * *

After dinner, Lucky and I stayed in the kitchen to finish the dishes. Olie, his Indian friends, and Phil—a pretty tired-looking crew—sat by the fire trying to talk themselves into a poker game. Rosebud had stayed home. I was stuffed with rich food, half drunk from too much wine—swilled toasting Lucky's dead elk—and exhausted from the afternoon ski.

"Why don't you drag that boyfriend of yours off to bed so we can play poker without him?" Lucky suggested.

"Why don't you tell him you prefer to play short-handed?" Uncle Bad Luck made an obscene gesture and scowled, his sour mood about poker losses now overriding this morning's elk euphoria.

"Are you going to help Olie get his elk tomorrow?" I asked as we rinsed the pans.

"Screw Olie!" Lucky pouted. "He can find his own elk." Then he softened a little, embarrassed that someone might have heard him. "Olie said if this snow keeps up, there'll be plenty of elk on the road in the next day or two. He'll just shoot one by the house." He passed me a frying pan to put away; it was still dripping.

"It's not dry," I scolded. But he was distracted.

"Olie's been holding unbelievable cards," he whined. "So have you. I bet I've lost two grand this week."

"Well, one way to look at it," I said, tired of his bad manners, "your elk only cost you twelve dollars a pound, dressed."

Lucky glared at me and stomped out of the kitchen. He threw a dish towel at Phil and yelled, "Go help your smart-ass girlfriend dry them dishes, Doc. God, she's got a mouth on her. Feminism run amuck!"

Doc Sloan came in and helped me finish up. Then I sat with the men until I couldn't stay awake. I said goodnight, kissed Phil, gave my uncle a little apology kiss on the forehead, and went to bed.

The wind was still blowing hard, and tiny pellets of snow, driven by the storm, rushed against the bedroom window. But the bed felt so cozy, and I missed Sloan. The wind roaring in the background was not like wind at all—more like the sound of water falling. I thought of the Sawtooth Mountains where Phil and I had backpacked a few summers ago, and a place there that looked down from a high ridge into a mountain valley.

We were making a steep descent. And on the way down, we stopped at the top of a near-vertical alpine meadow. Above us, from the base of the peaks, a snowfield fed a stream that plummeted through the meadow to a large lake in the valley. The velocity of the stream, which splashed against its rock-strewn bed, created a ribbon of mist and a shower of sparkling water drops above the stream's course. The spray danced in the sunlight, making rainbows that mingled with the myriad wildflowers that decorated the green mountainside.

With hands joined, we delighted in the beauty before us. Phil became giddy; he glanced at me and released my hand, then stepped through the mist to the stream's opposite side. He picked handfuls of yellow and blue lupine, and threw the flowers into the air.

That was the signal! Run to the lake along separate paths on either side of the dashing water. The meadow's steepness immediately overcame our strides and we ran much faster than intended. The romp was soon out of control. We plunged downward at an ever-increasing speed, each reckless stride covering thirty feet.

"I can't stop!" I cried out. "We're going into the lake!" I screamed, feeling both the fear and thrill of the fall.

Phil reached through the mist and took my hand. Though I knew he was there, I couldn't see him. "We can fly now, Shel," he said. I was filled with warmth as I sensed him within me—part of my body, merged except for his hand on my wrist. And we did fly! Now his arm disappeared into my arm. I flew on alone, skimming across the lake, my clothes swept off by the flight. I was thin, my breasts small, and I touched the water all along the front of my body as I flew. The lake was warm and tasted of salt. I felt great joy.

Suddenly I sat up.

"Go back to sleep," Phil said softly. I lay back down and cuddled against his back in our spoon position, my face in his blond hair. "I love you, Shelee," he said. In the quiet, I listened for the storm, and the wind now sounded lighter; the snow sighed at the bedroom window.

"Phil," I said, trying to explain my dream, "we were one body." He reached down and touched me. I was quite wet. I pushed against his hand. "It was *our* dream, Phil. Is that possible? A joint dream, merging and all?" He pulled me over on top of him.

"Merged like this?" he said, slipping inside me. I came instantly—the rainbow colors splashed in the still-dark room—he came at the same time, our lovemaking over in less than a minute. I lay on top of him and we stayed together, catching our breath and feeling each other's warmth.

Then I realized there was something quite special about this time—about the way I'd come. "Talk about rude, quick sex," I said. I rolled over so he could hug my back, my hip resting in our damp spot. I love the slick, wet feeling between my legs after we make love. Warm thoughts made me smile.

"I'll just give you a key," Ferris Olsen said, fiddling with the lock. There were tracks in the snow leading from the mailbox to the back door. The two men assumed that someone had a key and was leaving mail in the house. It was about one A.M. and snowing. Jonah Thornton leaned against the entryway and held the penlight for Ferris. Olsen carried four key rings, each with more than thirty keys on them, arranged according to lock brand. Jonah shielded the area with his coat to minimize the light leakage as he flashed the light briefly each time Ferris tried a new key. The evergreens in Sloan's backyard provided additional cover.

In less than three minutes they had gained entry and carefully brushed the snow off their feet before stepping in. Ferris removed a piece of masking tape from inside his lapel and marked the successful key. They walked through the kitchen and stopped briefly to riffle through the mail stacked on Phil's table. Jonah grinned at *The United States – Canada Journal of Child Psychiatry*, caught momentarily in the dimmed flashlight beam.

"Listen, Thornton," Ferris said at the front door, flicking his light on the deadbolt, "if he's home and uses both deadbolts, this key won't do ya. Let's jimmy a window so's you can always get in."

The two men went into the basement and looked over Phil's workroom and laundry. Ferris pointed to a basement window. "Old latches," he said, "that's what I'm lookin' for. We'll fix that window over the washing machine so you can get in without makin' noise dropping to the floor."

Ferris pulled the window open and extended the latch. Next, he took a keyhole saw out of his bag and sawed a short, angled slice off the latch extension. He tested the shortened locking piece, then filed the cut surface. He used a lead fishing sinker and pencil lead to darken the fresh metal to match the rest of the latch. He meticulously brushed the shavings onto a tissue and wiped things clean.

"Now watch this," Ferris said. He pushed the window shut, closed the latch, then retracted it slightly. "It looks like it's locked, don't it? Like the latch is all the way closed? Pull on the handle." When Jonah pulled and the window swung open, the latch handle remained down.

"Pretty slick, Ferris. So I push it shut and it looks like it's locked. Let's go do the same thing to the redhead's place." When they walked back to Ferris's car in the alley, it was snowing hard—no need to cover tracks.

The operation at Shelee Osbornson's house was much the same. Jonah played briefly with one of the cats, holding it affectionately after it meowed and brushed his leg. "Your time's a-coming, too, kitty," he whispered in its ear. Jonah also made an interesting discovery—something he figured might come in handy one night.

The two men drove back through the snowy streets and pulled into the lot at the all-night supermarket where Thornton had left his car. "Sure appreciate all your help," Thornton said. "Make copies of them keys, and I'll get 'em from you at Krystol's next week."

"They make keys at this market if you—"

"Naw, I don't want to wait," he said. "I've got a long drive home. Stop by my car and I'll get the $500 I owe you." They pulled up next to Jonah's Buick. Thornton got out and brushed the snow off his car's left side. He opened the door and pulled out a small backpack. Jonah got back in next to Ferris and fished in the pack for the money.

"Jesus Christ, Jonah, close your door. It's freezing!"

But he needed the door open to reduce the concussion to his ears. "My kids gave me this pack for my birthday," Thornton said. BOMP! BOMP! He'd pressed the revolver against Olsen's right side to muffle the two shots he pumped into him. Then he pulled the dying man's coat over his head and shot him once in the ear. He had chosen well, Jonah thought, putting the .357 magnum back into the pack. That .38 wad-cutter ammo hadn't been too noisy.

He quickly grabbed the tool bag containing the house keys off the backseat and closed the door of Ferris's still-running car. He felt pleased with himself as he drove from the parking lot. Ferris was well known to the local police and he'd probably just done them a favor.

A few blocks later, Thornton pulled into another market, parked near the entrance, and got out. I don't want to drive back home in this snow, he thought as he found some change in his pocket; and St. Paul's not too far away. He stomped the snow off his boots as he walked over to the pay phone.

Jonah knew it was late, but what the hell. He dialed Sugarspoon's number.

## Forty-five / Phil

It was noon, and Olie and Lucky had just returned with a large mule deer doe. "Well, that fills my doe tag," Olie said. "I'll keep the loin steaks, the rest is Slooper food."

"You know, that painting looks pretty good on your mantel," Shel said to Olie, looking at her small poker painting now resting above his fireplace.

"Sure is pretty," he said.

"Glad you like it; the painting's my thanks for your hospitality," Shel told him. "I'll order a frame for it at the gallery in Lodgepole tomorrow."

Olie smiled and ran his hands through his hair. "What a nice gift! I love it."

Shelee hugged Olie, then stepped back smiling, too. "Our trip and this setting has inspired me to try something new. And my first effort should stay here with you. Handle it by the edges; it'll be wet for two or three days."

The next morning, Shel and I volunteered to dig the vehicles out of the snowdrifts. We started the engines and let them run. Then we pulled both rigs into the backyard and, using Olie's truck winch, maneuvered the frozen elk carcass from the tree and lowered it onto the Suburban's roof rack. After lashing it on, much to Shel's disgust we tied the antlered head next to the hulking corpse.

"I hope Lucky doesn't decide to mount that thing for the farm," Shel said. "Maybe it will fall off on the way home."

"An elk rack is a badge of honor," I said with a laugh. "Even in Minnesota." I drove Lucky's car back to the driveway while

Slooper bounded about like a snow dolphin cresting a sea of drifts. Lucky, his arms full, came out of the house.

"Thanks for diggin' the vehicles out," Lucky said, stepping back and grinning at his elk head. Shel returned from the backyard, driving Olie's pickup.

Lucky gestured at the elk. "Looks pretty damn good up there, don't it?"

"I'm reserving judgment," she said, getting out and kissing her uncle.

Finally, with all of our stuff on board, we thanked Olie, piled into the car, and headed the Suburban in the general direction of Minneapolis. Snow from the car's hood swirled around the windshield as Lucky honked goodbye.

Our first stop was Lodgepole. Lucky and I gassed up while Shel went to the High Country Gallery, ordered a frame for Olie, and purchased a Kampino landscape with her poker winnings. Shel came back all smiles and put the wrapped painting carefully in the back.

As I drove north to Roscoe, we conducted a brief travel conference and agreed to retrace our southern route to I-90 East. Then my crew fell asleep. When we got to the junction at Roscoe, I glanced briefly at the north-pointing Billings signpost, then turned southeast toward Wyoming.

"Did I miss Belfry?" Shelee asked, stretching her arms now, her fingers curling around my neck.

" 'Fraid so," I said, "we're already in Wyoming. How do you like those mountains?" The west face of the Bighorns, an army of white peaks ahead of us, seemed to march across the sky as we motored east. "Let's come out here for a vacation next summer. Lunch in Sheridan okay?"

"Yes to both," Shel said, glancing back at Lucky who was still sound asleep. "Any thoughts about my dream, Doctor?" she asked, stretching again.

"I'd say it's about hope. Creative hope at several levels. Your artwork . . . our lovemaking," I said quietly.

Shelee reached across the seat, lacing both her arms around my right arm, hugging me as best she could. "I love you so," she said. "Pull over, we've never made love in Wyoming.'

Lucky stirred from his nap, holding one hand in front of his face. "It's damn near one o'clock. Let's eat."

After a quick lunch, we turned Lucky loose on the interstate. I sat in the back while Shelee read or talked with Lucky. Lucky spun the radio dial, looking for music or maybe news. ". . . genetic psychology," we heard a male voice say.

"Genetic psychology, my ass," Lucky said, mimicking the voice. "Never heard of it." He turned off the radio. "You ever heard of it, Doc?"

"Nope," I said with a vacant grin, "but I *am* listening for encrypted agenda." Lucky looked back at me and shook his head.

"Well everybody else has," Shel informed us. "We're riding beneath a perfect example. You people should watch more TV."

"Oh?" Lucky said. "You talkin' about that three-hundred-pounds of elk steak up there?"

"I'm talking about the head—the elk head. More specifically the antlers. Men need to kill other male animals to preserve their own breeding prerogatives. Hunting and warfare," she said.

"Oh, bullshit!" Lucky mumbled.

"What's more, men prefer younger women for the same reason—better able to breed. And women prefer rich men—better able to provide for their offspring. "Genetic psychology," Shelee twittered, "says everything we do is motivated by our need to spread and protect our progeny. You've probably never heard of sperm wars?"

"No, and neither have you," Lucky grumbled. "This better get better."

Shel was on a roll. "The French hate English because foreign language and culture represent intrusions to their collective genetics. That's the basis for most racial and ethnic hatred."

"Now you're talking crazy," he said. "There ain't no connection between hunting and prejudice. Any fool can figure that out. . . . Look," he said, pointing across the interstate to a large flock of Canada geese funneling into a stubble field. "Look at all them birds. I may need to shoot some honkers when we get home. Where's my shotgun?"

"In my basement," Shel answered.

"Maybe with that Thornton guy around, you better keep it loaded," Lucky said.

Shelee shook her head. "I don't want ammunition around the house, so I left the shells at the cabin."

"Well now, look'ee there," Lucky said. "That's a perfect example of some genetic phenom." He directed our attention to a duo of rusting combines on a hilltop, a junk-heap statue that looked like screwing dinosaurs.

"Those farmers should send their scrap to the Hirshhorn Museum in Washington," quipped Ms. Attitude, just as we crossed into South Dakota—a day's drive from home. "They could get *millions* for their junk."

## Forty-six / Phil

Willow McLendon sat in my office; her demure, wispy brogue—well suited to her fragile appearance—was rapidly putting me to sleep. Willow, an actress in her early fifties who'd received an Academy Award a few years before for her leading role in *A Way to Remember*, had been "referred" to me by Gloria Burns. We were halfway through her fourth visit and going nowhere.

In her first, and only productive session, she started with complaints that some scenes in her current movie project were stimulating some depressing memories for her.

"There's this character," Willow said, "who's the coordinating editor for the newspaper's investigation into SAPOR. And he has this problem where he goes nuts at about age forty, you know, a subplot. Anyway, I'm in several of the scenes with him where he starts doing nutsy stuff and it actually made me sick to my stomach. The guy reminds me so much of my second husband who really did go crazy at forty. I have a knot in my gut right now just thinking about it."

"Tell me about him," I said.

Willow sipped her coffee. "Danforth Brusnner. Maybe you remember him?"

"Vaguely."

"He's still around; gets some fair acting parts. He was in some British-African adventure movie last year. Anyway, we were married about six years, and I thought we had a pretty good relationship, considering the work and the Hollywood environment. But then, when he was almost forty, he started disappearing—then reappearing abroad."

Willow rose from her chair and walked around the office as she talked, stopping when she wanted to emphasize a point. She made only guarded eye contact.

"Well, he'd call me from Paris, Australia, or any damn fool place. Sometimes he was with a woman, other times with his foppish male chums," she said, stopping in her tracks, but looking at the floor. "The rotten bastard gave me the clap and I divorced him. It was a horrible experience." She began to pace again. "Do you know, he sometimes took so many drugs he'd forget my name in the middle of a conversation? He was a sexual sociopath, but most men are.

"I puzzled about Brusnner's conduct for a long time," she continued, "figuring the movie industry did it to him. But lately

I've learned that many people go crazy around age forty, men and women."

"It's a complaint I often hear," I said "Behaviors range from mild quirkiness to complete insanity."

"In *SABOR*, the editor sees an idiot psych and gets help. But I think these people stay pretty much nuts for the rest of their lives. Is it realistic to think that the shrink helps the fellow in the movie?" she asked.

"It's been my experience that psychiatric intervention can aggravate the problem," I said. Willow's own treatment history was probably getting in the way here, I decided. Patients who are treatment-wise are often the most difficult to reach. "So where are we going with this?"

"It's like a fatal accident where the victim goes on living," Willow said, ignoring my question. She stopped pacing and looked at the ceiling. "They become the zombies of destruction! They destroy everyone around them. It would be better if they just fucking died!" She smiled—not at me—and started moving around the room again.

"Those are strong words," I said.

"That's why I quit acting for three years. My career was about as good as anyone's, but the negative publicity made me crazy. And I just said to hell with it."

"Well, how is it troubling you now?"

Now, clearly the actress, Willow's brogue deepened as though my question had reminded her of that. "There was so much more going on with me and Danforth," she said, dramatically waving her hands. "We even tried the open marriage thing during the first few years. But it sort of got out of hand. You ever try that?" she asked. I shook my head, though she did not look my way or pause.

"I've decided couples who do that really don't love each other," she said, "or they have major problems. Swingers may think they love each other, but it doesn't last. Anyway, it's pretty stupid in these days of AIDS."

Unexpectedly, she sat down. "Oh, I don't know what's bothering me," Willow said with a sigh. "John-David, he's my current husband—he's done some quirky things that frighten me."

"What sort of things?" I asked.

"He's fifty-seven, not forty," she said vaguely. "His weirdness isn't important. It's only my viewpoint that's a problem," Willow concluded, reaching a self-analysis dead end.

During the next three sessions, Willow talked peripherally about her life and seemed to have no clear sense as to why she was seeing me. I decided to accept the ambiguity as part of the process. Though she continued to describe her history, it was always with tangential deliveries about feelings or insights. I believed Willow was capable of significant introspection, but we never got there. Her actress-self always exercised control.

I wanted to examine the ritual nature of her personal narratives, but now I sensed our sessions had little salutary value—perhaps it was time to give up on therapy.

"Willow, I am confused as to why you're here," I said. "Help me understand the direction of our conversations."

"I enjoy talking with you, Dr. Sloan. Is that a problem?"

"No, but for the past three sessions, I've heard none of the discomfort you expressed in our first meeting. So what is it we're trying to accomplish?"

"Do we have to always be working on something?" she asked, subtly flirtatious.

I got up and moved behind my desk, pacing slowly wanting to choose my words carefully. "It's my advice that our session for next week be put on hold until you can better identify your reasons for being here."

She walked over and gave me a perfunctory hug. Her brogue dissolved. "Well, thanks for listening to my prattle," she said. I opened my door for Willow and was pleased to see Manny settling into the outer office.

"Hello, Mr. Weston," Willow said, her hand resting on the doorknob. "Phil, I'll think about your suggestion and call you. Thanks again," she said, closing the outer door behind her.

I regretted not reaching Willow and knew she would not be back to see me again professionally.

Manny came into my office and sat down, smiling broadly.

"Great smile," I said. "What's up?"

"Two things. First, I'm rewriting *Mikie and Mike.* Mike is now a Native American in an urban setting."

*"Yes!"*

"Second, you would be doing Connie and me a big favor and a grand honor if you and Shelee would join us for dinner at the Coles'." He shoved his hand at me, palm first. "I know what you're going to say, but listen to me: How unusual would this be, after all the times we've spent together?"

"That's just the point," I said. "I need to tell—"

"But you, more than anyone, are responsible for the evolution in my writing—and in me!" he interrupted.

"Manny, my friend, you accomplished this yourself. You are one of the most disciplined men I know."

"Not without your help, Phil."

"I'm honored that you're inviting us," I said. "But where do the Coles fit into this?"

"Aren't we *suspicious,* Doctor? It's at their house, and Burns-Cole has bought my new novel. Gloria knows I see you; we're working on the guest list together."

"They bought *Mikie and Mike*?"

"Uh-uh. A brand new one."

"How could you have completed a new book in such a short time?"

"The book's nowhere near finished," he said. "Maybe 20 percent, but I know where I'm going with it. It's all right here." He pointed to his head.

"I thought you didn't like doing social things."

"You're avoiding an answer, Phil."

"Of course I accept," I said with a smile. "I don't even need to check with Shelee on this one; I know she'll be pleased to attend—we both will."

"Good."

"I have some news," I said. "I believe you don't need to come in anymore . . . unless you want to."

"I've been feeling the same way, Doc." Manny sighed heavily, then gave me a sad smile and an awkward nod. "But now can we be friends?" he asked tentatively.

"Absolutely."

## Forty-seven / Shelee

Phil handed his car keys to an attendant in front of the Coles' Minneapolis mansion. "With Thanksgiving less than a week away, this dinner party will be a real test of self-control," I told him.

"I'll keep that in mind myself," Phil said and rang the bell. "Nice layout," he whispered as the door swung open.

The place was full of celebrities, many of whom we'd met at the Coles' summer party. I searched for Ms. Billion, and fortunately for her, she wasn't present. But the Neals were there, home for the holidays from Tokyo.

"We're stationed with the Cole interests in Japan for the next six months," Serena explained.

"Then we *are* going to move here," Wayne added. "We sold our town house in D.C."

The dinner setting was surprisingly informal, a superb buffet of salads, side dishes, and entrées presented on long tables in a room adjacent to the dining hall. The Westons were seated next to the Coles, and I was pleased when Manny came up and asked us to sit next to them.

"To be more specific, Dr. Osbornson, I'd like you to sit next to us, on our left," he said.

I nodded and smiled, thinking to myself, now Dr. Sloan may sit at my left hand—or *on* my left hand.

A short program was placed in front of each diner, informing us that Manny's new novel, *Wrong Man Twice?* had been "purchased by Burns-Cole for both publishing and movie rights. Emmanuel Weston, Esq., will be treating our guests to a short reading after dessert."

"Why not before dessert?" I asked, fingering the leather-bound manuscript resting on the dinner table in front of Manny.

"It's pretty graphic, Shelee," Connie Weston said, her eyes twinkling. "Best wait until after dinner."

I lifted the cover and tried to peek at the first page. Phil nudged legs with me, then thunked his wine glass to mine.

"Another fine choice, Duncan," Phil said, raising his goblet of Nevada City, '86 Douce Noir.

"I had you two in mind when I selected it, Dr. Sloan," Duncan said and smiled, lifting his glass.

I, now distracted from my mischief, did not smile. "You're dead meat," I growled quietly to Phil. Manny patted my hand and slid the manuscript under his salad plate. I considered further incursions, but thought better of it.

Dessert included an absolutely sensational, cheek-cramping Key lime pie served along with coffee and after-dinner drinks. Then, after the Coles' household staff seated themselves around the dining area, Duncan gave a brief introduction:

"And now, honored guests, for your pleasure—and ours—I present America's master storyteller and mystery craftsman, Emmanuel Weston, reading from his newest novel."

Manny stood and slowly opened the manuscript, setting the drama. "Tonight I'm reading the first two chapters of *Wrong Man Twice?* I trust it will be short enough that no one will faint or fall asleep." He smiled, and the audience laughed and applauded.

As he began to read, his canorous, baritone voice moved to an unsettled, urgent tone.

Janis Sproul knew an innocent would likely die in the night now spreading across the city. When the stench had billowed up from the factories, the Loda River fog came with it. Nicolai called it "concurrence," fog from the putrid river rolling over the gray buildings in early afternoon. Vapors of madness, *chodstvo*: concurrence, another street person murdered—last night a child, the crime covered up and silenced.

Janis paced across the room, two-and-a-half strides if she took small steps, in the dismally cold *razvalina* sector apartment, her haunted eyes watching as the evening light faded through grimy windows. Nicki was out there somewhere, she thought, hoping for photos and evidence. He wanted to outguess the killer, the *zulek* street thugs, and the police—and maybe intervene.

Her thoughts raced, then scattered into the gloom. Why were the crimes being concealed? It had to be more than bureaucratic villainy. Westerners couldn't conceive how lawless Russian cities had become. My god, she thought, I'm so isolated. Waiting, waiting to coordinate the search. What a joke, coordinate with who? Retired *chief melecea*, Alexi Andriaovitch, who'd befriended and helped them, had not checked in for over a week. Had the *zulek* taken him out, too? She grabbed the receiver from the ancient phone and listened for a dial tone that was not there. Phones worked less than half the time in Vostov. What if Nicki needed to call? Cursing the circumstances that brought her to this fearful place, she slammed the receiver down.

Janis had arrived in Moscow a year ago, assigned to cover the new Russian Stars hockey team, the sweetest assignment a sports reporter could ask for—a ten-day stint at most. At age thirty-six, Janis had become *The Times's* hottest sports journalist. And why not? She was a natural. She had been a track and lacrosse star at Swarthmore and had majored in English and foreign affairs. Her family had always been involved in sports, and her brother was a major league pitcher. What's more, she could speak Russian. That's what got her here, the goddamn language skill!

When Janis got to Moscow, *The Times* had put her up at Hotel Rosseya, the best in town. At nine on her second morning, she was just heading out to Red Square to visit the Stars' practice rink when C. Price Newsome, the newspaper's editor in-charge-of-everything called. He wanted a favor. The famous trial lawyer, Dewey Remling, hired by *The Times* to cover the Simornik trial was sick, he said.

"In fact, he's two floors above you, heaving his guts out!" Newsome told her.

Amazing, she thought, the paper was paying Remling a million bucks to cover the Simornik trial and write a book about it. "But I don't know anything about the trial," Janis protested.

"Not to worry," Newsome said. "It's only for a few days; and it's your byline, Janis, until our friend Dewey takes over."

"What about the hockey—?"

"We'll have someone from the Moscow bureau do backgrounds on the Stars," Newsome said, interrupting her, "so you'll be up to speed when you go back to hockey. I have confidence you'll do a *great* job for us."

Reluctantly, Janis agreed and jotted down the particulars. *The Simornik trial,* she wrote, then rushed to keep up with Newsome. They talked for a few minutes and she had two pages of notes by the time they hung up. Then Janis-the-Brainless sat down on the bed in wonder. She had just agreed to cover the trial of the worst serial killer in current history!

The new Russian Justice *Beurokreja* was conducting the trial in Moscow for hordes of reporters, even though the industrial port city of Vostov, about a thousand kilometers south of Moscow, had been the killing ground. By moving the trial to Moscow, the politicians were sucking up to the press to avoid exposing Vostov's reeking pollution problems. Besides, the Vostov *Beurokreja* had long been in a state of great embarrassment, ever since arresting, trying, and executing the wrong man seven years earlier. And it soon became evident to Janis that news coverage of the trial was being stupidly pumped up.

On the first day of the trial, Janis met Nicki. Brilliant, freaky-crazy, the shell-shocked-in-Afghanistan, Nicolai Simornik, son of the accused. And Nicki said his father was *soshol s uma*, nuts, a schizophrenic who confessed to the murders, even fabricated evidence and stories to incriminate himself.

Now, sports reporter, Janis Sproul, impossibly in love with Nicki Simornik, suspended by her newspaper, pursued by god knows what, was trapped in a fog-bound, one room *razvalina* flat waiting for some unknown thing to happen. Worst of all, of course! WORST OF ALL, OF COURSE! The killings had continued all year, covered up by the authorities, the victims labeled missing persons or runaways. Moreover, schizoid Boris Simornik, within a month of hanging—the executioner's clock ticking—was obviously the wrong man. But the pompous *Beurokreja* would never admit to another mistake.

Janis poured herself a Scotch—never liked vodka—and noticed that she was down to the final two inches of her last bottle. Through the paper-thin walls, she could hear the occupants breathing in the next apartment. Shuddering fear rose in her throat—and something else! The feeble strip of light at the base of the apartment door was no longer continuous. There were shadows in two places.

Just then the phone made a metallic clatter and Janis, distracted by the shadows under the door, put the receiver to her ear. "*Allo, Allo?*" A click—nobody was there. But now she could hear the dial tone, a sound that further chafed her nerves. That's it, she decided, deal with shadows! She held the *Chineré* pistol by her side, unlocked the door to the apartment, and cracked it open. "I'll scare them off," Janis mumbled to herself, struggling with her fear. The shadows didn't move. THEY COULD NOT MOVE! She shrieked at the specter of death—two pairs of it standing. Four shoes, four socks on four legs, cut off at mid-calf; gore leaked down, brick red on deadly white. She faints.

Nicki was there and he stroked her face. "You're lying in the doorway? Janis, *libimaja,* what happened?"

Janis drew her knees to her chest and covered her face—crying. "The legs! Don't you see the legs, Nicki? Who could do this?"

"What legs?"

Her head and neck felt suddenly painful—she was fully conscious. There was a bitter taste in her mouth.

"My god, they're gone!" she said, pointing to the bloody outlines on the floor. "There were severed legs standing by the door, Nicki!" She groped around. "My gun, it's gone, too! Someone was here."

> **M**orning came finally, without sun, gray and cold—gray and cold inside the flat, except in the bed where Nicolai held her.

Manny closed the folder at the end of the second chapter. "Only one more thing I'll reveal about the story," he said to the guests. "Someone needs to single out the killer, but for a most peculiar reason. But you'll have to see the movie or read the book." He beamed at Gloria, who returned an admiring, satisfied smile. Everyone applauded and Manny sat down.

"Now do you see why it was best to wait until after dessert?" he said to me, settling in his chair.

"I wish you would have read more," I said. "I want to know what happened."

"The Westons are moving to the Cole-Burns Moscow headquarters," Gloria announced to our end of the table, "to finish the book."

After dinner, I visited with several people, then went over to a group where Phil appeared to be the center of attention. It seemed he was leading a discussion about current self-help/philosophy books. "The essentialist language of these books mirrors the child frozen in his unresolved state," he said. "The accompanying myths enable the reader to break through personal boundaries and to view resolution." Phil had attracted quite a crowd.

"What's the point of repeating the parables in so many forms?" someone asked. "These books take themselves so seriously."

"Repeating gives the reader more opportunities to personalize the experience," Phil said. "And repetition reinforces healing." Phil looked thoughtful as he sipped his port. "Their serious tone, which is usually reserved for the author's concepts, provides an embedded polemic to the allegories, because the myths are often presented with considerable whimsy. But what *isn't* recognized is that these books minister to children's broad range of fragility." Phil's audience went glassy-eyed.

What is this abstruse bullshit? I wondered. I took Phil's arm and smiled. "*I* don't understand what he just said, and he's *my* roommate." Everybody laughed.

"Everyone is emotionally fragile," Phil offered, "but in different ways and to different degrees throughout their lives. The thing that will disable one child might have a different effect on another. One sees that in families all the time—each member has a *different* experience growing up in the same family.

"So some damaged children become murders, others financiers, artists, or whatever. Look at Ingmar Bergman—out of his childhood trauma came insight, beauty, and a magnificent body of work."

Phil's Blazer was damp and chilly as we drove away from the Coles'. I snuggled against his arm, as best I could across the gap between the bucket seats. "You are a Renaissance man," I said, "and I want your body when we get home."

"Of course you do," Phil said and grinned cheerfully.

"I'm leavin' early tomorrow to go goose hunting," Jonah Thornton told his wife, Mary. "And I'm spending the afternoon out at the rest home." He gathered up his things as she told him her plans, not listening to her at all. Jonah knew her plans from the phone recorder. Mary was going to visit her brother, a short drive away in Browerville. She was taking the truck and would be gone until Sunday night.

Once on the road to Minneapolis, Jonah turned nervously to glance at the duffel bag and suitcase on the rear seat. He had $15,000 in cash, a false passport, and all the documents he needed to disappear permanently. When he got to town, he drove by the redhead's house. But there were no vehicles and, assuming she was at Sloan's, he went there to check. Sure enough, her green station wagon was parked in the doctor's driveway. He drove back to the redhead's.

It was four A.M. Thanksgiving morning when Thornton returned to Osbornson's. He parked two blocks away from her house, walked down the alley to the woman's yard, and entered the back gate.

An empty house was a lucky break, he thought as he let himself in through the basement window and closed it carefully behind him. He located his hiding place beneath the stairs that led to the first-floor hall. He settled there for a few moments, behind some wine cases, to make sure that he would be well hidden. The hall door to the basement was held open at the stairhead by a red bootlace looped around the doorknob and tied to the bannister. Jonah knew he could not move once his guests arrived.

Osbornson's two house cats padded down the basement stairs to greet Thornton as he lay down for a nap on a dusty, braided rug by the lower landing. He used his jacket for a pillow. One of the pets used the litter box a few feet away. He slept until seven, when the alarm on his watch awakened him. Jonah's holstered .357 lay beside him; one cat used it for a pillow. He got up stiffly, stretched, and urinated in the laundry sink.

Jonah reviewed his plans as he searched around. He found a small plastic bucket—a good piss pot for his spot under the stairs. He knew from the week's telephone conversations that Dena Lewis and his daughters would be coming about noon and planned to go to the redhead's parents' for Thanksgiving dinner later in the day. Except, he smiled to himself, he figured to kill all of them with the fancy pump shotgun he'd found previously in the professor's basement. Jonah loaded the weapon, patted the four extra buckshot shells in his jacket pocket, and zipped the shotgun back in its case. He finished eating a candy bar and made himself comfortable.

## Forty-eight / Shelee

"No breakfast?" I asked. "Are you feeling okay?"

"My stomach's really upset," Phil complained. "I just *can't* be getting sick on Thanksgiving. Think I've got a fever, too. You take off, there's nothing I need but rest."

"Bad timing, sweetheart. Maybe you'll feel better this afternoon"

"Hope so. I'll see you and the girls at your house. If not, I'll call. It's time for me to soak in a hot tub."

Phil shuffled to the back of the house, while I gathered up the Thanksgiving groceries that we'd bought the day before. We had met for lunch, shopped for food, and then spent a quiet evening at his house watching a movie.

I loaded the groceries into my station wagon, looked in on Phil reclining in his tub, kissed him, and drove to my house. It was time to start the Thanksgiving cooking.

When I got home, I put some groceries away in the fridge. I left the cranberry packages on the drain board and organized others on the counter. I would start with the cranberry sauce, I decided. I fed the cats their morning food, soaked the cranberries in the sink, and went to the basement to select the wines. My white wines were stored in an old root cellar behind the furnace. The reds could tolerate warmer conditions; they were stacked in wooden crates underneath the basement stairs.

I selected three great white wines, an Italian Thurgau—no German wines for *my* mom—an old Vernaccia, and a solid, Australian Chardonnay. Phil was bringing the red wines from his collection—if he's well enough to come. If not, I would take some reds from here.

The three girls arrived with an interesting-looking Japanese-style salad, and flowers for the table. "Thanks, ladies," I said, putting the flowers in a vase. The girls were uneasy at first but relaxed after my hugs. We heated up some soup and gabbed through lunch. Then I put them to work. When I called to check on Phil, he answered on the first ring.

"I'm just sitting here with Rose and Lucky, watching the OSU team get killed. I'm too sick to go to your folks. Sorry."

"I'm sorry you're still sick," I said. "The girls will be disappointed."

"I still want to send the wine over to your folks," he said. "Could you come by and pick it up? It's been set out to warm."

"That's sweet, Phil. But you don't need to—"

"I would feel better by contributing, Shel. I'll be there in spirit."

"Bad pun."

"Also, I'd love to say hello to the Stone Lake ladies. So plan to come by. Oh, Lucky says they're going to Rose's folks for dinner. They'll be to your mom's sometime after seven o'clock."

"Already knew that," I said. "Ask Lucky if he wants me to bring him the shotgun."

I could hear my uncle in the background. "Tell her I've given up hunting for the year," Lucky said.

"Okay," I said. "We'll be over in a little while." I rang off.

The food Jonah had been smelling all morning and planned to eat after killing them was forgotten when he heard the Osbornson woman's call to Sloan. He knew that leaving the redhead's house in the daytime would be dangerous; but if he could catch them all together at Sloan's, it would be worth the risk. Then he'd be on his way to points south.

Jonah watched from a basement window as the professor's station wagon backed out of the driveway, then listened while his daughter's car drove off. He left the house by the back door, took his .357 out of its holster, and laid it on the seat of his car. He made the short drive to Sloan's neighborhood. Jonah patted his gun as he turned onto Blaircross Road. As soon as he cruised by the house, he knew that his plan had failed—there was an unfamiliar Chevy Suburban parked in the driveway, and the neighbor kids were making a snowman in the yard across the street.

He fingered his quarry's house keys on their separate key ring and decided to head for his mother's rest home at Rawlings Creek. He'd just kill them some other time, he thought, maybe at night next week. Should he give up on this bullshit? he wondered. Sveen had said that a guilty plea could net a five-year sentence, and that he could be out in two.

Thornton sighed. Oh hell, there was still time to get a Thanksgiving dinner at his brain-dead mother's place.

The Tuesday after Thanksgiving weekend was an unmitigated disaster. Phil stayed at my house and, after oversleeping because our power had gone off, we awoke to an infamous Minnesota ice storm.

With the electricity back on, we rushed through our morning chores. Phil left right after breakfast. I dumped the dishes in the sink and hurried out the door. Fortunately, I'd parked my station wagon in the garage, so I didn't have to scrape ice for five minutes like Phil had to do. Backing out the drive, I remembered an art folio that I needed, so I rushed back into the house, grabbed it, and jumped into my car, now parked by the curb.

I was still fussing with my seat belt two blocks from my house and, as I approached a stoplight, an older, white sedan with a sole male driver—right on my tail—appeared in the mirror. The next thing I knew, my beautiful green station wagon was sliding through the intersection onto Cedar Lake Drive. No cars were coming in the westbound lane, but a big delivery truck in the eastbound smashed into my car's right side. The door buckled and I could feel it—actually see it in slow motion—come across the seat and smack into my right leg. The station wagon spun around and crashed into a light pole, throwing me hard against the steering wheel. When the ambulance took me away, the policeman said, "No one hurt but you, ma'am, and *you're* lucky to be alive."

My hospital room and the corridor outside were full of people—Phil, my parents, my sister and Tim, Rose and Lucky. After three hours of emergency treatment and X-rays, my bandaged leg was put in traction. Our family doctor, Clayton Mallory, shooed most everyone out. But I insisted that Phil stay.

"Well, you're in one piece," Clayton said, "and you're going to be 100 percent, but to get there, you'll need an orthopod, and I want you to be examined by a second internist. Here's the situation: Your right femur has a clean break five inches above . . ."

I went into shock, the room faded to a purple-flecked gray, my stomach headed for the basement. Dr. Mallory held one hand, Phil held the other.

After I revived, Clayton continued. "You've heard the worst news, so here's the rest: Your leg is banged up, and it's a miracle there's no damage other than one break. But a broken femur is a big deal—we'll talk about that in a minute." I stayed conscious this time, my innards going only halfway to the basement.

"Your lower abdomen is severely bruised," he continued. "There's a little internal bleeding, but no real organ damage. But you're going to be sore as hell for a while. And I want to be sure of my diagnosis, so I'm having another doctor examine you."

I began to cry, and Dr. Mallory patted my hand. "I'll talk with your family; you're going to heal up fine. Be back in a few minutes."

"Oh, Phil," I wailed, "what am I going to do?"

## Forty-nine / Shelee

I never knew I had so many friends. There was a stream of continuous visitors. Finally on Saturday, five days after the accident, I was only a day away from going home. I had ugly blue-and-green bruises, a four-inch incision at midthigh and a smaller one on my hip. My leg had a thing called an intermedullary rod in it—right down the center of the bone. No cast! The orthopedic surgeon said it was the best choice. I could start to use crutches in about five weeks, back to school after Christmas break, limited walking maybe six weeks after that, and get the rod taken out in late spring.

Did it sound bad? Not when Phil said he was moving in to take care of me. While explaining this to my sister, I was surprised when Marion from the frame shop peeked in.

"And I've got to talk to you about your monastery painting," Marion said after the usual hospital-room small talk. "The painting's caused quite a stir."

"That's nice to hear."

"It's very masterful, Shel; but more than that, everyone who's seen it feels it's an important work. I think so, too, though I can't put my finger on it."

"I intended it that way," I said and smiled. "Will you ladies please help me change position?" I lifted with my elbows and Abby, Marion, and I adjusted my poor, sore body.

"You know, someone told Liz Carbonnader about the piece," Marion said, smoothing my covers, "and she came in yesterday. Liz didn't know what kind of shape you were in, so she gave me a release for you to sign. Says she wants to do a story on it, pictures and all. Call her if you want. What did Liz mean when she talked about researching the faces?"

"I believe she's on to something," I said and smiled again. "Is it framed yet?"

"Yes, and it looks terrific. I want your permission to put it on display. She's on to what?"

"One hint: There's a serving maid in the painting—only woman there—a historical figure, famous turn-of-the-century American painter. . . . You've got my permission to display the work, but it's not for sale—not yet anyway. The painting has a name: *Salon du Monastère.* There's another hint."

Marion handed me the *Post Express* release form and a pen. I signed it and handed it back.

"I guess I'd better run now," she said. "By the way, are you going to do any more representational paintings?"

"You bet," I said, "I have more than a month before I can go back to school. So, I'm staying home and painting.

"Down, but not out," I said to Abby after Marion left.

"It's going to be like living together," I said to Phil as we drove home from the hospital Sunday. "Thanks for all your help. I love you so much."

"I love you too, Shel. I guess sex is out."

"Yeah, Phil, while you're driving," I said, reaching over to give him a private caress. "Dr. Mallory said lovemaking will help my leg heal. What the hell are we going to do about Christmas? You know I asked Dena and the Thornton girls over for Christmas Eve." I broke out in a cold sweat and my heart skipped a beat. "Phil, I just remembered." I put my hand to my mouth

Phil looked at me. "Remembered what? What's wrong?"

"I ran the light because I was looking in the mirror. There was a guy on my tail. White car."

"Did he look like Thornton?" Phil asked.

"I don't know. Middle-aged, that's all I remember."

Phil took my hand. "There's nothing we can do about it now. Christmas is going to happen. Why don't we stay with our plans, if you feel up to it?"

Well, I felt up to Christmas and a lot more. I lurched around the house in the wheelchair and had my painting stuff moved from upstairs to the dining room. Finally, I gave up on the stupid wheelchair and started hobbling around the house, holding on to the furniture. Then I talked the orthopod into letting me use crutches on a limited basis. I also rediscovered the luxury of a bathtub.

A week after I'd been home, Elizabeth Carbonnader's *Post* article about the *Monastère* painting came out—she gave it excellent coverage. I had a lot of visitors but found it irritating—I was enjoying painting and wished to be alone, except when Phil was there. But when Gloria Burns called to say she was on a secret mission, I eagerly invited her over.

"I hope your drinking isn't curtailed," Glo Buns said, handing me a bottle of beautiful '88 Vouvray.

"Nope, it isn't, Gloria. Thanks. What's your secret mission?"

"Has Marion said anything about the delegation viewing your *Salon du Monastère* painting?"

"What delegation?"

"From the art institute and the Cole-Burns Corporations. Well, Duncan and I for the latter. . . ." Gloria let her words hang in the air for a moment, then continued. "If the painting's for sale, have you set a price for it?"

"No, have you?"

"Shelee, dear, let me explain our offer." Gloria began to walk slowly around the room, appearing to choose her words—though I figured she had it well rehearsed. "Since I'm on the institute's board, and also represent our corporation, we—Cole-Burns that is—want to purchase the painting for the institute. But we want our corporate collection to benefit, also. So we'll display it on alternate years. Your second painting in their collection—our first."

"I'm really honored," I told her, now finding my couch uncomfortable. I hobbled over to the recliner that Phil had recently brought from his house. I eased myself down and extended the leg support.

"There's one minor problem," she said, "but we think we have a solution."

"What's that?"

"We want to agree on the sale, but put the money in escrow until after the spring show. We wouldn't close the sale until then."

I shrugged. "Go on."

"I guess I'd better quit beating around the bush," Gloria said, her words coming faster. "Here's the deal: We're prepared to pay eighty thousand dollars for the piece—everybody just loves it—but everyone also wants it to be in the spring show. You know the problem with the rules?"

"That only *artists* can submit *unsold* works to the show?" I said.

"Yes."

"I'm glad I'm sitting down," I said with a smile. "Will the escrow get you around the unsold condition? Sounds a little fishy."

"It gets worse," Gloria continued. "This is the institute's hundred-year anniversary, and there's going to be a Centennial Prize in addition to the usual awards. We think *Salon* is a contender."

"No shit!"

"So we'd like you to submit the painting with a five hundred thousand dollar price tag, and . . . well, assuming it doesn't sell, we'll close the eighty-grand purchase after the show."

"Have you got the contract with you?" I asked, pointing to her thin leather briefcase.

"Right here." Gloria unzipped the case. "And a check for eighty thousand."

"Are you going to make the deal public?"

"We haven't decided yet," she said, handing me the papers. "Can you keep it quiet?"

"Sure, considering that however this turns out, it's favorable to me." I still couldn't believe the damn check. Finally, I said, "Keep the check, Gloria; however, I'd like to hang on to the contract and think about it. As I said, I'm truly honored."

"Of course, Shel, take your time."

## Fifty / Phil

Shel was managing quite well with her crutches and pushing her recovery at every opportunity. I rearranged the furniture to make her movement around the house easier. Living together was delightful, although I missed some of my own home's conveniences. In a couple of weeks, after the holidays are over and Shelee can bend her leg more comfortably, we plan to shop for her new car. Despite her newly found wealth—wackily in escrow—she was considering an economy van, a green one, of course.

Trish Lathrop came over in the afternoon to help with the Christmas Eve preparations. She was on the outs with her boyfriend and seemed a little down.

"Where's Will?" Shel asked her.

"He's with Seth, but he'll be over later."

"You know Seth is welcome to join us," Shel said.

"Thanks, but he's moonlighting tonight. Some security job. Says he gets double-time pay and needs the money."

"No financial problems, I hope," Shelee said.

Trish laughed. "I don't think so. He just goes all-out for Will's Christmas presents. Spends a fortune on the kid. Then he's got some big deal planned for Will's birthday in February."

"What is it?" I asked.

"I haven't a clue," Trish said with a sigh. "But one thing I do know, while Seth was a terrible husband, he's a great dad."

It was late afternoon on Christmas Eve when Jonah Thornton drove to Minneapolis. He was having dinner with his mother at the rest home, he had told Mary, and would be back at the farm by nine. She planned to spend the afternoon and evening with her brother's family, then Christmas day with him. She had even smiled at Jonah and said he seemed less angry. He couldn't help smiling back, but only because she amused him. Jonah knew Mary was pleased that her daughters would be with their new friends on Christmas Eve.

"I'll call up there at your mother's if I'm going to be late," she said as he was leaving.

"Suit yourself."

By morning, it wouldn't make any difference, Jonah thought. Everybody would know he'd killed that bunch. He got into the car and put his .357 magnum under his coat on the seat beside him. Maybe he would not have to use the revolver if the shotgun was still in the basement. Jonah smiled to himself—he was going to do 'em in with their own gun. He felt the shells in his coat pocket. Enough for a group killin', he was sure; show them smart-ass college girls. He'd keep that fancy old shotgun, too—and torch the house—it would be a shame if all that paint thinner went to waste.

Thornton had been away from his daughters for so long now that he regarded them coldly, as simply a threat to his freedom. No way was he going to end up like Morton Lewis, he decided. He'd visited Lewis at the state prison and just the thought of it pissed him off—he hated the Lewis girl, Sloan, and his redheaded girlfriend. That redhead's car wreck was only a show-stopper, he thought—it merely extended their miserable lives for three more weeks. But what the hell, there were always delays to contend with. As Jonah neared Minneapolis, he was getting hungry and wondered if anything decent would be open tonight, what with the holiday and all.

Dena Lewis and the Thornton girls showed up just after five, bringing food, flowers, and presents. The girls chatted excitedly as they put their presents under the Christmas tree.

"Where's Heidi and Fritz?" Trudy Thornton asked first thing.

"They're at home tonight," Shel explained. "Their grandparents are in town for Christmas."

"Where from?" Trudy asked absently, peeking around under the tree.

"St. Louis."

Trudy looked up and put her hands on her hips. "Well, it would be nice if Heidi and Fritz were here," she said.

About six o'clock we served a pickup dinner of filet mignon and scampi, side dishes courtesy of our guests, and a couple of our best wines. We opened some presents during dessert; wrappings littered the floor. We were a pretty loud bunch, singing and laughing, having a good time.

"Telephone," I heard Shel say. I picked up the phone in the hall. It was Will calling for Trish.

"Trish," Shel shouted over the noise, "Tell Seth there's extra food if he wants to grab a bite here." I turned down the stereo.

Trish returned from the kitchen and set the phone back on the table in the hall. "They've already eaten," she said. "Seth is going into work, but he's dropping Will off in a few minutes."

We cranked up the stereo and continued to open presents. Because I was sitting by the tree, it was my job to pass out the gifts.

"Who's next?" Shel called to me.

I leaned over for a gift. Except for Andy Williams on the stereo, the room was suddenly dead silent. I turned to see a man standing in the hall holding a shotgun.

"Daddy!" Trudy screamed. "What are you doing here?"

"Who is he?" Trish said to Shel in tears.

Jonah Thornton rapped the shotgun against the doorway and then walked into the room. "I'll ask the questions, blondie. He nudged Trish's chin with the barrel. "Who's getting dropped off?" When she didn't answer, he whirled suddenly and blasted the Christmas tree. The girls screamed and huddled on the couch. The room filled with dust. Thornton pumped out the spent shell and slammed the action shut. He nudged Trish's chin again. "Talk!" he said.

"My son," she cried. "He's just a child."

"I guess we'll have time to wait for him," Thornton said as he walked to the front window, pushed the curtain aside, and looked out. "All of you sit down and shut up," he said with narrow intensity, motioning with the shotgun. Then he pointed it directly at me. "You, Sloan, get over on the couch with the rest of them."

I moved to the couch as he tracked me with the shotgun; then I recognized the gold trigger guard—it was Lucky's gun. My heart was pounding with fear and anger. I wanted to kill Thornton, just get my hands on his bloody neck.

Trudy sat on the floor in front of her sister and Dena. The two young women held the sobbing girl against their legs. "Daddy," Trudy cried, "please don't hurt us, Daddy." But Thornton ignored her. He walked calmly across the room, looked over the stereo controls, and turned off the music. He kept one eye on us as he glanced out the window again. His manner was matter-of-fact, chilling.

"All of you stand," he demanded, motioning again with the 12-gauge. "And Trudy, keep your goddamn mouth shut or you'll be the first to get it!"

I stood at one end of the couch, turned slightly, hoping for an opening as Thornton looked us over, staring in turn at each of us, holding the gun ready. "Stand back, Sloan," he ordered, stepping in front of me. "You're too fucking big to mess with." He also moved back, probably reading my thoughts.

His eyes clouded for a moment, then he said, "Merry Christmas, Doc." I saw the blow coming, but reacted too slowly. He swung the gun and smashed the left side of my head with the flat of the stock. I went down in a heap.

The side of my head and ear hurt terribly, but the rug felt so good on my face and the pain began to fade. I knew that I needed to rest. Somewhere, from a long way off, there were people screaming. A thing nagged at me slightly—I was supposed to do something, but I just couldn't recall what it was.

## Fifty-one / Shelee

My mind raced madly around, not believing what was happening. When Thornton hit Phil, my thoughts cleared, became focused. I had to stay aware, do something, but what? Jonah was going to kill us all. Could I use my leg? I wondered.

Poor Phil was lying on the floor, his eyes partly open, and blood was leaking from his mouth. He twitched occasionally. I was so scared—maybe he was dying.

I couldn't bear to live without him. Yet I didn't want to die; there was still so much for me to live and love. I felt some calmness; my life had been full—quitting now would be okay. But being killed by this rapist bully with my uncle's shotgun! I felt sorry for Lucky, then suddenly hated my cats. One was stalking around in the Christmas tree mess, and the other was playing with the wrapping paper, both oblivious to our danger. My ears were still ringing from the gun blast.

Thornton sat on the arm of the recliner, steading himself with one leg, letting the chair rock slightly. He looked over at Phil and grinned hatefully.

"Please, Mr. Thornton, tell us why you're here," I pleaded.

Thornton glared at me, sullen as a bull. He waved the shotgun, flaring his nostrils. "This gun will do the telling," he said.

Trish gasped and we all looked over. Her ex-husband was standing in the basement doorway with a pistol leveled at Thornton.

"Don't move!" Seth ordered. "Drop the gun!"

Jonah in a quick motion, first as if he were going to comply, lowered the shotgun toward the floor, then blasted Seth Cooper.

Seth jolted back against the doorjamb and crumpled to the floor. Trish and the girls cried desperately as Thornton walked over to Seth, poked him with the gun barrel, and booted his body down the stairs. We could hear Seth thudding against the steps into the cellar. Thornton kicked his pistol after him.

"One more dead cowboy," he muttered, ejecting a shell, replacing it with two from his pocket. My heart shuddered, first for Seth, then for us. When Thornton reloaded the gun, I kept thinking about how I use it—it should have only one shot left.

"Okay, all of you get close on the sofa." He motioned with the gun. "Kinda like a family portrait, only this ain't no camera." He lifted the vase from the coffee table and threw the water and flowers in Phil's face. "You, too, Sloan—I'm getting low on shells. I want you to see your girlfriend die."

Phil struggled but could not get up. Finally, he pulled himself to a sitting position next to the couch, then slumped sideways to the floor. My heart rose a little when I imagined he'd faked this last move.

Jonah backed up; his gun was leveled at us. Dena and his daughters gibbered fearfully, pleading with him. As he stepped backward, I saw my old Jesusa cat. Her tail twitched under some Christmas wrap behind Thornton, and his right foot came down directly on her. She shrieked and bolted. Jonah fell onto his back and the gun discharged into the ceiling.

"The gun's empty!" I screamed. "Get the son of a bitch!" I jumped up, falling full force across the coffee table as my leg collapsed under me. The pain, beyond anything I'd ever felt, ripped through my entire body. Trish and the two older girls pounced on Thornton as he tried to get up. He swung at them with the shotgun, knocking them loose; then, leaving Lucky's gun on the floor, he stood with one foot on it, ripped his jacket open and pulled a revolver from his belt. Plaster littered the room.

"The gun ain't empty, lady," Thornton said, "and I got a backup. Now let's get on with this." He used the pistol to direct us to the couch. Phil, who had returned to a sitting position, raised his arms and tried to say something, but his voice was faint, his words garbled. I could barely move, and as I tried to crawl around the table, my leg knotted up in the middle of my thigh, doubling in size.

Dena, Trish, and Carol dragged themselves off the plaster-and-paper-strewn rug and slumped back onto the couch. They pushed the coffee table away and pulled me next to their legs. Phil was sitting on the floor at the far end of the couch, his head against the cushions. He appeared barely conscious. My leg and belly were in agony, and I cried, too. I was about to die and I couldn't even hold Phil. I couldn't even reach him. And for the first time I felt defeated; I hardly cared what happened.

But dear Trudy, who was still standing, began screaming. She was not yet ready to give up, and in a convulsion of suicidal fury, threw herself across her father's gun arm. "You can't do this, Daddy! These are my friends!" she screamed.

Jonah appeared to enjoy her attack. He grabbed the revolver with his free hand and shoved it back in his belt. Then he picked Trudy off his arm by her hair and smashed her face with his fist. She went limp and blood rushed from her nose. She reached up to hold Jonah's arm again, perhaps trying to take some of the weight off her hair. I closed my eyes, seeing how a grasshopper holds tightly to a fisherman's finger even as he's running it through, threading a hook into its head and body. My eyes snapped open. Thornton reared back to strike his daughter again.

But something caught my eye—a faint movement near the basement staircase. I could see Seth Cooper on the top step, trying to steady his aim at Thornton. I held my breath. He fired a shot into the rug near Thornton's feet. Jonah dropped Trudy and frantically reached for his revolver, then stooped for the shotgun.

"Don't!" I heard Phil hiss, now holding Thornton's revolver and weaving precariously on his knees. Thornton reached for the shotgun and Phil fired. The blast was deafening. Thornton pitched face-first across his daughter. Phil sat back against the couch, still pointing the gun at Thornton.

I heard something clatter in the hall. I looked as Seth shoved his pistol across the wood floor in our direction. Then he nudged himself up to the landing, gave a sad, bloody smile, and rested his head on his outstretched arm.

"Oh, god, Seth!" Trish blurted and ran to kneel over him.

Carol and Dena rushed to Trudy, pulled her from under Jonah's body, and put her on the sofa. She was drenched with her father's blood.

Phil pointed at Thornton. He hissed the word, "Gun."

Dena Lewis picked up the 12-gauge and dumped it behind the couch. Phil handed her the revolver and she dropped it there, too. Then he crawled by me, stopped, and began to gently feel my leg. He looked terrible. I lifted his hand away, gritting my teeth at the pain.

"I'm not going to die," I said, "go help Seth."

Phil, momentarily confused, got halfway to his feet, then returned to his hands and knees. He crawled to Thornton and rolled him over, then listened to his chest. Thornton's breathing was heavily labored, and with each breath he made the worst sound I've ever heard. It was as though there were bubbles in his chest.

Phil hesitated, then crawled toward Seth. "We need three . . . no four ambulances," he mumbled. Transport four . . . uh, five injured. Call the police." He could hardly speak, appearing in agony with each word, holding his chin when he talked. "Get ice for Trudy's face," he said.

When Phil reached Seth, he had Trish and Carol pull him onto the hall floor. He yanked Seth's shirt open to examine the wounds. "No wonder," he mumbled as he ran his hand across Seth's bulletproof vest. Phil and Trish undid the vest and lifted the front half over Seth's head. Phil ripped the bloody T-shirt and examined Seth's chest, then felt his neck. "He's bleeding into his lungs," Phil said. "Trish, I'll need help with him. Can you do mouth-to-mouth? My jaw's broken."

Then he wheezed to Dena Lewis who was talking on the phone, "Tell them major pulmonary trauma!"

I repeated our address for Dena.

"It's already been reported," she replied. "There's help on the way."

"We need help for Seth *now!*" Phil yelled, pointing at him. "Make sure they understand that!"

When he turned his attention back to Seth and started Trish on the resuscitation routine, I noticed a piece of tissue paper lying next to them. Seth's face, now framed in the black vest, was whiter than the paper. Trish came away after a few puffs, her face covered with blood.

"It's *okay,* Trish," Phil said, tears running down his cheeks, "he saved our lives. I'd do it if I could!"

Carol came from the kitchen with a wet towel and handed it to Trish. "I'll take over," she said, and knelt down. Jonah Thornton's terrible chest noises continued, his blood soaking into my carpet.

Someone knocked at the front door, and Trish, wiping her face, opened it to see her son, stricken and wide-eyed. A few neighbors stood behind him.

"Will, oh Will!" Trish cried. "I was worried sick about you." My heart went out to her as she quickly put her arm around Will and ushered him back outside.

"But what about Dad?" I heard him say as she pulled the door closed.

A couple of neighbors tended to Trudy, who was now sitting up, while Phil, Dena, and Carol worked over Seth. Except for Thornton's frightful breathing, the room was deathly still. Everyone watched as Phil held Seth's nose and set the breathing rhythm with his free hand.

There was a commotion on the porch, and Will came bursting through the front door with Trish trying to hold him back. "My dad's been shot," he cried as he ran toward his father. Poor little Will, his arm around his mother's waist, now watched with the rest of us.

After a few minutes, Phil listened to Seth's chest, then shook his head. "It's no use," he said hoarsely. "No use . . . no one can save him—he's gone."

The cops and medics arrived, did a cursory triage, checked both gunshot victims, then focused their work on Thornton. I felt overwhelmed with hatred. "Let that bastard die!" I shouted. But they hurried him into an ambulance, covered Seth, and tended to the rest of us.

## Fifty-two / Phil

Death felt like a thing sitting in the middle of my chest. I'd watched Seth die and shot to kill Thornton. I lay in the hospital bed trying to find anything that made sense amid the pressing confusion I felt. We all had come close to death—so close that I couldn't shake the weight of it.

"Phil," Shelee cried when she saw me. Two orderlies had wheeled her in and were now easing her into bed. A nurse lingered for a few minutes, attaching an IV to Shel's arm. "Oh honey," Shel said, "I can't stop thinking about Seth and Will."

"I know," I said. "I've been lying here wondering how Seth knew we needed help." I had to talk through my teeth because my mouth was restricted by a jaw restraint.

"How did you get Thornton's gun?" Shel asked.

"I guess it fell out of his belt when he was struggling with Trudy," I said. "I just looked down and there it was. I wonder if Thornton's alive."

"You think it's okay to call Trish?" Shel asked. "I won't be able to rest until I talk with her. The look on Will's face—it just breaks my heart." Shel wept, and I got out of bed and held her.

"Let's call," Shel said and wiped her eyes. She dialed the phone, and I felt her stiffen as she waited for Trish to answer. "Abby," Shelee said. "What are you doing there?" I continued to hold Shel as she talked. There were long pauses where she just listened. Tears streamed down her cheeks and she wiped them with a tissue.

"I know," she said, several times. "Thanks. I love you, too, sweetie," she said and hung up.

"Trish is on her way here," Shel said. "Will's finally asleep and the three girls are staying there, too." She reached up and touched my face. "How bad are you hurt, sweetheart?"

"Oh, oh, here come the MPs," I said as a nurse entered with some meds for Shelee.

"That's right, Dr. Sloan," the nurse scolded. "You have to get back in your own bed right now—you're supposed to be lying flat." She gave the pills to Shel and checked her IV.

"Why flat?" Shel demanded as I got back into bed. "What's wrong with him?"

"My jaw's not broken," I cut in. "Just dislocated." I felt light-headed and the room faded briefly.

"Thank you, Doctor," the nurse said, straightening some of Shel's apparatus. "He's going to be fine."

"Then why flat?" Shel asked the nurse as if I were nowhere around. She gulped her pills and took a long drink of water.

"You'll have to ask Dr. Mallory," the nurse said. "Or him." She pointed to me and left.

"My inner ear is damaged," I said. "And . . ."

"Are you going to lose your hearing?"

"No, but I can't hear on that side now. The damage isn't permanent; just some fluid and swelling. And I'm going to be dizzy for a while."

"What about me?" she asked next. There was a soft knock at the door and Trish Lathrop came in. Shelee reached for her friend.

"Oh Trish, I'm so sorry," she sobbed, dissolving in tears. "I guess we'd be dead if you hadn't been there. . . . If Seth hadn't shown up. And Trudy; how's Trudy? She's a hero, too."

"Her nose is broken, but she'll be fine . . . physically," Trish said, sitting on the bed, her hand resting on Shel's cheek. "They're all home with me. Abby's been wonderful to help out."

"I know," Shel said. "I called your house. I feel *so bad* for Will!"

Trish sighed heavily. "I don't know how Will is ever going to get over this." She choked back tears for a moment, then buried her head in Shel's shoulder. The two women hugged and cried.

"Phil, how are you?" Trish asked after a few minutes, wiping her eyes.

"I'm really doing all right," I said. "Did Will tell you anything about Seth?"

"It's so sad." Trish started to cry again. "You know, Will just hates Seth's cooking," she said through her tears. "So he talked his dad into going to McDonald's. I guess they opened their presents while they watched a Christmas video after dinner." Trish began to sob and Shelee hugged her. After a few minutes, Trish dried her eyes and blew her nose.

She took a deep breath. "Their Christmas was too short, Will said, because they had to leave before the video was over. They were walking to the door when they heard Thornton shoot the Christmas tree. They ran back to the car and drove around the corner. Will said his dad took off his watch and gave it to him. He told Will to go to the neighbors if he wasn't back in ten minutes."

"How did they get into the basement?" Shel asked.

Trish shook her head. "I don't know. Will just said that Seth grabbed a flashlight and took off for the house. He thought he saw Seth draw his gun when he turned into the yard."

"My god," Shel said.

A face looked into the room, and Clayton Mallory, along with Shel's parents, filed inside. Trish Lathrop hugged Shelee goodbye, then walked over to me and kissed my forehead. "Thanks, Phil," she said with a sad smile. "I need to go home and relieve Abby."

Inga went over to Shel and hugged her. Then she sat down next to her and stroked Shel's forehead. Stewart kissed Shel and came over to me.

"You doing okay?" he asked, patting my shoulder.

I nodded as Shel asked Mallory about her leg.

"Your leg's not broken," Dr. Mallory said. "The bone is fine, the fracture's not damaged."

"I sort of figured that out," Shel said, "no traction. But what then?"

"That lump you feel. That's your quadriceps, the main extensor. It's torn and will have to be surgically repaired."

"Why?" Shel cried softly. "Why won't it just heal on its own?" She got very quiet.

"The muscle's torn completely through," Clayton said. "It has to be stitched together to heal properly. Your surgeon will be in tomorrow morning to explain it thoroughly. We'll get you stabilized and operate the day after tomorrow. You should be out of here by Friday or Saturday."

"My abdomen is so sore," Shel said. "Christ, I was just here a month ago. Anything else wrong?"

"Your abdomen is bruised," Mallory said, "but no worse than last time. Just aggravated some of the previous damage. It'll heal. But now you both need rest. I'll see you in the morning."

Inga came over and kissed me. She took my hand. "Your mom and stepdad will be here tomorrow," she said. "We love you, Phil."

"Thanks, Inga. I love you, too."

"Where's my uncle?" Shel asked.

"He's spending Christmas with Rose at the farm," Stewart said. "The roads are terrible, he'll be in tomorrow. We've kept him updated."

A nurse came in to check on us. "We better go," Stewart said, promising to return the next day. "We might bring a small Christmas tree," he said. "And don't worry, we'll take care of the cats and clean up." He let the door swing shut.

"The cats," Shel said. "I forgot about them. Jesusa's a hero, too." The nurse gave me an odd look and left the room.

"How did we end up in the same hospital room?" Shel asked, her words beginning to slur from the medication.

"I requested it, then wrote out an order when they hesitated."

"I'm glad you did," she said. "I feel so doped up. What time is it, anyway?"

"A little after midnight."

"Do you know anything about Thornton?" Shel asked quietly.

"Nothing, sweetheart. Nothing."

"You had to shoot him. You know that, don't you?"

"I know."

The police showed up about ten the next morning—two officers—one was Kathleen Murell. My jaw and ear hurt more than ever.

Detective Murell, dressed in a padded jumpsuit, took off her parka and extracted a pad and pen from an inner pocket. She did not bother to introduce her colleague. "Dr. Sloan, Ms. Osbornson, we're sorry about what happened. Unfortunately, we need to ask you a few questions."

Shelee glared menacingly at both of them. "Is Jonah Thornton alive or dead?" she asked.

"Mr. Thornton is still in critical condition," Officer Murell said. "But he will live to stand trial."

A wave of panic swept over me as I remembered Jonah Thornton standing in Shel's hallway. "I hope he's not in this hospital," I said.

"No, he's not, Dr. Sloan," Murell said. "He's in Ramsey General under police guard."

Shelee looked distressed as Kathleen Murell recounted the incident. "Mrs. Cooper told us—"

"It's Patricia *Lathrop,* Kathy," Shel declared icily. "She's *dead* Mr. Cooper's ex-wife. Where the *hell* were you people when we needed you last summer?" The other cop, a man in uniform, shifted from one foot to the other. "You people couldn't find jack shit in a sewer," she yelled, "yet you're *here* twelve hours later, on a major holiday!"

"I can understand you're upset," Detective Murell said evenly.

"No you can't," Shelee said, flopping back on her pillow and staring grim faced at the ceiling. Murell turned to me then, just as two nurses came in.

"You'll have to step outside for a few minutes," one nurse told the cops. They checked our vitals and changed Shel's IV bottle. "How's your pain?" one of them asked Shel. "Need a shot?" she added, nodding toward the door.

"I'm all right," Shel said.

The nurse put a fresh pitcher of water next to Shel's uneaten breakfast. "Please eat" she said. "Nothing to eat or drink after five P.M. because of your surgery tomorrow. Drink now, you need the fluids."

Shel narrowed her eyes and shook her head. "I'm on a diet."

"Well, at least eat your dry cereal," she said cheerily. "Would you like some fresh milk?"

"No thanks," Shelee said and waved goodbye to the nurses.

"Murell's an arrogant cunt!" Shel snarled. "Why didn't you say something?"

"What's to say?" I smiled painfully. "I agree with you completely."

The phone rang. "Hi, Mom," Shel said. "We're doing fine; don't worry. . . . Oh, no, we can open presents at Phil's house next week—I'm moving in with him."

I looked over in surprise and Shel smiled at me. "Yes, cats and all." I smiled and nodded. There was a tap on the door, the cops were back. "Gotta go," Shel said. "Okay, see you in a bit. I love you, too."

"Dr. Sloan, we need to ask you a few questions," Detective Murell said, looking at her notepad, "then we can be on our way. Were you aware that Jonah Thornton had a sucking chest wound?"

"Yes."

"Right-side chest wounds like that can be fatal if not given immediate first aid. Are you aware of the procedure?"

"Yes," I said. "My first concern was Seth Cooper. Can't all of this wait?"

"No, this is an important case," the uniformed cop said as Shelee shifted in her bed.

"The first-aid technique is pretty simple, Doctor," Murell added, "just a couple rags soaked in cooking oil."

All of a sudden to everyone's surprise, Shelee's water jug and food tray went flying through the air, the contents scattering along her bed. "We were fresh out of cooking oil!" she yelled as the tray and pitcher clattered against the door, barely missing the cops—they had not anticipated her fusillade.

"Jesus Christ, lady, you've just assaulted an officer," the uniform said, stepping forward. "Lighten up, it's Christmas."

"THEN YOU'VE GOT TO BE OFFICERS *FIRST,*" Shelee shouted, "not a bunch of stupid, fuck-headed bozos!" I had never seen Shel so angry. "*SECOND,* if you want Christmas, here's some holiday color, *ASS-WIPES!*" She pulled back her bed covers, and yanked up her gown. Her leg was ghastly!

The man jerked his head away. Kathleen Murell stared at Shel's leg, mottled with gray, red, and blue, swollen larger than her torso, pushing the other leg off to the side.

"That's it!" Shel yelled, covering herself, eyes brimming with fury. "Charge me with assault or get the hell out of here! Get it up, or get out!"

The nurse pushed the door open, crunching debris against the wall. She was followed by Lucky and Trudy Thornton. Trudy carried a miniature Christmas tree, no higher than eight inches. Lucky's eyes were wide as he surveyed the scene. "You'll have to leave," the nurse told the cops for the second time that morning. "You've upset my patients." The cops were happy to be off the hook and left without a word.

"What the hell's going on?" Lucky said. "Having a temper tantrum?"

"I'll get an orderly," the nurse said. Shel rolled her eyes and hid under the covers.

Trudy, who had been standing behind Lucky, came forward and put the tree on Shel's table. "Shelee," she said. Shel uncovered her face.

"Oh, Trudy!" she said, "I'm so sorry, honey. I don't know what to say. You're so brave." Tears streamed down Shel's cheeks and she pulled the child close.

"It's okay," Trudy said shyly as the orderly came in, mop in hand. "I don't know why my dad was so awful," she said, tears running down her cheeks, too. She boosted herself onto Shel's bed and put her bruised and puffy face on Shel's shoulder. Shel stroked her hair. Shel's folks came inside then and smiled hello to us. They stood by the door with Lucky.

"I'm sorry your leg's hurt so bad," Trudy said with a sigh.

"How are your sisters?" I asked, recalling that they now referred to each other that way.

"Pretty good," she said. Trudy nodded to Shel. "They're over at Mrs. Lathrop's. But I wanted to come see you and Shelee." Shel looked away for a moment and covered her eyes.

"Patricia Lathrop and the older girls will be in this afternoon," Stewart offered. "Trish called and asked us to bring young Trudy in this morning."

"What a terrible Christmas," Shelee said. "What's going on with my house?"

"Oh, I got over there last night and just couldn't stand the mess," her dad said. "We went by two hours ago; the police had removed the barriers." He glanced at Trudy. "So I've got a cleaning crew in there, with a man from Seth Cooper's agency supervising."

"On Christmas?" Shel said.

"Seth's security company called first thing this morning," Stewart said. "*They* found the cleanup crew. An outfit that works any day—any time."

"Amazing."

I looked over at Lucky, now standing silently by the door. His eyes looked tired, and his nose, flattened long ago by punches, intensified his look of bleak sadness. He gazed at his niece, lost in his own thoughts.

Dr. Mallory came in accompanied by another physician who he did not introduce. "We need to examine Ms. Osbornson," he said and helped Trudy off Shel's bed. "Are you Trudy?" he asked. She nodded. "I understand you're quite a hero, young lady," he said, taking Trudy's hand for a moment and giving her a broad smile. Trudy looked confused and I thought she might begin to cry again. They pulled the curtain around Shel's bed as everyone shifted around the room. Lucky held the door for Trudy and they walked out into the hallway.

I heard Mallory introducing his associate to Shel, the doctor who would perform her surgery in the morning. Then Clayton came out and said he wanted to examine my face and ear. When Shel's doctor left for his rounds, Shel called from behind her curtain. "Will he live?"

"Oh, yes," Dr. Mallory said, pulling the curtain back to include her. "In fact, I'm discharging him." Then he turned to me. "But no driving for a week or so, Phil," Clayton said. "Until your dizziness is gone. I want to see you before you get behind a wheel."

While Clayton was examining me, my mom and stepfather showed up, further crowding the room. "We'll drive you home," Mom said after a brief reunion.

"Great," I said and glanced over at Shelee, who now looked miserable.

"Shel, honey, these are for you." My mother handed her the card and a bouquet she'd laid on my bed. Shelee smelled them graciously and opened the card.

"How sweet. Thanks," Shel said and Mother hugged her, then put the flowers in a vase on the window ledge.

"How are you?" my stepfather asked, shaking my hand.

"Could be better," I said.

"Well, you can get dressed now," Clayton Mallory said. "I'll see you in a week or so." He waved to the others and left.

"Shel," I said, "I'll have Mom take me to get some things and I'll be back in time for dinner." Shelee brightened considerably. "And I'll stay here tonight," I added. "And you and Mom," I said to my stepfather, "can stay at my house."

"There's no dinnertime for me tonight, Doctor," Shelee said with a slight sneer, "but you may come back anyway."

## Fifty-three / Shelee

Phil returned as promised, with yesterday's mail and today's newspaper.

"Tell me," I asked, "did you know about Thornton's wound? The first-aid treatment?"

"There was a bullet hole in his chest and out his back," Phil said quietly. "First aid for him wasn't important to me. As I told the cops, Seth Cooper came first. Absolutely."

"How do you feel about Thornton being alive?"

Phil shook his head. "I'm not sure what I feel."

"It's still Christmas," I said wearily.

"Yes, and the night before your surgery. But let's forget both for now."

"We'll pretend that Christmas is next weekend," I said. "New Year's will be our Christmas this year."

Phil smiled and kissed my cheek.

"Why did she risk it?" I asked.

"Trudy?"

"Yes."

"Bravery, perhaps," Phil said. "And rage—she's a very angry child, and rightfully so. Most likely, she felt indestructible."

"How's that?" I asked, adjusting my poor, aching, now hungry, body.

"That's how some abused children cope with assaults by all-powerful forces. They come to believe that they cannot be destroyed. Her belief probably saved our lives.

"Seth's funeral's on Thursday," Phil said. "I suppose I'll go with your folks. What a mess. . . . Oh, they found out how Thornton got in. He fixed a window in your basement to look as if it were locked when it wasn't. Your dad repaired it temporarily. That's how Seth got in, too. His footprints were on top of Thornton's in the snow by the window."

"Thornton's a swine," I said. "How did he get inside in the first place?"

"The cops found skeleton keys on him. One of them fit your back door. They're going to check mine."

"Goddamn spooky. You talked with Kathy Murell?"

"No, Stewart talked with two different detectives who stopped by your house."

"Lucky came back after everyone else left this afternoon," I said. "He's acting really strange."

"He's in some sort of shock," Phil said. "He offered to be my wheels, as he puts it, till I can drive. Maybe I'll get some insight."

"How're your folks?"

"Fine." Phil smiled sadly. "I'm depressed. And my face hurts. I shouldn't complain, but I saw death, Shel, death worse than mine. Have I fooled myself, believing that I understand anything—when I was unable to take action to save you or to save myself because of fragility? We're just a biological analog, so limited in our capacity to exist."

"Remember," I said, "you're not alone, sweetheart. We've just been through hell." I patted the bed. "There's room for two here. Come lie next to me. We'll hurt together. It's gonna take some time."

"I had the dream again," I said to Phil, "like the one in Montana, but it changed—really changed." The hospital folks had been in to prep me for surgery; now I was waiting for the inevitable gurney.

"How was it different?" Phil asked, holding my hand, waiting with me.

"Well, first, it was in Norwegian, you know, my grandparents' language, but no one spoke. And I was alone, you weren't there."

"It's a Lutheran dream."

"Don't joke! Listen, the next part is so bizarre. You know the part about your hand?"

"Yes."

Two attendants pushed through the door with a gurney. "Time to head downstairs," a fresh-faced kid said with way too much enthusiasm.

"I'll finish later," I grumbled, so full of painkiller that I didn't feel any fear, though I searched through my body for it. "See you later," I said.

"Sooner than you think," Phil responded, now able to smile a little better than yesterday. "I'm dressing down, Shel; see you in recovery." He kissed me and squeezed my hand. "I love you, Shelee Osbornson."

* * * * *

The rest of the day was a total blur. I only remember Phil in the recovery room helping the nurse put an oven-warmed blanket on me. I felt cozy and safe with him there.

I woke up for real, about three o'clock the next morning. Phil was sleeping soundly in the other bed. Starving, I rang for the nurse, and she brought me some food, just cold cereal, orange juice, and hot chocolate—but damn it tasted good.

In the morning, I woke to the sound of a real breakfast when a nurse brought trays for both of us. I looked over to see Phil already dressed and sitting in a chair. He was watching the KCB morning news with the sound turned down. A dim, December sun struggled through the venetian blinds. I didn't like the tone the nurse used when talking with my Dr. Sloan.

"Open them blinds," I commanded. "How'd the operation go?"

"Just fine," Phil said, turning off the TV. "Now all you need is time to mend." He got up and gave me a much-needed kiss.

"And get fat," I said, munching a piece of toast. "Thanks so much for being here, but keep away from that blond nurse. What am I going to do about exercise?"

"In a few weeks you'll be on a physical therapy regimen. They'll come up with something."

"Ain't soon enough," I said, lying there, feeling my leg—afraid to look. It felt as big as ever, but with the lump gone. I decided to wait, since it only hurt a little. "Why am I talking like my Uncle Lucky?" I asked.

"Because he was here."

"When?"

"About one A.M.," Phil said. "I was asleep, or trying to sleep."

"Talking Norwegian, right?"

"That's right."

"So weird. He did that when I was in the hospital as a teenager. What did he say? Thought I was dreaming again." I began eating my oatmeal after pouring a full mini-pitcher of coffee cream into it. To hell with the milk—I needed *real* nourishment.

"Well, he crept in quietly. It was like the soft rustle loving parents make when peeking into their child's room. Then he asked me, 'You asleep, son?' I was too drowsy and didn't respond. He patted my shoulder and went over to you and rambled on as if he were in Norway."

"What did he say?"

"He sounded utterly sorrowful. I don't have a clue, but he repeated a phrase several times . . . something, um . . . 'Min daughter, or min yings daughter.' Like a lamentation from *Götterdämmerung*."

"*Min datter, min yndlingsdatter*?" I asked incredulously.

"Possibly. That sounds like it."

"Fascinating! That means, My daughter, my darling daughter. . . . He thinks of us as his kids, doesn't he?"

"Yup," Phil replied. "I know I really love the old fart, that's for sure."

"That response have anything to do with your stepdad being in town?" I asked.

"Could be. Tell you what, why don't *you* take over my practice—since you'll be sitting around for a while."

"Don't get snotty with me—I asked that with love. You're the one who says, 'The work between children and their parents is never done.' And I *am* planning to paint." I mopped up the remains of some yellow scrambled stuff with my last piece of toast. "What's wrong with these people, can't they serve real eggs in here? And at these prices! You want to hear the rest of my dream?"

"No, not if I wasn't in it," Phil said.

I ignored him and continued. "So I'm flying, but you're not there. Did I tell you about your hand?" Phil shook his head. "In place of your hand—which had been holding my wrist—was that little girl's face."

"What little girl?"

"The one in the photo at Lucky's . . . the 'little lilac girl.' So her face is on my wrist as I fly across the lake, this time going up, into my *Salon du Monastère*. And the air is full of insects, beautiful ones, like those giant midges from up at Lucky's. What do you think the dream means?"

"It means you'll be bugged by a small child who learns to paint while flying," Phil said.

"Perhaps I should take over your practice, unless your clients are into sarcasm."

Phil shrugged. "I repeated the first thing that came into my head. I'm remembering you don't like relational introspection."

"Maybe a brush with death can change one's perspective," I answered.

"Maybe I'm beginning to understand your reluctance to delve into your unknown self," Phil said. "At some level you might feel it puts your creativity at risk—more peril than opportunity. But what's really more important," he said with a wry smile, "pushing the subject is my stuff and my problem, not yours."

## Fifty-four / Phil

A flood of visitors, starting with my parents, finally drove me from Shel's hospital room. My folks headed back to Racine after dropping me at Shelee's house. I was amazed at the amount of work that had been accomplished in two days. The front room rug was gone, its hardwood floor exposed, the couch had been taken out, and the holes in the wall and ceiling were patched and drying.

"You guys have done a lot of work," I said to Stewart and Lucky. "What can I do?"

"Nothing, here," Lucky said. "We've decided seeing Shelee laid up is too damn depressing. So you hold down the fort with the women at the hospital, we'll keep busy here."

"The Stone Lake crew came by here before lunch," Stewart said.

"Did they go inside?"

"No. I think they wanted to, but they just couldn't do it. They went over to the hospital to see you and Shel. I guess they're heading home after the funeral tomorrow." He took off his plaster-spotted glasses and wiped his brow on his sleeve. "Christ," he said, "when I think of how it could have turned out."

I shook my head. "I know. I've thought about that myself." I put my arm around his shoulders. "We'll get through it; just do the best we can."

"I should have killed that Thornton bastard," Lucky said, anger holding back tears. "How could he have raised two such fine kids? That Trudy girl, she's somethin' special." He began to sputter, quickly turned his back to us, and stomped into the kitchen. "I hope we're not out of beer," he shouted.

"Did you know Seth Cooper very well?" Stewart asked.

"No. It's embarrassing, but we didn't have a very favorable impression of him. He was sort of goofy. And that's a sad piece for me, because in the past several years I've prided myself on being nonjudgmental and open to everybody's stories. Including the weird ones," I added as Lucky rejoined us, sipping a beer.

"Then you must like listening to my stories, bub," Lucky said. "They're pretty weird."

"I never made that kind of connection with Seth," I said with a shrug. "That's what's got me puzzled."

"Well I'm goin' to the funeral tomorrow," Lucky said, "an' give thanks for his heroic soul and yours—and I *never* pray. Everybody's going. There's even a police contingent from Duluth. He used to be on the force up there."

Dena Lewis and the two sisters showed up. I stepped out on the porch to talk with them and wondered about their willingness to come so close to such recently threatening surroundings.

"If we hadn't spent Christmas Eve with you," Dena said, "we'd probably be dead right now."

"I'm not sure I understand," I said.

"The police showed us a map they found in Mr. Thornton's car. It had our address and location on it. Yours, too."

I just shook my head. We talked for a few minutes, then they left. Though the front door had been ajar, they showed no interest in looking inside.

"How're you feelin'?" Lucky asked after I stepped back into the house.

"I'm still pretty dizzy. But I can hear a little in my left ear now. Can you give me a ride to my house? I'm supposed to meet the cops there about two-thirty. Then I want to get some work done."

"Sure," he said.

"Let's get Chinese and take it to Shelee," I suggested in the car. "We'll eat with her tonight."

"Now you're talkin'." Lucky smiled, quickly over his aversion to seeing Shelee in the hospital. "I'll tell Rose I'm eatin' with you guys."

"Thanks," I said when we got to the house. "I ll call you when I'm done." I thumped him in the shoulder.

Two metro policemen showed up, looked around, and spent some time talking with me. Fortunately, neither one was a Shelee-abused Christmas cop. They tried Thornton's keys in both of my doors. I got the chills when one of them showed me a key that fit the back door. They spent less than a minute in my workroom and found the window he'd jiggered above my washing machine. My stomach churned and I decided to put off telling Shel about it.

"How about pale, lemon yellow for the front room?" Shelee said, bending the corner of a cardboard paint swatch and passing it to Lucky. "Here's the color."

"We took the carpet and the couch to the dump," Lucky said.

"Good," Shel said. "Want to hear who all came by today?" She recounted the list, which included the Westons and Gloria and Duncan.

"They were sorry they missed you," she said to me as we ate ice cream from the hospital cafeteria. I was stuffed with Chinese food.

"I don't know what I'm going to do about my house." Shel frowned with disgust. "After the dust settles, I might put it up for sale." She began to cry and I held her hand. "You know, I really love that house. . . . I can't thank you enough for all the work you've done, Lucky."

"Happy to help," he said.

Seth Cooper's funeral, held in a small Episcopal church in Cottage Grove, was filled to overflowing. I rode with Shel's parents and Lucky in his big Suburban. Trish was there, of course, with Will, her folks, the Stone Lake women, and an older couple—Seth's mom and dad from Duluth.

Seeing Will with his grieving grandparents shocked me back into the tragedy all over again. It simply hurt my face too much to hold back tears, and strangely—going through some baffling throwback behavior—I didn't want people to see me crying. So I sat in the reception area and listened to the service through the open doors, then moved back to the sanctuary during the eulogies. Remarks by a police captain from Seth's hometown gave me further reason to wonder about the man who crawled up the stairs half dead to help us.

The graveside service was brief, mainly because the temperature was near zero; and even though the sun shone brilliantly off a thin cover of snow, a slight breeze sent chills through everyone. Afterward, there was a buffet lunch in the church annex.

We who were at Shel's house the evening of the shooting did not look like the usual after-funeral reception folks. Trudy Thornton and I were the most visibly banged up, Dena still had obvious facial bruises and a cut on her forehead, and Trish wore her fading black eye with honor. I talked with Seth's parents, wanting to assure them that Will and Patricia were part of our extended family. But then I felt awkward about it, so I said nothing. Will showed me Seth's watch and explained that his father had given it to him before going into Shel's house. At that point, I had to wander off.

My conversations with several uniformed guards from Seth's security agency, and the police captain from Duluth, disturbed me deeply. I was looking for Lucky, hoping to leave fairly soon, when a *Post* reporter came up to me. There had been two television crews earlier, but they left just after the graveside service began.

"Dr. Sloan? Hi, I'm Ruby Norris from the *Minneapolis Post Express*. May I ask you a few questions?"

"I guess so," I said reluctantly. "But first, why has the *Post* story only referred to a 'Robbinsdale residence'? We're almost three miles from Robbinsdale. That's kept us away from a lot of unwelcome publicity."

"You can thank Elizabeth Carbonnader for that," Ms. Norris said. "She's friends with Shelee . . . uh, Professor Osbornson."

Well, if Shel wasn't friends before, I thought, she is now.

After answering some reasonable questions from the reporter, I found Lucky, Inga, and Stewart, and we went back to town.

Later that day in her hospital room, I told Shel about what I'd learned at the funeral. "Seth was so quirky, always groping for his gun. It's obvious now. There was a shootout in Duluth nine years ago and his partner got killed."

"That's terrible," Shel said. "What happened?"

"Nobody told me any details. They just said he moved to Minneapolis after he couldn't work as a street cop anymore."

"So the business with the holster was posttraumatic whatever?"

"Probably," I said. "It's beyond me why I didn't at least consider it. When I think how we used to joke about him."

"I was much worse than you," Shel said, tears coming to her eyes. "I was so rotten about Seth, always siding with Trish. I wonder why she never said anything about Duluth. Now I feel worse than ever."

"Me, too. My only excuse is, I don't do shrink all the time. Oh, shit! I just don't know. . . . When are you coming home, babe?"

"Clayton said possibly Saturday. You don't mind me staying with you?"

"Absolutely not," I said, "pussycats and all."

"God! What am I going to do about my house, Phil?"

"You'll figure it out."

## Fifty-five / Shelee

"Is there any way I can defer that eighty thousand dollars into next year?" I asked Phil. It was the third week in January, and Phil was sitting at the dining-room table fooling with income taxes on his laptop computer. I was supposed to go back to work on Monday and had been practicing with my crutches. Phil started to say something when the doorbell rang.

"I'll get it," I said. I clumped my way to the front door and opened it to a solid-looking man in a heavy, green-and-black checkered jacket.

"You must be Professor Osbornson," the man said, handing me the Saturday paper he'd picked up from the front porch. "I'm Deputy Hartung from Stone Lake. May I come in?"

Matthew Hartung's glasses fogged the moment he stepped into the house. "Hello, Dr. Sloan," he said, entering the front room. "I thought I'd drop by for a minute while we were in town." He took off his glasses, fished in his pocket for a handkerchief, and polished the lenses. "My family and I came into town for some shopping." He walked toward Phil, extending his hand.

Phil looked up from his work, closed the computer's lid, and said nothing. I was uncomfortable with Phil's silent gaze at

Hartung. Phil continued sitting, his hands folded on the computer.

Deputy Hartung stepped back, now addressing me. "I know you both have been through a terrible experience. I just thought I'd come by and see how you were doing."

"We're recovering," I said.

Then he turned back to Phil, anguish swept across his face. "Look, Dr. Sloan . . . I'm *sorry,* my department's sorry. We just dropped the ball! We all feel responsible for what happened. And I make no excuses. If we had done our job, we'd have known that Thornton was violating his bail conditions."

Phil unlaced his fingers, gestured with quiet futility—palms up, silent.

"Maybe I should have called first. . . . Maybe I shouldn't have come," he said, turning to me, unwilling to accept Phil's silence. "I hope you two are doing okay. . . . If it makes you feel any better, we've tightened our procedures. . . ." His words trailed off.

The computer made a tiny beep as Phil opened the lid and looked back at his work. "I guess I'll be going," Hartung said softly, turning for the door.

I leaned on my crutches and looked through a side window at his light blue van; I tried to smile. "Thanks for coming by, Deputy Hartung," I said. A woman sat in the van's passenger seat and three kids bashed around behind her.

"Sorry," he repeated, closing the door as he left.

"Hartung's got the sort of car I want, Mr. Silence.'

"My jaw started to throb the moment he walked in," Phil said. "I've nothing to say to him or to anybody in the cop business."

"He definitely got your drift. Guess it's better than throwing things."

"Maybe not, who knows?"

"I'm impressed that he at least came to talk with us. Was his apology genuine?"

"I don't care," Phil said. "When it's a life-or-death matter, one must always do his best. His apology was hollow, sincere or not."

I watched them drive off, then picked up the paper and joined Phil at the table. "What were you going to say about the eighty thou?" I asked. He was absorbed in his work.

"I don't remember," Phil said and looked up.

"Well, it's going to be embarrassing to put a half-a-million price tag on that painting," I said.

Phil smiled. "It's an extraordinary piece of work. If it sells for that price at the show, you can be embarrassed all the way to the bank."

"Is there a personality disorder called tooth fairy syndrome?" I asked.

"Uh-huh."

I left Phil alone and leafed through the paper. I searched the city news section looking for something about Jonah Thornton. He was in jail awaiting trial, and none of us were looking forward to having to relive Christmas. I soon found a short article about him.

"Well, I'll be damned," I said, spreading the paper on the table so Phil could see. "That bastard Thornton's pleaded guilty."

Phil looked up from his work and stared across the room. "That's a blessing," he said. "Now we don't have to go through a trial."

I finished reading the article. "It says he'll get a mandatory life sentence and cannot be paroled for thirty years."

Phil looked at me. "I was hoping for that. There's no wiggle room for premeditated murder in this state."

"But he wasn't stalking Seth. So is it still premeditated?"

"I think it's still classified that way," he said. "Does the article say anything about the child assault charges?"

"No. Just says there were charges pending in Jefferson County. You don't seem very pleased."

"All of this should never have happened," Phil said quietly. "But I feel safer knowing he'll be put away."

I suddenly felt dismal and began to cry. "Even so," I said as Phil took my hand, "I'm putting my beloved house up for sale. I just can't move back there."

## Fifty-six / Phil

Early spring—a time of hope and change—graced the Twin Cities with its usual share of wet snow. And as I drove home from work one evening, my windshield wipers slapped at high speed, barely clearing the splattering flakes. Interestingly, Shelee sounded somewhat upbeat on the phone and offered to fix dinner. When I asked about her visit to the doctor and whether she could start walking without crutches yet, she put me off. "I'll tell you this evening," she said.

Shel had decided not to buy a new car until she could drive. I was hoping that the doctor would let her start walking and that it might improve on her recent, contrary moods. We had talked about shopping for a car, and perhaps this would be the weekend.

Shelee was working at the sink, her back to me, when I walked in. She was washing something and her crutches were nowhere in sight.

"How are the roads?" she asked as I hung up my coat.

"Bare and wet, like your butt's going to be."

"Oh, Phil, I hope so," she said in a peculiar tone.

A cane leaned against a chair next to the sink. Jesusa and Fellini sat attentively on the chair, tracking her every move. Shel remained with her back to me.

"Well, no crutches?" I said, now in the middle of the kitchen. "Looks like good news." She said nothing. "Dinner smells sensational," I continued.

"Thanks . . . elk stew," she replied, barely looking around. "It is good news, Phil. Be with you in a second. Open that wine will you? Pour yourself a glass."

"Nice choice," I said, cutting the capsule from a bottle of 1981 Merlot. "*Very* nice choice. What's the occasion?"

"Will you marry me?" Shelee asked suddenly, still not turning around.

"My god, of course! Yes! *Absolutely!* What brought this on?" I set the bottle down and moved to hug her. She raised a wet hand and it quavered in the air. "You don't have to tell me," I said. "I love you, Shelee. Of course I'll marry you."

She turned to face me then, crying and smiling at the same time, drying her hands. I was dumbfounded. "You *have* to marry me, Phil. The doctor . . . the accident . . . how could I know?" She wiped her eyes with the dishtowel, now smiling more than crying. "You won't believe . . . I'm pregnant."

Later on that evening, we went for a short walk to celebrate everything. I helped steady Shelee as we went down the front steps—still in joyous shock over the evening's events. But Shel wasn't quite ready to try her cane in the snow, so we just stood on the front walk. We watched as the clouds were swept away by a buoyant west wind. The outside glistened with its fresh coating of wet snow, and a new moon spun out of the clearing sky. Shelee leaned against me and I took her hand. Did I imagine? Grass wet and thick along the rivers. New songs sung in lilac trees. The honeyed scent of cottonwood balm.

*– End –*

"You, little traveler! You have made the journey, the Long Journey. You now know the things I have yet to know. You, little traveler! You were given a name, a true name in my father's lodge. Good Medicine, Little Traveler! You are truly a Paddle Person, a Paddle-to-the-Sea!"

– Holling Clancy Holling

"Don't let the cookie-cutters define your art."

—Shelee Osbornson

© *Erin S. Griffin — Studio West*

Paul Cohn grew up in Portland, Oregon. He worked his teenage summers on ranches in eastern Oregon and Idaho and, after graduating from Oregon State University, had a 20-year career as a nuclear engineer.

He lives in Montana, close to where parts of his first novel, *Shelee and Me,* take place.

***Shelee and Me*** at your local bookstore.

Or order by mail: Burns-Cole Publishers
P.O. Box 5275
Bozeman, MT 59717-5275

***Please print clearly. This is your mailing label.***

Name ______________________________

Address ______________________________

City/State ____________________ Zip __________

Send additional copies to:

Name ______________________________

Address ______________________________

City/State ____________________ Zip __________

☐ Check/money order (no cash or C.O.D. orders, please)

☐ Please send an author-signed and numbered first edition (add $2.00)

Inscription, 10 words or less (please use back of this coupon).

Please send me______ copies of *Shelee and Me*:

| | |
|---|---|
| @ $11.95 each ($16.95 in Canada) | $ __________ |
| Add $2.50 each, shipping and handling | $ __________ |
| Add $2.00 each for signed/numbered first edition | $ __________ |
| **Total** | $ __________ |

*Prices and availability subject to change without notice.*
*Please allow four to six weeks for delivery.*